D0496058

Note on the author

Anne Dunlop lives in Bahrain. Again.

The first time, she flew as an air-stewardess, mixed with the jet set and suffered from jet lag.

This time she is the trailing spouse of an international expatriate and is yummy mummy to four little sweethearts.

Quite often, in the very hot weather, Anne feels homesick for Ireland.

Enchanting Alice is her sixth novel.

Cork City Libraries
WITHDRAWN
FROM STOCK

Cork City Libraries
WITHDRAWN
FROM STOCK

Acknowledgements

Thank you to Saba for keeping house and children while I was trying to write.

For Sam and Lila

1

It was the regional finals of Ireland's Emerald, the biggest beauty pageant in the country and pretty girls in sturdy bathing costumes were trying to impress the judges with their brains, beauty and home-making skills, for this was 1971 when an Irish girl wasn't worth marrying if she wasn't fit to look after a husband.

The qualifying heats had quickly sorted out *Mná na hÉireann* from the frivolous chaff. There'd been competitions in baking bread and scrubbing shirt collars, in singing, reciting and playing a musical instrument. Now the finalists had been asked to demonstrate their "feminine charms" in an evening dress they'd made themselves.

There were two outstanding entrants in the Derry final.

A big blonde country girl fair bursting out of her frock called Kathleen Temple had scored top marks in every qualifying heat. She radiated confidence, for she was handsome and capable in a hand-stitched dress *so* suitable for almost every social occasion she was likely to be invited to.

"You're in safe hands when you're with me," she told the interviewing judge, and she winked.

Giving her a close run for her money was Jane Costello from Derry City. Jane hadn't scored half as well as Kathleen in the qualifiers. Her bread was heavy and her shirt collar remained stained. She couldn't play a musical instrument, not even a tin whistle, and she'd told the judge, in all earnestness, that "first base" was when you allowed a boy to fondle your breasts through your jumper – "if he can find them," and she'd started to giggle.

So she was useless in the kitchen and a dead loss at entertaining the clergyman when he came to tea and she was probably quite fast in the back seat of a car, but in her favour she was beautiful, with long, fine bones and translucent skin; her eyes were violet and her dark hair fell thick and shining to her waist.

"My ambition in life is to marry for love, and to live happily ever after," said Jane.

Kathleen and Jane stood quietly side by side on the stage of the Electric Ballroom while the judges made their decision. It was the final countdown.

There was a pounding in Kathleen's head and she tried desperately to maintain a serene and sphinx-like aura, and not to pant with nerves and desperation. Desperately, desperately she wanted to win. She *needed* to be Derry's Emerald. It was her passport to freedom. If she could qualify for the finals in faraway, cosmopolitan Dublin, somebody might see her and offer her an escape route from the heavy-duty drudgery she'd been born into: pre-dawn milking in a stinking cow byre, throwing bales in her bra, carrying her father and her brother Michael cups of tea and slabs of soda bread every couple of hours . . .

Kathleen was neither naïve nor romantic. She knew this was her one big moment, the fork in her road. If she failed tonight she might end up marrying the first man who asked her, just to get away from Temple Farm.

Kathleen's evening dress had been refashioned from her mother's only pretty dress, her wedding-dress, silver-grey bombazine with an acre of taffeta skirt; such a good colour for a blonde. She'd been still deftly stitching at it while Michael revved up the Rapier and their father, a religious maniac, shouted, "*'Remember the Sabbath day, to keep it holy!'* Exodus 20, verse 8! I expect you pair home before midnight!"

Kathleen dominated the stage. Her shoulders were pinned back, her chest was inflated and her chin was high. She felt like Scarlett O'Hara the day she went to sell herself to Rhett Butler, dressed in her mother's green velvet curtains, to pay the taxes on Tara.

"And the winner is Jane Costello!"

Jane was barefoot and elegantly draped in a black halter-neck frock. Her thick, shiny hair hung loose about her face; she was the only finalist wearing false eyelashes.

She was crowned Derry's Emerald and they gave her a green sash and a silly-looking sceptre. The local paper took her photograph.

Kathleen's friendly smile of congratulations remained fixed until the show was over and the also-rans had been helped down from the stage. Only when she was locked into a toilet cubicle did she allow her face to relax into rage and pain and humiliation. Her corset was killing her and her heart was breaking. She'd been beaten by a cheap little thing from the town. She wrung and wrung at her tidy lace handkerchief, wishing it was Jane Costello's neck.

Finally Kathleen composed herself and went back into the dance hall. To find her brother Michael dancing with Jane Costello. They quickstepped together like a pair of sticking-plasters – slow, slow, quick, quick, slow, slow – it was love at first sight for both of them.

Michael Temple's hands were calloused and rough, though the nails were fastidiously scrubbed. His smile was crooked and his eyes were shy. Most of the time he hid behind a gruff voice and a rough manner but sometimes the mask slipped, his face softened and his eyes gave him away as sure as if he was talking with them. Women found him irresistible and at dances they quickly learned to do the asking, which was just as well because he'd never have had the nerve to do it himself.

So Michael was never short of a girlfriend and it was universally agreed among those who talked that there wasn't one who wouldn't have risked her reputation in the back seat of his Rapier. They only had themselves to blame if he could never remember their names afterwards . . .

The minute he saw her Michael knew Jane Costello was different. She was the first girl he'd ever really noticed, the first girl he'd ever asked to dance, and not just because she was the Derry Emerald.

"Can I take you home?" he asked, though it was twenty miles over the mountain to Derry along a dark and winding road and it was already a quarter to midnight and there were a clan of Costello women standing waiting for Jane, for she was only seventeen, and Michael's reputation for promiscuity stretched right across deepest South Derry, from Temple Farm and the wetlands of Lisglasson, via the Electric Ballroom, even to Derry's walls.

Jane was from the steep streets of Derry where there were railings to stop you slipping and nervous passengers kept car doors ajar on the climb out of the city in case the car stalled and started to plummet. Granny Costello lived at the bottom of a steep street, with the rest of the clan tucked into the terrace, higher and higher up the hill. Jane lived right at the top with a fabulous view of the River Foyle and beyond it to green Donegal; she had particularly good legs from the hill-walking.

The first night he came courting, the Costello women were waiting for Michael. They invited him, with menaces, to join them in Granny Costello's front room, where he was plied with strong tea and hard questions.

"And where are you actually from?" asked Granny Costello, for she'd lived all her life in Derry and anywhere beyond its walls was unexplored and foreign-sounding.

"Top left-hand corner of Lough Neagh. There's a little village just up the road, called Lisglasson."

"I've never heard of it," said Granny Costello which was hardly surprising for Lisglasson was off the beaten track, lying low in the shadow of the Sperrins. It was a cul-de-sac, a dead end, the back of beyond. "And your intentions?"

"My intentions aren't honourable, but they're sincere."

Everybody approved of his answer – smart but not smart-ass – and, as summer stretched, Michael's Rapier was rarely off the road. Either he was popping up to Derry to visit Jane or Jane was popping down to the Electric Ballroom to meet Michael.

He even took her to Dublin for the final of Ireland's Emerald.

"Come with us, Kathleen!"

"No, thank you," said Kathleen sullenly. "I don't wish to play gooseberry."

"But you won't be a gooseberry! Jane is booked to stay in Flowers Hotel. She's sharing a room with the Donegal Emerald and there's a bodyguard outside the door. I'm staying in a B&B."

"No, thank you," said Kathleen again and she spent the entire weekend playing gloomy crashing music on the piano in the parlour and sticking pins into Jane Costello's newspaper photograph that was in the *Derry Journal* when she won the regional final.

In spite of her, Jane came a respectable fourth and won a shopping voucher for a hundred pounds in Clerys.

"I still think she was the most beautiful girl there," said Michael and the courting continued while the hay and the harvest were shamefully neglected and the cows went half-milked. Michael's father, Old Dave, shouted a lot and quoted the fifth commandment and made dastardly threats about disinheriting. Michael's mother, Cecily, muttered about prodigal sons and happy endings and confidently reminded everyone that there had been other girls, some of them every bit as pretty as the Derry Emerald, and not one of them had lasted longer than a couple of months.

"Wouldn't we think there was something wrong with him if he wasn't chasing after a cheap little thing from the town?"

Hence the sensation when Michael ca
during ten o'clock tea, after the morning milki
in September, that he was going to buy an enga
Jane Costello.

"I can't understand why you're all so surpri
been passionately in love with her since the nigh   ...ie Derry
Final? Haven't I been ardently courting her all summer? Yes, I
certainly mean to marry her, sooner rather than later, perhaps
after the potatoes and before the lambing."

His mother said, "You've not gone and got her pregnant,
have you?"

"Not yet!"

"You don't seriously mean to *marry* him, do you?"

Jane flashed her ring at her mother and aunts, her sisters
and her granny: the Derry clan of Costello women. They
were crammed together into Granny's front room for the big
announcement and the silence afterwards was quite deafening
for no one had expected Jane's unlikely romance to last
beyond the first frosts of winter, when the mountain road
between Temple and Derry would become impossible and
impassable, and out of sight is out of mind when you're
seventeen.

Jane said, "After the potatoes and before the lambing – we
thought Valentine's Day . . ."

She was flushed and happy, so young and lovely and in
love. The engagement ring sparkled on her finger. But she
was only seventeen. And he lived at the back of beyond, turn
left at the foot of the mountain.

Somebody was going to have to say something.

Finally her mother spoke.

"What about the cookery course that you've only just started at the Catering College? You were really looking forward to that. You'd have to give it up if you married Michael and moved away from Derry."

Then everyone else chimed in.

"Could you not wait for a year, or two? Or five years?"

But she wouldn't listen. And to be fair to them, they hadn't really expected her to. She was from a clan of women who had all married young and stuck with their husbands, for better and worse, till death parted them.

"There's always the bus! I'll be able to come back and visit you."

The wedding was a spectacular affair; the Costello clan spared no expense. There were thundering crescendos of church music and choirboys in frilly smocks and four clergymen officiating. Jane's white satin wedding-dress cost a hundred guineas. She had six bridesmaids in navy blue. Her side of the cathedral was packed with tall, dark-haired beautiful Derry women, every one of them in a brand-new outfit. It was a fashion parade the like of which Cecily had never before seen in her life. She sat, quiet and unadorned, in a new coat with a real fur collar, staring fixedly ahead, wishing herself invisible.

"Which one is Michael's mother?" whispered the Costello women, for the Temples and the Costellos had never been officially introduced, not even for a cup of tea to discuss the wedding arrangements: "*What's there to discuss? Doesn't the bride's family pay for everything?*"

"She's a little brown mouse!" said the Derry women.

Cecily could feel their pity that she'd come to her only

son's wedding with grey hair, in a second-hand hat. "Do you rightly," said Old Dave who was wearing an ancient morning-suit that was mouldy under the arms.

Sat beside her was Kathleen, who had refused point blank to be a bridesmaid, though Jane had asked her nicely.

"No, thank you. I'm not a bridesmaid sort of girl," said Kathleen and, when she saw the six nymphs of bridesmaids who'd said "Yes, please!" with their faces painted and their hair teased up into bouffant styles, she sank deeper into the pew and was *so* thankful that she'd refused. She'd have been horribly out of place in that slinky, city line-up, an Irish Draught plough horse in a field of thoroughbreds. She wasn't wearing even lipstick and one of Jane's bridesmaids had such bright white hair that it gleamed at the front of the church, brighter than the light bulb over the altar.

The wedding reception was at the grandest hotel in Derry. There was free drink and after a couple of quick ones Michael stood up and spontaneously announced that he was the happiest man alive.

"That's the drink talking!" Cecily muttered but she had the grace to twist her cross little face into an approximation of a smile for the photographs.

Cecily had good reason to feel sour for it was the rural tradition in Ireland that the newly weds move into the farmhouse and live with the old pair. From now on Jane would sleep in Michael's bedroom, she would be welcome to sit in the parlour; she'd have part of a shelf in the scullery to store her own food. Jane was marrying Michael, but the reality was that she would be living with his mother.

Nobody asked Cecily or Jane if they objected to this

claustrophobic set-up, as intimate as marriage but with none of its compensations. Nobody asked if they felt they could tolerate each other in sickness and in health, for better, for worse, until death parted them.

This was the rural Irish tradition. If you didn't like it, you didn't marry a farmer.

The Costello women, town people born and bred, loudly voiced their objection to wee Jane being made to move in with her mother-in-law.

"A young couple need their own house."

"Nonsense!" said Old Dave. "Temple is big enough for everybody."

"I give it three months," said Kathleen.

2

Jane put on her wellies and went for another walk. This was her life now, the wearing of wellies and the taking of walks, for Cecily Temple didn't allow her to do a hand's turn about the house. Not that she minded, not at all, for it had always been a standing joke along the steep Derry streets that wee Jane wouldn't have noticed unswept floors and dirty dishes if they'd hit her between the eyes.

And there was a motto among the Costello women: *"Keep him satisfied between the sheets and he'll not notice the dust under the bed."*

She had offered her services, of course, the first day after the honeymoon, when Michael and she had driven the whole way back from Dublin without stopping for even a cup of tea, to find Temple in uproar and Cecily and Dave in the middle of an agricultural crisis: the pregnant ewes in the Forty Acres had found a hole in the hedge and broken out.

"A welcoming committee!" said Michael when they came

cantering towards him down the small grassy road that took you to Temple from Lisglasson, then meandered on at its own pace along the side of the lough and up the mountain. "With mad Dolly in charge, they'll be in Dublin before I get them stopped!"

He'd promptly jumped out of the car and joined Cecily and Old Dave in the chase after his pregnant girlies, abandoning his new wife without a backward glance.

It was a sign of things to come.

Jane climbed into the driver's seat and drove herself up to the house, where she sat patiently waiting for her new husband to come back for her. Call her old-fashioned, but she was expecting him to carry her over the threshold of their new life together.

"What are you doing, sitting out here in the car?"

It was Kathleen.

Kathleen worked in a bank in the town. The country bus made a special detour every morning and afternoon, through Lisglasson village, to pick her up and set her down.

"I'm waiting for Michael," said Jane.

"Then you'll be waiting a long time – I saw him from the bus – the ewes turned right into Lisglasson Estate, now they've a thousand acres to get lost in . . ."

Jane got out of the car and followed her sister-in-law into the kitchen where they found a marmalade farm cat sunning herself on the kitchen table and casually licking at an uncooked piece of mutton.

"That ewe dropped dead the day you got married – we've been eating at it for a fortnight now . . ."

Jane was an adventurous cook with a talent for sexing up simple ingredients. She rolled up the sleeves of her mini-dress and tied a bag apron round her waist. Quickly and without

12

fuss she made vichyssoise, *gratin dauphinois* and a soufflé. She roasted the scrag end with onions.

The dinner was sitting ready for them when the farming three came back with the ewes. Michael was soaked to the knees from wading through deep water. Old Dave was wheezing horribly.

"I've made the dinner," said Jane. "I hope you don't mind, Mrs Temple."

Cecily silently regarded the feast, neatly set out on the kitchen table, and the pretty bunch of snowdrops, pulled from the kitchen garden, nicely arranged in the milk jug. She felt suddenly territorial.

"Well, *I* don't want any of your fussy French muck."

It was their first night together at Temple. Jane and Michael lay rigidly side by side in the Irish double bed. Michael's feet hung over the end of the footboard. Jane wore an ankle-length nightdress; her husband's pyjamas were buttoned up to his neck. The bedroom door was firmly shut. On honeymoon they'd made love twice a day and slept naked, plastered against each other, a fortnight of delicious discovery. Michael had eaten two fried eggs every morning to keep his energy levels up.

"Please, can we hold hands?" Jane whispered.

"Keep your patty fingers to yourself! I have to get up at six to do the milking!"

Jane was trying to go to sleep like a good girl and not to obsess about the possibility of never having sex with her husband again when a cacophony of enormous, unapologetic, rip-roaring bellows startled the quiet night.

"Wake up, Michael, wake up! I think your bull has broken out!"

Michael grunted in his sleep. "My father snores, you'll get used to it."

Later that night, just as Jane was dozing over, Cecily came frantically knocking at the bedroom door.

"I'm having a heart attack, Michael! You'll have to go for the doctor!"

Jane frantically nudged her husband awake. "Wake up, Michael, wake up! Your mother's having a heart attack!"

Michael grunted again in his sleep. "My mother sleep-walks, you'll get used to it."

Jane wasn't so sure. "I'll get used to it the way the soldiers got used to the trenches during the First World War!"

Jane's first walk every morning was into the village with Kathleen. Generally they didn't talk because Kathleen wasn't a morning person; she was the sort of girl who, when you said "Good morning" before ten or ten thirty, would answer, "Is it?"

"You must be very clever, to work in a bank," said Jane.

Kathleen shrugged for it wasn't easy having brains and ambition when you lived in the back of beyond and your father was a religious maniac. Her teachers at the grammar school had suggested medicine and had offered to coach her for the entrance exam to Queens but Old Dave wouldn't hear of it.

"No daughter of mine is going gallivanting to university, to learn the ways of the wicked world, and turn her back on a decent, God-fearing upbringing."

This was Kathleen's first real chance at escape from the cows and the muck. Desperately she'd argued with Old Dave.

"But I'd be doing good in the world if I was doctor!"

"You'd be doing good in the world if you learned to *'honour thy father and thy mother: that thy days may be long upon the land which the Lord thy God giveth thee.'* Exodus 20, verse 12!"

"Him and his frigging commandments," said Cecily, who was sympathetic to Kathleen's aspirations but couldn't help her, stuck as she was in the back of beyond with a maniac she'd vowed to obey.

Since leaving school Kathleen had worked in the bank at a tiny desk, in a dull little job that filled up the time until Prince Charming arrived to rescue her. There'd been opportunities for promotion but she hadn't even considered them. This was not meant to be her life, only an interlude at the start of it. She barely passed the time of day with her co-workers.

"Stuck-up cow," they called her and she didn't care.

Once Kathleen's bus was gone, Jane strolled through Lisglasson village which had been built by the first Lord Glass in 1732, or so it was carved on the magnificent stone gateposts at the top of the street, through which you could see up the long straight mile to the house. It was Palladian and very beautiful; it looked like a wedding-cake from a distance.

Michael had solemnly told her, "There's been a Glass at Lisglasson since Cromwell!"

The village school was part of the estate and the private chapel was down by the lough shore. It was boggy even on the best days and could only be reached for Morning Prayer in wellies. Over the centuries other bits had been added on – a shop, a post office, a football pitch, a pub.

"What more does a man need, apart from a woman to share it?" said Michael.

Jane was only seventeen. She'd never been this far into rural Ireland before and she thought Lisglasson enchanting. She wouldn't have been a bit surprised if a coach and four had swept out of the enormous gates, attended by liveried footmen with ladies inside wearing crinolines and bonnets, or if the rabbits had started to talk, or fairies come out of the picturesque cottages.

What a fantastical place to come for a visit, to buy an ice-cream and drive on, back to civilisation.

The most difficult part of Jane's marriage was the weekend for there were no weekends at Temple: the cows were milked twice a day, every day, even Sunday.

"Are you telling me that you don't get a day off – ever?"

Michael stroked Daisy's nose. He had fifty milking cows and he knew them all by name for they stood gently tethered in the byre all winter, munching at the hay he carried to them. He took them for a walk in the afternoon, for a breath of fresh air, down the rutted farm lanes, between high, beautiful hedges. He carried the milking equipment to them. He treated them and tended them as gently as a mother with her children. Always, the cows came first.

"I was hoping that we could go for a run to Derry, to see my mother on Saturday? And maybe go out for a wee dance to the Electric Ballroom after?"

Michael shook his head.

"Early to bed, early to rise," he said.

For three ghastly months Jane lived at Temple, vainly trying to reconcile herself to sharing a house and her life with in-laws who cordially hated her.

16

"You're imagining things," said Michael. "Nobody hates you."

So Jane tried to make friends with Kathleen but sulky, spiteful Kathleen's idea of sister-in-law friendship was to borrow Jane's clothes without asking, spill things down the front of them and return them stained and unwashed, without an apology.

Michael said, "Don't take it personally, she's only jealous because you won the Derry Emerald and caught a husband and she's turning into an old maid."

"But it's not just my clothes – clothes can be washed. It's the way she never makes eye contact. I think she doesn't like me."

"Give her the benefit of the doubt," said Michael who didn't like conflict, not that he was a sissy, but his sister Kathleen had a piercing reputation for screeching and sulking and Michael never crossed her.

Then Jane tried to make friends with Cecily.

"Please let me make the dinner tonight, Mrs Temple."

Cecily poked at the pig's head bubbling in a saucepan on the range.

"What's wrong with the good plain cooking you get here, three times a day, free?"

Even the house hated Jane. The water was always cold when she took a bath. There was always a draught where she was sitting. Twice she tripped at the top of the steep narrow back stairs – only that she managed to grab the banister rail she'd have broken her neck. And every morning, noon and night the house whispered, "Get out, you're not wanted!"

One morning Jane put on her wellies and just kept on walking along the quiet country roads choked with meadow sweet. She walked the full length of the wall at Lisglasson and on through Derryrose village and across the big main road from Derry to Belfast. On and on, past fields of cows and country graveyards and huddles of council cottages. There wasn't a soul to be seen and nobody from Temple came after her.

Finally she reached the edge of the prosperous town where Kathleen worked. It had a grammar school, a hospital, a public swimming-pool, a cinema and a large ugly sprawling council estate called Sperrin View.

There was no central heating in Sperrin View and everyone burnt turf from the mountain, five bags a day, even in early summer. The turf smoke lay heavy over the houses, the condensation never dried on the windows; the estate was known locally as Stove Pipe Town.

Jane walked slowly through Stove Pipe Town in her wellies. She thought it noisy and jolly with children running and playing and mums sitting together in tiny gardens, smoking and sunbathing in their bras. Temple was so splendidly isolated in comparison, up a long lane, surrounded by empty fields. Stove Pipe Town, with five hundred people and a hundred houses could easily fit into the corner of the Forty Acres and there'd still be part of a field left over.

Deep in its heart, with houses to the right of it and houses to the left of it and houses in front of it, was a bleak terrace. In the middle of the terrace was an empty house. There was a *"For Rent"* sign erected in the ramshackle front garden.

A tall solemn-faced woman came out of Next Door.

"Hello there!" she said. "Have you come to look at the house?"

Susie was born when Jane was twenty and living in her council-house exile, to all intents and purposes a single mum

18

because Michael was five miles out the road at Temple from six every morning, seven days a week, milking cows, eating with his parents and trying not to think about the screeching chaos that was his current state of married domestic bliss.

Jane was frantic on the doorstep every evening. "Susie won't stop crying. She doesn't sleep long enough in the middle of the day for me to boil myself a potato . . ."

By now, Michael could barely recognise the glittering emerald he'd married, she was so horribly morphed into a skinny, anxious, highly-strung sort he didn't even fancy.

And though willing he couldn't help her because Susie didn't know him and hadn't liked him almost from the point of conception. Every night that first frantic, noisy year Michael stoically tied one end of a piece of baler twine to his foot and the other to the side of the rocking cradle at the bottom of the bed and taught himself to sleep with his foot in perpetual motion, rocking the rocking cradle because sometimes Susie stopped crying when she was in perpetual motion, probably because she was too dizzy to cry.

"If only you were around in the middle of the day to help me! If only your parents would allow us to build our own house on the farm!" Jane waved some sketches under his nose. "I sketched out some ideas this morning . . . And before you ask, I was rocking Susie's pram with my foot at the same time!"

Courteously Michael inspected the pencil drawings. They were sleep-deprived and surreal, impractical and beautiful. Just like Jane in fact. Tall slender houses with tall slender windows, flagstone floors, open fires and a kitchen made of industrial steel. Susie's bedroom was in a Rapunzel turret with padded walls . . .

"There's no bathroom!"

"Because people don't pee in fairytales!"

Michael shook his head and sighed and explained again how Old Dave had retorted to repeated requests for another house on the farm: "We don't need another house here at Temple. I'm an old man – I won't live for much longer. Soon I shall be dead."

"And what will your mother do then? Will she oblige us and die the same day as your father?"

Michael was an optimist. "Maybe my sister Kathleen will be married and she can go and live with her . . ."

"Bless your innocence," said Jane sarcastically.

3

Jane denied it emphatically afterwards – she swore Patrick was an immaculate conception – but at some stage during that first awful year Susie must have slept. Because on Susie's first birthday Patrick arrived.

"I don't know how it happened either," Michael boasted happily since there was no denying that from birth Baby Patrick with his crooked smile and shy eyes was the picture of his dad.

The birth of Baby Patrick should have finally had a miraculous softening effect on the old pair out at Temple.

Jane waited with joyful anticipation in her hospital bed for the tremendous announcement. *"You've produced a son and heir. Please come in from the cold. Of course you can build your own house if you want to!"*

But it never came. The Temples didn't even visit her.

Michael was encouraging. "My mother said 'That's nice' when I told her you'd had a boy but she's very tied up with Kathleen's birthday party . . ."

21

Kathleen's twenty-first was the talk of the country. There was to be a marquee and a band. Rich cousins were coming from Fermanagh. Every eligible bachelor in South Derry was invited.

"Isn't it going to be rather cold for a marquee?" Jane asked him, for it was January and there was a foot of snow on the ground.

"It was on special offer. We've told everyone to wear a fur coat."

Jane stroked the tiny hand of her tiny newborn son. Every muscle in her slender body ached from the rough handling of her endless labour. Who was it said the first baby was the worst? They should have been present when Baby Patrick was born and his mother had almost split in two with the exertion of delivering him.

"I *am* invited, aren't I?" she asked.

Michael had been stoically present the whole of the harrowing night, barking words of encouragement, with his gruff mask firmly in place, but his eyes had been wretched at the sight of his darling wife's terrible suffering. Jane was a brave girl and she hadn't wasted energy screaming her head off, but once with her face pressed into the hospital pillow he'd heard her whisper, "No one dies from this pain, do they?" and the thought of losing her had chilled him far more than any howling or swearing.

Doubtfully he said now, "You're hardly in a fit state for dancing . . ."

Jane flicked her fathomless eyes at the bold Michael. Tough guy! She'd been convulsed in agony, gasping on the gas and air, but she'd still seen his anguish as the midwives in the delivery room became increasingly less matter of fact in their handling of her labour and began to mutter to each other about emergency C-sections and whether they should phone for the consultant.

"But am I *invited*?"

Michael was firm. "Of course you are, but everyone will understand that you can't make it. You have two very small children and I'm going to be busy talking to my aunties."

Jane drove herself home from hospital the day of Kathleen's twenty-first. Michael didn't need the car; he was staying overnight at Temple. He had dropped Susie and the car keys into the hospital on his way to the farm.

"Mummy, Mummy!" sang Susie and she buried her face in her mother's neck and sniffed contentedly.

Jane whispered, "Poor little you, and poor little me, and poor little Baby Patrick. I don't think we'll even be missed . . ."

She folded her two little babies into her arms and cried bitter tears.

It is testament to the fact that Jane really loved Michael that she did not, that day, pack the car with Susie and Patrick and leave him. For she had a broadminded and indulgent family she could have gone home to and, unlike many women of her generation, she had a mother who even urged it.

They came in a convoy over the Glenshane Pass, Jane's mother and aunts, her sisters and old Granny Costello who was nearly ninety and crippled.

They told her, "You made a mistake when you married him. Those Temple farmers are very odd people – is it true that they never take holidays?"

"And is it true that Cecily Temple hasn't had a new pair of stockings since your wedding?"

"And is it true that they've not got a washing-machine?"

"And is it true that they're charging an entrance fee to

Kathleen's birthday party and they plan to raffle her off at the interval?"

"It's too late to lecture me now," said Jane.

"It's never too late," said Granny Costello who'd finally divorced her husband on his deathbed after forty-five years of bad feeling.

Jane's mother said, "Leave him, love, and come home to Derry. I'll help you look after my lovely wee grandchildren, and you can go to the Catering College which is what you always wanted to do and maybe you'll meet a nice city boy who won't mind that you already have two little children . . ."

Then everyone else chimed in.

"Michael Temple is a nice lad. Give him a chance while he's still young to marry a farmer's daughter who knows her place. In a couple of years you'll both look back and laugh at the folly of your youth . . ."

"*Get thee behind me, Satan,*" said Jane.

"Famous last words," said the Costello women.

Kathleen tried on her one good dress, the silver-grey bombazine with an acre of taffeta skirt that she'd worn in the final of Derry's Emerald. It was still a pretty dress, if a little bit frumpy, but today it was horribly tight. Kathleen could hardly breathe and the zip was wedged only halfway up her back.

Easy tears sprang into Kathleen's eyes. They were tears of anger and desperation and despair. She didn't have another dress to wear and it was definitely too late to go on a starvation diet. Her fabulous birthday party, the talk of the country, was going to be a flop because she was a big fat blob.

And her hair was a mess. She had no hands for hair so she simply couldn't manage the new fashion for flattening it with an iron – there was a singed bit at the front . . .

24

"What am I going to do, Mummy?"

Cecily was killing the fatted calf for her only daughter's twenty-first and the marquee and the band were only the start of it. She'd been out on the tractor with a chainsaw, felling every superfluous tree on the farm while Old Dave and Michael built an enormous bonfire with the wood in a paddock beside the marquee. For a week she'd been roasting turkeys and boiling hams (half price now that Christmas was over). Now she was buttering twelve loaves of bread with the ambitious intention of making a mountain of sandwiches for the interval when the raffle was called.

Cecily spoke sharply to her daughter. "What can you expect when you ate so much over Christmas – roast potatoes, gravy and stuffing, trifle? I watched you, Kathleen, I even warned you: *a moment on the lips, a lifetime on the hips*!"

"You're not very helpful, Mummy."

Cecily lost her temper. All this effort and the ungrateful girl couldn't even fit into her frock!

"Stop fussing about how you look! If you've got nothing better to do, get up those stairs and strip the bed in the spare room. The Fermanagh millionaires have just phoned to say they're staying the night."

Never one for self-control, Kathleen roughly barged out though the scullery and into the back yard where she screeched ear-piercingly into the frosted air. Cecily sniffed disparagingly at her daughter's theatrics and continued to butter the bread. It was her maternal opinion that though Kathleen was clever she had no personality, no sense of humour and no charm. And if they didn't catch her a husband at her big splash of a birthday party she was going to be stuck on the shelf for the rest of her life, a spinster and a millstone round her mother's neck.

(Not for the world would she have admitted it but the

awful thought of living with Kathleen forever often sent Cecily discreetly sleep-walking round the house in the middle of the night, muttering, "I'm having a heart attack, you'll have to go for the doctor . . .")

Kathleen felt a bit better after the big scream. She'd even thought of somebody who could help her. The January dusk descended early. She hid her singed hair under a headscarf, squashed her big belly into a fitted coat and slipped away from Temple. Nobody noticed. Old Dave and Michael were milking in the cow byre. Cecily was half-cut in the kitchen, gleefully concocting a welcome drink which tasted only of fruit juice (to please her husband's puritanical morals) but delivered a poteen kick when swallowed.

Kathleen drove cautiously into Stove Pipe Town. She wasn't quite sure where the house was. It never once occurred to her that she was imposing herself on a woman who had only recently and harrowingly given birth and she wasn't even bringing a baby present!

Jane answered the front door in her dressing-gown. Her face was pale; she was bent over like an old woman.

Temporarily shocked out of her self-absorption Kathleen's hand flew up to her mouth.

"You look like death warmed up!"

Jane grinned. "I feel like I've been run over by a bus. Take a word of advice while you've still a choice in the matter and never marry a man with a big head, just in case his son inherits it!"

Kathleen had no idea what Jane was talking about. Could she still be under the influence of the drugs in the labour ward? The words "Please help me!" were forming in her mouth, but before she could force them out Jane shuffled slowly away, down the dark hall and into the living-room, which seemed to be full of tall, beautiful, dark-haired Costello women, passing the bundle of new baby between them.

"Bless him, but he'll be tall and strong and good-looking," said the old hag sitting on the best seat in front of the fire with her feet up, nursing Susie.

"And the women will come from miles in the hope of catching his eye."

"And he'll never be short of a few bob."

"And he'll marry for love and live happily ever after!"

Kathleen, overwrought to the point of madness, exclaimed, "And he'll prick his finger with a spindle on his sixteenth birthday and fall asleep for a hundred years!" She burst into hysterical tears.

The Costello women looked at each other, then at Jane. They didn't speak, but the words "Told you so – mentally unhinged – it's still not too late to pack the car and come home with us" vibrated in the hot perfumed air of the living-room.

"What's the matter, Kathleen?" Jane asked gently. "Is it stage fright?"

"It's my hair."

Kathleen pulled off the headscarf to show them the burnt place. Then she dramatically unbelted her coat and allowed her belly to spill out.

"And my belly! I'm too fat to get into my frock!"

The Costello women studied her quietly; their keen eyes missed nothing. Kathleen felt like a cow in the sales ring at the market yard. She wouldn't have been a bit surprised if one of them had run an appraising hand over her bottom or pulled back her lips to look at her teeth.

Finally one of them spoke. She was an older version of Jane, she might have been Jane's mother, but there were so many of them and they were all blessed with such ageless beauty, it was hard to tell. It had been the same at the wedding – Cecily had suggested they wear name tags, with the family tree connection written underneath.

The Costello woman said, "Sure that's only the smallest bit of a burn! Haven't I anxious women coming into my salon every day of the week with chunks burnt out of themselves? Come out to the scullery with me till I find a pair of scissors and I'll soon have that wee bit of a burn tidied away out of your hair!"

Then Jane said, "You've not put on that much weight, I think my black halter-neck frock will fit you . . ."

"But you're far thinner than me!"

"The fabric drapes but you'll need a pair of high heels to carry it off. What size are your feet?"

Kathleen shook her head firmly. She was five foot ten in her bare feet and very self-conscious about her height. All her life she'd stooped a bit: "Coming down to your level!" she'd joke even though it wasn't funny. And she always wore clumpy-heeled shoes which ruined the shape of her shapely ankles and excellent legs and made her bum look like it was trailing along the ground.

"I couldn't possibly wear high heels. I'd tower over every man there!"

The old granny by the fire said, "Aren't we all the same height when we're horizontal?"

Then the rest of the Costello women offered their opinions:

"You've a very symmetrical face – it'll carry a lot of make-up."

"Big earrings always look good with big hair."

Kathleen hesitated. "You're not going to make me look cheap, are you?"

"You wish!"

An hour later Kathleen Temple was beautiful. Her blonde hair was exquisitely ironed, framing a flawless complexion and enormous seductive painted eyes. Her large capable hands looked less mannish with the fingernails filed and polished. Jane's black halter-neck frock was a show-stopper. When Kathleen threw back her shoulders her huge breasts reared up in magnificence and her muscular legs were endless on the top of a pair of borrowed Derry stilettos.

The Costello women carefully inspected their handiwork.

"If you wear regular pants under that thin black dress you're going to have VPL," said one. "Would you prefer no knickers or a panty girdle?"

Kathleen couldn't stop looking at herself in the mirror over the fireplace. A voluptuous siren smiled back. Was it really her?

"No knickers!"

Finally she was ready to leave.

Jane said, "You can borrow my fur coat if you like. I don't need it and it's probably the only opportunity you'll ever get to go out in a fur coat with no knickers!"

"She never said 'thank you'," said Granny Costello once Kathleen was gone, trailing a miasma of strong perfume and stronger hairspray in her wake.

Jane shrugged. "What can you expect from a pig but a grunt?"

4

Operation Catch Kathleen a Husband was ten minutes to blast off. And you could be sure there would be at least one carload of rude guests who would turn up on time. Cecily hoped there was a special place in hell for them. And for the Fermanagh millionaires who were sleeping over and expected a red carpet. What was wrong with the B&B in town? She'd suggested it, she'd even offered to phone and book them a room but Dave's sister, Rose, wouldn't hear of it.

"Nonsense, Cecily!" said Rose. "Temple is big enough for everyone."

And since Michael was sleeping in his old bedroom Cecily was going to have to sleep with Old Dave who she hadn't shared a bed with for years.

"I'm sorry, Dave," she'd said, after the children were born, "no offence and I know I'm not perfect either, but once I tune into your snoring I'm awake all night . . ."

"Can't you poke me so I roll over on my side?"

"No."

Old Dave had been banished to a cold bed in the spare room at the top of the house. In desperation he'd tried everything to stop snoring: sleeping tablets, herbal pillows, a gum shield, clothes pegs on his nose, a sharp pastry cutter sewn into the back of his pyjamas, even a faith healer. Nothing worked.

"Can't you wear earplugs, Cecily darling?"

"I could, but the bed would still vibrate."

You can say what you like about Cecily Temple – and many people did, for she was a sharp-tongued, tactless woman – but Cecily understood the simple things in life and she knew that nobody wise would leave a warm fire and the television on a bitter January evening and go out to a party unless there was free drink, lots to eat, and plenty to gossip about.

"The brass neck of her, charging an entrance fee!"

Admission was by invitation only and Cecily had been ruthless with the guest list. This was a party to catch Kathleen a husband so any local girl who was pretty and unattached simply was not invited. Only the stout girls and the spotty girls and those unfortunate enough to have squinty eyes and buck teeth were welcome.

Engaged girls and married girls were making up the numbers because they had already caught husbands and couldn't be classed as competition.

(And wasn't it just as well that beautiful Jane Costello, Derry's Emerald, was languishing after a twenty-two hour labour, a high forceps delivery and fifteen stitches and was physically unable to upstage the Birthday Girl?)

"Why can't I invite my friends, Mummy?"

"Because they're prettier than you."

Surrounded by the cosmetically challenged, Cecily hoped it wouldn't be quite so obvious that Kathleen's vibrant, youthful bloom had started to go off her. Perhaps no one would notice the permanent frown of discontent between her eyebrows and the stubborn jut of her chin. Telling everyone to wear a fur coat had been inspirational for huddled inside a fur coat it would be less obvious that Kathleen's voluptuous chest was becoming shelf-like and her magnificent curves were running to fat.

"Some men like a big bird," Old Dave pointed out. "Something warm to cuddle up against in a cold bed in winter . . ."

"Some men might be afraid of her rolling on them and squashing them to death."

Cecily was many things, but she wasn't a snob and she'd cast her net wide in her conscientious effort to catch Kathleen a husband. Every eligible tinker, tailor, soldier and spy was invited to the party, but no farmers, not even rich ones, for after thirty hard years with Old Dave Cecily wouldn't have wished the life of a farmer's wife on anyone, even a daughter she was desperate to marry off.

"Whyever not?" asked Rose, who'd come from Fermanagh bearing gifts: a box of groceries for Cecily, a string of pearls for Kathleen, something that looked like a large teddy bear elaborately wrapped in blue tissue paper for brand-new Baby Patrick.

Cecily had already enviously remarked on Rose's new fur coat; this one reached right down to the floor and had an elegant hat to match.

"Bertie took me to Brown Thomas at Christmas and told me to pick anything I wanted!"

Bertie was a builder and he was rolling in money, which he loved to spend on Rose; "my princess" he called her. He cheerfully paid for her to go to a health farm once a week for all the works.

It might have been easy to make fun of Bertie and Rose for they were all cash and no class, except that Rose looked twenty years younger than Cecily and her flamboyantly made-up face wore an expression of contentment that bags of money can never buy. Even now, Bertie was still blowing her kisses across the kitchen table . . .

"Why did you not marry a farmer, Rose?"

"I fell in love with Bertie."

"That's exactly what I always tell Kathleen! That it's just as easy to fall in love with a rich man as a poor man . . ."

It was the appointed hour. Old Dave lit the bonfire, the band began to play. A thousand fairy lights twinkled in the marquee as Cecily took up position, modest and unadorned in her good coat with the fur collar, a rictus grin of welcome plastered firmly to her face.

The stout girls and the spotty girls flocked into Kathleen's birthday party, where they were invited to sit on bales of straw, and offered nudge-nudge wink-wink fruit punch from gorgeous Michael Temple who was squashed into a fitted dinner jacket, his handsome head bulging over the top of the bow tie Cecily had pulled too tight.

"Be still, my beating heart!" giggled the stout girls and the spotty girls. There'd been a wake when he married Jane Costello; hearts had been broken and tears were spilled.

"The wife's at home tonight with a new baby," they whispered to each other.

"And you know what they say – you're never the same again *down there*, after you've had a baby . . ."

Michael took another swig of nudge-nudge wink-wink

fruit punch. He could feel a dozen hungry, lascivious eyes piercing his back and his buttocks. Without Jane by his side he was naked and vulnerable and he knew his mother expected him to dance with every one of these wallflowers, even the girls he wouldn't normally go near with a bargepole, even the brass-necked hussies who would press themselves against him and grind their hips into his hips when they were dancing.

This was the reason she'd insisted he come to the birthday party.

"I don't want to come," Michael had said. "I want to stay at home with my wife."

And Cecily had wept hysterical tears and thrown a couple of saucepans and threatened to drown herself in the river if he didn't show up and divert attention away from the shower of eligible bachelors, hand-picked to marry Kathleen.

"It's not like she's swimming in sex appeal, or rotten with money. Don't you realise we're going to have to *trick* somebody into taking her?"

Now Michael took another anxious gulp of the nudge-nudge wink-wink fruit punch. Soon he would be partially pissed and comfortably anaesthetised and fair game for women he wasn't fit for.

Auntie Rose had been admiring Kathleen's extraordinary birthday cake, the shape of a milking cow, with a pink icing udder, on a pedestal up on the podium. From her vantage point she could see Michael nervously necking the nudge-nudge wink-wink fruit punch. His face was hard but his eyes were anxious as a coven of ugly women licked their lips and closed in on him.

"Come and dance with your Auntie Rose!" she said and she swept him away.

"Thanks, Auntie Rose."

She grinned. "It's a common mistake that people make, to think that the morals of plain girls are superior to those of their prettier counterparts – how do you think I caught your Uncle Bertie?"

Cecily began to relax as the marquee filled. The band was playing marching tunes and the stout girls and the spotty girls, many of whom were officers in the Girls' Brigade, had arranged themselves into marching formation. Old Dave, who'd been a sergeant major in Crete in 1945, stood to attention at the edge of the dance floor and roared drill instructions . . . could there have been a jag too much poteen in the fruit punch?

Already she could spot two of South Derry's most eligible bachelors: Arthur Stewart whose father owned a furniture empire, and Rupert Glass, the only son of Lord Laurence Glass who owned Lisglasson estate.

Arthur Stewart was Cecily's first choice of a husband for Kathleen. He was a tall, fattish man who wore a swanky sports coat and slicked back his hair like Elvis. Cecily wasn't usually charmed by salesmen, she thought them oily and ingratiating, but Arthur was an only son and Stewart's Fine Furnishings had branches all over Ireland. It was said Arthur had a breast fixation and an evil reputation for savaging women's nipples and this was reason he hadn't yet been snapped up and married. Cecily chose to ignore this scurrilous rumour. What sort of silly girl would allow a man to bite till he drew blood? It wasn't like he tied them down – Cecily had checked – and one good hard smack across the back of the head of any man (or dog) would soon cure him of biting . . .

Failing that, Rupert Glass would have to do, though Cecily

had little time for the aristocracy, finding them even odder and meaner than herself. She'd once been fleetingly friendly with Lady Glass when Michael and Rupert were small boys and Michael was invited to the Big House to play. She'd taken him, dressed in his best shorts, with his curly hair carefully flattened with spit – to find Rupert filthy and frolicking in a pink crimplene trouser suit, and Lady Glass halfway down a bottle of gin.

"Rupert has only sisters, four of them, older than him. Pointless creatures! I was so utterly desperate for a son I took special herbal supplements flown in from London and ate special food. Every two hours I took my temperature, my *vaginal* temperature, and when the thermometer said I was 'optimum' and I was sure I was ovulating I whistled for Laurence and we copulated."

"Disgusting," said Cecily who didn't like sex.

Lady Glass had trailed a diamond-encrusted finger along Cecily's flushed cheek.

"I don't like sex with men either," she whispered and her face was so close Cecily could almost taste the gin off her breath.

"I think it's the inbreeding," said Cecily but she refused to rule out Rupert as potential husband material, simply because his mother had questionable sexual preferences. And didn't Lady Kathleen Glass have a lovely ring to it?

There was a hush in the marquee when Kathleen made her grand entrance. Cecily's heart sank into her sensible shoes. What had the irritating girl done to herself? She was radiant and she looked about eight foot tall. And she was acting like a film star at the Oscars, pausing and posing at the door of the tent with her chest stuck out and a painted hand stroking her generous hips. Jane Costello's good fur coat was hanging seductively off her shoulders.

The band began to play "Happy Birthday". Kathleen strode onto the dance floor, swinging her hips, trailing the fur coat on the ground behind her. It was her finest moment.

At the raffle Kathleen was won by Rupert Glass. No one was vulgar enough to suggest that the raffle had been rigged!

"Take me, I'm yours!" said Kathleen coquettishly (half a glass of fruit punch had gone to her head). When the band started up again and the guests were dancing he took her to the back seat of his car, parked behind the hay barn.

Kathleen was feverish with excitement. This was her first proper court in a car. She was dressed to kill. She was wearing stilettos. She wasn't wearing knickers.

Rupert was rather pleased with himself too. It was the way Kathleen was pressed against him and the way she kept laughing at everything he said and the way she was allowing him to grope her all the way up to the top of her stockings and the way she was moaning with pleasure and opening her legs. It was anyone's guess what she'd let him grope if his car wasn't basking in a bright full moon. Perhaps he should take her for a little spin to the lough shore . . .

Next morning Kathleen's lips were still stinging from Rupert's rough kisses and her body was still tender from his rough hands.

"What's first base?" was the only question she hadn't been able to answer in the etiquette section of the Derry Emerald.

"Take care, my girl," warned Cecily. "Why would Rupert Glass buy the cow if he can get the milk for free?"

Kathleen tossed her head defensively. "Oh really, Mummy!"

But the faintest tremor of doubt slipped into her soul and when Rupert didn't call her that day or the day after or the day after that, and when she occasionally saw him driving past (when she just happened to be walking alongside the demesne wall of Lisglasson, dressed in her tightest bell-bottom trousers) he lifted his hand with a formality that made her wonder if he even remembered who she was. Kathleen vowed that the next man who won her in a raffle would be made beg for it on bended knee.

"*There's none so prudish as a reformed whore,*" muttered her mother and she got out her address book again and began to compile another list of '*Suitable Husbands For Kathleen*'.

But, having fallen heavy at the first fence, Kathleen lost her confidence and abandoned all hope of marriage as the obvious escape route from Temple.

She decided to concentrate on her career.

When the position of assistant to the bank manager became unexpectedly available Kathleen leapt at the chance. Boldly she applied for the job.

There was a violin softly playing when Kathleen went for her interview with the bank manager. Victor Rich – they called him "Rich Rich" – was a very tall man, slightly stooped with the habit of leaning over to listen to short employees. But there was no stooping when he stood up to shake Kathleen's hand. In her new high heels she was almost tall enough to look him in the eye and an electric shock shot up her arm when he touched her.

At first Kathleen didn't recognise the signs of love. When she looked at Mr Rich she saw only the most famously tragic man in South Derry whose lovely wife had walked out on him twenty years before but people were still talking about it.

Those who were charitable said, "She was a city girl. Country living was never going to suit her."

Those who were less charitable said, "She took drink and her head went."

Kathleen thought the shivers going up and down her spine when he was near her were sympathy.

5

Two babies are ten times more work than one. Even when one of them is a good baby. You'd have hardly known Patrick was in the house. It was almost as if he was trying to make up for the trouble he caused being born.

"Do you think there might be something wrong with him?" Jane fretted, because after the Susie experience she couldn't believe there were babies who slept for longer than twenty minutes and Patrick only ever woke once at night for a bottle and always brought up wind when he was finished. When he was awake he was content to rest quietly in his bouncy chair and watch Susie throwing tantrums on the floor in front of him.

"Jealousy," diagnosed Old Mrs Somerville from Number 12. "She's jealous of the new baby so she's attention-seeking."

Jane was still weak from the delivery. Her stitches were taking forever to knit. Her breasts were leaking and the tablets to stop the milk flow were making her nauseous. There wasn't a bite of food in the house and she couldn't get out to the shops. Michael was away at Temple in the Rapier and wouldn't be home till dark. By then the shops would be shut, even Keane's on the corner where the bread was never fresh.

Tears of desperation pricked Jane's eyes. "Poor little Susie! It can't be easy for her. What can I do to stop her feeling threatened?"

Mrs Somerville was brisk. "Nothing you can do, dear, though I've always thought a good hard smack . . ."

Jane's world began to blur and shrink. All day she was kept busy with the babies and the repetitive grind of mothering them: sterilising bottles, boiling nappies, wiping snotty noses, cleaning dirty bums, policing Susie to ensure that she didn't try to suffocate Patrick, or sit on his head. (As well as the general domestic drudgery of cooking and cleaning, washing and drying, ironing . . .)

At night she belonged to Michael. After the six-week watershed, when her physical bruising had healed, normal service was resumed in the bedroom. The first time, they made love gently in the pitch dark, with whispers and sighs and guiding fingers. Not because they were afraid of hurting Jane; it was Susie they feared in the room across the landing. She slept so fitfully that the rhythmic creaking of her parents' bed, or the gentle slap of its headboard against the wall, even for five minutes, was enough to wake her up and keep her awake half the night, screeching in her cot until Jane yielded and brought her into the bed where there would be demands for bobo and dodo and all the sundry other things used to plug the orifice that the noise came out of.

Jane's body was still beautiful. She'd carried two babies without a stretch mark to show for it. Yet the pitch black lovemaking excited Michael far more than anything they'd ever done with the lights on, for without sight his other senses were heightened and he could savour the smell of her skin, the taste of her mouth and the heat in the secret folds at the top of her thighs.

Afterwards he whispered, "I never realised that I don't need to see you to desire you . . ."

She smiled into the dark at his innocence. "Have you never heard that expression – *'you don't look at the fireplace when you're poking the fire'*?"

"That's not what I meant!"

"I know it isn't."

Normal service with one minor adjustment. The memory of Jane's long night of suffering labour was still fresh. "Don't ask me ever to face that again," she said so their lovemaking was now strictly recreational – sex for exercise, sex for fun, sex for the sake of it; can't hear anybody complaining.

Spring came, the lambing started. Sometimes Michael was gone from six in the morning till ten at night.

"Lucky you!" said Diane from Next Door. "My Gerry gets home from work at tea-time and he expects me to drop all and roll out a red carpet for him. And if I don't have his dinner on the table he sulks with me. Once he sulked for a whole week and I had to sleep on the sofa in the living-room there was such an *atmosphere* in the bedroom."

"Men are only good for one thing and sometimes that's a disappointment!" Linda from Number 14 was a full twelve stone of animal instinct and urges. Her husband had escaped quite early on in their marriage when he realised she was a nymphomaniac and he was never going to be able to satisfy her.

Another Saturday night. Jane sat alone in her council house, all dressed up with nowhere to go, watching happy-ever-after television, waiting for Michael who didn't wear a watch. There was no appointed hour for his homecoming; he finished farming when the farming was finished.

It was lonesome, the waiting. Diane and Linda invited her to Tupperware parties and baby-clothes parties to pass the time. At the weekend they wanted to take her shopping.

"Come with us to Derry – we'll call in on your mammy for a cup of tea."

"I wish," said Jane, "but Michael farms on Saturday and I can't leave the babies."

"Bring the babies with you!"

"I wish," said Jane, "but I want to bake Michael a cake. It's our anniversary – we met thirty-three months ago today. I remember it like it was yesterday – the happiest day of my life."

"I'm so glad I didn't marry for love," said Diane to Linda and they were gone, bouncing out of Stove Pipe Town in "My Gerry's" Ford Capri with go-faster stripes.

Jan With The Pram they called her in the town, for she was never seen but she had the two babies with her, squashed in beside the groceries, and on the rare occasion that she wasn't physically attached to it her body was still braced from the weight of the pushing.

"Your young husband is asking for trouble, leaving a beautiful woman like you unattended," warned Old Mrs Somerville.

It was just an average Tuesday, a miserable wet day and the living-room was trashed, the fire was smoking, the windows were steamed up, condensation ran down the scullery walls and nappies bubbled in a cauldron on the gas ring.

Last night Susie had woken up twice, screaming with sore ears, but Jane couldn't get her to the doctor, in the rain, for an antibiotic. Now she was high on infant painkillers and performing a war dance round Patrick who wasn't sure whether to smile or defend himself.

"Please be careful with the baby, darling," Jane warned from the scullery where she was scraping carrots.

Unheeding, Susie rushed forward, whooping. She tripped on the edge of the bouncy chair.

It happened in slow motion. Jane dropped the carrot and leapt to catch the cauldron of nappies on the gas ring as Susie lurched towards it, arms flailing, a scream caught in her throat. Jane narrowly missed burning her own hands and the tender parts of her wrists but she saved Susie the best part of a serious scald. Only the wash of the boiling water tipped over the rim and splashed onto Susie's plump, bare forearms.

"Mummy, Mummy!" screamed Susie.

There was no telephone at Temple. Michael couldn't be contacted, even in a crisis. Jane gathered up Susie into her arms and frantically turned to her neighbours for help.

"She'll have to go to the hospital," said Diane and she ran to the call box at the end of the street to phone for an ambulance.

Mrs Somerville came to sit with Patrick, Linda offered to walk out to Temple to tell Michael.

"But it's five miles," said Jane who had Susie in the bath and was throwing cold water over her, though she wasn't sure if cold water was the proper first aid for a scald.

"Five miles, nothing, I'll be there in an hour."

"In that skirt and heels?"

"Some dirty old man is bound to stop for me!" said Linda and she sashayed out of Stove Pipe Town in her mini-skirt and her platform sandals, blowing smoke rings from her cigarette.

The story of Linda's mercy dash became the stuff of legend round Stove Pipe Town. As predicted, she was picked up at the edge of the town by a country boy the size of a small mountain who had muscles in places where other men didn't have places. He was bouncing along in a tractor with some farming thing attached to the back of it.

"You're a long way from home!" he said when she climbed up into his cab.

(It rather depended who she was telling the story to whether at this point she included unnecessary details about the bit of in-your-face flirting that went on when she was asking Man Mountain for a lift.

"You're just the man I'm looking for!"

"Come and sit on my knee and we'll talk about the first thing that pops up.")

Linda had enjoyed bouncing through bucolic countryside in the tractor. The dirty grey hedges were covered in hawthorn blossom. She spotted bold daffodils and shy primroses, catkins and frolicking lambs. The air was fresh and full of promise. This was the rural Irish equivalent of driving through city streets in a flash sports car with the top down. Man Mountain's shirtsleeves were rolled up to the elbow. His hands were the size of dinner plates. He wasn't wearing a wedding-ring. Linda had never felt so romantic in her life. When the tractor swerved off the main road and she was thrown against his broad hairy chest it took superhuman self-restraint to remember that she was a Good Samaritan on a mission and to resist her animal instinct to prise his dinner-plate hand from the tractor's steering wheel and place it on her naked white thigh while fastening her hot lips to his generous, red, laughing mouth.

Too soon, the ride of her life was ended. Man Mountain slowed down in front of a magnificent pair of ornate, wrought-iron gates, forbidding in height but lying drunkenly open.

"Temple's at the top. Good luck!"

He was gone with a roar, in a belch of black exhaust fumes.

Linda walked briskly in through the gates and past a picturesque but seriously dilapidated gate-lodge squatting in a riot of overgrown garden, with ornate facia-boards and diamond-shaped panes of glass. The avenue was canopied with ancient stately beech trees. Temple Farm was much grander than she'd been expecting, but what had she been expecting? Jane never said anything about her husband's home place, except that the house wasn't big enough for the old pair, the newly weds and Kathleen. Linda and everybody else had pictured a modest thatched cottage with roses round the door . . .

"It's *huge*," Linda told Diane afterwards, "like a mansion. It's three storeys high, and there are eight windows at the front, and every window has at least fifteen little panes of glass . . ."

Linda didn't know her architecture. Temple was a classic example of a three-storey over-basement Georgian tall house with what an estate agent would describe as "having retained all of its period features". There was a classic fanlight above the front door and the sash windows had their original uneven glass and rotting frames.

"I went up to the front door and I knocked and knocked and knocked. Nobody answered. To be honest I thought I was at the wrong place, for there was no sign of a farmyard and I was afraid to go wandering about in case somebody shot me for trespass. So I just stood there and shouted

46

'Michael, Michael, it's Linda! Come here this minute! Your wee daughter Susie has had an accident and Jane is at the hospital waiting for you!' Finally the front door was opened by an old woman in a woollen hat and wellies, carrying a black lamb and a stout bottle with a big rubber teat on its lip. 'Who are you and what do you want?' she said and when I told her she pointed past the big house and further up the avenue. 'Michael is at the yard,' she said and she shut the door in my face."

Finally Linda found the farmyard. By now she was exhausted and thirsty, subdued with anti-climax and more than a bit nervous about meeting Michael. It wasn't that she disliked him. She had no reason to dislike him for he was always polite when he spoke to her. It was just that Linda was a woman who prided herself on catching and holding the attention of every man she encountered. By hook or by crook she always had something to make a man look twice whether it was her tight T-shirt, short skirt, bleached hair, long fingernails or dirty chat. Michael ruined her sexual confidence because he had eyes for no one but Jane. He might not even know her name. He might not even recognise her . . .

Linda lit a cigarette, so useful for calming the nerves, and hesitated. The farmyard was pretty and old, the stone buildings were whitewashed, the barn doors were painted red. And there seemed to be sheep everywhere, knee deep in straw, making a terrible racket.

Michael emerged from an outhouse. His arms were smeared with blood and mucus, his jeans were covered with filthy plastic trousers. He was dragging a couple of baby lambs along the ground. The mother ewe followed, bleating desperately, begging him to let go of her babies.

"Come on, Dolly," he murmured in a soft, rough voice. His guard was down, his face was gentle. This was his world; he was up to his elbows in sheep having babies.

So Linda was not in the least bit outraged or surprised when she told him the sorry tale about Susie at the hospital and he said, "But I'm lambing ewes! I'm busy! What does she expect me to do?"

Jane sat in the hospital, holding Susie's little burnt hands and ignoring the gorgeous young doctor giving her the eye. Waiting for Michael. There was a terrible pounding panic in her heart and her stomach fluttered with nerves. Of course he'd come. The very minute Linda made it to the farm and passed on the awful news he'd drop all and come.

Morning stretched into afternoon and Michael didn't come.

The hospital nurses were kind and brought her cups of tea. They knew Jan With The Pram – everyone did.

"Can't you get the hold of him?"

"He farms."

They nodded sympathetically. They knew.

Susie was bandaged and sedated and allowed to go home.

"Bring her back every day," said the gorgeous young doctor, "and we'll change her bandages and inspect her wounds. Would you like me to drive you home?"

Jane flashed her violet eyes and he blushed. "Thank you."

By the time Michael finally came home, smelling of sheep and defiance, Jane had learned to stop needing him and a brittle crust was beginning to grow round her heart. Something rose-tinted and cherished in their marriage was scalded when the cauldron of nappies splashed on Susie.

6

Falling out of love with Michael was a gradual thing, not like falling in love with him which had taken a heartbeat. Jane stopped getting up at six in the morning to make him tea before he went to Temple. She stopped changing into clean clothes and composing herself into a smiling and serene wife when he was due home. She stopped cooking his favourite food and asking him about his day. She stopped trying to show an interest in the incomprehensible mysteries of farming; a tiny yawn slipped out when he was explaining the fine-tuning of his new forage harvester.

Glancing thoughtlessly into the bathroom mirror when she was brushing her teeth she saw a sad-eyed, anguished woman staring back. Yet she turned her back on him when she finally got into bed.

Michael joked, "What's the difference between having an erection and leaving the light on? I can sleep with the light on!" and after a proprietorial fumble, he was content to roll over and fall asleep.

This insidious loss of intimacy made Jane even more unhappy. In the middle of the night she woke up to silently worry if her marriage was over.

After a week without sex Michael cracked.

"This would never have happened if you lived at the farm."

Jane flicked her eyes at her husband. "What would never have happened? I wouldn't have been boiling nappies? Susie wouldn't have tried to pull the cauldron down on top of herself? I wouldn't have had to sit alone at the hospital all day with a scalded toddler and everybody staring at me, whispering, 'Does that woman even have a husband?'"

Michael sighed deeply. It was now two years since Jane had packed her bags and told him she was leaving Temple. Of course he'd tried to stop her.

"You haven't given it much of a chance."

"I know when I'm not wanted!"

For two years he'd been sitting on a fence, quite a comfortable fence, waiting for someone to blink first – either his father to change his mind and agree to the building of a new house on the farm or for Jane to swallow her pride and humbly return to the bosom of his family.

Michael said, "You shouldn't be here by yourself, utterly isolated with two small babies, trying to keep all the balls in the air at the same time. If you lived at Temple you'd have my mother and Kathleen to help you . . ."

He wondered why she laughed.

Another long evening alone. Just like the one before and the one before that. Susie and Patrick were bathed and bottled and finally pinned down for the night. There was a pile of dirty dishes waiting for her in the scullery. Patrick needed bottles made up. Susie needed bandages washed. Michael was still lambing sheep; his dinner needed to be dished up, covered and put into the bottom of the oven until he came home.

Everybody needed everything.

Just for a change Jane sat down for a think.

Leaving Temple and moving to the council house was supposed to be a temporary adventure in her happy-ever-after with Michael, a breathing space from the unfriendly unfamiliarity of the farm; time out. Her nice brown leather suitcase, bought for her honeymoon, was still sitting under the stairs in the hall.

And it wasn't so bad in Stove Pipe Town. She could walk to the shops, she could cook what she wanted, she could watch what she wanted on the television (there'd always been such a row at Temple when Old Dave insisted that they watch *The Farming Programme* and everyone else was desperate for *Coronation Street*).

Two years had just flashed by, thanks to screaming Susie the first year, and Susie and Patrick the second year and Michael since she'd married him.

The long evenings alone had gone to Jane's head. There was nobody to talk to, so she'd started to talk to herself.

"Do you think that it might be possible that my whole life might flash by, summer and winter, seed-time and harvest, silage-cutting and lambing, and I might not even notice it passing?"

It was time to accept that Old Dave Temple was never going to change his mind and allow them to build a new house on the farm.

The prosaic reality was that she lived in Stove Pipe Town

with her children and was likely to remain there for the rest of her life.

Jane unpinned from the drab wallpaper the surreal and sleep-deprived sketches of her tall, imaginative, beautiful country house, canopied with pretty trees, ponies grazing in a paddock, a view of the river, vegetable gardens, fruit bushes and a few hens scratching.

She neatly filed them away in her suitcase and put her suitcase into the roof space. It was a symbolic gesture.

The noise woke Susie who immediately began to screech. "Mummy, Mummy!"

Jane tiptoed into the small bedroom and lifted Susie gently into her arms. Susie snuggled into her mother's neck and sniffed contentedly.

"Kiss kiss," said Susie.

Mrs Somerville said the reason Susie refused to sleep the whole night in her cot was because Jane ran to her and lifted her out of it the second she woke up and started screeching.

"If you ignored her, she'd soon stop screeching!"

It was so simple when Mrs Somerville was explaining it. Put Susie in the cot with her bottle and teddy. Speak in a calm measured voice: "You're going to sleep in your cot, Susie, and you're staying in your cot the whole night." Walk out of the bedroom and resolutely down the stairs. Don't look back. Under no circumstances stand dithering outside the bedroom door. Switch on the television. Start the ironing. When Susie begins to screech put cotton wool in your ears. Go into the scullery and scrub out the oven. If Susie continues to screech, go out into the back garden and start digging.

"Show no weakness," said Mrs Somerville. "Remember, the blessed lamb can smell your fear."

"But if I ignore her she'll scream until she makes herself sick!"

"Only a couple of times. She's a smart little thing, she'll soon learn."

It was sensible advice, even Michael thought so, but Jane couldn't bring herself to try it. All the sensible advice in the world could never compensate for the satisfaction of comforting the small, warm, sleepy child who called for her.

"Mummy's bed," said Susie and Jane carried her, without protest, to her own room, and tucked her in even though it would be a horrible squash when Michael came home.

Jane stroked her daughter's dark curls and whispered, "We live in Number 10, Sperrin View, Susie. This is our home."

Susie snuggled down, smiling. "Love you, Mummy." She didn't care where she lived as long as her mummy was with her.

Now that she was resigned to living in Stove Pipe Town forever, the scales fell from Jane's eyes and she took a long hard look at her council house.

Downstairs there was a very basic living-room furnished with cracked lino, drab wallpaper and an orange plastic sofa bequeathed by the previous occupants. The living-room opened into a back scullery just big enough to hold a twin tub and a gas ring.

Upstairs there was a bathroom and two bedrooms ubiquitously decorated with brown curly carpets.

The excuse that love is blind may have explained Jane's tolerance of cracked lino and depressing wallpaper, but how could she never have noticed before that the brown curly carpets reeked of wet dog, cheap cigarettes and stale urine?

"Stinky poo," said Jane, who spent too much time alone with the babies.

When Michael got home from the farm, smelling of sheep, tired out as usual and desperate for an hour's peace in front of his dinner, Jane said: "Please will you bring the cattle trailer home with you tomorrow night? I want to pull up the brown curly carpets and throw them out."

"Why?"

"Because I want to buy clean carpets."

A nasty, damp feeling of suppressed panic crept into Michael's belly. First no sex and now "I Want". And his dinner was cold! What was happening to sweet Jane, his Derry Emerald? She was turning into a tyrant! Before he knew it, he'd be a henpecked shadow of his former self like Gerry from Next Door who handed over every penny of his pay-packet on Friday and wasn't able to go out for a pint with the lads from work unless Diane gave him pocket money and her permission; who said "Yes dear, no dear, three bags full dear!"

"Tomorrow night is out of the question," said Michael and he threw himself down on the plastic sofa and promptly forgot all about it. "What's for dinner, love?"

The following evening Michael came home from the farm to find the brown curly carpets lying in a foul heap in the front garden.

Jane was nonchalant. "Diane from Next Door helped me. Once we got started it was the easiest thing in the world to pull them up. Come and see what was under them! The loveliest floorboards! Let's paint them and paint the walls as well. I've started to strip the wallpaper on the landing but it's very hard to get it off, there must be ten layers. The bottom layer is newspaper from 1940 and I think it's been glued on . . ."

"I didn't want you to lift the carpets," said Michael quietly.

Out of the corner of his eye he could see Diane from Next Door's curtains twitching with a fabric form of excited epilepsy as she spied with relish, but pretended not to.

"I thought you might say that," said Jane.

"How did he take it?" asked Diane from Next Door. "Was he angry with you?"

Diane had rather a crush on Michael. She called him "the housewife's choice" and without fail she went silly and giggly when she saw him. "It's not just me!" she'd excuse her guilty reflection. "Even Mrs Somerville fancies him and she's a hundred if she's a day."

Gorgeous or not, Diane had very uncompromising views on the sanctity of marriage and the marital vow of "cherish" in particular, and she'd been frankly horrified by the state of the brown curly carpets. "My Gerry" was a bit short in the leg and a bit foggy between the ears, but he always did his best for his family (and he always did what he was told).

"Your husband should be ashamed of himself, allowing his wife and children to walk on such filthy carpets!"

Jane had laughed. "You've not seen the squalor of Temple! They don't even have carpets – they have rugs that are so threadbare you can see the floorboards through them. I think they've been there since the house was built!"

Diane sniffed with disgust. "You've said yourself that nobody wise could live there . . ."

She'd spent the previous evening with the sound turned down on the television and her ear pressed to the common wall that joined the Temple's house to her house, in a lather of righteous indignation, listening for a row and poised to rush next door and give Michael a piece of her mind if he dared make a squeak about the lifting of the curly brown carpets.

Jane laughed. "Of course he wasn't angry! He prefers to pretend it isn't happening. He's sweeping the whole thing under the carpet!"

"What are you going to do?"

Jane shook back her long black hair. "I'm sure I'll think of something!"

That evening when Michael came home from the farm the brown curly carpets were still lying in the front garden. When he opened the front door he tripped over a pile of clothes. They were his clothes, stacked up in a tidy pile.

"Go home to your mammy," said Jane. "I don't need you any more."

Slowly Michael packed his clothes into a bin-liner bag while his wife stood over him, watching. Jane was dressed in a tight vest top without a bra which was always guaranteed to arouse him sexually. What was it about hard nipples through thin fabric?

This was the most exciting thing that had happened to him since they'd married, almost as good as the long, hot summer of the Derry Emerald when he'd been driven to distraction by the tantalising way she'd sat primly in the Rapier with her legs pressed modestly together: "No, Michael, that's not nice, keep your hands to yourself," while her fathomless violet eyes had encouraged him to keep on trying. Right up to the moment he proposed, and even then, he hadn't been totally sure if she'd accept him . . .

Jane ran careless fingers through her fantastic hair and watched Michael hungrily eyeing her breasts. She knew the effect she was creating. Hadn't she spent half the afternoon practising for this moment?

"Hurry up, Michael, and get out! I want to have a bath before bed. I'm covered in wallpaper paste!"

56

"Let me say goodbye to my children first," said Michael softly. "I'm going to miss them so much."

"You couldn't pick them out of a line-up."

Jane lay back in the warm bathwater with her eyes half closed, silently congratulating herself on a job well done. Playing hard to get with her husband hadn't come easy. All her life she'd been a straightforward girl, uncomplicated and devoid of hidden depth. What good had that done her?

This new, sharp-tongued version of Jane suited her new sharp-tongued circumstances. Why not treat Michael mean? She had nothing to lose.

An hour later she was lying in bed, watching the stars through a gap in the curtains, valiantly trying to ignore Susie who had woken up crying. Again.

"Mummy's bed," howled Susie.

Jane had already been twice into Susie's bedroom, after five minutes and after ten minutes to calm her and reassure her: "Mummy loves you, darling, go back to sleep."

Now she had to leave her for a full fifteen minutes before tiptoeing back into the bedroom to repeat, "Mummy loves you, darling, go back to sleep." This had to be repeated ad nauseam at increasing intervals until Susie learned to sleep in her own bed.

Mrs Somerville called this method of mother abuse "controlled crying".

"It's not doing the blessed lamb a bit of damage. Wouldn't you be up half the night with her anyway, if she was sleeping in your bed?"

Jane was counting the seconds left till she could go to Susie – one hundred and forty-four – when she heard the rumble of the Rapier – heavier than usual, with the scraping noise of the cattle trailer attached.

What a relief but also what a disappointment! All joking and bravado aside, was marriage really little more than a battle of wills and clever skirmishes? The art of ambushing her husband with her breasts when they disagreed – the disillusion of happy ever after.

"I see the carpets have gone," said Diane from Next Door.

"More than the carpets," said Jane.

7

Jane's victory in the Battle of the Brown Curly Carpets was only the start of it.

All summer she wrestled with the revamp of her council house, scrubbing and painting, pulling up, throwing out and sanding down. Finally the little house was cheerful, comfortable and child friendly. All that was left was to burn the plastic sofa and buy something new.

"How do you propose to pay for it?"

They were standing outside Stewart's Fine Furnishings on Main Street. Jane and Susie were holding hands, Patrick was hugging Jane's hip. Michael was bringing up the rear with an empty pushchair.

"Don't cross the road without me, Susie darling, in case a car drives over you."

"Don't wander away from me, Susie sweetheart, you might get lost."

"Stick close beside me, precious Susie, don't let the bogey man steal you."

It was August, the back end of the sales, and she'd proposed this walk after Sunday lunch because she wanted to show Michael the nicest sofa ever that was in Stewart's window. Jane had been walking slowly past Stewart's for a month, watching the price of the sofa gradually receding. Now it was the last week of the sale, the sofa was half price and the Autumn Collection had started to squeeze into the window . . .

"Don't you think it would be perfect for our living-room? It's exactly the same shade of emerald green as the brocade curtains Granny Costello gave me!"

Michael said, "It's a very nice sofa, Jane. How do you propose to pay for it?"

Jane took a long hard look at her husband. This was Michael with the two hundred acres, Michael who milked fifty cows, Michael who worked every day of his life, regardless of weather and weekends, who hadn't taken a day off since she'd married him, not even the afternoon of Granny Costello's funeral, when she'd had to go by herself on the bus to Derry nursing a Tupperware box of ham sandwiches and Susie and Patrick, one on each knee . . .

"I thought you would pay for it!"

Michael's face closed down. Suddenly his eyes looked tired. There were flecks of grey in his thick hair, and he wasn't yet thirty.

What was it about townie women that they refused to understand rural Irish traditions?

Maybe he should have explained it a bit better to her before they got married, except she might never have agreed to marry him. Until his father died Michael wasn't much better than a slave about Temple. He was at Old Dave's beck and call, night and day, and Old Dave was in control of everything. He chose the new bull, he decided what day to cut the barley, he paid the rent for the council house. Michael didn't own even the clothes on his back.

"You'll have to ask my father for the money," said Michael.

"But I'm married to you, not your father," said Jane and something small and magical and terribly important in her marriage got left behind on Main Street when they turned for home.

That night Jane had a curious dream. She was the Derry Emerald again, barefoot in her famous black halter-neck frock. She was smiling and posing with the crown and the sceptre for newspaper photographs, watching Michael who was watching her. She recognised him immediately, though in her dream she didn't know him. He stood at the edge of the crowd, his shy eyes were calling to her and she easily edged her way over to him. They stood quietly side by side, his toe was touching her toe; she was ashamed because her feet were dusty.

Finally he said, "Can I have your phone number?" but she didn't have a pen or a piece of paper to write it on.

He stood very close to her when they were talking, her heart thumped with anticipation, but her teeth weren't brushed, so she couldn't raise her beautiful face to kiss him, though she wanted to.

Jane woke up with a shock. She was breathless, her guts were fluttering and her nipples were hard. Was this really her husband she'd been dreaming about? This lump in the bed beside her, lying flat on his back, snoring, with the blankets kicked off; the man who wouldn't buy his wife a new sofa?

In her dream she'd burned to kiss him, now she was awake she couldn't stand him.

What a relief when Susie woke a few minutes later for her midnight serenade: "Mummy's bed!"

Next morning Jane felt unwell. Not vomiting unwell or high temperature unwell, or even women's problems unwell.

Michael asked, "Do you have a pain somewhere?"

She shook her head.

"Can you sit up?"

She shook her head.

"Well, what's wrong with you then?"

He was vaguely exasperated. Sickness was a physical thing. You had pain, you took a painkiller, the pain went away. *Sulking* was when you lay in bed, refusing to move, because your husband refused to buy you a new sofa.

"I'm going to have to go. The man's coming to cut the barley."

Jane lay perfectly still, her face turned to the wall. She could hardly hear him. There was ringing in her ears, she felt numb from the hairline down, her arms and legs were too heavy to lift, tears leaked unchecked and trickled over her face.

"Please stay at home with me, Michael."

But he was already gone. The front door banged, Susie and Patrick woke up. It was another new day; once more into the breach.

"Mummy, Mummy!" Susie was on top of her, snuggling and sniffing, kissing her hair with butterfly kisses, tugging her shoulder so she'd turn round from the wall.

Nothing. Jane wouldn't move.

"Mummy sick? Sore tummy, Mummy? Poo, Mummy?"

Clearly and simply Jane said, "I have a pain in my chest. I think my heart is broken."

Across the landing, trapped in his cot, Patrick began to cry. He was only a baby; he wanted his bottle, his morning hug, his mum.

The crying in the cot roused Jane. It was an automatic reaction, a Pavlovian response: they cry and you comfort. She got out of bed and went to Patrick.

The morning routine proceeded: the feeding, cleaning and dressing of children, the dressing of Jane, the answering of Susie's impossible questions. How could a child who was not yet two, with a vocabulary of maybe a hundred words, manage to ask so many questions? But today something was different.

For the first time in her marriage Jane was depressed. It was a new emotion and she wasn't wearing it well. She felt as if someone had taken an egg spoon and smartly tapped the one weak spot in her happy-ever-after. All her efforts to make a fabulous palace of the council house and to create an enchanting alternative to Temple were a waste of time when Michael wouldn't, couldn't, buy her a new sofa.

"And it's not only the sofa! It's the way he steadfastly resists every decorating initiative I take! He hasn't painted one skirting-board all summer."

They were in the bathroom, now aquamarine with a sea-green Roman blind on the window, made by Linda who was a surprisingly dab hand at the sewing.

Jane was brushing Susie's teeth.

"He wouldn't even help me tile round the bath and the wash-hand basin. I had to teach myself how to do it. Gerry from Next Door helped me with the pointing . . ."

Susie nodded in sympathy. She didn't much care for

Daddy either. His hands were rough and he smelt horrible and when he was around Mummy didn't pay her half as much attention . . .

"Stinky Daddy," said Susie.

Jane nodded. "You're right! He does stink and his jaw clicks when he's eating, and he always puts the empty milk bottle back into the fridge instead of washing it out. And he sweats on me when we make love . . ."

Knock knock.

It was Old Mrs Somerville, discreet and kind, famously married for thirty happy years.

"I'm just popping down to the shops. Do you want me to get you anything?"

Jane said, "I think I've everything I need, thanks."

Susie spoke up. "Mummy needs a new heart. Mummy's heart is broken."

Mrs Somerville gently stroked the top of Susie's head with her freckled hand. She was a lonely old lady with all her family grown up and gone and though much sought after and respected for her mothering advice – and what wouldn't she know after rearing six children of her own? – she fastidiously minded her own business with respect to everything else.

Living next door, with only a wire fence to separate them, she'd had a ringside seat for the Battle of the Brown Curly Carpets and the subsequent arguments and huffing and raised voices, all summer, while Jane was fixing up the house. Mrs Somerville knew Diane vociferously encouraged Jane and had even helped her with the painting. She knew Linda had been badmouthing Michael around the council estate since her mercy dash to Temple, when Susie was scalded and he wouldn't leave the sheep. But she had resolutely taken no

64

sides and had passed no remarks. Mrs Somerville was an old lady. She'd seen it all before, heard it all before; once long ago, she'd even lived it.

Pleasantly she said, "I can't help but notice, my dear, that your honeymoon is finally over! I'm amazed, given the circumstances, that it lasted for as long as it did!"

"How long was your honeymoon?"

"We had a weekend in a boarding house by the sea. Then Ben's widowed mother moved in with us. Poor old thing doted for years before she died. She kept running away in her nightdress to the police station to file official complaints that I was bad to her, that I beat her and starved her. And she used to shoplift sweets. It was very embarrassing – we had to set up accounts in every shop in the town . . ."

Jane was thoughtful. "Well, I suppose that's something to be grateful for. Cecily Temple will never want to live with me!"

Mrs Somerville left for the shops and Jane's morning routine proceeded. She sweated leeks and onions in unsalted butter, thinly sliced some potatoes and simmered everything together in real chicken broth, made from the carcass of yesterday's roast.

Patrick watched from the safety of his high chair. This was where he sat every day when she was cooking. She'd handed him some chopped leeks to play with. It was the most useful way of keeping him busy while she was busy.

"Mrs Somerville says there's never really a death blow to signal the end of the honeymoon. Instead it's the relentless drip drip drip of small disappointments, and one day you wake up and realise that your heart is full of disappointment and your marriage is weighed down with disappointment."

When the soup was ready Jane puréed it and gently stirred in some cream. She poured half into a clean saucepan and covered it with a cloth. Diane from Next Door was a huge fan of Jane's vichyssoise and, after all the painting all summer, it was the least she could do, to share with her.

She lifted Patrick out of the high chair and onto her hip.

"Ma ma ma ma ma ma!" said Patrick.

Diane from Next Door was a sensible, pragmatic woman, devoid of delusion, the salt of the earth.

Diane said, "My honeymoon was in April 1965. I was pregnant with Ernest. Gerry took me to Donegal and we stayed in a B&B. It rained every day, except for the day we went to Glenveagh National Park, when it snowed."

There was a whimsical pause while Diane reminisced.

Jane said, "And then what?"

"After my honeymoon? Then it was time to find somebody else to love. First Ernest, then Valerie, finally Tim . . ."

Ernest was sitting at a table scattered with schoolbooks. He was studying though it was the summer holidays.

"Ernest has his eleven-plus exam in November. If he passes he'll go to the grammar school. We've been going over past papers all summer. I'm timing him and we practise exam techniques."

Valerie had beautiful manners. She won badges in school for being clever and kind. She took Susie firmly and kindly by the hand and led her, unresisting, to some cushions on the floor, to join a row of dolls with picture books open in front of them.

"Valerie wants to be a teacher when she grows up."

Tim, who was still a baby, sat quietly surrounded by cushions off the sofa, staring into the middle distance. The wireless chattered quietly beside him.

"Tim's listening to the *Money Programme* on the wireless while he digests the Omega 3 fish-oil capsules I gave him with his lunch. They don't stink as much as fresh mackerel from the market stall but they've exactly the recommended daily requirement of Omega 3 – I checked it in the books."

"Mackerel?"

"Mackerel is a rich source of Omega 3 fatty acids. That means it makes your brain grow."

The *Money Programme* finished, the wireless was switched off.

"Music," said Diane.

Immediately Valerie jumped up and produced a violin. Ernest stopped studying and sat down at an ancient piano, squeezed in between the window and the television. There were a few minutes of discordant tuning up of the violin. Then, on the count of three (from Diane) the children began to play.

"'Duet for Piano and Violin'. They've been practising it all summer. The books say classical music can dramatically improve a child's IQ."

Jane buried her nose in Patrick's dark hair and listened politely. She knew all the cruel jokes her neighbours made about Diane. They called her 'The Control Freak' and they said her children were machines, and of course everyone knew Diane's reputation for a hard hand. Though her heart was in the right place. And her children were a credit to her.

Their school reports glowed: they showed great leadership, they were very mature, they were helpful and popular, they mixed well. It was impossible not to be blinded by the shine coming off the school reports because Diane had them framed and they hung in the hall of the council house, where other people had three flying ducks, or a row of coat hooks.

When you entered Next Door she drew your attention to them: "Mrs Smyth says Valerie has done good work and made progress this term . . ."

"Duet for Piano and Violin" was finished. Diane applauded enthusiastically.

"Oh, my darlings, that was *superb* – wasn't it superb, Jane? Even the really difficult bit in the middle where you usually go wrong, Ernest, you got it right today. Oh my darlings, I'm so *proud* of you!"

She opened her arms, and they ran to her. She enveloped them in hugs and kisses. There were tears of triumph sparkling in her eyes.

Diane said, "I really regret not trying harder at school but I was far more interested in shifting boys and backcombing my hair. I was clever – everybody said so. I wanted to be a teacher when I grew up but I didn't have the brains to know to learn. Everyone thinks I'm mad, my obsession with the children's education, but I know for a fact that I'd never have ended up here – in Stove Pipe Town with My Gerry if I'd learned at school . . ."

8

Jane's depression evaporated. How could she feel depressed when she had two adoring, adorable children, flesh of her flesh, to love and nurture and mould into acceptable, attractive human beings? With Diane as her inspiration, Jane stopped grieving for her passionate prolonged honeymoon and allowed her mothering ability to grow wings.

"Of course it's not going to be easy," Diane told her solemnly. "Your children are only babies. It might be years before you reap the rewards of the efforts you put in now. I remember it was one crisis after another when Ernest and Valerie were small. Every day there was falling over, falling out, screaming and sickness. And that was only me!"

Jane rescued Patrick from the cupboard he was wrecking. She wrestled a pencil from Susie who was trying to autograph the living-room wall. Stoutly she told them, "We may live in reduced circumstances, my darlings, but it simply gives us more scope for imagination. We don't need a new sofa to be smart and popular and accomplished."

Diane agreed. "What would you want a new sofa for? They'll only spill on it and vomit on it and scribble on it with felt-tip pens . . ."

Soon the council house was filled with educational books and library books and every day Jane stoically sat, colouring in and building alphabet blocks while Mozart played in the background. It was chaos at the start. The Mozart was as foreign to Jane's ear as tribal music or jungle drums. Susie was interested only in running wild, singing at the top of her voice, while Patrick preferred to eat the crayons than colour with them.

"How's it going?" asked Diane.

"I'm exhausted! I think those horn concertos were hunting me in my dreams last night."

Diane grinned. "It's still early days . . ."

Soon drawings by Susie and Patrick were displayed on the living-room wall and photographs of Susie and Patrick were crammed onto the narrow fireplace. There was no room any more for the official framed wedding photograph of Mr and Mrs Michael Temple. Jane tidied it away, into a cupboard, the innocent bride in stiff white satin and the husband she'd married for love.

It wasn't all learning of course. Diane said it was also important for pre-school children to socialise with their peers so Jane encouraged Susie and Patrick to make friends in the street.

For Patrick there was Tim from Next Door and for Susie a little girl called Claire Kavanagh whose dad had a silver lorry with a bed in the back. He drove to France every week and brought her home beautiful French clothes in dark velvets and patterned satin, with ribbons and bows and pin tucks; she was the most exquisitely dressed child in the town.

The very first time he saw her Patrick fell in love with Claire Kavanagh. She was a pretty little thing, with a provocative sense of occasion. She posed in front of him, with her hand on her hip, in a white knitted mini-dress and matching beret, in knee-high shiny white plastic boots, exotic and very French till she opened her mouth and said, "He's a big fat baby, Mammy!"

Nonplussed, he stoically stumbled after her while she and Susie ran away from him laughing and shouting, "Chase me, chase me, Patrick Temple!"

"Love at first sight," said Claire's mum. "It never happened to me."

"I wouldn't recommend it," said Jane with a wistful smile.

Up the street were a family of ten – their mother was dead and their father was out of work. Their surname was McBride and they ranged in age from thirteen to three.

"One child a year for ten years, it's no wonder Maeve died in the end." Diane's eyes always filled with tears when she talked about Maeve. "Even Oliver wanted to stop after five, but you couldn't have told her . . ."

It was like a kibbutz in the McBride house. The older children minded the younger children and everyone pulled his or her own weight. There never seemed to be a cross word said. After school and at weekends they spilled out onto the street with a fist of bread and jam; they were barefoot, half of them. They played an involved and complicated imaginary game together; the silver tops from the milk bottles were currency and the youngest two, Bare Bum Isaac and Mary of the Sorrows, were pushed everywhere in a rusty pram.

Sometimes Oliver played football with the older boys,

throwing in the ball and passing so they could score goals between posts made of rolled-up jumpers. Jane watched him covertly from behind her curtains.

Linda said, "His sisters offered to help him when Maeve died. They said they'd take three kids each and rear them like their own. It was a big offer when you think about it, for they already had families and Oliver said, 'No, thank you. They're my children and we're a family and I'll make do.' Then Social Services tried to persuade him to have them fostered. But he wouldn't hear of it. 'No, thank you. They're my children and we're a family and I'll make do.'"

"Not very practical, of course," said Diane. "He can't work with so many children to look after so there's no money coming in. It's quite obvious that there have been no new clothes bought since Maeve died. He's almost totally threadbare and the poor little children look like ragamuffins. I always pass on what Ernest and Valerie grow out of."

Every day Tim, Claire, Isaac and Mary were made welcome to play between three and four in the afternoon. Mozart was given a rest and Achilles' Heel, a hot Belfast rock band, was put on the record player instead. Jane and the children danced and sang – "*My brother was a bad man, My brother was a thief, My brother stole my woman . . .*"

"Who's that singing?" asked Diane. There was something about the lead singer's voice, something sexy and city which eased the rigidity of her ramrod backbone, and loosened the poker up her arse. Diane wasn't sure she liked the feeling.

"Bobby Flood, he's gorgeous, I'm his number one fan!"

Every afternoon there was a cup of tea for the adults and soup and potatoes for the children. It wasn't charity, they didn't have to eat if they didn't want, but they were all made to sit together at the table and encouraged to say, "Please may I have a drink of milk?" and "Please may I leave the table?"

In Isaac's case it was usually: "Please may I have some more?"

Afterwards they made chocolate Rice Krispie buns together. Baking-chocolate was melted in a glass bowl, balanced on a saucepan of boiling water, the Rice Krispies were mixed in with a wooden spoon, the bun cases were filled. Trays of chocolate Rice Krispie buns hardened in the fridge while the children sat on the scullery floor, licking the bowl and the spatula, their faces smeared joyfully with chocolate.

At four o'clock, she timed everything fastidiously, Jane clapped her hands and said, "You'll have to go home now, children! Susie and Patrick need their nap . . ." and away they went, modestly and quietly, hand in hand down the street, in their bare feet with runny noses, ruddy cheeks, and tangled hair – Isaac and Mary from the family of ten, who had no mother.

"Poor wee souls," said Claire's mum. She was fastidiously buttoning Claire into a pale pink lambswool coat, so she wouldn't catch cold as she was carried, wrapped in her mother's arms, up the street. "It's no wonder Mary is always in tears!"

Gently Jane wiped faces and hands. It was the same ritual every afternoon. A bottle of hot baby milk for Patrick, a cup of cold cow's milk for Susie, then Susie got into the pushchair with her teddy bear and Patrick was put in his pram with a blanket over the top to make it pitch dark – and like a stalwart windmill Jane efficiently rocked both of them to sleep.

"You're some woman!" said Diane and she meant it as a compliment.

The healthy feeding of Susie and Patrick had always been Jane's favourite obsession; now she was obsessed with brain food. Every Thursday she queued at the fish stall in town to buy mackerel, though the taste of it made her gag.

"There must be some way I can cook it so it doesn't taste like oily fish . . ."

Jane explored her cookery books, seeking out recipes for mackerel. She was pleasantly surprised with what she discovered.

"What a versatile fish – I had no idea! And particularly delicious with old-fashioned fruit. I think we should dig over the back garden and plant out gooseberry bushes and rhubarb. By next summer we'll have our own fruit, and I'll be able to stuff the mackerel with rhubarb, or bake the mackerel and serve it with a gooseberry sauce. Until then we'll just have to make do with mackerel fried in oatmeal."

Michael lay with his feet up on the plastic sofa – such a comfortable sofa! He was faintly bemused.

"Why can't you buy your gooseberries and rhubarb from the greengrocer like everybody else?"

"You think we shouldn't eat organic fruit because we live in a council house?"

Jane went up the street to ask for gardening advice from Oliver. He had ten little mouths to feed so he grew all his own vegetables in military rows in his back garden. He had potatoes, leeks, peas, beans, spinach and nasturtiums which grew like mad over the fence: "You can eat the flowers of the nasturtium."

He was a nice man, very modest. There was suffering etched on his face and his jeans were tied to his thin body with a piece of washing-line.

"Can I borrow a spade?"

Oliver had a soft spot for Jane, or should that be a hard spot? He could sense something lonesome about her, even with Susie and Patrick clinging; it called out to his own isolation. When she explained that she wanted to plant out some gooseberry bushes and crowns of rhubarb he insisted on doing the digging for her.

"A delicate little thing like you, the digging would kill you."

Oliver brought Isaac and Mary with him, when he came to dig the garden. They sat quiet and content along the wire fence. Isaac sucked his thumb, Mary played with a rag doll. From the kitchen window Jane watched him handle the spade like a craftsman. He stopped only once to wipe away Mary's tears with the tail end of his shirt.

She took him out a cup of tea and he joked, "Mary never knew her mother. When she's older I'm going to tell her I found her under a gooseberry bush!"

"How can I thank you?" He was right, she'd never have managed the digging herself, never in a hundred years, not with Patrick sitting on her hip and Susie swinging from the end of her hand.

Oliver tramped in the last gooseberry bush and tickled Patrick under the chin. Here were the best-fed children in Ireland with rosy cheeks, shiny hair, big bones and an impressive and extensive culinary vocabulary: "*Vichyssoise* is the French name for leek and potato soup."

"I'd love to taste some of that fancy French muck you're so famous for," said Oliver. "I've heard you're a fabulous cook."

When Michael got home from the farm, smelling of cows, tired out as usual, and desperate for an hour's peace in front of his dinner, Jane said, "Oliver says the gooseberry bushes and the rhubarb would establish and flourish much faster if the soil had organic animal fertiliser dug into it."

"Oliver?"

"Oliver from up the street – how do you think I got the digging done?"

In fairness, Michael hadn't thought about it, he was so busy at the farm. They were building a milking-parlour, fully automatic, ten cows could be milked at once, five up each side, and Old Dave wanted to expand the herd so he was gone gallivanting every day, shopping for milking cows while Michael baled the barley and milked by himself in the old-fashioned cow byre.

Jane and her gooseberry bushes; it sounded like a music-hall joke but he was too fatigued to even indulge her. He threw himself down on the plastic sofa – such a comfortable sofa!

"What's for dinner, love?"

Jane regarded her husband. Michael had fifty milking cows and two hundred ewes dropping organic animal fertiliser from their back ends day and night. It was the least he could do, she felt, to shovel up some into a bag, and bring it home for the garden.

"Mackerel Curry," she told him and she felt the faintest echo of malicious pleasure to watch his face fall for the mackerel curry made with pineapple chunks out of a tin was very possibly the very worst of all Jane's mackerel variations. Michael wasn't a fussy eater, he had proved this often by eating dried-up and indigestible dinners, left sitting for him in the simmering oven for hours when he was delayed at the farm. But he was growing tired of mackerel; it gave him indigestion and made his armpits smell.

Jane added, for spite, "Susie and Patrick thought it was delicious."

"Susie and Patrick are little children! Their taste buds haven't developed yet!"

"Diane says by the time their taste buds develop their brains will also be working!"

"Susie and Patrick don't need organic fruit and exposure to classical music and structured play dates and special diets! When I was their age I sat all day in a playpen. My mother still has it in the attic. She says we're welcome to take it –"

"No, thank you. Diane's books don't approve of playpens."

"Well, hark at Lady Muck!" Cecily was quick to take offence. "If that Susie had been safe in a playpen instead of running riot round the house she'd not have pulled a cauldron of boiling nappies over herself."

Michael was strangely comforted by his mother's sharp remark. You always knew where you stood with Cecily for she made it her priority in life to find fault with everything and everyone. You could see the knife coming from miles off.

Cecily said, "Young women these days have far too much free time on their hands. I blame sliced bread and washing machines. If Jane was baking bread and hand-washing-clothes and wringing them through a mangle, as I did every day when I was her age, she'd have no time for delusions of grandeur."

"I'm almost afraid to go home," Michael admitted. "I'm afraid of what she'll think of next – ice-cold bathing to stimulate the nervous system, dining on boiled mackerel while standing on our heads . . ."

Cecily smiled ghoulishly. "You've made your bed, my son. Now you must lie on it . . ."

What no one had foreseen, not even Cecily at her most alarmist, was that the mackerel and the Mozart might work their magic on Jane and that she'd quickly graduate from entry-level classical music to Italian opera. Now every time you went into the house it was *Carmen* this and *La Bohème* that and Jane singing along, "*La La La . . .*"

"I haven't a clue what they're on about – he could be singing that he loves ice-cream for all I care! Can't you hear the *passion*? He makes me cry every time I hear him . . ."

Or sitting with her nose in a book, devouring literature: Jane, who had never read anything but recipes. She was particularly fond of stories about doomed lovers.

For a week she raged about the disgraceful way "poor Karen" was left alone on her farm in Africa while dashing lover boy was off shooting big game and flying his aeroplane, no strings attached.

The next week she was in floods of tears because Cathy Earnshaw's boyfriend wasn't good enough for her: "He was a cheap little thing from the town."

The week of *The Wings of the Dove* there wasn't a dish washed or a bite of dinner made. The book was up and Jane was utterly absorbed within the love triangle: "It's a lesson to us all – Michael, are you listening to me? *Never, never, never* take someone's love for granted . . ."

Michael looked up from his takeaway fish and chips, for all the world like a pig looking up from the trough. As far he could determine (he was too afraid to ask), Jane seemed to have only a couple of pages left to read. Please God when *The Wings of the Dove* had flown back to the library his Derry Emerald would come to her senses and proper mealtimes would be restored. Michael never thought he'd say it but he was starting to miss the mackerel.

"Why don't you read a nice cheerful book next? Where they marry for love and live happily ever after?"

She solemnly regarded him, her husband the literary philistine: "Can you recommend one?"

He laughed at her. "I've never read a book in my life!"

Of course, this was the wrong thing to say. He realised it the minute the words were out of his mouth – come back, words . . .

She was severe. "Diane says it's very important to set a good example to your children. We cannot expect them to be interested in reading, if we don't read."

9

Patrick and Susie's joint birthday party was the social highlight of the council-estate year. It was on New Year's Eve and everybody on the street was invited.

"Something to look forward to!" said Diane for nobody worked between Christmas and New Year and she was dreading a dead week of undiluted "My Gerry".

It was a fancy dress party because Susie wanted to be a fairy; Patrick was going to be a pirate. For a week Jane worked on their costumes, fashioning fairy wings from two wire coat-hangers wrapped in tinsel and sewing jaunty patches on to a pair of ragged pyjama bottoms, artistically frayed with Linda's pinking scissors. She cut an eye patch from the cornflakes packet and Susie coloured it in with black crayon.

Michael lay with his feet up on the plastic sofa watching her. It was miserable and wet outside, with snow in the rain. There was hardly a thing to do round the farm. And now they had a thoroughly modern milking-parlour the milking was half the hard work it had always been, even with double the cows. There were times in the day when Michael found himself standing with his arms the same length, wondering what to do next. It was during one of these interludes that he'd had the inspired idea of taking his wife out on New Year's Eve, to the Electric Ballroom, if Jane could find someone to baby-sit.

Jane looked up from her sewing. "Since you're doing nothing, would you help me with Pass the Parcel? The prize is a Ladybird Book, *The Enormous Turnip*. We need to wrap it up about fifteen times to give everybody a turn. Go Next Door and get yesterday's newspaper from Diane – it's pink so it'll look pretty."

Reluctantly Michael got off the sofa, pulled on his wellies and waterproof waxed coat and went outside onto the street. It was deserted but for a selection of McBride children, wearing no coats and barefoot, faces turned to heaven, trying to catch snowflakes on their tongues.

"We're coming to your party! We're going to be the Von Trapp family. Dad's going to dress like a nun and we're going sing 'Climb Every Mountain' . . ."

Diane was full of cold. Her eyes were red-rimmed; she was lying in state on the sofa Next Door. A blanket covered her, there was a pillow at her head and Ernest and Valerie were fussing.

"I've made you another cup of tea, Mummy."

"Let me fill up your hot water bottle again, Mummy."

"My Gerry" was enveloped in an apron. "They say 'feed a cold and starve a fever' so I'm making an Ulster Fry for her – I'm cooking bacon, sausages, eggs and potato bread."

Michael stood to attention. He resisted an urge to salute. Even from the depths of her little illness he could feel the force field of Queen Diane's contempt for him, the man who didn't put his family first, the most vilified husband in Stove Pipe Town, worse even than the wife-beater in Number 18 and the alcoholics at the end of the terrace.

"Please, may I have yesterday's pink paper? I'm going to make Pass the Parcel for the party."

She sneezed. "You mean the *Financial Times* – certainly! I order it special from Keane's corner shop and read it to Tim in bed when he's sleeping. I want him to be an investment banker when he grows up . . ."

On New Year's Eve, for the first time that winter, it froze. Michael's feet were like blocks of ice on the cold concrete of the milking-parlour floor. He stood in a bucket of hot water when the cows were quietly milking; it thawed him out a bit.

When the milking was finished and the yards were scraped and the cows were fed and he was at last relaxing in his mother's kitchen with a cup of strong tea and a plate of soda bread and jam, with his feet thrust into the warming oven of the Aga, he said, "I won't be in for my dinner today, Mother, I'm going to the children's birthday party . . ."

Cecily looked up from her baking – soda-bread flour and buttermilk – it was hardly rocket science. She hid it well but she could feel her heart starting to sink. What was it about this Christmas week that it was the loneliest week of the year for her?

Old Dave was away to the market yard at the windswept foot of the mountain: "Come with me, Cecily! We'll take the scenic route home."

Kathleen had high-tailed it down the avenue to catch the first bus to civilisation before the sun was properly risen.

"Gallivanting again!"

"Come with me, Mother! It's the first day of the sales. The shops are full of bargains! I'll buy you lunch!"

(Kathleen loved pretty clothes and since her promotion most of her pay-packet was spent on them. The end of every month was the happiest day in her life when she caught the bus from the front gate of Temple and it whisked her away from the cows and the muck to the bright lights of civilisation and she didn't come home until every clothes shop had been carefully inspected, everything that caught her eye tried on and every penny that was burning a hole in her pocket spent.

Of course Cecily was horrified by such extravagance. *"Fine clothes don't make a fine lady,"* said Cecily.

"I'm afraid I'm going to have to disagree with you, Mother. I've always found myself to be a much nicer person when I'm well dressed. You should try it sometime!")

It was only ten o'clock in the morning. A long, long day stretched ahead of Cecily, with nobody to cook for and nobody to squabble with – what was she going to do with herself?

"But this is the first cold snap we've had this winter!" she said to Michael. "I thought you'd be spreading slurry – hasn't the ground been too soft before to drive the tractor and tanker over it?"

Jane was making congolais when Michael came home from the farm. She was whisking egg whites with sugar in a saucepan till they were frothy, then mixing in desiccated coconut with a wooden spoon. From his high chair Patrick helped: a paintbrush was dipped in butter and he greased the baking trays in spite of himself.

"Party!" shouted Susie when the trays of congolais came out of the oven, toasted on top and soft in the middle, delicious hot or cold. She busied herself about the living-room dusting at the plastic sofa with a lump of wet toilet roll.

Michael hardly ever saw his wife in the middle of the day, when her eyes were still bright and her face was fresh, before the sheen of exhaustion descended and her clothes got smeared with baby food.

"You're early!" She kissed him.

"It's a flying visit. I won't be home for the party. I'm going to have to spread slurry."

Jane waited to feel something, disappointment perhaps, that the father of her children could not take two hours off on New Year's Eve to attend his children's birthday party. But she felt nothing.

"Oh well, never mind. It's only a birthday party, there's one every year."

He smiled at her. "We'll still go out together tonight?"

It was Diane's idea that everyone club together and buy one large present for Susie and Patrick. The obvious choice was a plastic toy kitchen fully stocked with plastic food and cooking pots, spoons for stirring, knives for chopping, a frying pan, a fridge . . .

"This is far too much!" said Jane for the toy kitchen had more gadgets than the real one she stood cooking in every day.

"Of course it's not too much when you've gone to all this bother for the party!"

There was also a present for Jane.

Claire's dad was just back from France. He brought her a string of garlic bulbs and a dozen pots of fresh herbs – they couldn't be got in rural Ireland and when she was cooking

Jane improvised with herbal scented dust out of plastic jars and tubes of minced garlic which she squeezed from the end, like toothpaste.

Jane stroked the leaves of the fresh herbs and smelt her fingers in ecstasy. So this was what basil smelt like, and thyme and chives and tarragon.

Jane wore her black halter-neck frock.

She told the children, "It's a fancy dress party and this is my most fancy dress!"

They crowded into her council house, all her neighbours, even Oliver from up the street who never went anywhere. As promised he was dressed like a nun and his Von Trapp children were spotless.

"I stood them all in the kitchen sink. And scrubbed at them with a Brillo pad!"

He'd brought her a bunch of leeks and a bucket of potatoes from his garden: "Could you make us vichyssoise with my vegetables?"

There was something about the way he said that and the way he looked at her in her black halter-neck frock when he said it and the way he was standing right in front of her when he said it with his thumb idly stroking the top of Mary's head. With a funny little jolt, the first since she'd met Michael, she realised it was sex talking. It was almost a foreign language, but easily the words came back to her . . .

She raised her hand to his face. "Smell my fingers."

He didn't touch her, he didn't have to. "Chives," he said.

"I'll put them in your vichyssoise."

"How did you manage to crack him?" Linda asked.

They were alone together in the kitchen, arranging food

85

onto serving plates: Quiche Lorraine, garlic bread, *profiteroles au chocolat* and congolais – fancy French muck by popular demand. Oliver's vegetables were lying on the draining-board; Oliver and the children were in the living-room head-banging to Achilles' Heel. A chorus of innocent children's voices was singing: "*One more drink and I'm anybody's, One more drink and I'm yours . . .*"

"What do you mean?"

"There's been a steady stream of women cooking that man big feeds since Maeve died, offering him a shoulder to cry on – and more! And he hasn't looked at one of them."

Linda tried not to sound resentful for she was one of the overlooked, who popped in to visit Oliver on a regular basis with a packet of biscuits and eyes full of invitation, and a few buttons extra undone on her blouse.

"We're just friends," said Jane.

"Men and women can never be friends. Because of sex."

"Mummy, Mummy – Patrick is cooking!"

There he was, her son, with Claire Kavanagh at his elbow for she was as fascinated by the plastic kitchen as Patrick was. Together they were stirring with a plastic spoon the plastic potato and the plastic leeks he'd thrown into the plastic saucepan, Patrick who'd been sitting on her hip or in his high chair watching her cook since he was born. And now he was cooking: carefully tasting with the tip of his tongue on the spoon and sniffing an imaginary aroma over the saucepan . . .

It was just as Diane had promised: if you show a good example to your children the rest will follow. What a pity Michael wasn't at home to see it.

Patrick looked up at his mum and smiled.

86

"Vichyssoise!"

It was his first word.

Susie and Patrick were still high on dilute-to-taste orange juice when Michael got home from the farm. Susie was running madly naked through the house; Patrick was furiously chasing after her, brandishing a water pistol.

Jane said, "Daddy's home. Give him a big kiss, kids! We've missed you, Daddy," but they ran straight past him. Patrick might actually have elbowed him out of the way.

"I'm sorry I missed your party," said Michael and he was sorry because he'd never had a birthday party when he was a small boy. Cecily wasn't that sort of a mother; there hadn't even been a couple of friends invited over to make the day special.

Jane said kindly, "They didn't even notice you weren't there. No one noticed you weren't there. Gerry from Next Door dressed up like a clown and chased them round the living-room, Claire's dad gave them the bumps and Oliver twisted their balloons to make animals."

Susie shouted, "I got a pink pussy! Patrick has a dog with three legs!"

They'd had Gerry from Next Door and Claire's dad, and Oliver – father substitutes, better than nothing.

It wasn't a success, their big night out. New Year's Eve never is. It's the most overhyped and overrated night of the year. The Electric Ballroom was packed and there was no room for dancing. Jane sat at a shaky table sipping Fanta orange, watching Michael boat-racing pints with Trevor Mountain at the bar.

Nobody looked near her, the frumpy woman in the corner

with '*Somebody's Wife*' stamped fluorescent across her forehead. New Year's Eve is a night for decadence not for small-talk.

"Where's your halter-neck frock?" he'd asked her when they were leaving and she was wearing a granny dress with a high neck. It was empire line and it billowed out from under her breasts; she'd worn it on formal occasions when she was pregnant.

"Susie vomited her birthday cake over it. It's washed but I couldn't get it dried in time, even with the hairdryer."

"Pity. I like you in that halter-neck frock."

Now Trevor Mountain was playing Fiery Arse at the bar. His underpants were at his ankles, a ribbon of toilet paper fluttered from his buttock cheeks, the toilet paper was lit with a match and he bolted a pint and pulled out the toilet paper to raucous applause.

Every night they'd ever been out together Trevor Mountain had tagged along too, his enormous body squashed into the back seat of the Rapier, his knees pulled up round his ears, chatting exhaustively, and his breath stank of drink.

She had tolerated him when they were courting for someone had to drive and it gave her a chance to practise. She'd never have passed her driving test but that Trevor lived halfway up the mountain and it was a series of hill starts and revving every evening while he fumbled drunkenly with the gate, when they were leaving him home.

Jane squirmed in her seat in the corner. She been on the go all day and she was exhausted. All her friends from the street were snuggled up on their sofas, with a nice cup of tea, watching New Year's Eve on the television and thinking fondly about the fun party they'd been to at Jane's house.

"My Gerry" would be tenderly tending Diane: plumping up her pillows, boiling the kettle for a wee hot whiskey choked with sugar and sliced lemons "for medicinal purposes, love . . ."

"You look tired," Mrs Somerville had remarked when she'd come to baby-sit.

"I'd far rather stay at home with my book," said Jane and she didn't feel even a tiny bit disloyal saying it. "Until I started reading about Constance Chatterley, I never realised that you don't have to be happily married, or even in love with a man to achieve the magnificent heights of sexual satisfaction with him."

Just once, towards midnight, when the unattached revellers were seeking out a suitable pair of lips for kissing, the modern disco music slowed down.

Michael set down his pint, wiped his mouth with the back of his hand and led Jane onto the dance floor. He only burped beer into her ear the once when they were dancing; when midnight was called, he kissed her.

Then he went back to the bar and started a rowdy sing-along: *"I'm singing in the rain, I'm singing in the rain, what a wonderful feeling I'm happy again – Trevor Mountain, take your shirt off . . ."*

10

'Michael Temple was a simple man. It was one of his greatest charms. When he was hungry he ate, when he was horny he shagged, when he was tired he slept. The rest of the time he was farming. There was no time left over for introspection, no space allocated to it in his daily routine.

The row about the six white hens was such a little row too, so insignificant, shiny and lightweight, sandwiched between other, larger, more important rows.

Jane asked Michael to bring her home six white hens from Cecily's flock and Michael said, "But where would you put them?"

It wasn't an unreasonable question when you considered the size of the council house.

Jane said, "Fine then, don't bring them," and she didn't mention it again.

She didn't tell him that the hens weren't for her. They were a gift for Oliver from up the street who had built her a small greenhouse in the back garden and helped her plant out the pots of fresh herbs that Claire's dad had brought from France. Now Jane had a regular supply of chives and the rest. It was a game she played with the children: "Smell my fingers and tell me what I've been touching . . ."

She'd wanted to pay Oliver hard cash for his work. It was the least she could do when he was so obviously strapped but he'd point blank refused, said he was insulted by the suggestion. Then she'd considered buying him a bottle of whiskey – it was unimaginative but better than nothing – until Mrs Somerville told her he didn't drink. Now she felt slightly beholden to him, which was uncomfortable, but exciting at the same time, since there's only so much vichyssoise a man can accept from a woman before he begins to expect the main course.

Oliver already had hens, brown ones. They lived in a cute clapboard henhouse, painted duck-egg blue; it stood on stilts in his front garden. The hens ran with a speckled rooster who woke the neighbourhood at six every morning. Michael called it "Mr Ding Dong" and used it instead of an alarm clock. Mr Ding Dong was adventurous and there were daily excursions out of the hen-coop and up and down the street, followed by his faithful hens. The McBride children were trained like sniffer dogs to hunt under hedges and behind bushes for rogue nesting places and abandoned brown eggs which they tested for freshness with a basin of water.

Isaac explained to Jane, "If they sink they're fresh, if they float they're rotten because when they're rotten they're filled with stink-bomb gas and the gas is so light it makes them float."

"What a clever little boy you are!" said Jane.

"My daddy told me," said Isaac.

The hens were a cottage industry for Oliver. He sold their

free-range eggs round Stove Pipe Town. It was one of his many ingenious ways for making ends meet. It was Jane's inspired idea that he expand his empire with white eggs.

"I'll guarantee that you get a whole new class of egg-eater, if you offer them white eggs."

They were standing together at the kitchen sink watching the children chase Mr Ding Dong round the back garden. He'd brought her the last of his potatoes and leeks to make vichyssoise; she'd made him a cup of tea. The tea was drunk half an hour ago; it was time for someone to make a move. They continued to stand at the sink.

Oliver's eyes were glued to Jane's feet, the least sexual part of her body. He tried to concentrate on what she was saying about Cecily Temple's famous white rooster who won competitions and charged a stud fee but it was difficult to think straight about anything when he was standing so close to the luscious curve of her neck, the kissable bow of her lips, the inviting swell of her breasts and the biteable curve of her ass.

Sometimes he muttered "Yes, yes," to encourage her to keep on talking, for once she stopped talking the moment would be broken and he'd have to gather up his children and go home.

Jane watched him from under her eyelashes. She knew she was flirting with him and that it was dangerous, but she couldn't help herself. Something was driving her, which she was too young and too inexperienced to understand.

Jane saved up her housekeeping and bought white hens from Trevor Mountain's mother who advertised in the local paper. Trevor Mountain offered to deliver them.

The very first person he saw, when he drove into Stove

Pipe Town was Linda loitering on the street corner, idly watching for a bit of excitement.

Quick as a flash she jumped up into the cab of his tractor. Be still my beating heart, he was even bigger than she remembered!

"You're a long way from home!"

He grinned. "And you're just the woman I'm looking for! I'm lost – can you tell me where Jane Temple lives?"

"Only if you let me sit on your knee . . ."

Trevor Mountain thought often of Linda: she was the first and only exotic whiff of danger he'd ever had in his tractor cab. He remembered in particular her smell. Cigarettes and cheap perfume are heady and intoxicating when you spend your days in the fresh air.

Linda directed him to Jane's house. She was standing on a scrubbed front step waiting for him. A solemn little girl, the picture of her mother, was holding her hand. A shy little boy with a crooked smile was peeping out from behind her legs.

Here she was, the fabled Derry Emerald, slender and dark and delicate, "trophy wife" written all over her. Delicious to look at but not much use for pulling calves.

He carried the bag of hens from the cab and presented them with a flourish; there was a twinkle in his eye.

"You can take the woman away from the farm but you can't take the farm away from the woman."

Jane laughed and laughed at how wrong he was but was too proud to tell him the truth – that she'd tried, briefly, to love a farmer and found it wanting.

Ireland was basking in sunshine and everyone was gone to the seaside, even Old Dave and Cecily who were travelling in an official capacity with the Sunday School Excursion. Old

Dave was armed with a hawthorn walking-stick. It was his self-appointed duty to keep the teenage youngsters of decent God-fearing parents out of the amusement arcades and away from the sand hills, where he'd once discovered them drinking cider and shifting.

So Michael was alone at Temple and once the milking was finished and the cows were walked back to the meadow he went on a bit of a gallivant himself to the market yard at the windswept foot of the mountain which was a picturesque place in the sunshine, though the wind still cut right through you if you weren't wearing a vest.

It was always the same crowd at the market yard. Michael didn't know their names but he knew their faces and they knew him. Some nodded and said, "Hello, sir!"

He was eyeing up some swollen heifers when he saw them coming – Trevor Mountain who lived with his mother and the Carson twins who'd bullied him at school.

When they drew close Jack Carson announced, "My wife likes a free-range egg every morning, hard-boiled with a bit of butter."

His brother Jimmy said, "My wife likes her free-range eggs fertilised. Ha ha ha!"

Jimmy's sturdy, competent wife – Michael remembered her from Pony Club, she had a coarse country voice and hearty country manners – had just given birth to their third son and Jimmy was at the market yard with the other two. The youngest one was riding piggyback on his dad because he wasn't big enough to walk.

Michael tried to ignore their peals of puerile laughter. No one else thought they were funny and Jack Carson was married to a pig in a frock . . .

But nobody likes to be laughed at.

He could feel a slow dull burning in the bones at the back of his neck, the introduction of a violent episode of blushing, the mark of the beast. It quickly crept round his neck and up into his face and down into his chest, until he was coated.

"Why the big red face?" asked Trevor Mountain.

Michael got into the Land Rover and drove home. His day was ruined. He was the laughing stock of the market yard.

The council house was strangely quiet. The remains of lunch were still on the table.

Michael noticed it wasn't mackerel. In fact it looked quite tasty – grilled chicken breasts and a tomato salad dressed with fresh herbs. Two teacups, a milk jug and a pretty pink checked tablecloth. There was an intimacy about the place settings – the adult couple cosy at one end, the children in a bunch at the other. Michael didn't like the look of that.

They were in the back garden. The children were jumping in and out of a paddling-pool, Susie and Patrick and the two little ragamuffins from up the street. Out of the kitchen window he could see Jane lying back on a stripy deckchair. She was wearing a pretty sundress. The top was a stretchy smocked cotton tube with spaghetti straps. It hugged the outline of her breasts and left nothing to the imagination.

She was laughing with Oliver from up the street who was impossibly tanned. His fair hair was bleached blond, he was naked but for a pair of threadbare shorts and surprisingly well built for such a thin man, virile, wiry. Michael watched him pull a handful of gooseberries from one of the bushes, carefully pick away the top and tail of each one, peel them and feed them straight into his wife's greedy mouth. There was fluidity to the movement and an utter lack of self-consciousness even though they were being overlooked by a dozen houses in the terrace behind.

Michael's stomach plunged.

Michael sat on the plastic sofa staring sightlessly at the living-room walls, painted by Jane in washable paint, hint of green to match the emerald curtains. They were festooned with children's paintings and every one of them was of Mummy covered in hearts.

Scattered across the floor were building blocks, picture books and children's shoes. Jane's latest novel of doomed lovers, *The Mill on the Floss,* was balanced on the arm of the fireside chair; Jane's favourite band, Achilles' Heel, was on the record player.

It was hard to believe Michael lived here, that Jane was his wife, and Susie and Patrick were his children, for the only piece of Michael in the room was his face in a framed photograph with Jane at their wedding. He'd spent the entire day twisting and twisting at the unfamiliar wedding ring on his finger, he hadn't wanted to wear it to start with.

"It's not very practical for a farmer," he'd said when she'd presented it to him, but she'd picked it and paid for it by herself, from her cash prize for winning the Derry Emerald, so he'd worn it to please her, but by the end of the lambing it was lost.

"Up a sheep's bum?" She'd been horrified.

"Can't think where else it might be," he said.

Jane felt her shoulders burning and went into the house to cover them. She found Michael sitting on the plastic sofa, staring sightlessly at the living-room walls. His face was such a strange purple colour that her first thought was that he was ill, or, God forgive her, that his mother or his father were dead, or both of them. Jane could think of no other reason for Michael to leave the farm in the middle of the day.

"Are you all right, Michael? What are you doing here?"

"I live here," said Michael.

Jane brought him a glass of water. She held it to his lips for him to drink. She felt his forehead and pronounced it a little hot. She got down on her hands and knees in front of him and took off his work boots, ugly brown things with yellow laces, and his socks; there was a hole in the toe of one of them.

"Why are there no drawings of me on the wall? Every one of them is of you, Jane. What about me?"

Jane assumed he was joking. So she made a joke back.

"I haven't taught the children the facts of life. They don't yet know that it was your sperm fertilised my egg. When they learn that, I'm sure they'll be overwhelmed with gratitude and draw you into the pictures . . ." Then she said softly, "I think you've had too much sun on your head – I think you need to lie down."

Michael lay wide awake in his bed. He couldn't sleep. He couldn't even close his eyes because every time he did he saw Oliver peeling gooseberries and feeding them into Jane's mouth.

"But you *know* he helps me with the gardening . . ."

Michael was a sensible man. He loved his wife, and she loved him. They were happily married; at the very least they were married. So why was he sleepless and obsessing?

Michael tried to console himself. He knew Jane hadn't done anything with Oliver, except be friendly. But where did friendly finish and flirting begin? And how many steps was it from flirting to fornication? And from fornication to a full-blown affair? How many degrees of adultery was the peeling and feeding of fresh gooseberries to a woman not your wife?

"You're very tense," murmured Jane. "Cuddle in and I'll stroke you . . ."

Her hand, always friendly, even during the Battle of the Brown Curly Carpets, slipped down between his legs. And rested there, lightly. This was their private signal, her intimate way of telling him she was willing, though she was fit to spell it out for him too.

But Michael was numb from the neck down.

Until now he had always priggishly assumed that those who committed adultery went looking for it because they were amoral and lascivious. Because they had no loyalty and no respect for their marriage vows. Because they were bad people who should never have been married to start with.

Never before had it occurred to him that temptation was always all around. It was up every street and over every garden fence. And it was a careless husband who allowed his wife to be tempted.

He had dazzled Jane with passion and persistence the summer of the Derry Emerald – and married her in haste. And given no thought to the business of living happily ever after.

11

There are few things that inflame a husband more than a bit of healthy jealousy. Michael stopped taking his wife for granted and couldn't bear to let her out of his sight. Even though it was summertime, the busiest season in the farming calendar, or so she'd always been told, he began to arrive, unannounced, on the doorstep of the council house at lunchtime. And he came bearing gifts: wild roses and honeysuckle pulled out of the hedge, ice-creams from The Savoy, fresh raspberries from Cecily's fruit gardens.

He set the table, he helped feed the children. On one auspicious mark-the-calendar occasion he even washed up afterwards and he only broke one plate.

"Are you spying on me?" asked Jane for she was so used to him not being around that his constant presence made her edgy. And he had a very tiresome habit of hovering right behind her when she was cooking and making helpful suggestions.

"I think that vichyssoise needs a few more chives. Will I run out and get you some from the greenhouse?"

Every evening he made a special effort to get home early and do some gardening.

"You don't need Oliver when you've got me!"

There he was, posturing with a push mower in the front garden, passing the time of day with anybody who walked past.

"Lovely evening, Oliver, wouldn't you say?"

Diane from Next Door stuck her head out of her living-room window and shouted by way of neighbourly greeting: "Typical man, cutting grass where everybody can see you while Jane is run ragged indoors putting the children to bed! I often ask myself, is there a book of rules given to every father in the delivery ward entitled '*How to look good while you wriggle out of helping your wife with this baby*'?"

"Let's go away," said Michael, "just you and me for a night . . ."

He pictured them together in an upmarket Dublin hotel with a telephone beside the bed to ring for room service and tea-making facilities in a cupboard and complimentary soap. A hotel where dinner was so impressive that even food-obsessed Jane could find no fault and where they would lie in bed dozing and say "Five more minutes or we'll miss breakfast."

Michael had always wanted to go back to Dublin with Jane, since the whirlwind weekend of Ireland's Emerald when, for a pound, a busker outside Trinity had quoted W.B. Yeats' "He Wishes for the Cloths of Heaven" – and afterwards, in Bewleys, he had proposed with the lines "*I have spread my dreams under your feet; Tread softly because you tread on my dreams* . . ."

They could go on the train and make an excursion of it. There would be city shopping on Grafton Street, afternoon tea at The Shelbourne, ducks to feed on Stephen's Green. In the higgledy-piggeldy streets they could buy delicious cheese, bouquets of fresh flowers and antique jewellery.

Jane said, "Can we go to the National Concert Hall and hear *Madame Butterfly*? I read in the *Irish Times* that it's fantastic."

"That's the one with all the high-pitched screeching?"

"You could wear ear-plugs!"

It was a lovely idea, romantic and exciting; a night away from the old familiar . . .

"But who will look after the children?"

They were cutting silage at Temple – Michael, Trevor Mountain and Old Dave – playing "chase me, chase me" round the Forty Acres. Old Dave drove the lead tractor with the forage harvester attached. Like a giant lawnmower it gobbled up the grass and spat it out into the trailer skilfully driven alongside by Mountain. When the trailer was full Mountain drove it up to the farmyard and tipped it out and Michael fussed up and down on the little Massey, tidying the grass into the silage house where it would gently ferment into heavy, wet, smelly silage, to feed the cows all winter.

The cutting of the silage was a festive occasion at Temple. Kathleen was made to stay home from her Saturday shopping to help Cecily roast a chicken.

"But it's the Summer Sales!" said Kathleen.

"It's always something with you."

Cecily blew a whistle from the back doorstep to formally invite the farmers for their dinner. Kathleen was made to stand by the kitchen table and say, "Another roast potato,

Michael?" and "More tea, Trevor?" as if they weren't fit to get up off their bottoms and help themselves. Such formality of atmosphere inspired small-talk in Trevor Mountain who usually preferred to hang his head over his plate and shovel the food in silence.

"How are your wife's hens?" asked Trevor Mountain.

"What hens?" asked Cecily.

Kathleen, standing truculently to attention at the end of the table, bearing a glass jug of milk, was in the perfect position to see the shadow that crossed Michael's face – Michael who had been mysteriously slipping away to the council house at unpredictable hours during the busiest season in the farming calendar.

Michael said carefully, "The hens weren't for Jane. They were a present for her friend."

"Which friend?" challenged Cecily. She could smell a hunt and her blood was up. She'd always had a talent for pushing Michael, pushing and pushing – any secret Michael ever had, his mother had managed to squeeze it out of him.

Michael's first impulse was to tell the truth. "Oliver from up the street, he's been helping with the gardening," but he knew this answer would cause an uproar at the kitchen table.

Cecily would shout, "If a man and a woman say they are just good friends, at least one of them is lying!" and Old Dave would quote something biblical about an adulteress being stoned at a well. Meanwhile Trevor Mountain would sit silent and deadly with his big ears flapping. And the very next time Michael was at the market yard there would be more nasty teasing by the Carson twins: "My wife goes looking for free-range eggs up the street . . ."

Michael cleared his throat. "I've been meaning to ask you,

Mother. I'd very much like to take Jane away for a night to Dublin. How would you feel about minding Susie and Patrick?"

"Susie and Patrick who?" asked Cecily and she was only half joking for everyone knew Cecily Temple didn't like children, that she'd reared Michael and Kathleen only because she'd had to; if she loved them it was only because it was her duty to love them. Everyone knew Cecily did not like the noise of children, or their neediness. She was not charmed by their quaint little speeches, or their sticky soft hugs.

"Children should be seen and not heard," she always said and she honestly thought she meant it.

Cecily's aversion to children was so universally acknowledged that Susie and Patrick had never been to Temple and had never met their grandparents. Hard to believe when they lived only five miles away, but without an invitation it might as well have been at the other end of Ireland.

"I never said they weren't welcome," Cecily insisted but the truth was that she never made them welcome either.

Michael wasn't going to allow the old grievances to deter him any longer. He was the man who had sat on the fence of his marriage for long enough, and had too easily accepted no for an answer: no, you can't build a house on the farm – no, you can't have the money for a new sofa – no, you can't get off early to attend your children's birthday party . . .

"Brace yourself, Mother. I'll be bringing the children to meet you tomorrow afternoon."

The car pulled in through the ornate wrought-iron gates, past the dilapidated gate-lodge and up the gravel avenue shaded by stately beech trees in bloom. Susie and Patrick had never seen anything quite so grand in their life.

103

"Daddy was born in a castle," said Susie in awe as they drove past the house. "Is our granny a queen? Are you Prince Charming, Daddy?"

Michael laughed, glancing at Jane. "Your mother used to think so!"

They parked in the farmyard and Michael gave them a guided tour of the new milking-parlour. It was something he was very proud of for Temple was an old farm and until the birth of the new milking-parlour its farming practices had hardly changed in a hundred years. They followed him down a rutted farm lane and he pulled buttercups and held them at their throats and told them if there was a gleam of gold it meant they liked butter. He pointed out Cabbage White butterflies and dazzling dragonflies and an exquisite blackbird, with a yellow beak, singing from a thorn bush.

Jane and Susie and Patrick held hands. They had no wellies and their shoes were ruined.

In the meadows they stopped to politely admire Old Dave's modern milking cows – leggy and business-like in black and white who lived all winter in the new cattle house, and ate silage and walked independently into the new milking-parlour, where their milk was suctioned off and removed by pipe to a temperature-controlled bulk tank.

"Come over and have a look at them," said Michael, but the children stood their ground, clinging tightly to Jane's hand. The largest animal they'd ever before seen was the Alsatian dog at the end of the terrace. Jane might have been able to persuade them to move, but Jane was terrified.

"Don't cross the field without me, darlings, in case a cow runs after you!"

"Don't wander away from me, sweethearts, you might fall into a hole!"

"Stick close beside me, precious children, in case the big bad bull eats you!"

Then they walked to the plantation and the Forty Acres and down to the river where Jane's hair got tangled up in a thorn hedge trying to pull blackberries to make jam.

They walked back to the house by the road and in through the main gates where Susie fell into nettles trying to get a closer look at the pretty gate-lodge.

"Let's kill and eat those naughty nettles – we'll make nettle soup tomorrow!" said Jane.

Bringing up the rear, dragging his feet with his hands thrust deep into his trouser pockets, and a scowl on his face, was Patrick. He was a town child. Jane had reared him to be streetwise and traffic-savvy – he recognised the breeds of cars but could not distinguish between a sheep and a collie dog.

"What do you think of the farm then, son?"

"It smells," said Patrick.

Sunday afternoon at Temple was a solemn affair. Old Dave sat rigidly in the parlour reading aloud bits from his Bible while Cecily drank stewed tea and ate her way through a shop-bought Swiss Roll and fretted noisily about Kathleen who she despaired of ever marrying off.

The big splash of a birthday party, with the marquee and the band, had been an expensive mistake. Cecily was honest enough to admit that. It didn't matter to Cecily that the invited guests had enjoyed themselves so much they now used Kathleen's twenty-first as the benchmark against which all other birthday parties were measured. Or that copycat parties with bonfires, raffles, bands (and fur coats) were shamelessly fashionable. All that mattered to Cecily was that Kathleen still hadn't caught a husband. With worse to follow: since getting promoted at the bank she'd stopped taking her marital status seriously. It was starting to dawn on Cecily that perhaps Kathleen didn't much care to get married.

"I'm a career girl, Mummy," said Kathleen. "I don't need a husband."

"Everyone needs a husband!"

"Why?"

"To stop people talking about you."

And how typical of Kathleen to choose banking, a profession which stank of spinsterhood and desperation – stop the world I want to get off – it was almost as awful as teaching.

"Why couldn't you be cute and get work as a nanny or a cook? It would give the illusion of a caring personality and domestic competence! Who wants to marry a woman who works in a bank?"

A man who works in a bank.

From his corner Dave read, "'*Take no thought for your life, what ye shall eat or what you shall drink; nor yet for your body, what ye shall put on. Is not the life more than meat and the body more than raiment?*' Matthew 6, verse 25."

Cecily gulped noisily at her tea; she stuffed the last of the Swiss Roll into her mouth.

"Easy for you to say, Dave! Now she's started wearing skyscraper high heels every day most men need a stepladder to get up high enough to talk to her . . ."

"'*Ask and it shall be given you; seek, and ye shall find; knock and it shall be opened unto you.*' Matthew 7, verse 7."

Knock knock.

There was a brief silence as Jane and the children were ushered into the parlour. The Farm Walk was over and Michael had insisted that they come in for a cup of tea.

"We don't want to impose," said Jane.

Michael said firmly, "It would be rude not to come in. My mother wants to meet her grandchildren. She may even offer to keep them so we can get away for a night to Dublin."

Cecily observed her elegant daughter-in-law with a jaundiced eye. Here was textbook perfection with two pretty little children and a basket of blackberries to make jam. Nanny and cook and married at seventeen. Things would have been so much easier and smoother in Cecily's life if she'd had a daughter more like Jane, to rear and marry off.

Susie and Patrick clung to their mother. They could sense Jane was nervous and that made them nervous. Temple was the largest house they'd ever been in, big enough to ride a bicycle round and never bump into anything. The parlour was particularly austere with a stiff, slippy horsehair sofa set, draped in embroidered antimacassars. The fireplace was enormous and boarded up to stop the draught, a two-bar electric fire flickered in front of it taking the subzero chill out of the air; the parlour was north-facing and never warmed by the sun. And the ceilings rose up forever. It reminded Susie, with her limited life experience, of the butcher's on Main Street.

Cecily took a couple of sugar lumps from the bowl. She twisted her cross little face into a ghoulish smile. She held out the sugar lumps in the palm of her hand as if to coax a pony who was hard to catch.

"Susie, come here!"

Susie took one look at scary granny with her scrawny face and bitter eyes and began to scream.

Jane was kind. "Thank you for trying, but I honestly don't think they'd ever stay with you, Mrs Temple. They don't know you and I've trained them to be wary of strangers."

"But I'm their grandmother!"

"Yes, I know. It's very sad, isn't it?"

12

Kathleen was lying on top of her bed counting the hours, minutes and seconds until Monday when she would put on her fragrant bank uniform and escape from Temple back to the bank.

Kathleen loved the bank now, and it wasn't just because of her promotion to the exalted position of assistant manager, though that had given her enough self-confidence to turn her back on the expectations of rural Ireland, where you were pitied and despised if you weren't cute enough to catch a husband.

Kathleen's failure to find a husband at her big splash of a birthday party was the best thing that had ever happened to her. There was no need any more to create the illusion of submissive and willing marriage material so she walked tall in her high heels and swung her hips when she was walking, she made eye contact when she spoke to you, she stuck out her chest, she smiled a lot, and she threw back her head and laughed uproariously when she was amused.

Frank from Accounts and Rosie and Michelle stopped calling her a "stuck-up cow" and instead said, "That Kathleen is a real laugh, isn't she?"

At the bank there were official tea-breaks, going out for lunch with the girls, whip-rounds for birthdays, team-building afternoons – and Mr Rich of course. For though she was a first-rate failure in the marriage market, Kathleen could still recognise Cupid's arrow: it was the weakness she felt in her water every time Victor Rich looked at her. And really, it seemed, without meaning to boast, that he liked her too because he always seemed to be looking at her and when their eyes met he'd quickly look away.

"Kathleen! Kathleen! The tea's wet!"

Kathleen peeled herself off the bed. Bubbled in delicious daydreams she floated down the back stairs and into the parlour to where Jane and the children were rigidly perched on the horsehair sofa, making stilted small-talk about silage and Cecily looked even more huffed than usual.

"I won't have tea, thanks," she said and she sat down at the piano and played "Moonlight Sonata" passionately and accurately from memory.

"Is that a hymn?" Old Dave sounded suspicious.

"Almost as good as," said Kathleen and Jane, perched opposite, sipping stewed tea, noticed her starry eyes and the soft smile which transformed her face into something lovely.

"Does Kathleen have a boyfriend?" she asked later.

"I doubt it," said Michael.

It was Monday and Kathleen was in a marvellous mood. Stretching ahead of her was a whole week away from the farm – a week close to Mr Rich of course who'd stopped beside her desk first thing and asked her if she'd had a good weekend.

"Not particularly," said Kathleen who had an unfortunate tendency to open her mouth and blurt out exactly what she was thinking. Cecily was always condemning her for it:

"When people ask you how you are – you answer 'Fine, thanks.'"

"But what if I'm not fine? What if I'm furious, or euphoric, or frantic or fabulous?"

"Nobody cares! Take my advice, dear, when people ask you how you are – you answer 'Fine, thanks.'"

Mr Rich said, "Not 'Fine, thanks'?"

She grinned at him. "*'Laugh and the world laughs with you, weep and you weep alone!'*"

"*'For sad old earth must borrow its mirth but has troubles enough of its own.'*"

Their eyes met. He had nice eyes and a nicer smile, sexy and mischievous – it took years off him. Kathleen felt a hot flush of excitement spreading from the pit of her stomach down into the top of her legs. Any more smiling and she'd be weak at the knees . . .

"Do you think he has a girlfriend?" she asked Rosie and Michelle for it was just possible that he quoted Ella Wheeler Wilcox at all his staff, but Rosie and Michelle had nothing juicy to tell her.

"He keeps himself to himself," they said.

He was the boss, he was divorced, he was far too old for either of them; flighty things, they went to the Electric Ballroom every weekend and courted strange men in dark corners and got great mileage out of it afterwards.

"The one with the short legs and the big shoulders groped my bum when we were dancing and I said, 'Don't do that, Trevor, that's not nice,' and he said . . ."

Kathleen went back to her own desk and furiously

fantasised about Mr Rich who was looking particularly handsome, in a dashing blue shirt with a long pointed collar. He must have been outdoors all weekend for his face was sunburnt – it made his teeth look very white when he smiled at her . . .

"Look at the big eyes of you! Like stars! What are you thinking about? *Who* are you thinking about?"

Kathleen laughed. "You'd never believe me if I told you!"

The bank shut at four and Kathleen's bus came at ten past. But today she couldn't think of one good reason to race back to the farm, for Trevor Mountain and the gang were still cutting silage and her mother would be almost half dead feeding them. By the time she got home they'd be ready for high tea and she'd be expected to change out of her fragrant bank uniform and carry it out to them, to the Forty Acres, with a picnic blanket for them to sit on.

It was Kathleen's caustic opinion, one of the few she shared with her mother, though she wouldn't have thanked you for pointing it out, that a farmer didn't need a wife, only a donkey to do the heavy lifting.

Instead, she decided to saunter through Stove Pipe Town to where Jane lived. She had a bag of clothes for Jane, summer cast-offs from last year, some of them still in fashion, all of them getting a bit tight, for the official tea-breaks and the going out for lunch with the girls and the team-building birthday cakes were doing nothing for Kathleen's waistline: "It's not the first wee bun makes you fat!"

She might never have got round to it, the culling of her cast-off clothing, but that she'd been trapped at home on Saturday, assisting with the silage-making. And she might never have thought to offer the clothes to Jane if she hadn't seen her on Sunday, pinned between Susie and Patrick on the horsehair sofa, a worn-out shadow of her former beautiful self. Brimming with new self-confidence Kathleen had been overcome by an unfamiliar emotion – she recognised it as a sudden rush of pity for Jane who was wearing machine-washable clothing and her hair needed washing.

"Where are you going with those clothes?" asked Cecily.

"Curiosity killed the cat," said Kathleen.

Kathleen strode confidently through Stove Pipe Town, stepping over dog poo and skilfully avoiding a stampede of speckled rooster and brown hens. Susie and Patrick's play hour was just ended and Jane's friends were taking their children home. There was a tall stiff woman with a hatchet face and a small, pretty woman carrying a child so exquisitely dressed with her hair in ringlets that for a second Kathleen presumed it to be a doll.

Kathleen stood well back in her fragrant bank uniform. "I've called at a bad time?"

"Just finished! Would you like some soup and potatoes?"

Jane fitted on the clothes while Kathleen ate her soup. It was not a part Kathleen had ever visualised herself playing, that of Lady Bountiful, but Jane's unfettered delight in her bag of clothes was infectious.

"I love Cork Ease shoes and these have never been worn!"

"Yes, well . . . I actually bought two pairs the same. I only realised when I got home from the shops . . ."

"Lucky you! I have a pair of Moses sandals that I bought in the Children's Department when Patrick was being fitted for his first pair of shoes. And a pair of fluffy slippers, and that's it –"

There were peasant blouses made of cheesecloth and butterfly tops with square necklines, trimmed with ribbon. There were crocheted shawls and cowboy boots and jeans and tie-dyed T-shirts and an exquisite off-white Gunne Sax dress – part hippie, part prairie, part Edwardian dinner party in thin, floaty chiffon trimmed with lace. Jane had often admired them in shop windows and magazines.

"You haven't even worn this!"

Kathleen smiled ruefully. "I'm not a chiffon kind of girl but of course I didn't realise that until it was bought and I got it home and tried it on and my mother informed me that I looked like a toilet-roll holder. I'm much better suited to trouser suits and wrap-over dresses and that white cheesecloth blouse is a headache, I swear it shrank after the first wash, and it has to be steeped in cold tea after you wash it, to keep its colour . . ."

Jane smiled warmly at her sister-in-law – she could hardly recognise her – and it wasn't just her beautiful clothes . . .

Impulsively she said, "You look lovely."

"Because I'm wearing make-up! It's still at the experimental stage. Mummy says I look like a clown. Is there lipstick smeared on my teeth?"

Jane carefully inspected the teeth. She shook her head. "Always blot your lipstick after you put it on, with a piece of toilet roll or a handkerchief. Then it won't smear!"

Next morning, at the bank, Mr Rich formally presented himself in front of Kathleen's desk and said, "Can I have a word with you, Miss Temple, in private?"

Come into my office, said the spider to the fly.

Inside, Kathleen stood nervously to attention, blushing in spite of herself, afraid to make eye contact with the boss for

Mr Rich's office was used only for meetings with clients, and the hiring and firing of employees.

"For some time now, I've been watching you, Miss Temple and I believe you're the woman I'm looking for . . ."

A delicious shudder sprinted up Kathleen's spine. "Yes, please!"

"Lord Laurence Glass is ridiculously in debt. He does his best, but frankly, nobody can afford to live in a monstrosity of a house like Lisglasson any more. It has a hundred rooms and there's not electricity in one of them. For years he's been selling off bits and pieces to make ends meet: out-farms, Lisglasson Lodge, the fishing rights on the lough. The hunting, the hounds, the huntsman and the horses were drafted last year. All that's left is the gamekeeper's cottage and the shooting. It's a sensitive case. Lord Laurence has his pride left, if not much else. I'm seeking a clever, tactful woman to assist me with the bankruptcy proposal . . ."

"Yes, please," said Kathleen and in no time they were composing an intelligent and practicable proposal that the shooting at Lisglasson be hired out to corporations and businessmen, creating a modest income for Lord Laurence, while the bank discreetly put up his estate for sale.

Together they sat at the conference table while he talked her through the proposal, side by side, carefully not touching, and Kathleen was overwhelmed with an urge to push aside the boring papers and sit astride him, to take his severe spectacles off his nose, loosen the tidy Windsor knot of his Golf Club tie and slip her fingers between the buttons of his carefully pressed shirt and run her nails over his nipples . . .

On Thursday, as usual, Jane joined the patient queue at the

fish stall. The Chinese restaurateurs were buying big plastic bags of fish-heads and haggling about the price and holding everybody up.

Across the street an elaborate, choreographed pantomime was unfolding. Victor Rich, smartly dressed and distinguished in a middle-aged, middle-class sort of way was repeatedly getting in and out of his swanky car and checking his watch. Hurrying along Main Street towards him, in skyscraper high heels with her face beaming, was Kathleen. As they got closer to each other Victor Rich straightened his Golf Club tie (again) and got out of his car at the precise second that Kathleen – wearing the serene expression of woman who has just had an orgasm – dropped her glove.

No way! Gloves! In 1975! What sort of romance novels did Kathleen read? Jane opened her mouth to shout "What century are you pair courting in?" – because, apart from period dramas on television, she'd never seen the like of it – but then she closed it again and watched instead.

"Miss Temple – your glove."

"Oh, Mr Rich! Please call me Kathleen."

(And full marks to Kathleen for pulling off a very believable impersonation of *virginal and coy*.)

"But he's an old man," said Michael. "There's no way she's in love with Victor Rich, you're imagining things!"

He was strangely disgusted by the thought of his little sister with Victor Rich and strangely disgusted with himself that he felt disgusted.

Jane shook back her long black hair, freshly washed. She rattled her big hoop earrings and jangled the silver bangles up her arm.

"Take them all," Kathleen had said. "They were another

impulse buy and another fashion mistake on me. I'm just not an ethnic type of girl . . ."

For the first time in a long time Jane had changed into clean clothes, Kathleen's best cast-offs, before Michael came home from the farm. For the first time in a long time she was composed into the smiling and serene wife he remembered from the start of his marriage. For the first time in a long time she kissed her husband full on his mouth and meant it.

"Who knows the workings of the human heart?"

Michael said, "I know these clothes are fashion but I still prefer you in the black halter-neck frock."

"You're a shocking man, Michael – addicted to the old familiar . . ."

13

Kathleen had to thank Jane for the fact that she ever made it to the altar with Victor Rich. It was also thanks to the ritual of the Sunday afternoon Farm Walk – such a fun way to spend Sunday once everyone had wellies! And always, afterwards, there was tea in the parlour, stilted conversation and passionate piano.

Until the week that Kathleen didn't appear from her bedroom for tea.

"Is Kathleen unwell?"

Cecily tossed her head and muttered something; it sounded like: "She's sick all right, sick in the head."

Afterwards Jane carefully carried the tray of china tea cups into the scullery to find Kathleen standing at the sink, sniffing ugly snottery tears. Her nose was horribly swollen with crying.

"Let me help you," said Kathleen and she plunged her arms into the hot water.

There was more painful adolescent sniffing and she shook her bushy thick hair over her face and muttered into it.

Then suddenly she began to shout.

"We worked really late on Friday to get the bankruptcy proposal finished and he gave me a lift home because it was raining and I'd no umbrella, and he didn't want me to get wet walking up the avenue and I invited him in for a cup of tea and when Mummy saw him she said: 'Isn't that old fellow a bit long in the tooth for you, Kathleen?'"

"To his face?"

"I was his special protégé, hand-picked! Now he's never going to speak to me again! I can't eat, I can't sleep, I can't stop thinking about him . . ."

Quietly Jane said, "'Better to be an old man's darling than a young man's slave', wouldn't you agree, Kathleen?"

More muttering from Kathleen.

Afterwards, thinking about it, Jane was sure she'd said, "Thanks, Jane."

That very next afternoon, after the bank closed, Kathleen arrived unannounced at the council house. Susie and Patrick's play hour was just ended, Hatchet Face and the doll had gone home. Jane was on the doorstep, chatting to a thin blond man. With a shock Kathleen recognised him: it was Oliver McBride who'd been the assistant manager at the bank when she'd started working there. Then his wife died, it was very sad, some sort of complication during the delivery, and the next they knew, he'd resigned and disappeared.

By the look of him, he'd been living on handouts, under a hedge.

"Mr McBride!"

She swept forward to speak to him for she'd never had a chance to say how sorry she was that his wife had died and she wanted to tell him how much everyone missed him. He'd

118

been so kind to her in the beginning when she was still a big awkward farmer's daughter who didn't know how to count in her head or how to talk to people. And when the figures wouldn't add up, and they never had at the start, he'd always said, "Chin up, Kathleen, it's not the end of the world!" and sometimes he'd bought her a bar of chocolate.

She'd have known him anywhere and recognised him for the gentleman he was even dressed in rags on a council estate.

Jane bundled the children into waterproof dungarees, wellies and coats and ushered them outside into the back garden.

"It has finally stopped raining and they really need some fresh air. But I know I'm going to regret it later that they're missing their usual nap."

Before the scullery door was even shut Susie said, "Excuse me please, Mummy, I have to pee," so in she came again and off came the wellies and the coat and the waterproof dungarees. Susie sat on the potty. When she was finished Jane patiently redressed her in the waterproof dungarees, the wellies and the coat and ushered her back outside into the garden. Peace descended in the council house.

All day at the bank Kathleen's heart had been breaking. It was the first morning in weeks that she hadn't accidentally on purpose bumped into Mr Rich on the front steps and the first Monday in weeks that he hadn't sauntered past her desk mid-morning and asked: "How was your weekend, Miss Temple?"

Mr Rich stayed locked into his office; he didn't send out for tea; he didn't invite anybody in. A depressing fog hung over the bank and Kathleen's co-workers kept their heads down, anxiously and diligently busy. No one loitered by the tea table.

The uncomfortable atmosphere was sensed by the customers, standing in tidy lines, lodging money and removing it. There was no small-talk and no fool chat and nobody enviously remarking on the plastic bag full of money the Chinese restaurateurs were lodging after a weekend of feeding punters with prawn crackers and fish heads.

"Maybe Mr Rich isn't feeling well," said Kathleen.

But tip-toeing past the firmly shut door she heard him shouting and the sound of his fist banging on the bank manager's desk.

"But he's usually so quietly spoken! I've never heard him raise his voice."

And she felt something shift deep in her belly – a twanging excitement in the bass cords of her sexuality . . .

Frank from Accounts whispered, "He was like this when his wife left him. I remember it well. He locked himself into his office for weeks, and when he wasn't in the office he was on the golf course, whacking balls and talking to himself."

Kathleen didn't know much about golf. There was a small dimpled ball and bag of sticks and the aim was to pick the right stick to hit the ball the right way so it landed in a distant hole. And of course golfers wore amusing clothes and talked about "birdies" and made jokes about the nineteenth hole. It sounded sociable and jolly, a fun way to stretch your legs if you were about a hundred.

Kathleen was overcome with curiosity.

"What was she like, his wife?"

Frank shrugged. "She took drink. Her head went."

Jane said, "You're going to have to make the first move, Kathleen."

"You mean throw myself at him?"

They were sitting comfortably at the kitchen table. Kathleen was on her second helping of baked mackerel with gooseberry sauce – her heart was broken not her stomach.

"I haven't eaten a bite since Friday," she boasted, "I haven't been able to *swallow* –"

Knock knock. It was Susie at the back door.

"Excuse me please, Mummy. Patrick has just pulled a sheet off your washing-line."

Slowly Kathleen followed Jane and Susie into the back garden. Patrick was in a muddy puddle, laboriously wrapped in fluffy white flannelette, huffing and puffing as he tried to walk with the sheet tangled round his legs. Diane from Next Door was leaning over the wire fence that divided the gardens, scolding him.

She'd been supervising Next Door's thirty-minute run-around. Ernest and Valerie were throwing and catching tennis balls with one arm and one leg tied behind their backs; Tim was juggling with bean bags. Monday was devoted to hand-eye co-ordination skills Next Door.

"Patrick Temple, if your sister told you to put your finger into the fire, would you do it?"

Jane said mildly, "They want to build a tent, Diane, they want to camp out. Would Tim like to come and camp out with them?"

Diane had the greatest respect for Jane but she was frankly bewildered by her stubborn inability to discipline her children or even raise her voice to them when they were naughty. That sheet in the mud was going to have to be washed again and the chance of another half-decent drying day was remote . . .

Susie tugged at her mother's elbow.

"Excuse me please, Mummy, why is Diane from Next Door such a crosspatch?"

Diane from Next Door rolled her eyes. Where did Jane get her patience? Every infuriating "Mummy, Mummy" was always politely answered, every ridiculous suggestion given careful consideration. Jane genuinely seemed to think that Susie's and Patrick's opinions were just as interesting and important as adult opinions.

She shook her head with gloomy foreboding.

"I dare say you've got your reasons but I think it's a big mistake to let children think for themselves. You'll never be able to control them when they're older."

Kathleen rapped smartly on Mr Rich's office door. It was first thing Tuesday morning and she hadn't slept a wink all night. She'd been far too excited. She was going to throw herself at Mr Rich and she couldn't wait a second longer.

He was on the phone.

"Allow me to reassure you, Lord Laurence, that Miss Temple and I, together, have done our utmost to protect the confidentiality of your situation."

Their eyes met. Afterwards, she swore to him that he blushed when he said "Miss Temple and I, *together*" and that's what had given her the confidence to lock the office door.

Kathleen stood in front of Mr Rich. Under her regulation blouse and skirt she was wearing her nicest underwear in ivory satin, trimmed with ivory lace; it had cost an arm and a leg. The woman in the lingerie shop, wrapping it up, had assumed incorrectly from the colour that it was for her wedding and had said, "If I was you, dear, I'd let him take this off very, very slowly . . ."

She was fastidiously doused in Chanel No. 5. The woman in the shop, wrapping it up, had whispered, "I call this bedroom perfume. Try it in the creases of your elbows and behind your knees."

On Kathleen's feet were her very best shoes. "Business or pleasure?" asked the curious woman who sold them to her, because in rural Ireland shiny black stilettos were only ever bought by women of suspect virtue.

"Both!"

Mr Rich finished his phone call and the receiver clattered onto the table. His hands were shaking.

(Afterwards he admitted that the bulging erection in his trousers hadn't helped either.)

"What can I do for you, Miss Temple?"

The words came out in a squeak. He already knew what she wanted.

She moved in on him. "Kiss me."

Afterwards everyone in the bank said it had been perfectly obvious from the very first day that Victor Rich and Kathleen Temple were perfect for each other. It was written in bold print across their foreheads. The painfully slow progression of their romance had been the subject of bets and animated tea-break conversations since Kathleen was hand-picked to assist with the bankruptcy proposal.

Those who were charitable said, "Isn't it lovely that two such unusual people can find love?"

Those who were less charitable said, "What a pity he's an old man."

That first kiss had taken most of the morning, for once their lips met something amazing happened, a chemical reaction, a magical spell. Kathleen's nerves melted away and

Victor Rich's strained formal good manners evaporated and they clean forgot that they were standing in his bank manager office with a tidy queue of customers on the other side of the locked door and Frank from Accounts waiting to be summonsed in for his monthly appointment to go through the figures. Their lips met and stuck together; their tongues touched and it was electric.

The phone started ringing. Victor Rich pulled the connection out of the wall.

She laughed and he smiled his mischievous, sexy smile. Then he pushed the papers on his desk to one side and lifted her up on to it. Kathleen wrapped her muscular legs around him and pulled him tightly towards her and they kissed again, and inhaled.

"You smell of very clean soap," she murmured.

His mouth hesitated behind her ear, where only an hour before she had fastidiously dabbed her bedroom perfume. "You stink of that stuff!" Cecily had told her at breakfast.

"You smell good enough to eat," he told her.

At first it was enough for Kathleen that Victor Rich and she were an item. "My boyfriend," she called him. They went for walks, drank coffee, held hands and kissed in secret corners. He drove her home from work, and took her out for dinner at the weekend. She tried not to take offence when an ignorant young waiter in an overpriced restaurant described Victor Rich as "your father" – "Your father is waiting for you in the lounge area . . ."

"I beg your pardon, he's not my father!"

"I suppose you can't really blame him." Victor was always reasonable. "I *am* old enough to be your father!"

"But you're not old, you're only fifty!"

"It's old compared to twenty-four."

Such a stupid argument: my age is bigger than your age!

She snuggled into the swanky leather interior of his old man's car, her young hand rested lightly on his old thigh. Expensive, gentle darkness enveloped them and they kissed deeply.

"I can't see your wrinkles when I'm kissing you."

"I can't see your spots."

Kathleen couldn't stop smiling. So this is what happy felt like! It was a hundred times better than shopping! She even stopped picking fights with her mother.

In the beginning cynical Cecily assumed that Kathleen and Victor Rich were using each other – Kathleen was sleeping with the boss and Victor showing off with a much younger woman. But soon it became clear, even to Cecily, that Kathleen and Victor were in love; they loved each other. Any day soon Kathleen was going to appear with an expensive diamond and announce her engagement.

Cecily knew she should've been pleased that finally her awkward big lump of a difficult daughter had found a man but instead she wanted to cry.

"Why don't you like him, Mummy?" asked Kathleen who was disappointed by her mother's lack of enthusiasm.

Unfortunately Cecily had never learnt how to express herself gently. Her worries displayed themselves as hysterical screeching and daily, dramatic threats to drown herself in the river: "He's an old man! In ten years you'll be a woman in the prime of life and you'll be trapped, nursing an old-age pensioner."

"But I love him, Mummy," said Kathleen.

Cecily started sleep-walking again, round and round the

house, banging on doors, insisting: "I'm having a heart attack, you'll have to go for the doctor!"

The Farm Walk tea ceremony was particularly fraught with Kathleen radiant at the piano, playing the Wedding March and Cecily screaming, "Old men sag! In bed it takes them all night to do what they used to do all night!" and Old Dave, in an affronted voice, booming from his corner: "'*Judge not, that ye be not judged.*' Matthew 7, verse 1!"

"My mother has gone mad," Michael whispered.

Only Jane didn't think that Cecily was acting out of character. Not that anybody asked her opinion but this was Cecily Temple whose mission in life was to make the path of true love as precipitous as possible and who, when she had successfully got rid of Jane out of Temple, after three vicious months, had gloated: "What can you expect from a cheap little thing from the town?"

Kathleen took refuge in the scullery, up to her elbows in dishes. With the door slammed shut she almost couldn't hear her mother shouting: "That old fellow has been married before! And his first wife left him! He couldn't make her happy, what makes you think he can make you happy? Do you even know why his first wife left him?"

She was holding out bravely against the bombardment but the strain was starting to show.

She whispered to Jane, "Maybe he is too old for me. Maybe I should be concerned that he's been married before. Maybe I should ask him why his first wife left him . . ."

14

They say that on the point of death you are bestowed with a celestial understanding of the mistakes and triumphs that make up your life. After Amelia left him Victor Rich had longed for one clean shot through his aching heart to put him out of his misery. Maybe then he'd understand why she walked out on their nice marriage and politely divorced him in Mexico and never a cross word between them.

They'd met at university. She'd come from privilege and education, the Dublin intelligentsia, reared on recitals at the National Concert Hall, exhibitions at the National Gallery, lectures in Trinity College. He was the son of a country doctor. His parents had implored him not to marry her: "You could never make her happy." But he was young and they were in love. He didn't believe them. He didn't want to believe them. Rural Ireland was a beautiful place, if you liked cows and grass. Family life was fulfilling, if you liked children.

Before long Amelia was pregnant, she'd made friends, she fitted in. A few eccentricities: she always had her nose in a book, even at formal bank parties and golfing get-togethers, she had a fondness for the drink and Lady Glass, her intimate friend, was quite obviously a lesbian.

Victor was a broadminded man and an indulgent husband. They were happy until she miscarried the baby, and suffered – suffered wasn't too strong a word – her Awful Epiphany.

He'd brought her a bunch of little white roses to the hospital; they matched her little white face.

He spoke gently. "The doctor says we did nothing wrong. We can try again in a couple of months . . ."

She spoke clearly. "I think this is the best thing that has ever happened to me."

"Hush, darling!"

"Before we have real children and responsibilities. Before it's too late."

At first he'd thought it was shock and bereavement talking. A miscarriage is still a dead baby and she'd been far enough on for them to know it was a dead baby girl. The nurses said, "Take her home and be kind to her, she'll get over it in time . . ."

But once she was well enough she left him.

"I'm leaving you, Victor. Please drive me to the station to catch the Dublin train."

He'd stood on the platform, willing her to stay, tears sliding down his cheeks.

"What have I done wrong?"

He'd been a good husband, reliable and kind, generous with money.

"That's not enough for me," she said. "What makes you think that's enough for me?"

Bitch.

"Why is it not enough for you?'"

"Rather ask yourself, for what sort of a woman is it enough?"

For twenty years his failed marriage haunted him. Things had happened of course, there'd been girlfriends and holidays and promotions at work, golf, but it all amounted to nothing. He amounted to nothing. For twenty years he was comfortably numb while men with less going for them met girls, married them, bought houses with them, had children with them. Lived happily ever after.

What had he done wrong?

It was only now, from the vantage point of age and experience and, finally, personal happiness with Kathleen that Victor realised he didn't have to wait for the point of death any more to fully understand the mystery of his first failed marriage. Within his darling Kathleen's family circle he had the surreal opportunity to watch its sad history repeating itself. This time the married couple were Jane and Michael, the setting was a council house, and there were extras – Susie and Patrick.

In the beginning Victor Rich was dismissive of Jane. She was just like all the other young mums out of Stove Pipe Town who he saw every day, uniformly dressed down in jeans and an anorak. In the morning they marched spotless, bright-eyed children to school with the cigarette smoke flying out of them. They clogged up the post office on Tuesday while they queued for their Family Allowance. They caused long tailbacks in the butcher's and the greengrocer's while they counted out their money for a pound of mince and a pound of carrots and a pound of onions and carefully checked their change. They had eyes in back of their heads to watch their lively little ones and they roared at them without embarrassment in public: "*If you don't get over here right this minute, when I tell you to, and let go of your sister's hair, I'll give you a clip round the ear!*"

So when Jane invited Victor over for dinner, the first time, to celebrate his engagement to Kathleen, he hesitated.

He didn't want to hurt Jane's feelings and he certainly didn't want to get off on the wrong foot with the only member of Kathleen's family who did not emphatically disapprove of him. But:

"Isn't it asking a bit much of her? She lives in a small house and she has two children. Anyway, I'd rather take you out for dinner; I'll book us a table at The Rainbow's End . . ."

Kathleen had laughed at him. "I'll give you five minutes alone with her, and if you're not in love with her by the end of it I'll have to assume there's something wrong with you!"

"I suppose she's attractive enough," he said politely but without conviction, "if you like that sort of thing."

Victor wore his navy blue blazer with the Golf Club crest on the pocket; a yellow spotty cravat was wound round his neck. He felt foolish and overdressed as he drove his company car through the grey streets of Stove Pipe Town, carefully avoiding kids on bikes, kids kicking a football, kids skipping and kids chasing each other. It was nearly eight o'clock at night. Did these children not have an established bedtime?

Kathleen was serene in the seat beside him. "That's the first time I've ever heard you sound like a grumpy old man."

"I'm nervous. It must bring out the grumpy old man in me."

"Nervous of what?"

Should he admit that he'd been awake half the night trying to remember the names of the actors in *Coronation Street*? She was bound to watch *Coronation Street*, everyone did . . . And would it be better at the very beginning of the evening to admit to not knowing one end of a milking cow from the other, or should he wait until the brandy and cigars when Michael might courteously ask his opinion on the introduction of milk quotas and the Common Agricultural Policy within the EEC?

"What if I can't eat what she's made? What if I can't think of a thing to say to him? I want so very much to make a good impression . . ."

Kathleen leant over and kissed the man who had successfully faced down Lord Laurence Glass in a bankruptcy board meeting.

"Win her over and he will follow. He worships the ground she walks on. That's Jane's house in the middle of the terrace – the one with the speckled rooster crowing from the fencepost."

"And the tractor parked outside the gate."

"Come in, come in, you're very welcome!" said Jane. She was wearing an extraordinary emerald-green cotton voile dress, overprinted in gold. There were rings on her fingers and bells on her toes. With her long dark hair and eye make-up she was breathtaking and exotic and her heavy perfume vibrated in the simple living-room.

A table and four chairs dominated the room; a plastic sofa was pushed against the window; a turf fire burned in the grate; Vivaldi was on the record player.

Victor Rich was suddenly relieved that he was an old fart who always dressed for dinner and always brought wine and flowers to a dinner party, even when the dinner party was at Number 10 Stove Pipe Town, in a house the size of his bank manager's office, where he worried that he might be mugged on the way back out to his car afterwards.

Kathleen said, "I knew that dress would suit you the minute I tried it on! I really wanted it to suit me, which is why I bought it and brought it home, but when Mummy saw me in it she said I needed only a crystal ball to tell fortunes . . ."

Jane explained to Victor, "This is my most excellent benefactor. But for the fashion mistakes of Kathleen I'd still be wearing my black halter-neck frock from out of the ark."

"I like you best in the black halter-neck frock," said Michael.

Michael Temple was exactly as Victor had imagined, no surprises there: he was ruddy-cheeked and broad-shouldered with few thoughts beyond the cows and the barley, shy until he'd a couple of drinks and even then it was like squeezing blood out of a stone. What Victor noticed most was that Michael never took his eyes off his wife, even when she was ignoring him, and when she spoke to him his face softened and his eyes beamed.

It was déjà vu, and he hadn't seen it for twenty years. It was exactly what he used to do with Amelia.

What an extraordinary evening and not just because of the food, though of course Jane was an excellent cook.

"I've not tasted better French cooking outside of France," he told her after the first plate of vichyssoise.

She said, "The potatoes and leeks come from an old friend of yours – Oliver McBride from the bank?"

"A very old friend," said Victor politely and he might have elaborated with some sort of professional explanation of how Oliver had been his second in command with a very real chance at manager, but that he noticed the shadow which crossed Michael's face and an alarm bell actually went off in his head. For Oliver McBride had been a thorn in the side of his marriage to Amelia from the very first time he'd taken her into the bank to show her off, after their honeymoon, when they were married a month.

"If Only" she'd called him.

"If only what?"

"'If he were the only boy in the world and I was the only girl.'"

At first he was pleased that she'd found a friend, to coax her away from the drink at banking functions and Oliver was courteous and pleasant; he always addressed Amelia with just the right amount of deference as befitted the wife of the bank manager.

Amelia said, "Do you know how few really attractive men there are in the world? I can hardly believe I've found one here in the wetlands of rural Ireland."

"But he's the son of a bog-trotting farmer! Fifty-two acres of mountain and three older brothers!"

"I do believe you're jealous!" said Amelia.

She'd reached that point in her marriage when making her husband jealous was the most fun she could have with her clothes on. If only Oliver had done something to give Victor a reason to hate him – if he'd held her too tight when they were dancing, or kissed her under the mistletoe, or touched her inappropriately. But he never had, and Victor, unfairly, never forgave him for it. The resentment lay buried inside him long after Amelia left. And of course he could have helped Oliver more when his wife died and the crunch came and he was forced to abandon the corporate ladder for a quieter life. But he hadn't. Victor wasn't particularly proud of himself when he thought about that.

The conversation turned to books.

Jane was reading *Heat and Dust*. It had won last year's Booker Prize and everybody was still talking about it – a story set in British India, of a deeply respectable Civil Servant posted to a rural backwater, with a spoilt wife who causes a scandal when she runs away with an Indian prince . . .

By now Victor was mellow with fancy French muck and fine wine. He knew it was pompous of him, the way he'd pointed out the vintage and the grape type when he'd handed the bottles to her and announced, "*Le Beaujolais Nouveau est arrivé!*" but these bottles had been specially imported from France; they were Beaujolais Nouveau, an immature wine intended for immediate drinking, and there was always the awful possibility that she might hide them away in a cupboard and save them for best. And by then they'd have diminished into vinegar.

"I know nothing about wine," she'd refreshingly confessed, without shame. "How do we open it? Does it have a lid?"

"Don't you have a corkscrew?"

How ponderous he sounded and he could have bitten out his tongue the moment he said it but in the end they'd found a corkscrew as an unused attachment on Michael's penknife.

"I thought that was for cleaning out the dirt from under my fingernails," said Michael.

Victor poured a dollop into a tumbler, swirled it gently and sniffed. He held the tumbler up to the living-room light bulb and pronounced, with satisfaction, that the wine lacked legs.

"And that's a good thing?" Michael asked.

"I smell bananas," Jane announced, "and pear drops . . ."

"I'm a pint man, myself," said Michael.

Afterwards, on the way home, Victor cautiously said, "Your brother is a very lucky man, Kathleen."

But he was remembering Jane's one artless remark of the evening: "I don't condemn Olivia for leaving her husband and running away with the Indian prince – do you? Lucky Olivia to get the chance, I'd be away like a shot."

This was the sort of striking statement Amelia had always made at rural Irish dinner parties after half a bottle of red and before pudding when the assembled guests would pronounce her "Fascinating!" and "Original" and she would earn for herself the reputation of "an asset to any table" for without her the conversation was quite often as tough as the beef.

It wasn't that Victor Rich fancied her – he didn't, she wasn't his type, but he became ever so slightly obsessed with Jane and her dull little marriage, never going anywhere, never doing anything, the cows come first.

The years passed and nothing changed, except that the children grew older. And they were charming – especially Susie, who was quite obviously a deviant eccentric – she wore odd socks, ate raw carrots and at seven was reading Modern Twentieth Century classics:

"The man in this book is called Sebastian and he has a teddy bear!"

Patrick was the star of Junior Football. There was free coaching at the town pitches; Oliver from up the street took him every week, with his own sons.

"Coach says I've the fastest pair of feet in Ireland," said Patrick.

Jane's dull little marriage remained externally serene.

135

Victor, watching quietly, wondered at its endurance and wondered if Susie and Patrick were the glue that held everything together.

If they had never been born, just as his daughter had never been born, would Jane too grow tired of never going anywhere, never doing anything, the cows come first, and take the bus back to the bright lights of Derry City leaving Michael without a backward glance, as Amelia had left him?

Victor Rich had a theory, which he hesitated to share, that Jane was a boiling pot, a time bomb. Beware the first Indian prince who happened her way . . .

15

"Come out with us at the weekend," Linda urged. "We're going to the Electric Ballroom. Achilles' Heel are playing!"

Jane sometimes went out with "the girls" – Linda and Diane and their gang of friends who rented a minibus to take them to restaurants and discos in Derry City where they dined expensively, knocked back a few wee drinkies, and danced in a circle round their handbags. Then the minibus drove them home, and it was a standing joke that Diane from Next Door who had remained defiantly sober and respectable all evening, and minded everyone else, would slip on the steps, on the dismount.

It wasn't for lack of trying that Jane didn't get out with them more but there was always a parenting crisis: measles, or a sore ear, or a finger slammed in a door.

"Mummy, Mummy," the children would sob and Jane, stricken, would say, "I can't leave them tonight, I don't think I should go."

She'd wash off the make-up from her face and change out

of her black halter-neck frock, back into crimplene trousers and fluffy slippers and they'd snuggle up on the sofa beside her, the exaggerated illness temporarily forgotten about, now the crisis of her leaving was averted.

Michael was convinced they did it on purpose. He called them "Jane's ball and chain". He declared they were so badly petted by their mother that they were content only when tied to her apron strings.

Michael very much wanted to break into the magic circle of Jane and Susie and Patrick but unfortunately he never could get it right, not even the simple rituals. When he bathed his children he put soap in their eyes, when he cut their fingernails he drew blood, when he read them a story they cried for Jane's stories, he hugged them in bed and he hurt them.

They howled with anticipation when they saw him coming.

"Mummy, Mummy!" screamed Susie who wriggled so violently in his arms that he dropped her.

Finally Jane said, "Stand back, Michael, I'll put them to bed myself."

"I'm trying my best," said Michael.

"You're certainly very trying."

Most of the time though she tried not to be petty with him, or spiteful. If she always took the children's side against him it was because she happened to think that the children were right and their daddy was wrong.

"I'd love to go and see Achilles' Heel," said Jane for they'd finally hit the big time with "Hell Raising Woman" – Number One in the charts – and they'd been invited on to *Top of the Pops* where Bobby Flood's performance had outclassed even the Rolling Stones.

Fame and fortune and a nationwide tour – Bobby Flood smouldered from every poster on every lamppost in Ireland.

He had created for himself a notorious reputation for drink and drugs and inviting floozies backstage. Excited girls were always throwing their knickers at him and fainting.

Sexual flaunting was still a new thing in rural Ireland and orgies utterly unheard of. The decent God-fearing people of deepest South Derry were not fans of Achilles' Heel. When it was announced that they were to play the Electric Ballroom an ecumenical moral righteousness group was hand-picked from the local churches. Led by a firebrand preacher they were going to picket the concert and passionately denounce Bobby Flood's lifestyle choices. Prayers would be said and rousing hymns sung with the spiritual intention of drowning out Bobby's synthesiser.

"I wish I could go!" said Old Mrs Somerville. "Except they'd never let me in through the door and at my age the excitement might kill me!"

"You must come, Jane!" insisted Linda. "I'll never get invited backstage unless you're with me – you're the sort Bobby Flood always goes for."

"He fancies farmers' wives with two little children?"

"He fancies beautiful women."

"I've nothing to wear," said Jane. Styles had changed and the black halter-neck frock was now so old-fashioned it was virtually vintage. Kathleen's cast-offs, though pretty and fashionable, were too conservative to catch the eye of a sex god.

"You can wear my clothes! Please ask Michael to let you go!"

Jane's violet eyes flashed. "Ask him if I can go? Don't you mean tell him that I'm going?"

On Saturday morning, once Michael had gone to Temple, Jane undressed and dispassionately inspected her nakedness. Susie and Patrick watched with interest.

"Mummy's got a fluffy bum," said Susie.

"And fluffy legs and fluffy armpits," Jane agreed thoughtfully. "And skin as rough as gravel. And my face is a thousand years old."

"Pretty Mummy," said Patrick firmly.

"You're quite right, Patrick! My scaffolding *is* in good nick and compared to Auntie Kathleen I still *have* a waist and a cleavage. There's very little that can't be fixed on my face by the intelligent and liberal application of make-up."

Jane spent the day plucking, shaving, exfoliating and begging her children to allow her out for the night.

"Please. Please. Please don't make a fuss when I'm leaving . . . and I won't ask again until Christmas!"

Susie and Patrick watched her, bemused. They ate the strawberry face pack between them when she'd finished with it. By tea-time sixty fingers and toes were painted Fuchsia Fun and Patrick was bouncing on the plastic sofa, wearing only Y-fronts and an embroidered bead choker. Susie's dark hair was set in rollers and she was drawing another picture of Mummy covered in hearts. This one had Jane smiling brightly in her black halter-neck frock, holding hands with Susie and Patrick. The detail was incredible – Jane had eyelashes and earrings and platform sandals. Diane from Next Door said that only a very bright child drew in eyelashes before the age of eight.

When Michael got home from the farm he found the living-room trashed and Jane standing oblivious in the middle of it, dressed to kill in her black halter-neck frock and it fitted as snugly now as it had when she was seventeen. She was carefully rubbing green camouflage cream into her cheeks, to cover up weather-beaten broken veins . . .

"Daddy's home! Give him a big kiss, kids. We've missed you, Daddy."

"What's the celebration tonight?"

"No celebration. I'm going out to see Achilles' Heel with Linda and Diane from Next Door."

Michael's heart sank. He wasn't usually a wet blanket but for an entire week Old Dave had talked of nothing but Achilles' Heel playing the Electric Ballroom, working himself up into such a lather of religious and moral indignation that he was worse than useless around the farm.

Today, instead of supervising the potato gathering, he'd taken two of the workforce into the house to help make a huge banner with a bed sheet which read *"Lead us not into temptation"*. Michael had been left behind in a boggy field in soft rain to do the work of four men. He was filthy and his back ached. How he longed to slip into a hot bath and lie there, dozing, till his dinner was ready!

"I never said you could go out!"

Jane's violet eyes flashed. "Because I never asked you!"

Michael sat down to his dinner. It was mackerel stuffed with rhubarb. He was allergic to rhubarb. It made his tongue swell up. She'd forgotten. His own wife had forgotten he was allergic to rhubarb.

Jane was defiant. "But *we* all love rhubarb – Susie eats it raw. Can't you scrape out the stuffing and leave it on the side of your plate?"

The minibus pulled up. The horn honked.

Jane took one last look in the mirror and pulled on her fur coat, just as Susie began to scream.

"Mummy, Mummy, don't leave me, Mummy!"

Hesitation was fatal. Jane fled down the garden path with her fingers jammed firmly in her ears, singing loudly at

141

the top of her voice: "*She's a hell-raising woman in a tight black frock – the heat of her body makes me hard as a rock!*"

The minibus stopped at Kate's Pub and Lounge Bar and everyone baled out. It was the first time Jane had ever been inside a public house. When she and Michael were courting, lounge bars hadn't existed and pubs were for men and loose women. Jane had sat in the Rapier, modestly, when Michael and Trevor Mountain went into the pub for a drink without her.

"What would you like to drink, Jane?"

Linda's war paint meant business and she was almost wearing a tight dress, held together with bits of string, it left nothing to the imagination. Even by Linda's low standards this one was shocking.

"Whiskey!" said Jane. It was the only alcohol she'd ever drunk and she'd only ever had a mouthful from Michael's hip flask. Michael had discovered from his legions of previous girlfriends that whiskey has a magical leg-opening effect on women.

Bobby Flood didn't expect to find hot tottie at the Electric Ballroom. The moral righteousness demonstration had cast such a shadow of public condemnation that the decent God-fearing people of deepest South Derry were refusing to allow their youngsters to go to the concert. Only Bobby's most devoted fans had enough brass neck to walk through the puritans' picket line. Ticket sales were so low Achilles' Heel had been tempted to cancel, but for the fact that the demonstration was generating unprecedented amounts of publicity. *Nationwide* and the *Belfast Telegraph* had sent reporters and Bobby, at his most sober and charming, with his sex appeal turned down to simmer was filmed and photographed offering the firebrand preacher and his disciples a free ticket each to the concert. Tomorrow the story would be splashed across every Sunday newspaper in the country.

Jane caught Bobby's Flood's eye the moment he stepped on stage. How could he fail to notice her when she was lit up with a diabolical whiskey-induced light that showed off the snug fit of her frock, her long legs and her clouds of black hair?

Bobby Flood licked his lips.

"He's spotted you!" screeched Linda when the stage spotlight rained down on them.

Jane smiled vaguely, out of her whiskey head. She felt as light as air and her body throbbed with the pounding drumbeat. She had no idea why the spotlight from the stage was trained on her.

She was dancing to "Hell Raising Woman" – Achilles' Heel had performed it on *Top of the Pops* and Susie and Patrick and Jane had held hands in a circle in front of the television and sung along to the catchy chorus:

"She's a hell raising woman in a tight black frock – the heat of her body makes me hard as a rock!"

Diane from Next Door, who had never thought an uncensored thought in her life, was hysterical with excitement. "He wants to dance with you! On stage! Look, Jane! Look! He's pointing!"

Jane was helped up onto the stage. Bobby Flood kissed her hand, then her wrist. He sucked her fingers. Jane clean forgot that she'd married for love and her ambition was to live happily ever after. With her fingers in Bobby Flood's mouth and her inhibitions already weak from the whiskey, she clean forgot she even had a husband.

"You're used to getting what you want," she said.

"You want it too."

"Oh yes!"

Sometimes even the most saintly of wives can be swept away. Breathless, Jane pressed her body against Bobby Flood's. She was suddenly keen to yield to the delicious temptation of a man who was used to getting what he wanted.

Next morning Jane woke with a head the size of Ireland and excruciating pinpoint pain behind her eyes. Her mouth felt like sandpaper and she was still wearing the black halter-neck frock. Susie and Patrick were snuggled into the bed, one on each side of her. Susie was still clutching her latest picture of Jane in her black frock covered in hearts.

"Don't open the curtains, Michael, the light's blinding me . . ."

Michael was smiling and tender. "It's still dark outside, darling."

"I have a headache."

"Caused by falling in through the bedroom door at midnight, stinking of whiskey, singing 'Hell Raising Woman'? Or by waking me up by pulling down my pyjama bottoms and climbing on top of me?"

"I did *what*?"

Michael kissed her on the lips before he left for the milking. "You're just like a horse, Jane – sometimes you need a good gallop . . ."

Slowly Jane got out of bed and dragged herself downstairs. The chaos of the previous evening was tidied away, the dishes were washed, the floors were brushed, the ironing was folded on top of the ironing-board – Michael had ironed even vests and knickers and towels. The table was neatly set for breakfast.

There was a drawing propped up against the kettle of Daddy covered in hearts, holding Susie's and Patrick's hands. Jane could see that Michael had done it himself. He'd written *"I hope you had a good night"* under it.

Jane could remember very little about the night before. They'd been in Kate's Pub and Lounge Bar – Diane, Linda, herself. They'd drunk some whiskey . . . After that everything was hazy and surreal, like a movie she'd seen years before or a dream she'd once been woken out of.

Had she really danced on the stage with Bobby Flood?

"You're going to be splashed across every Sunday paper in Ireland – *'Hot Bobby Flood and his Hell Raising Woman!'*"

Linda was looking rougher than usual. Her make-up from last night was still smeared across her face and she was hanging out of her dressing-gown. And she couldn't stop smiling! What an amazing night! In she'd walked, through the puritans' picket line, with her arms folded protectively across her skimpy dress, feeling slightly foolish and self-conscious and the first person she'd seen was Man Mountain, out of his head and off his face, pigging at the front of the ballroom.

"You play a mean air guitar," she'd told him and he'd swept her into his beefy arms and offered to play her too, all ten fingers, against the wall at the back.

"What a 'paramedic'!" said Linda, laughing. She made it sound like a term of endearment.

Jane said, "Did I really dance on stage with Bobby Flood?"

"For the whole first set! You were amazing! Can you really not remember? It was like sex standing up. Diane had to go and sit down at one stage she was so alarmed to discover hidden depths in a neighbour she's known forever!

Where did you go during the interval? We tried to get backstage to look for you, but the bouncers wouldn't let us through . . ."

Jane shook her painful head. "I've no idea."

She couldn't remember a thing.

16

Victor Rich and Kathleen were at the Derryrose Golf Club. This was their Sunday ritual – nine holes before lunch and the carvery in the Club House afterwards – everything you can eat for a fiver and the roast potatoes were delicious. Then Victor networked with the old boys and Kathleen made polite conversation with their wives "who were golfers when lady golfers were still ladies . . ."

Right at the start, when they were still newfangled, and trying to impress each other, Kathleen had coyly offered to caddy for Victor.

"Maybe I'll even learn to play!"

Victor had assumed she was joking. "You're too young for golf!"

But she'd hoisted his bag up on to her shoulder and marched on ahead of him to the first hole. He'd watched her passionately. She was beautiful in manicured parkland, with her broad shoulders thrown back and her heavy hair swinging, her stride strong and long; she ate up the ground.

"That bag's too heavy for you!" he shouted after her.

Over her shoulder she'd told him, "Wasn't I reared on a farm, Victor? Didn't I grow up throwing over bullocks before breakfast?"

So he'd taught her the basics as a bit of a joke – the swing was only an excuse to put his arms round her in public, the putting to hold her hands between his hands. Before long she'd "got it" or maybe the golf had got her. Physically strong to start with, she could soon out-drive every lady golfer in South Derry, and many of the men.

She might have become a great golfer, if only she could learn to keep calm and focused during her short game, but Kathleen had a habit of losing her temper, kicking disobliging balls and swearing at them if they didn't roll directly across the green and into the hole. And should the ball get lost in a bunker . . .

On lazy Sunday afternoons in the bedroom Victor buried his face in the soft pillows of her generous breasts and Kathleen pulled him into her and held him with her strong muscular legs and he teased "Every shot is a compromise between length and precision."

"Just like life, really . . ."

Golf was the all-consuming passion of their lives together. A weekend away was unfulfilled if there wasn't a bit of golfing thrown in. The Royal Portrush on the North Antrim coast was Kathleen's favourite, not for its fantastic views of the Atlantic, but because it suited her. It was full of character and without blind spots, and it was tough, especially on blustery days when the wind was gale force and it was only her solid driving skills that ensured the ball went anywhere.

"I love it here best in the whole world," she told Victor, who romantically proposed on one knee at the fourteenth, called "Calamity".

They had their wedding reception at Derryrose Golf Club. What a fun occasion that had been with a special green cake and photographs taken under an arch of driving irons!

Their honeymoon was spent at the British Open. The official highlight was getting Jack Nicklaus's autograph and it hung, framed, in the Member's Bar. The unofficial highlight was sex three times in one night and Victor didn't have a heart attack afterwards.

It was hard to believe, now, when you saw them together that Victor was twenty-four years older than his wife, because the longer they spent together, at work, at home, at play, it was as if their age gap reduced. And not because they consciously made foolish artificial efforts at it: Kathleen dressed in tweed and polished brogues, Victor with dyed hair and blue jeans. They didn't have to, it happened naturally. Love and intimacy smoothed out the angry frown lines on Kathleen's face, leaving behind intelligence and gravitas, love and intimacy put the bounce back into Victor that he'd lost twenty years before. They were shiny happy people and ageless.

Kathleen and Victor were enjoying a coffee together when Basil showed them the Sunday papers. *"Bobby Flood and his Hell Raising Woman – Mystery Brunette Steals the Show."*

"Don't tell me that's not the beautiful woman who was at your wedding! She's hard to forget once you've seen her!"

Kathleen recognised the black halter-neck frock immediately and the most of Jane inside it. If she looked closely, and honestly she was trying not to, she couldn't help but see that what looked remarkably like a small pert breast had broken free. It was provocatively cupped in Bobby Flood's hand. He was standing right behind her, pressed against her, with his legs spread, the microphone on its stand jutted from their fused bodies like a phallus and it didn't take much imagination to guess what he was singing about. Achilles' Heel were famous for their filthy lyrics.

Kathleen said quickly, "It's not her. Sorry to disappoint you, Basil. Jane was with me last night. We went to a cordon bleu cookery demonstration. But it certainly looks like her."

Victor frowned quizzically at his wife but he waited until Basil had moved away before he said, "Of course that's Jane on the front page of the paper!"

"Jane with her breast hanging out!"

Victor finished his coffee and fastidiously dabbed at his mouth with a napkin. He crossed his legs, rested his folded hands lightly on his knee and stared through his spectacles down his long nose at Kathleen. This was his professional face, the one he used with Lord Laurence Glass when he was trying to convince him that it would be a great deal easier to sell Lisglasson if he would actually allow interested parties into the house. An oil sheik had arrived once by helicopter, the whole way from the Ritz in London, with Beluchi bodyguards dressed head to toe in black and wielding sub-machine guns – so important and exciting – and Lord Laurence had hid at an upstairs window and thrown potatoes at them until they got back into their helicopter and flew away. . .

Kathleen's lip dropped. "Why do I get the feeling that you're about to say 'I told you so'?"

They'd been waiting for this moment, both of them, since the very first dinner party at the council house when Victor had hesitantly remarked, "Your brother is a very lucky man,

Kathleen," and Kathleen had flashed back, "I've no idea what she sees in him either but she always insists that she married for love and it's her ambition to live happily ever ater."

Victor's lips had twitched. "What a noble intention! I promise I won't say 'I told you so' when she explodes with an Indian prince . . ."

Banking, golf and marriage were the cornerstones of Kathleen's life. The rest of the time was spent not thinking about not having children. Victor and herself – best not to think about it. Let nature take its course while she carved out for herself another role, that of indulgent auntie to Susie and Patrick.

It had started as a bit of an accident on a sunny Saturday when she was at a loose end for an hour between waving off Victor to a bank conference and leaving for a Ladies Golfing thing at the Royal Portrush.

There was just enough time for a quick visit to Stove Pipe Town to drop off another bag of cast-off summer clothing. Kathleen and Victor were recently back from a week in Spain and she had a Spanish doll for Susie, a Spanish football strip for Patrick and an itsy bitsy teenie weenie yellow polka-dot bikini for Jane – Kathleen's best intentions to lose a stone of weight before the holiday had never materialised and she'd felt more comfortable sunbathing in a reinforced swimsuit.

"Busy, busy, busy!" Kathleen burst into the council house, to find Susie and Patrick crouched behind the plastic sofa.

"We're not here," said Susie.

It had just spilled out of Kathleen's mouth, unrehearsed, not even thought about: "What a pity because I wanted to take you to the seaside!"

151

Of course that brought them out from behind the sofa! In a flash they were standing in front of her with buckets and spades and swimsuits. Too late Kathleen learned the first law of talking to children – never say something you don't mean. Help!

"Where's your mother, children?"

Patrick said, "Mummy was talking to herself, into the mirror –"

"It wasn't talking." Susie corrected him. "It was poetry!"

And standing there, in a pair of scuffed white sandals, with a silly-looking Flamenco dancer doll under her arm, Susie quoted an entire Shakespearean sonnet from memory. Kathleen listened, amazed. Susie was word perfect, right to the end.

"*If this be folly and upon me told, I never wrote and no man ever loved.*"

Patrick said, "And then Mummy started to cry. And Susie and I clapped. And when she saw your car she ran upstairs and told us to hide."

"And she was shouting, 'Don't tell your Auntie Kathleen or she'll have the men in white coats come to take me away!'"

Before Kathleen could quite decide if the children were telling her the truth or if she'd stumbled into the parallel universe of their imagination, Jane appeared down the stairs, serene and lovely as always: "What an unexpected pleasure! How nice to see you! I was just washing my face . . ."

Kathleen had taken Susie and Patrick to the seaside with her and, after the Ladies Golfing thing she bought them ice-cream and taught them to play crazy golf and treated them to tea in the Clubhouse. More little stories slipped out. They told her how Mummy ordered lots and lots of crazy things out of the Club Book: a satin negligée, camisole knickers, long black opera gloves, a white fur coat. She hid them in Susie and Patrick's wardrobe and when Daddy was at the farm she pranced through the house in them, stopping occasionally to pose in front of the mirror at the top of the stairs and talk to herself in a high, funny, sing-song voice.

When anybody came to the door she hid, except for Oliver from up the street – she invited him in when she was wearing only her see-through silk negligée and he'd said, "Jane, you need to get out more. Go and get dressed like a good girl . . ."

"They're not old enough to make up something like that," said Victor, when she told him about it afterwards.

Kathleen picked up the newspaper again. How thoughtful of Basil to leave it lying. She studied again the incriminating photograph of Jane. Then she read the feature accompanying the photograph.

It was an interview with Bobby Flood, the charismatic lead singer of Achilles' Heel: Mr Pin Up. He was a city boy from a tough Belfast neighbourhood, with generations of shipyard workers as ancestors. His grandfather had helped build the *Titanic* – it wasn't something Bobby boasted about. He'd worked in the shipyards, too, with his brothers, his uncles and his father, after he left school, before he became a rock star.

It was a gritty life with few frills, a hobnail boots sort of life with his lunch box under his arm. And a young wife from when he was seventeen – Millie was pregnant and her father had threatened to bash out his brains with a crowbar if he didn't marry her.

A lesser man might have given in gracefully and resigned himself to hard work and warm slippers but Bobby was hungry for the Big Time. He worked in the shipyards all day, sang in working men's clubs at night and left Millie sitting at home in a pokey terraced house with the ring of respectability shining on her finger.

There was no denying he had talent. Even Kathleen, who preferred Beethoven, couldn't hear his voice without her head growing hot and her legs starting to shake. But talent was only the start of it.

"One per cent inspiration, ninety-nine per cent perspiration," said Bobby because for ten long years, before the Big Time, he'd toured the highways and byways of Ireland with Achilles' Heel, playing every out-of-the-way dance hall, church hall, town hall and GAA Club that would let him in.

The million-dollar question: "Was it all worth it, the climb to the Big Time?"

He'd missed his only son's birth, he'd missed birthdays, wedding anniversaries, Christmas. Sometimes there was only a handful in the audience to sing to and there were a lot of long lonely nights in the early years when he'd sought comfort in the undemanding arms of the solitary ageing women who hung at the fringes. They were never in a hurry to go home and they were easily spotted, sitting, staring unsteadily into their drinks when the lights came on at the end of the evening.

Bobby said, "If you don't start at the bottom, you can't appreciate the view when you get to the top."

Now here he was, arrived at the Big Time, with a reputation to match and it was almost impossible to associate his words with the picture of him and Jane – "*When interviewed Mr Flood said, 'I think South Derry is the most picturesque part of rural Ireland I've ever visited . . . I'm a family man at heart and I easily grow tired of the touring . . . I hope to settle down soon . . .'*"

"So this is Jane's Indian prince," said Kathleen.

154

17

It was Sunday lunch-time. Michael was home from the milking. Jane had been cooking all morning. They were dining on braised pork with prunes and vegetables harvested fresh from the greenhouse.

"Did you know, Dad, that the 'Pope's eye' is a small circle of fat in the centre of a leg of pork or lamb?"

A blackberry and apple tart was warming gently in the oven.

"Mummy made us walk *miles* yesterday to find these blackberries. She wouldn't come home until the basin was full, and she wouldn't let us throw in red berries or green berries because she said they weren't ripe enough to be in a tart."

The Temples' big old car pulled up outside the council house.

From behind the net curtain Jane and Michael watched Old Dave fastidiously check the locks. Old Dave had never lived anywhere in his life but Temple, he felt vulnerable and

exposed in this concrete jungle. He sincerely believed that
when his back was turned hard men with crowbars would
slip out of the shadows to steal his tyres and drain his tank
of four-star. Cecily was huddled deep into her coat with the
fur collar. Her face was anxious. She was expecting urchin-
like children to surround her, pull at her Sunday best and
demand money from her in high, famished voices.

"How do they know which house we live in?" asked Jane.

"Dad asked me directions this morning."

Old Dave was the best type of Bible-thumper because, as
well as teaching Sunday School, attending Bible Study and
singing in the church choir, he practised what he preached.

Old Dave loved his enemies, and patiently bore the cross
of being married to an unrepentant sinner who refused to be
gently directed towards the paths of righteousness. At the
first whiff of a sermon Cecily always stuck her fingers in her
ears and shouted, "You're a sanctimonious old man and I'm
not listening to you!"

When he was chosen to represent 1st Derryrose at the
moral righteousness demonstration (beating the organist and
the minister's wife in a secret ballot) she had cynically said,
"If you're not careful you might enjoy yourself, Dave. The
devil always has the best tunes."

"You're just jealous!" said Dave.

Old Dave hadn't noticed Jane in the audience at the
Electric Ballroom until she was hoisted up onto the stage.
He'd been too busy writing down the names of those from
1st Derryrose whom he recognised. Tomorrow morning he'd
take the list with him to church, and quietly and tactfully
corner their parents . . .

"Look at that Jezebel!" shrieked the firebrand preacher

when Jane began to dance with Bobby Flood, the vertical expression of her horizontal desire . . .

Dave's first emotion was one of overwhelming relief, that his daughter-in-law, in her skin-tight dress, with her hair all over her face never darkened the door of a church. Nobody knew she was Michael's wife. He had only to "Tut tut" a bit and shake his head and his sterling reputation as the pious head of a decent God-fearing family would remain untarnished, his secret safe . . .

"Am I my brother's keeper?"

Achilles' Heel's latest release, "My Brother's Keeper", had a rhythmic drumbeat. The Electric Ballroom went dark and a spotlight played on a huge spinning glass ball, throwing a million sparkles across the dance floor.

Old Dave experienced a sudden crushing pain in the centre of his chest, which spread to his arms, throat and back. Frightened and in pain, his body went into shock. The Electric Ballroom blurred and swam hazily in front of his eyes, his body temperature dropped and he began to shiver.

The lights came back on, the music started, the moment passed. But the damage was done. Old Dave had felt the hand of God grabbing his heart and squeezing. It never once crossed his mind that the flashing lights, the loud music and the excitement might have given him a little bit of a heart attack.

Old Dave and Cecily stood awkwardly in the middle of Jane's living-room. They were silently appalled by her featureless house in the bleak terrace and by her cramped living conditions. Why was the kitchen table in the living-room? Was there no room for it in the kitchen?

The kitchen table at Temple was so long that the old pair,

sitting at either end, had to pass things by rolling a tea trolley to each other.

Jane said, "This is an unexpected pleasure. Are you staying for lunch?"

Susie said, "We're having roast pork with prunes. It's delicious but it makes you run to the toilet to poo!"

Patrick said, "I gathered all the blackberries *myself* for the sweet . . ."

Cecily Temple shuddered delicately at the words "toilet" and "sweet". It was exactly as she'd argued this morning when Old Dave described Jane's overt exhibitionism at the concert: "What can you expect when Michael insisted on marrying a cheap little thing from the town?"

"That vulnerable young woman is married to our son. She is the mother of the heir to Temple. She *begged* to be allowed to build her own house on the farm. But we cast her out, away from the calming influence of decent God-fearing people. We allowed her to take the broad road that leads to destruction!"

Cecily stuck her fingers in her ears. "You're a sanctimonious old man!" she'd shouted, but she'd shouted it with affection.

Old Dave cleared his throat and drew himself up to his full height. His heart was fluttering and his face was very pale. Everyone watching assumed he was overwhelmed by the momentousness of the occasion.

"My wife and I would like you to come home to Temple."

That very afternoon, once Old Dave and Cecily had been offered a cup of tea (they declined) and courteously escorted to their car, and waved off with meticulous assurances that they couldn't possibly get lost in Stove Pipe Town on the way out and even if they did get lost the locals all spoke English and were mostly friendly, Jane climbed into the roof space and resurrected the sleep-deprived sketches from years before.

"This is the sort of house I want, Michael, but we'll have to add in another turret for Patrick. And a bathroom of course . . ."

Michael looked at the faded pencil drawings. But he couldn't see them. There was a blurring in front of his eyes that might have been tears but was probably a symptom of mild shock. Never in his wildest dreams had he dared hope for this happy ending. What *had* Jane been up to on the stage of the Electric Ballroom? Maybe it was better never to find out.

"Aren't turrets rather fairytale?"

That very afternoon the Farm Walk went only as far as Jane's proposed building site at the end of an unused lane, on a flat patch of ground where a farm labourer's cottage had once stood and fallen. The overgrown hedgerows were choked with rosehips, apple trees and wild plum had seeded and run riot, the wind whispered through slender birch and sturdy beeches.

Michael protested. "But this is the machinery graveyard! Buried here are threshing machines and ploughs and things that kick up hay from a hundred years ago."

Jane smiled indulgently at her husband's whimsical tone of voice. How typical of the Temples to choose the most tranquil and picturesque spot on two hundred acres to dump machinery!

"And the horsebox?" she asked.

"For Kathleen's pony. The floor's rotten."

Susie and Patrick let go their mother's hand and ran joyfully through long wet grass and soft mist, shouting "Let's play hide and seek!"

Jane raised her voice as they disappeared behind a rusted mark one forage harvester.

"Don't cross the garden without me, darlings, in case you're attacked by the ghosts of antique machinery!"

"Don't wander away from me, sweethearts – if you get cut you'll need a tetanus jab!"

"Stick close beside me, precious children, until Daddy clears away the machinery!"

Sunday afternoons had quickly become boring at Temple since Kathleen married Victor Rich. Cecily had nothing to complain about any more and she rather missed it. She'd tried to stir things up at the beginning, after the wedding, when they'd call in, dressed identically in diamonds, on their way home from the Golf Club.

"I wouldn't leave it too long, Kathleen, to get in the family way. That old fellow you've married won't have many strong swimmers!"

"Thank you for the advice, Mother."

"Anything stirring?" she'd ask, until it became clear, even to her, that nothing was stirring except distaste in Victor Rich's face when she mentioned it.

"I think our Kathleen has married an extinct volcano," said Cecily.

Their visits got fewer and fewer. Now they hardly ever called and every Sunday afternoon stretched endlessly, broken up only by a few carefully orchestrated squabbles with Dave, until it was time for Jane and the children to be ushered into the parlour for the tea ceremony ritual after the Farm Walk.

Today was even longer and lonelier than usual for Dave was utterly exhausted after his late night at the rock concert, his little bit of a heart attack and his change of heart which

160

had caused him to extend the hand of Christian friendship to his prodigal daughter-in-law. It was all too much for him; he'd fallen asleep on top of his Bible.

"Wake up, Dave, and talk to me!" Cecily commanded but he was fast asleep, snoring softly and the pages of the Bible fluttered slightly as he snored.

A couple of times Cecily thought she heard them arriving, Jane and Michael and the children, but it was only the wind slamming a door shut, and the farm dogs barking at a fox. They were later than usual and she was irrationally irritated, though the house visit after the Farm Walk had always been a casual arrangement.

Finally they burst into the parlour, bringing fresh air and exuberance. Jane had a basket of windfall apples, and the last of the rambling roses in her hair. She was pale – her late night was also catching up with her.

"We've been to pick a site," said Michael.

"We want to build in the machinery graveyard," said Jane.

"That's the stupidest thing I've heard all day," said Cecily.

Jane solemnly regarded her mother-in-law. Cecily was a wicked little gnome in her shapeless housedress and old aged stockings, her hair clumped like silage on top of her head and the same colour, her false teeth smeared with Swiss Roll. She bit back a sharp retort to the effect "I know it's not to everyone's taste, but nobody's asking you to live there!"

Instead she politely said, "Where do you think we should build, Mrs Temple?"

Cecily couldn't have been more wrong-footed if Jane had pounced on her and slapped her. Her mouth opened and shut a couple of times, like a fish out of water, gasping unfamiliar air into its lungs. Then she jumped up out of her chair and

161

ran upstairs, locked herself in her bedroom and screeched with genuine feeling: "I think I'm having a heart attack – you'll have to go for the doctor!"

Déjà vu. It was just like Jane's honeymoon all over again, when no matter what she'd said, or done, or hadn't done, Cecily had thrown a wobbly every day and there had been slammed doors and screeching in abundance until Jane had packed her bags and bolted.

"What have I said to upset her this time?"

Michael shook his head. He was already defeated. She was his mother and he wouldn't hear a bad word said about her.

It took loyal Susie to announce: "She's just jealous because we're getting a lovely shiny new house and she has to live in this pigsty."

And loyal Patrick to add, "Granny Temple has a big fat nose and you're beautiful, Mummy."

Afterwards Jane liked to say that the building of her new house at Temple was the most cynical time of her marriage.

"Maybe Mum's right," said Michael. "Maybe we should knock down the old gate-lodge and build a modest brown and white bungalow . . ."

Before he left for milking Jane made her husband a cup of tea.

"Come home as soon as you can. I'll be waiting for you . . ."

She kissed him with tongues and touching and sent him off to Temple half-cocked and fully excited. Michael made sure he was home to read Susie and Patrick their bedtime story and to kiss them goodnight because once they were asleep Jane ran him a bath and carefully soaped his body. That night they made love twice and slept together naked.

Michael took two white eggs, hardboiled, in the pocket of his coat to Temple.

It was just like his honeymoon all over again, but this time he appreciated it. And Jane got full backing from her husband for a new house in the machinery graveyard.

"I showed my mother your pencil drawings. She thinks the turrets are stupid and pretentious, the stainless-steel kitchen is an unnecessary extravagance and the flagstones will be very cold underfoot . . ."

Next morning Diane said, "If you'll excuse the vulgarity of the next remark, My Gerry and I didn't get a wink of sleep last night, with the noises you and Michael were making in your bedroom. You do appreciate that our bedrooms share only a dividing wall in the terrace. We haven't heard the like of it since you were first married!"

What Diane really wanted to ask was what *exactly* they'd been doing at midnight when the electricity supply to Stove Pipe Town had begun flashing just as Jane was exuberantly reaching orgasm. The combined effect had excited "My Gerry" into a passionate frenzy and in Diane's opinion, once a week was quite enough and even then only after a couple of strong G&Ts.

"Sorry about that." Jane didn't look even a tiny bit sorry. "Michael was flicking on and off the bedroom light, while we danced naked to 'Hell Raising Woman' . . ."

"Stop! Too much information!"

Suddenly Jane's outrageous performance at the Achilles' Heel concert, up there on the stage with everybody watching, was much more than the lighthearted antics of a seriously drunk woman . . .

"I wasn't completely naked, Diane, I was wearing a bow tie round my neck."

Diane felt faint.

"It's only for a little bit longer, Diane. I promise. Once the plans for the house have been drawn up and finalised and once I've got my own way I'll behave again!"

"Mum says, 'Why do you want to build at the end of a long lane? What's the point of spending a fortune of money on turrets when nobody is going to see them?'"

Jane's hand crept quietly to the top of her husband's leg. It rested lightly on the bulge in his jeans and with gentle, controlled stroking soon he began to squirm and arch and lose his train of thought and then frankly he'd have agreed to anything she wanted – turrets, battlements, a moat and drawbridge . . .

18

For a week Jane hadn't been feeling a hundred per cent but she couldn't have told you what was wrong. It felt like a hangover, except she didn't drink. It felt like the old exhaustion of broken nights with a small baby, except the children were big now and better sleepers. And it felt like something else, but she couldn't quite remember what.

After walking to and from piano lessons, eating dinner, checking homework, packing schoolbags and polishing school shoes she'd felt so dizzy she'd almost passed out on the toilet seat waiting for the children to bath themselves before bed.

It didn't help that Susie had spilt bolognese sauce down the front of her school jumper, trying inexpertly to twist spaghetti onto a fork. Three times Jane had said, "Let me cut it up with a knife, you can use a spoon to eat it," and three times Susie had insisted, "I've got it onto the fork this time, Mummy!"

"There's too much on your fork," said Jane and the whole thing had slithered off before it reached Susie's mouth.

"Oh for . . .!" Jane clamped her lips tightly together to stop the word shooting out. She made a fastidious point of never swearing in front of the children but she could tell, just by looking, that the bolognese sauce was going to stain horribly. It was never going wash out.

When Michael got home from the farm he found her up to her elbows, in the sink, scrubbing at the stain for a third time. Jacqueline du Pré was playing Elgar's Cello Concerto, Jane's latest novel from the library, *The Country Girls*, was propped against the taps. If Michael had been a sensitive, artistic type of husband he might have been worried by today's taste for the tragic, but he was tone deaf and he couldn't have told you whether Jane was listening to happy music or sad music. To him it was just a noise in the background. And as for the book – he didn't even notice it, he was too busy eagerly caressing his wife's bottom and nuzzling into the ticklish place beneath her hair, behind her ear.

"I've never made love to a woman wearing Marigolds . . ."

Pressed against the scullery sink they kissed hungrily.

She whispered, "Your children are up in bed waiting for you to read '*Chapter 6 – Noel's Princess*'. Hurry back . . ."

Jane hung the stained, wet jumper on the wires in front of the fire. She'd never experimented with Italian sauces before, French cooking was her thing, and she had no particular interest in starting but for the bottle of olive oil and the packet of real Italian pasta that Victor and Kathleen had brought her home from Venice: "Just a week away to celebrate five blissful years of marriage."

Jane had started on the school lunches – soup in a thermos flask, boiled eggs and raw carrots – by the time Michael finished bedroom duty and came back downstairs.

"The kids say you fainted in the bathroom. Maybe you

should go and see a doctor? Maybe you're run down. Maybe
you need a tonic?"

"Maybe you should come over here and examine me . . ."

Next morning she was sick again. And Susie's school jumper
was still stained.

"Look, Mum, I've made myself some toast. I buttered it . . ."
Patrick was covered in butter. It was in his hair and his
eyelashes.

"Have you buttered your face as well?"

She could hear her voice getting higher, thinner, more
strained and her heart was palpitating horribly in her chest.
Any second she was going to snap, like an elastic band, and
start screeching at him, though she didn't want to, and all the
books emphasised what a mistake it was to send your child
off to school chastised and unhappy. It was so difficult to
concentrate on reading, writing and arithmetic when lurking
was the sad little thought that Mummy, more precious than
diamonds, was displeased.

She'd actually cried a bit yesterday when she read that.

Patrick laughed. "I was being a dog. I ate it off the floor
like a dog – *woof woof!*"

"Go and wash your face again, Patrick."

"My face is clean, Mum."

"Mummy."

"My face is clean. *Mummy.*"

"Your face is filthy. It's covered in butter. And there's sleep
in your eyes, I can see it from here."

It was a quarter to nine. She was going to be late. They
were all going to be late. She was going to have to pussyfoot
apologetically into school again with her tail between her
legs and Patrick's teacher, ferocious Mrs Forsyth, was going

to be so brisk: "Tough morning, Mrs Temple? Oh well, never mind. I only marked the roll in pencil. I can rub out his 'absent' and change it to 'present' . . . it's no trouble at all . . ."

And she'd take Patrick by the hand and lead him into the classroom. Cluck cluck. Poor little fellow . . .

"Get your coats on, children. What does it matter if your school jumper is stained with bolognese sauce, Susie? Who cares about a dirty face, Patrick? Now, go, go!"

Jane struggled to the bathroom and began to vomit unpleasantly into the toilet bowl.

The children followed her, curious.

"What's wrong, Mum?"

"Mummy?"

Could she not even vomit in private? Jane shut her eyes to stop the room spinning. What was this sickness?

Jane was lying on the top of her bed, listening to soothing Chopin, thinking beautiful thoughts and feeling fractionally better when Diane brought Susie and Patrick home from school.

"Look Mum, Mrs Forsyth has sent you a note!"

Which said: *Patrick does not know the words 'help' or 'yes' in his reading.*

"Patrick, darling," Jane raised her voice, "please bring me your reading book!"

"I'm kicking a football, Mum!"

"Patrick!"

"Patrick!"

"Patrick!"

Today she hadn't the energy to chase after him, and pin

him down and read the page over and over again with him, '*Here are our friends, Peter and Jane*' till he could recite it, even if he couldn't read it. Patrick's homework was the most stressful part of every day and it wasn't just the reading:

"Six and what make ten, Patrick?"

"What does 'what' mean, Mum?"

"You were spoiled with Susie," Diane told her. "Girls are far smarter than boys and far easier taught. It's a sick joke that men rule the world . . ."

On the back of the note Jane scribbled "*You're his teacher, you teach him!*"

Next day after school:

"Look, Mum, Mrs Forsyth says I'm special!"

Proudly he handed her his shiny new folder that said *Special Needs* on the front of it.

Tonight he had no reading homework, just some remedial colouring-in. And a polite request that he learn his alphabet A to Z. Thank you.

Tears pricked Jane's eyes. How could Patrick have special needs when she'd fed him mackerel twice a week every week since he was born to make his brain grow? For six years she'd been reading to him, building blocks with him, doing jigsaws with him, listening to Mozart with him, singing the alphabet song with him . . .

When Michael came home from the farm he found her with her head buried in her hands, almost asleep on the plastic sofa, muttering "H, I, J, K, L, M, N, O, P . . ."

Susie and Patrick were cuddled up together on the fireside chair, Susie was reading "*Chapter 7 – Being Bandits*".

Susie said, "Patrick couldn't remember the alphabet song. He forgot 'M' fourteen times, I counted, and Mummy said a bad word, actually a number of bad words, and banged her head off the living-room wall. I think she's gone mad, like Mr Rochester's wife, and I'm watching her so that she doesn't try to set fire to the house."

Michael said, "Who is Mr Rochester? Is he the man in Number 4?"

Once the children were in bed Michael made his wife a cup of tea and gently said, "So he needs a bit of extra help with his reading, Jane – so what! I was useless at reading too. I was fifteen before I could tell the difference between 'b' and 'd'."

"So it's your fault!" She tried to smile, but she was too tired. She was asleep before she'd finished her tea.

Jane dressed carefully before going to see Mrs Forsyth, with no flesh showing for it was only two months since the Achilles' Heel concert and people were still pointing and staring at her when she walked down the street . . .

Kathleen had said, "And they'll still be talking about you when you're in a bath chair with a blue rinse. Don't you know that country people are famous for their very long memories?"

"One night of indiscretion and I'm marked for life? How very unfair!"

This meeting had been Diane's idea. To show Mrs Forsyth that she was a parent who cared about her son's learning difficulties.

"Of course I care!"

"Of course you do! But Mrs Forsyth doesn't know that and Patrick is at a social disadvantage, living in Stove Pipe Town. Some kids who live on this estate really do have special needs, with no father around and the mother too worn out to give them enough attention. Then there's your dubious reputation to consider. After that big splash across the Sunday papers with Bobby Flood . . ."

"Charming! One night of indiscretion and Patrick is marked for life!"

So Jane had made an appointment for the afternoon, after class. She wasn't generally so sick in the afternoon. She prepared carefully what she wanted to say and practised in front of the mirror and in front of Diane.

Diane said, "Ask her first off if it's a behavioural problem. Boys are notorious for messing. Even Ernest had to be tied to his desk at the start to help him concentrate."

"Perfect Ernest with eight A grades at O Level?"

"Even Ernest! It's one of the main reasons Oliver from up the street gave up the big job at the bank when Maeve died. He was afraid his shower of boys would develop behavioural problems if they didn't have a strong male role model. And no teacher would be able to control them."

"And if it's not a behavioural problem?"

"Then ask her if Patrick has been formally assessed for special needs, by an educational psychologist, and if so, can you see the assessment? Then ask her what he does in the Special Needs classroom, and what the rest of his class are doing when he's in there, because if he's missing important work, how can he ever catch up with them? Ask her how long Patrick will remain in the Special Needs classroom. You don't want to think that he's in there forever and you're in a panic wondering if he'll ever be released!"

Jane said, "You're amazing! How did you think of all those questions, off the top of your head?"

Diane shrugged, "I think of little else but education, morning, noon and night. My Gerry says I'm obsessed. But let me tell you, Mrs Forsyth is *tormented* daily with parents from the posh end of town, barging into her classroom, all guns blazing and blaming her if their little darling doesn't get top marks, or a seat at the top table. You can hear them at the school gate, every morning: 'My little Fiona always gets all her spellings right,' and 'My little Sebastian is brilliant at long division.' It's more competitive than Miss World! And the rest of us, out of Stove Pipe Town, standing there with our heads down, too humble to boast about our own brilliant children . . ."

It was the smell that got her, the second she stepped in the door of the school. Jane had a very keen nose – Victor Rich was always testing it with glasses of wine: "Guess the bouquet" and she always got it right. Today the bouquet was full-bodied, a fruity combination of school dinners, Dettol and urine. Beads of perspiration broke on Jane's forehead and her stomach heaved. Oh no, it was coming back up again, the little bit of lunch she'd coaxed down –

She made it to the Girls' Toilets just in time, retching loudly over the miniature bowl in the tiny cubicle. The toilet roll was stiff and translucent, like tracing paper. There were bossy signs everywhere, reminding her to wash her hands when she'd finished.

In the end Michael took her to the doctor himself, though she kept protesting, even in the waiting-room, that there was nothing wrong with her.

Dr Hennessey repeated the symptoms. "Nausea, vomiting, exhaustion, flashes of temper, increased libido, heart palpitations. Please go and pee on this stick, Mrs Temple."

"No way!" said Jane. She looked horrified. "You're not serious!"

Michael had never been with his wife before on the two previous occasions that she'd discovered she was pregnant, so he was unfamiliar with the diagnostic procedure. He actually thought it was the good doctor's clever way of getting her out of the room for a couple of minutes while he privately told Michael what was really wrong with her.

Soon it became clear that Jane was expecting another baby.

"Congratulations!" said Dr Hennessey.

"But how can that be?" Jane asked her husband. "We're always so careful!"

Not that it really mattered. She was expecting a baby. The doctor thought July. Counting back made it an October conception.

Michael thought for a moment. "The Achilles' Heel concert was in October. Don't you remember you came crashing in through the bedroom door, stinking of whiskey, singing 'Hell Raising Woman'. We didn't use contraception . . . there wasn't time . . ."

He was thrilled with himself. As if it took a special talent to impregnate one's wife when she was on top of him.

He said, "You took advantage of me, Jane."

Now Jane really did feel sick. The night of the Achilles' Heel concert was all a bit of a blur, and that was the way she wanted to keep it. Because she had an uncomfortable feeling that if she would only allow the forgotten memories to surface there might be more to that memorable evening than she cared to remember.

19

What was the worse case scenario?

That Bobby Flood was the father of the baby she was carrying.

The thought haunted Jane. It hovered all the time at the back of her mind and woke her up at night. She lay in the semi-dark, listening to Michael's untroubled breathing and the great weight of her guilty conscience mocked her. It poked at her, sly and painful, when childless Kathleen enviously remarked, "Another baby, you're so lucky!"

"And I know for a fact that it wasn't the Immaculate Conception this time!" said Diane from Next Door.

This pregnancy should have been a triumph, for finally all the higgledy piggeldy pieces of her life were fitting together. It was bitter irony that one foolish night and its consequences could spoil everything.

Desperately Jane wished she could remember what had happened during the interval at the Achilles' Heel concert, after she'd danced on stage with Bobby Flood and before rejoining Linda and Diane in the main hall of the Electric Ballroom. But only if she could remember sitting nicely in Bobby's dressing-room, sipping tea and making small-talk, comparing notes about their children. It was said that Bobby Flood had married his childhood sweetheart and they had a son, Alex.

But what if she was able to stretch back her mind through the fog of drink, and she remembered a horrible, tiny snatch of something else that would confirm her worst fears? That she did have sex with him. It didn't bear thinking about. It was better not to think about it.

Jane was worried sick and sick with worry. Her morning-sickness – "What can you expect, you're expecting!" – became morning, noon and night sickness and soon she was nauseous all the time. She couldn't cook, she had no energy or urge to wash herself. Food and drink made her vomit. She lay, dazed and dirty, in her bed, aware that the children were downstairs getting themselves out to school – the smell of burnt toast made her retch – but she was unable even to raise her voice to remind them to wear aprons and keep their uniforms clean. Every morning Susie brought the basin upstairs, in case she vomited, once the breakfast dishes were washed up.

Michael told his parents, "She's not feeling well. She can't keep food down."

Cecily said, "Go home and tell her it's her imagination. I didn't have time to be sick when I was pregnant. I *didn't have time to be sick.*"

Sometimes, when Jane was resting in a trance-like state, Satan came and sat on her shoulder and whispered, "What does it matter? Who will ever know? Even if you did have sex with Bobby Flood, you made love to Michael just after. Unless you go looking for a DNA test nobody is ever going to question the paternity of your baby. There's nothing remarkable about Bobby Flood's physical appearance to distinguish his offspring, except perhaps his green eyes. His ears don't stick out, he doesn't have webbed feet or a tail. For all his fame and fancy ways he's as Irish-looking as you . . . *you* won't even be able to tell if Bobby Flood is the father . . ."

"But I'll always wonder!"

Old Dave had been to the Saturday market at the windswept foot of the mountain. He'd stood with a hump on his back among leather-skinned, purple-faced farmers; his woollen hat was stretched down over his ears; there were neatly folded pieces of newspaper in his wellies to keep out the damp.

This was where Dave went every Saturday but just in case Cecily (or Michael) thought he was gone gallivanting and enjoying himself he always took the trailer though he rarely put his hand in his pocket, and never on impulse.

This endless dull, damp winter was getting to Dave. He had a chest infection and a barking cough. Some mornings his arms were too heavy to lift and it was only habit that propelled him out of bed and into the milking-parlour where he wasn't really needed any more. Modern technology had made the milking a one-man job, he knew he was only in Michael's way, though Michael would never say.

The chip van at the market yard sold the best cup of tea in Ireland. Dave walked around the car park with his tea. He passed the time of day with a country woman who sold jam and eggs and an old dear, the mother, who was half-blind and bedridden – she sold exquisite Aran jumpers. She told

Dave the knitting gave her something to do until the television came on in the afternoon.

There was a mentally handicapped man who sold hens and bantam roosters while his elderly father looked on with pride and straightened him up when he listed a bit to one side. This week the elderly father was selling a litter of pups. Dave had often noticed the pups' mother and admired her. She was beautifully marked and very modest. Today she was tied up with a piece of baler twine.

The old fellow told him, "My Meg is a strong-eyed working sheepdog. The pups are crossed with a dog called Fly, the most intelligent dog on the mountain. You could send him five miles to find sheep and he'd bring every last one of them home, wagging their tails behind them!"

Dave bought a collie bitch from him. She was bright-eyed and early maturing, he longed to keep her and call her Ruby. Unfortunately Cecily was dog-hater and refused to allow them into the house. Half a dozen times he'd tried to win her over, with a fun-loving terrier, a handsome retriever, a jolly spaniel, an elegant hound, even a pedigree corgi because he knew she was a fan of Royalty. Not one of them made it past the honeymoon period. The spaniel and the retriever had filthy toilet manners, the terrier and the hound chewed shoes and rugs, the corgi bit her. Every one of them had been ignominiously dispatched to the great outdoors, the corgi by air, on the end of her toe. Now Dave had half a dozen farm dogs roaming round the yard. He thought of them as his colleagues, they were not his friends.

There was no doubt that this little darling, enthusiastically licking his rough old hand with her hot pink tongue would end up outside too if he brought her home to Temple.

"I'd love to have you," he told her softly, her ears were

silky and very soft, "but there's already one bitch in my house."

Dave stopped his Land Rover in Stove Pipe Town. Jane's house didn't look any bigger this time than it had on his last tremendous visit.

"I'll have to breathe in and hold my breath when I'm inside," he whispered to Ruby.

In the window of the front room there was a festive Christmas tree, fully tinselled and floodlit. He could see paper chains hanging from the ceiling and a Yuletide Log on the fireplace, garnished with real holly and a fake robin. It was the only tree left on the street. Christmas had been over for more than a week.

Patrick was kicking a football aimlessly along the pavement. He was wearing his Spanish football strip.

"Saturday football was cancelled because of the fog, Grandpa. Oliver from up the street has taken his kids to the swimming-pool. He asked me did I want to come, but I've got a verruca and I'm not allowed to swim until the doctor burns it off my foot."

"Aren't you cold, young man? You're not wearing a coat."

"It's even colder inside! I'm kicking my ball to keep warm."

Dave left Ruby in the Land Rover. He needed to ask Jane's permission before he gave her to the children. He knocked the front door and Susie answered. She was wearing her coat and a tam-o'-shanter.

"You're just in time for tea. Do come in."

She led the way into a chaotic living-room, choked with black soot and ashes. Dirty laundry was piled up in a corner. Christmas cards were scattered everywhere and schoolbags disgorged their contents onto the floor.

Grandpa Dave was politely ushered to a seat at the small table. A plastic teapot, full of cold tea, was set in front of him.

"Mummy doesn't allow us to boil the kettle."

Thickly buttered bread was piled up on two plates and two packets of ready salted crisps had been tipped out onto the tablecloth.

"Linda gave us the crisps, as a present. Mummy doesn't allow us to eat crisps, but when it's a present it's rude to refuse, don't you think, Grandpa?"

The lunatics had taken over the asylum.

Quickly the children made sandwiches. They carefully crushed crisps into the butter, rolled the bread and crammed it into their mouths. Grandpa Dave could tell, from their dignity and dexterity, that this wasn't the first time they'd been left to fend for themselves at tea-time.

"Help yourself, Grandpa Dave!"

He did his best but the house was freezing – he was almost too chilled to chew.

"Would you like me to light the fire?"

"Yes, please! Mummy doesn't allow us to play with matches."

Grandpa Dave lit the fire. He tidied away the tea things. He washed up. He brushed the living-room floor, straightened the rug and pulled the curtains. Surely, wherever she'd gone, Jane would be back soon? It was dark outside. Other families were home from the Saturday shopping. They were settling down with chip-shop chips and Saturday television. Where was Jane?

"What's next, children?" He tried not to sound anxious.

Patrick said, "I have a page of reading, a page of writing and a page of sums."

Susie explained. "Patrick's not academic, Grandpa. His Christmas school report said 'adequate' and 'average' and 'Patrick tries hard but he's never going to set the world on fire'. His teacher says he should do extra schoolwork every day over the holidays to help him catch up with the rest of his class. Diane from Next Door gives him lessons because she's far more patient than Mummy."

Patrick said, "If I don't get out of the Special Needs classroom when I grow up there will be guttersnipes on street corners who will point at me and say 'Look, there's Patrick Temple, he's stupid!'"

Susie added, "You can use as many fancy words as you like and dress it up any way you want. Everyone knows that children who are sent to Special Needs are stigmatised."

Grandpa Dave felt suddenly sad. It was hard to believe that such cynical, world-weary words had come out the mouths of these innocent children. Susie was only just eight, and Patrick was only just seven. The pup outside in the Land Rover was their birthday present, provided Jane allowed it.

Patrick climbed onto his grandfather's knee and kissed his leathery cheek with soft child lips. "Please will you help me with my reading?"

Grandpa Dave, unused to unforced affection and caught off guard, suddenly softened. He'd almost forgotten long ago when Michael had run to him for hugs, without maternal prompting.

"Of course I'll help, but I've no reading glasses with me . . ."

They sat down together on the plastic sofa. Patrick's dry little hand rested lightly on the top of his grandfather's big rough one as they followed the words across the page. Patrick tried his best for he wanted to impress his grandfather but his reading was very poor, he couldn't recognise even the simplest words. Patiently Old Dave helped him with an unfamiliar word in one line but Patrick had forgotten the word again by the next line.

Stoically they persevered together to the end of the page while Susie crouched down on her hunkers, studying the thousand-piece jigsaw of Buckingham Palace on the floor.

She remarked, "Diane from Next Door says in a less ambitious world Patrick would slot comfortably into the middle stream of a comprehensive school, and jog along unchallenged and maybe learn to read and write along the way. But in Northern Ireland there are no comprehensive schools. There are grammar schools for those who pass the eleven-plus exam and high schools for those who don't. Diane says that everyone likes to pretend that it's not a big deal, but academic selection hangs like a big black cloud over the head of every little Northern Irish child, and over the heads of their parents."

Grandpa Dave kindly said, "Your father failed his eleven-plus. He went to the High School and I think he *enjoyed* it. They teach woodwork and metalwork, practical subjects for practical boys, and I know they have a very good football team. They won the Schools Cup last year, I read it in the paper."

"That's what Daddy told us but Mummy says, 'You think my Patrick is only fit for manual labour?'"

Old Dave stroked his grandson's soft hair. He couldn't help but think of the old man at the market yard and his mentally handicapped son, who he thought so much of. He could feel a biblical quotation springing to his lips, something about counting your blessings, but instead he quietly said, "Jesus was a carpenter."

"Was he, Grandpa Dave? Mummy says he was a king."

Finally Old Dave asked the question. "Where's your mother, children?"

They looked at him in surprise. Didn't he know?

"She's upstairs in bed," said Susie.

Susie led the way up the narrow stairs.

"Mummy, Mummy, Grandpa Dave is here!"

The sight of Jane brought unexpected tears to Old Dave's eyes. He could see immediately that she was very sick. Her body was emaciated and her face was grey and lined with exhaustion. She was lying on the top of the bed, awake and muttering, unaware that they were in the room.

"I'll know if the baby has tuneful howling. I'll know if the baby develops a taste for infant painkillers . . ."

Susie said, "Daddy tried to get her to drink some water this morning, with a spoonful of sugar in it but she vomited it straight back up over him. I gave her my teddy bear to hug."

Grandpa Dave plucked the skin on the back of Jane's hand. It stayed in a ridge. "She's very dehydrated. We better phone for the doctor. I think she's going to have to go into hospital. They can put her on a drip, to rehydrate her. And maybe they can give her some tablets to help her start eating again."

Susie's small hand crept into her grandfather's big one. "But who's going to look after us, if Mummy goes into hospital?"

"Your dad?"

Susie was firm. "Daddy wouldn't know where to start. He doesn't even know how to use the washing-machine. Would you help him, Grandpa Dave?"

He was flattered. "Of course I would. And Granny will help too."

Jane sat bolt upright in the bed and announced, "I think I'm having a heart attack, you'll have to go for the doctor!"

20

For seven years Lisglasson had been for sale and every year
the house got harder to live in. After the ceiling fell down in
Lord Laurence's dressing-room outrageously bold rats had
come out of the attics and taken over the first-floor
bedrooms. But for the ferocious Pike and Spike who slept
with them, Lord and Lady Glass would have been eaten alive
in their beds.

The noise of shrieking battles between the terriers and the
rats gave Lord Laurence nightmares. Every night he woke
thrashing and sweating.

"For God's sake, pull yourself together," said Lady Glass,
"or the men in white coats will take you away."

Lord Laurence's stiff upper lip trembled. "I dreamt I was
blown to pieces by a thousand-pound bomb out of a Stuka
and my dismembered body was hanging on barbed wire and
rats were feeding on me . . ."

"Wishful thinking," said Lady Glass who'd been frankly
disappointed when Laurence returned home from World

War II, bad with his nerves, but blemish free; she'd been having such fun without him.

Every night when he woke Laurence sat rigidly terrified in his splendid four-poster bed – it dated back to the days of Queen Victoria – anxiously drinking tea from a thermos flask and peeing into a bottle with a screw neck. He was far too afraid of the rats to get out of bed and find a loo.

During the day he kept his trousers tucked into his socks, in case a rat ran up his leg. He was turning into a nervous wreck.

"Let's move into the gamekeeper's cottage," said Laurence but Lady Glass was a tough old bird with a lifetime's experience at keeping up appearances.

"No surrender," said Lady Glass. "There's been a Glass at Lisglasson since Cromwell!"

"Not for much longer," said Laurence and he didn't have enough pride left to keep the note of hope out of his voice. "Not once the estate is sold."

His wife gently said, "Let's stick it out until we get Prudence married off. Then we'll sound the retreat."

Prudence was their final unmarried daughter – forty-two and never been kissed. Lady Glass was diligently scraping the bottom of the aristocratic barrel in her efforts to find Prudence a husband. So it was with great rejoicing she finally announced her engagement to an old-aged pensioner who owned half the Highlands.

"And he can trace his ancestry back to the court of King James!" boasted Lady Glass.

They got married in the summer when natural warmth and natural light flooded through the spotless ballroom windows of Lisglasson – Lord Laurence had spent a week up a ladder cleaning them while the Mother of the Bride furiously polished at the parquet ballroom floor and Mary, their housekeeper, cooked in the kitchen in her wellies.

There were two hundred swanky guests – in morning-coat, kilts and Ascot hats. They dined on Lisglasson pheasant and not one of them thought to ask why the Father of the Bride had his trousers tucked into his socks.

"Thank you for a wonderful wedding, Mummy," said Prudence, now Lady Prudence. She helped her ancient old husband into the family helicopter – there was a crest on the driver's door. Lady Glass modestly averted her eyes when his kilt blew up in the breeze from the propellers.

"I wish they'd get a move on," said Lord Laurence for black clouds were massing over the top of Lisglasson and he was impatient to get back into the house to replace the basins and buckets and jugs and commodes carefully positioned, X marks the spot, to catch the furious drips coming through the holes in the roof, once it started to rain.

It was the end of an era. The daughters were all married off.

Laurence and Lady Glass graciously surrendered the upstairs of the house to the plague of rats and set up camp in the West Wing which was south-facing and closer to the kitchens; Mary didn't have as far to walk with their dinner.

This was the most comfortable time of their lives. They still had the grandeur, and they could still impress when they had to – the christening of another grandchild, a pony club rally. The rest of the time Laurence dozed in front of the racing on the television while Lady Glass read holiday brochures and fantasised about the marvellous jet-set existence they would lead once Lisglasson was sold. She could finally gloat about the advantages in life to having four daughters.

"We'll spend three months every year with each of them. Jenny says we're welcome to use their plantation house in Antigua at any time except December and Antonia says the castle in Tuscany is always free except during the summer months. Prudence *insists* we spend Hogmanay in Scotland with them, but that sounds rather chilly. And sweet Sylvia says she'd love to have us all the time, but especially at Christmas when the children are opening their presents."

Laurence grunted. "What a frightening thought!"

Now their only headache was Rupert, who they'd made the foolish and expensive mistake of educating to be a gentleman in the romantic hope that he'd do something impressive with his life and meet an heiress en route. It was one of the many reasons they were bankrupt, his public school had cost a fortune. But Rupert wanted to work in television. He aspired to becoming a presenter.

Lord Laurence said, "I suppose we should be grateful that he's willing and able to diversify. There aren't many only sons who could so casually turn their back on such an inheritance. There's been a Glass at Lisglasson since Cromwell."

"And please God," said Rupert, "that you are the last! Surely there must be somebody with more money than sense who wants to buy it?"

This was exactly the same thing Victor Rich said to Kathleen at every board meeting and crisis meeting and brainstorming at the bank when they reviewed the sale of Lisglasson – "Surely there must be somebody with more money than sense who would want to buy it?"

In seven years, since the estate had been put up for sale, there had been only a couple of serious shoppers.

The first was the oil sheik. Rotten with money, they said, and so flamboyantly wealthy he could abandon a limousine in the desert when it ran out of petrol. He was seeking a base in Ireland, from which to breed Irish racehorses. He told Victor Rich he had a passion for steeple chasing. A date was fixed for the viewing and Kathleen was sent on ahead to brief Lord and Lady Glass on oil sheik etiquette. So they'd know how not to cause offence.

It was not a successful interview. Lord and Lady Glass were not used to being dictated to. They sat in stony, patrician silence while Kathleen advised that Lady Glass should not offer her hand for shaking, and that neither of them, for whatever reason, should show the sheik the soles of their feet.

"Don't offer him food or drink with your left hand, and don't offer him ham sandwiches!"

"I don't think we'll offer him anything!" said Lady Glass.

"And please lock up the dogs, and please hide the gin bottle."

That was the final straw. "How bossy! Who does she think she is?"

When the sheik arrived they were out in their kitchen garden, digging potatoes for dinner. Covertly they watched his helicopter land. Disdainfully they observed his bodyguards leap out.

"Show off!" whispered Lady Glass, and together they crept back into the house and up the stairs to a first-floor bedroom with the bucket of freshly dug potatoes.

When the magnificent sheik climbed out, Laurence took aim . . .

The chance of securing a private sale became increasingly remote. Victor Rich began to explore commercial options. One of these was Emerald Heritage, a holiday company based in America with a special interest in old-world nostalgia. Already Emerald Heritage owned a number of charming, well-preserved Irish Big Houses and throughout the year they organised ten-day trips to Ireland for wealthy, educated, pleasure-loving Americans seeking something a little bit different.

"I took the liberty of writing to Emerald Heritage," Victor told Lord and Lady Glass, "and they'd like to come to view. If they like what they see they'll buy Lisglasson from you, lock, stock and barrel. They've made generous offers for other Big Houses in Ireland – they'll give you more than the house is worth."

"Why?"

"Because Emerald Heritage will expect to buy you too. You are a vital ingredient to the success of their business. They will expect you to remain at Lisglasson and to entertain the paying guests. You'll be paid a stipend for your trouble."

"You mean they'll want to buy us as well as the house? How exciting!"

"I don't understand," said Lady Glass. "What do you mean by entertain? Are we expected to juggle for the guests?"

The Emerald Heritage woman had addressed Lady Glass as "My Lady" – she looked like somebody who read books on etiquette. She particularly admired the private chapel by the lake. But she'd been unable to drink the cup of tea that Mary had gone to such fastidious pains to make for her.

"Is there something wrong with the tea?"

"Not the tea. The milk. It's sour."

They were huffed. "Should that matter?"

In the end though, Emerald Heritage hadn't wanted Lisglasson. It wasn't interesting enough, they said. No history.

"But there's been a Glass at Lisglasson since Cromwell! What are they talking about?"

So Emerald Heritage quoted examples from their other properties in Ireland: the Big House where an unfortunate small sweep, sent to climb the chimney with a gorse bush tied to his ankle, to clean it out, had got stuck. His handler had lit a fire in the grate to smoke him out – panic was the prescribed method of making children move faster in the good old days. But the child had suffocated in the chimney.

"Our house is not good enough because we are not murderers?"

Or the house with the friendly ghost. A woman in white who sometimes got into bed with the guests, especially after they'd been drinking the local poteen-based cocktail.

"Well, I could do that," said Lady Glass.

The disappointment of not being chosen by Emerald Heritage threw Lord and Lady Glass into a depression. It's fair to say they gave up hope. Even Mary left them, seduced away from their employment by the bright lights of the Village Spar. Regular hours and regular pay, who could blame her?

Mary was their last daily link with the outside world. Now they sat at an endless game of Scrabble, bickering about the rules for contractions and proper names and foreign words.

They were mad, the pair of them, poor old ostriches, with their heads stuck in the sand. Too proud and too haughty to consider anything easier.

Rupert plagued them with kind-hearted offers of a warm, easy retirement. "Please give it up. Come and live with me in London."

If it hadn't been for their weekly jaunt into the village to collect their pension they might have quietly wasted away and died and no one would ever have remembered them. They'd always lived such a segregated existence, up a long lane, behind a high wall, unwilling and unable to casually mix, so that many of the local people, their neighbours, assumed they'd abandoned the estate and retired to England. Nobody remembered, or cared that there'd been a Glass at Lisglasson since Cromwell.

"Omelette, darling?" Laurence had been up since dawn, walking his grounds, the lord of the manor, gathering early-morning mushrooms – before the poachers got them! A quick detour via the hen house for half a dozen bantam eggs, still warm – before the foxes got them! Now he was standing at an exquisite but filthy floor-to-ceiling window, gazing out at the spectacular view of the lough and the private chapel, whisking together an omelette for breakfast.

"Heat is the enemy of eggs," he informed his wife's prostrate form.

She was still asleep on the daybed, fully clothed, nursing the mother of all headaches. She'd had the headache for years, since the Tall Two from the bank had arrived with their bankruptcy proposal.

Laurence said, "I saw eight magpies in the garden this morning but I can't remember the rhyme. Do think it's a good sign?"

After breakfast Lady Glass got dolled up to the nines, in her diamonds and her picture hat, and swept into Lisglasson Post Office to collect her pension, while Laurence waited for her in the antique car with a Biggles hat pulled down firmly over his patrician nose, flicking at dust on his immaculate three-piece suit.

The small post office was packed. She tried to queue-jump

her way to the front but the local people, her neighbours, were having none of it.

"Get to the back of the line!"

She was outraged. "Don't you know who I am?"

Afterwards they squandered her pension on iced buns and beer in the old man's pub in the village. They drove home, pissed as newts, once the money was finished. No one remembered who they were but everyone knew to get out of the way of their car.

Kathleen and Victor Rich were parked up at the front of Lisglasson's grand sandstone colonnade entrance portico, chatting and patiently waiting for the antique car to cough up the avenue.

Kathleen said, "I don't know why you wanted me to come. You know Lady Glass doesn't like me."

Victor stroked his wife's hand with the tips of his fingers. They always maintained a professional distance when they were working, but just sometimes he cracked and touched her.

"You were there at the start of the project. It was your bright idea that they live off the proceeds of the pheasant shoot until the house was sold. Not that you received any thanks, or even an acknowledgement! Or for any of your other efforts to get this monstrosity sold – above and beyond the call of duty."

Kathleen preened slightly in the passenger seat. Victor was right. It was thanks to her that finally they'd found someone who wanted to buy Lisglasson!

"We should really thank Jane," she said because it was Jane's outrageous performance at the Achilles' Heel concert and the subsequent splash across the Sunday newspapers which had excited Kathleen's interest in Bobby Flood. She couldn't have told you why but every time since that she'd watched him on television or seen his picture in the paper her head had grown hot and her hands had started shaking. Something tremendous built up inside her; she'd thought perhaps it was hormones.

Finally, sitting in the bank, wrestling with figures and the Lisglasson problem, she'd had her eureka moment.

She burst into Victor's office.

"Knock knock!" said Victor.

"Remember the photographs of Jane splashed over the Sunday newspapers after the Achilles' Heel concert at the Electric Ballroom? Do you remember the incongruous interview that Bobby Flood gave the evening before – it was underneath the photograph?"

"No," said Victor.

"Well, I remember, now! He said he thought South Derry was the most picturesque part of rural Ireland he'd ever been in – and I also remember him saying that he was tired of the touring and hoped to settle down soon. Put two and two together – what does it spell?"

Lisglasson.

21

Jane was still in hospital, semi-delirious on a drip, when the tremendous news broke. Bobby Flood had bought Lisglasson, cash, no questions asked. It was splashed all over the local paper. *South Derry to Have its Own Rock Star.* There was a photograph of Lord Laurence shaking hands with Mr Flood on the front steps of the Big House. Both men had their trouser legs tucked into their socks.

Jane was so sick she also missed the backslapping and big feeds to celebrate the completion of Mission Impossible. The enormous bunch of flowers sent to her, courtesy of the bank, she naturally assumed was just a kind gesture from her brother-in-law because she was in hospital and not a special thank you for the unwitting role she'd played in Kathleen's eureka moment.

But she managed only to miss the first flush of euphoria sweeping through South Derry as she lay safe in the hospital, wrapped up in herself, blissfully ignorant. For there was no escape. Every visitor and every nurse had a fresh instalment in the soap opera. The Flood family had been to church on Sunday and Bobby had sung in the choir. Alex Flood had been seen out riding with the minister's daughters, twin girls, but he seemed to favour the gentle one with the faraway eyes.

Unlike Lord and Lady Glass the bold Bobby intended to be a very hands-on member of the local community and the first thing he did was issue an open invitation to anybody who had a terrier or a hunting dog to come and hunt it through the upstairs bedrooms of the Big House. Those rats which were not killed in action but which managed to escape out of the house would be shot by the local gun club.

He himself would be blowing a hunting horn and his son Alex would lead the charge with his pet fox.

"Can nobody talk about anything else?" Jane snapped when Michael told her that he was taking two of the farm dogs with him, the fun-loving terrier and the elegant hound.

Michael indulged his wife's sharp tongue. Sick people were always self-obsessed.

When she got better she'd be just as dazzled as the rest of them, at this small bit of excitement sent to break up the tedious routine of their daily lives.

Finally Jane got out of the hospital, fully rehydrated and successfully able to keep down a cup of tea and toast, though it had been touch and go for a couple of days after Bobby Flood's arrival in South Derry when her guilty conscience had sent her into relapse.

To discover that the world had kept on turning without her and she was not as indispensable as she'd always assumed. And most astonishing of all: her darling children hardly seemed to have noticed that she wasn't there.

"We've been on our holidays."

"Where did you go?"

Susie said, "We went to Temple. And we slept in Daddy's old bedroom, in the double bed where he slept when he was a little boy and Granny made us porridge every morning for our breakfast and when I said I didn't like porridge she put a big dollop of jam in it and then I did like it."

Patrick said, "Grandpa Dave took us to school in the Land Rover and we both sat in the front seat and Ruby sat in the back and when school finished he bought us Polo Mints in the shop on the way home."

Jane had suddenly come over all weak. She couldn't have felt more confused if she'd come out of a long coma to discover that Susie and Patrick had been kidnapped and brainwashed.

"Ruby?"

"Ruby's our dog!" They were so proud of themselves. "She's only a baby still and she lives in the back of Grandpa's Land Rover on a little bed that we made with a blanket and straw and we feed her every day and pet her and *please,* Mummy, can we keep her?"

Grandpa Dave became a regular feature at the council house. He arrived most days about lunch-time to check if Jane was well and whether she was well enough to cook for herself and the children. Some days she was quite well, thank you, clean and dressed and beginning to bloom, but there were other days when nausea overpowered her; quite often these coincided with a Bobby Flood moment.

And he seemed to be everywhere.

On Tuesday he was at the pool when she took Susie and Patrick for their swimming lessons. The girl behind the desk whispered, "He's getting fit for his next tour. Feast your eyes on that, Mrs Temple – doesn't he have a fantastic body, and aren't his Speedos skimpy!"

But Jane preferred to keep her head well down in the viewing gallery even though there was absolutely no chance that he could even see her, hidden as she was among the other gawping young mums. Afterwards she told Michael that the overheated chlorine smell in the changing-rooms had made her feel faint, so Grandpa Dave offered to take the children swimming in future.

On Wednesday he was ahead of her in the doctor's surgery when she went for her antenatal check-up.

"He has Venereal Disease," whispered Linda who worked as the doctor's receptionist, "from shagging groupies at concerts . . ."

"You're not serious!"

As if she didn't have enough to worry about! Now she had to find time to worry that Bobby Flood had infected her with a dirty disease, as well as everything else.

Linda laughed at her stricken expression. "Of course I'm not serious! There's nothing ailing the bold Bobby, not now he's off the drink and the drugs. He has a little bit of a cough. Too many fags, I told him, and he said it was hardly worth his while waiting for the doctor when I had already diagnosed his illness. Do you want a glass of water? You look like you're going to faint!"

On Thursday he was ahead of her at the fish stall. At first she didn't recognise him because he looked just like everybody else – cold and a bit fed up because the Chinese Restaurateurs were taking forever as usual. Then it was his turn and he asked for cod and she immediately recognised his harsh Belfast accent, so unlike the soft country voices of South Derry. Their eyes briefly met as he turned to go. And he recognised her, even though she was thin and sick. He smiled and opened his mouth to say something and she panicked, turned on her heel and quickly walked away, comforted only by the fact that she was wrapped in an anorak and you couldn't tell she was expecting a baby.

"You forgot the fish!" said Old Dave. He'd called in, as usual, and found her sick on the sofa.

"I didn't feel well enough to stand in the fish queue this morning," Jane told him.

On the sick days Old Dave gamely rolled up his sleeves and did the cooking for her. Most of the time it was boiled potatoes, bacon and cabbage, but on Thursday when the fish market was in town it was potatoes, bacon, cabbage and mackerel fried in oatmeal.

"I don't want to relax your high standards. We both know Patrick's brain needs all the help it can get."

Jane had grown fond of her father-in-law. He couldn't cook for toffee of course, and he favoured sow's bacon which was mostly fat and an acquired taste, and quite often the cabbage was boiled into mush. But he was brilliant with potatoes, quite the cordon bleu, and he took fastidious pride in keeping the cooking water at the correct temperature, not too hot, by throwing a cup of cold water in. He was the only person she knew who could perfectly boil a large floury potato and keep its skin intact. "Very delicious with salt and butter!"

Old Dave said, "Do you want me to stop at the fish stall in future and bring the fish with me?"

"Before or after you collect the children from school?"

On Sunday morning he came bouncing by in the big old car to take the children to Sunday School.

"We sing pretty songs," Susie told her friends, "about purple-headed mountains and sunbeams . . ."

"And they tell us thrilling stories about giants and battles and brave little boys who become heroes!"

Within weeks all the children on the street were politely knocking on Old Dave's car window and begging to be taken to Sunday School, even Mary of the Sorrows and Bare Bum Isaac who both were taken on to Mass afterwards.

Linda liked to stand at the street corner and watch the Sunday morning procession of happy children eagerly waiting for Grandpa Dave.

"Here comes the Pied Piper in his Jesus Bus!"

"Do you know Jesus, young woman?" Dave asked her solemnly and she giggled and said she'd heard his name taken in vain the odd time.

"He's a bad colour, do you think it's his heart?" she said as the Jesus Bus pulled slowly out of Stove Pipe Town, with the children inside loudly singing "Onward Christian Soldiers".

While Jane languished and Old Dave nursed, Michael concentrated on the building of the new house at Temple. Proper plans were drawn up, they were in sympathetic keeping with Jane's imaginative sketches. Builders were engaged. Mr Maguire, a settled traveller who dealt in scrap metal was invited into the machinery graveyard and offered anything he wanted.

"I'm sure he should be made to pay you for that stuff," said Cecily when the lorry, heavily loaded, chugged past her kitchen windows.

"I'm only grateful that he doesn't charge me for taking it away. And there's just as much again waiting down there for him."

All that now remained was to clear the site and the

building work could begin. When asked, Trevor Mountain said he'd come on the first dry Saturday and bulldoze everything away.

The first dry Saturday was Valentine's Day. It was Jane and Michael's tenth wedding anniversary.

Mrs Somerville said, "Ten years is tin. How appropriate! I think you deserve a medal, Jane. You've been a very patient woman!"

Jane was feeling quite well. Bobby Flood had gone on tour and she was eager to get out to the farm and witness the grand site clearance.

"Maybe I should squeeze into my wedding dress and Michael could carry me over the proposed threshold? And his mother can wear her good coat with the fur collar and loudly announce 'We don't want a cheap little thing from the town round Temple!' And his father can shake his head sadly and say 'We don't need another house here at Temple. I'm an old man – I won't live for much longer. Soon I shall be dead.'"

Linda was at a loose end. Saturday can be very lonely when you're single and on Valentine's Day she felt her pariah status most keenly. She was a married woman but she had no husband. Even Diane had got a Valentine Card from "My Gerry".

"Come out with us to the farm," said Jane. They usually spent Saturday together, she and Linda, because Linda was not at work and Michael was. They were two misfits in the general pattern of regular lives. Until Jane had conceived and taken ill they'd often walked to the library or to the corner shop to buy cigarettes.

"Has my life come to this?" asked Linda, as she climbed

into the back of the Land Rover with Susie and Patrick and a dog. "Playing tag-along in somebody else's marriage?"

"If you don't like your life you should change it," said Jane. This was what she always said when Linda felt depressed and dissatisfied. This was why she was dragging Linda out to the farm, against her will, on a cold Saturday.

"Sure who would take me? I've got a bad reputation the length of my arm!"

Cecily had been watching for Susie and Dave from the kitchen windows. Ever since Michael had come in from the milking and told her he was going back into town to collect them. She'd baked them their very own loaves of soda bread, one with an "S" in caramelised sugar for Susie and one with a "P" in chocolate chips for Patrick. They'd especially loved her soda bread when they were staying with her: "Granny, it's delicious!"

When Susie and Patrick had been brought to her the night the ambulance took Jane to hospital Cecily Temple was a scary old woman with a scrawny face and bitter eyes. Susie and Patrick wanted to run away screaming, except there was nowhere to run.

Susie whispered to Patrick. "We've fallen together into a fairytale and Granny is the Wicked Witch. There will be gruel to eat and rags to wear and an attic to sleep in!"

Patrick was an optimist. He whispered back, "Fairytales always have a happy ending."

Cecily watched them whispering and felt rusty long-forgotten yearnings. Funny pain. But she was a stiff old woman and she'd never learnt how to talk to children. Silently she handed them cups full of warm milk, straight from the cow, and slabs of soda bread, thickly buttered.

"Granny, it's delicious!"

For a week they unwittingly worked their way into her heart which was a stale place, seldom used. Every day there was a new emotion, or an old emotion revisited. A rush of pride when they complimented her soda bread, surprising tenderness when they cried for their mother. By the time Jane was well again and they were gone she'd grown used to them. Within Cecily's limited emotional landscape this was the same as loving.

"Was Granny good to you, when I was in hospital?"

They hesitated, too young and too well loved to read between the lines: "She wasn't bad to us."

So when the Land Rover pulled up in the courtyard at the back of Temple and everybody piled out, it didn't occur to anyone – not Michael, not Jane and certainly not the children – to run into the house to say "Hello" to Granny. And of course Cecily was too proud to call to them from the kitchen.

Half ashamed, she greedily watched her grandchildren from behind the kitchen shutters while they chased Ruby, running and laughing, down the shaded lane. She listened hungrily for their childish excited voices. One fell over and the other called for "Mummy, Mummy!"

Had her own children ever ignited such passion in her? It was so long ago now she couldn't remember.

Alone in the damp, solitary, decaying splendour of Temple Cecily realised she wanted to make friends with Susie and Patrick, but she did not have the common sense to realise that first she must make friends with their mother.

22

Trevor Mountain was a happy man because he believed himself to have the best of all worlds. He lived at home with Mammy and she cooked for him, cleaned around him, washed his clothes and wouldn't hear a bad word said about "my Trevvie". Just look at the magnificent lunch-box she'd sent him out with this morning! You wouldn't get a wife doing that.

As far as sex was concerned, there was always the Electric Ballroom on a Saturday night, and somebody prepared to dance with him. Of course they always ran a mile afterwards when he told them he lived with Mammy.

This was Trevor Mountain. Fair, fat and forty, the oldest swinger in town, a man with every Saturday morning free and too stupid to realise the significance of it.

Trevor had finished bulldozing and the site was cleared but for an ugly skinny bit of a tree that poked unattractively at the sky. He was sitting with his feet up in his digger, eating a Mars Bar, admiring a job well done, when Michael and Jane and the children arrived and Jane's friend Linda, for whom

Trevor harboured a special affection. His hardworking heart gave a little skip when he saw her. He always looked for her first, when he went to the Electric Ballroom, and he was always fleetingly disappointed when she wasn't there.

"Good morning, Trevor."

He climbed down from his digger and stood awkwardly in front of them, with his hands in his pockets, wishing he could think of something memorable to say, but the sight of Linda made him tongue-tied. He wished he was French so he could kiss her on the cheek; he longed for her to look at him.

"Lovely morning and a lovely site for a house, if you like trees and silence."

Jane said, "You've missed a bit."

She pointed to the ugly skinny bit of black tree, poking up at the sky. It was exactly where she intended her threshold to be.

"I can't move that. I'm sorry."

She didn't understand. "Why can't you move it? Is it tangled up or attached to something? Can Mr Maguire help you? He'll be back later, won't he, Michael – to take away the rest of the scrap-metal machinery?"

Trevor said, "I've already spoken to him. Mr Maguire won't touch it either."

"Why not?"

"It's a fairy tree."

At first she thought he was joking with her for this was Trevor Mountain with his mighty shoulders and broad chest, who had tattoos and an agricultural contracting business, who whistled at women in short skirts. It was not possible that a man so brutish could believe in fairies. She had an urge to laugh, but suppressed it.

"What is a fairy tree?" asked Jane.

Everybody started talking at once, Michael, Trevor, even Linda who was from the town but chatted daily to country people in the doctor's surgery. They all knew about the sinister magic of a fairy tree.

"The tree will cry out and bleed if it's cut down," they told her.

"Well, that is very sad for the tree," she said, for she was determined to indulge them if they were teasing her, "but –"

"You don't understand," said Linda. "The person who cuts down the tree – the fairies put a blink on him."

"A blink?"

"Have you not heard of the man who pulled out a fairy tree and as he pulled it from the ground a hare ran out from among the roots, he turned his head to look after the hare as it ran away and his neck got stuck, looking left, *for the rest of his life?*"

Jane shook her head. No, she hadn't heard and she'd been quite happy not knowing. Rural Ireland was choked with myths about pots of gold at the end of rainbows and banshees who wailed to foretell the death of those whose names began with Mac or O. So charming and top of the morning to you but – Jane said, "That's where I want my front door. Just where the tree is standing."

"You'll have to move the front door," said Trevor Mountain.

That evening Cecily and Old Dave walked slowly, hand in hand, through their frozen garden in the moonlight. Dave had a touch of indigestion after his dinner and a headache. His big, rough farmer's hand was clammy but Cecily didn't remark on it. They strolled to the bottom of the garden and out through the kissing gate, down the shaded lane to the machinery graveyard, now cleaned up and cleared away. The builders were coming on Monday.

Cecily said, "She's picked a pretty site but I'll never speak to you again if you tell her I said so."

Dave kissed his little wife. His breath was sour but Cecily didn't remark on it.

"I declare, Cecily, I think that's the most Christian thing I've ever heard you say!"

"And you'll probably wait for the rest of your life before you hear me say another!"

For months Cecily and Old Dave had been pretending that Dave's indigestion was caused by Cecily's cooking, that his breath stank because of a stomach upset (also caused by Cecily's cooking) and that he was clammy because he was overheating in his longjohns.

Old Dave's time was up, and they both knew it. The little heart attack at the Electric Ballroom had been only the start of a series of little heart attacks. Dr Hennessey wanted him to go into hospital for a professional diagnosis but Dave didn't want to waste the end of his life in a hospital, under surveillance, attached to monitors and machines, popping pills. Just as he had lived, he wanted to die, without fanfare and without fuss, at Temple.

So he was following the same routines as he'd always followed. Every morning he rose to do the milking with Michael and every Saturday he went gallivanting to the windswept market yard at the foot of the mountain. He took his grandchildren to church every Sunday and of course he'd been calling on Jane. "Visiting the sick," he called that.

"You're over exerting yourself, running after them," said Cecily.

Cecily wasn't prepared to give up her husband without a

fight. Surreptitiously she was cutting back on the salt in his diet and every evening she ground up half an aspirin into his bedtime cup of Horlicks. She was studying the theory of CPR from a library book practising secretly on her dressmaker's dummy when Dave was at church.

Old Dave had been getting ready to go to the market yard when Jane hunted him down. He hadn't really felt up to the drive, maybe he'd only drive as far as there and turn back and if anybody asked he'd say there was nothing worth buying, not even early pet lambs.

Jane was in a state of near hysteria. Her eyes were sparking and her hair was cracking, she was full of nervous energy and adrenaline.

"What's the matter, my dear?" he asked her.

Jane didn't want an ugly fairy thorn scratching against the new house. She didn't want to move her front door. She didn't want her gravel driveway built around it. She didn't want it to be a feature in her garden. She wanted rid of it and she wanted rid of it now, before the builders arrived on Monday and filled her head with more superstitious nonsense so she became too afraid to even move into her own house which she'd been waiting ten years for . . .

"Please come and talk sense into Trevor Mountain and make him knock down the ugly tree. You're a god-fearing man – I know *you* don't believe in bleeding trees and fairy blinks . . ."

Dave allowed himself to be dragged down the shaded lane, to where Trevor Mountain was standing belligerent, with his mighty arms folded across his broad chest and a look of stubborn sulkiness on his face.

Solemnly Dave inspected the tree.

"This isn't a fairy tree," said Old Dave. "It's a wild plum."

"Go and cut it down yourself then," said Trevor Mountain.

That very night Old Dave was gently snoring when God grabbed his heart and squeezed. He had been gently squeezing for months, since the first squeeze at the Electric Ballroom. "Tonight I mean business," said God.

Dave's heart was hardly stopped when Cecily dashed into the bedroom, with her hair in curlers and the sleeves of her flannelette nightdress rolled up. She'd been fast asleep at the far end of the landing, tuned into the snoring and comforted by it. But, as always, half-listening for it to stop.

One breath – "Breathe, Dave!" five compressions – "Breathe, Dave!"

He was smiling as she frantically tried to revive him. Funny, afterwards, how much comfort she got from the fact he was smiling when he had his last heart attack.

The Sunday School children were lined up in an orderly row at the end of the street, faces shining, shoes shone. They were cheerfully testing each other on the shorter catechism, and Mary of the Sorrows was already in tears because she'd dropped her collection down a drain.

For the first time ever Old Dave and the Jesus Bus didn't arrive at the appointed hour.

"I don't know why he's late today," Jane said quietly to Linda, "and Michael's not back from the milking yet either."

Linda took a final drag of her cigarette and stubbed it out under her high-heeled boot. Suddenly it seemed like the most natural thing in the world for her to assume the reins of command.

"Onward Christian Soldiers!" she said. "I'll take you to Sunday School this morning."

Cecily wore her good coat with the fur collar. She sat possessively by the open coffin. She was rigid with grief. Old Dave was dead. The End.

Susie and Patrick were led in to say goodbye. They were solemn and curious. They kissed their dead grandfather without flinching.

"He's smiling!"

Jane said, "That's because they're throwing a big party for him in heaven, to welcome him home. With cake and buns and lemonade. He's got lots of friends up there. His mummy and daddy are waiting for him."

"Will he miss us?"

"Not as much as you'll miss him."

Cecily's face remained rigid but she was curiously comforted by the thought of Dave at a party in heaven. Imperceptibly, at that moment, her opinion of Jane Costello changed, and she never again referred to her as a cheap little thing from the town.

Trevor Mountain was first in the door at the funeral. He was squashed into a double-breasted pinstriped suit, bought before the onset of middle-age spread. He was wearing his most pious of funeral faces. He sat beside Cecily at the head of the coffin shaking hands and accepting condolences though he was no relation, God forbid, but he had a vested interest for he sincerely believed himself to have had a near death experience.

"It could be me in that coffin today but that I believe in the curse of a fairy tree!"

"My father had a heart attack," said Michael. "My father had a weak heart."

Michael was remarkably composed. It was the farmer in him, which helped him to unquestioningly accept the cycle of birth, breeding and death – he lived with it every day on the farm. He didn't feel a debilitating weight of grief, as his mother did, just a light airy emptiness at his elbow, where Old Dave had been standing for a lifetime.

Trevor insisted, "If I hadn't stood my ground when your wife wanted the tree cut down, it would be me in the coffin today, not your father, rest in peace."

He helped them with the coffin, he was strong enough to carry one end by himself. Michael, Victor Rich and Uncle Bertie from Fermanagh took the other end between them.

"If he's not careful he'll split his trousers with all that bending over," said Jane.

Cecily didn't like being a widow.

Suddenly everyone wanted to be kind to her. Victor Rich and Kathleen visited every afternoon, once the bank closed. They bossed her about her own kitchen.

"Just popping in on the way home," said Kathleen brightly.

Cecily was breathless. When Victor's car pulled up she'd had to dash upstairs to pull back on her stockings. And resentful. Now she was going to have to share her Swiss Roll.

"I hope it's not an inconvenience?" said Victor.

Victor was so polite it was sometimes like a foreign language when he spoke. Cecily had lived all her life among farmers who belched and farted without excusing themselves so Victor frightened her a bit, especially when he stood back to let her out of a door first, or held doors open for her or stood up when she came into a room. The temptation to stick out her tongue at him, in nervous defiance, was sometimes overwhelming. Except that Kathleen would never have forgiven her and would read more into the tongue than was intended and she'd weep until her heart broke and accuse Cecily of mental torture and Victor would have to pay out a fortune of money to some sort of fancy brain doctor to teach her how to feel good about herself again . . .

"Go and sit down, Mother, I'll make you a cup of tea."

"What's wrong with the way I make tea?" She burst into frustrated tears. "I may be a widow but I still know how to boil a kettle!"

The tears pleased Kathleen and Victor Rich. "Let it all out, Mum, that's good."

Then there was the ghastly minister's wife, Mrs Reverend Simms, who'd fetched her and driven her to a Golden Oldies Morning at the church. More tea and buns (this time they were homemade tray bakes).

What fool honestly thought that eating iced buns in the company of a bunch of silly old women could possibly compensate for the raw and visceral grief of losing your husband?

"It's better than ending up in a Valium haze, don't you think?" said the sharp-tongued bottle-blonde sitting beside her.

Cecily recognised her vaguely as Jane's friend Linda from Stove Pipe Town.

"Are you a widow?"

"I wish!" said Linda.

The afternoon of Dave Temple's funeral, Linda had a visitor to her council house. She hadn't gone to the funeral of course, it wasn't a woman's place, if you weren't a near relation, but she'd made sandwiches for Jane to take and kept her curtains pulled as a mark of respect. When she got home from the doctor's surgery there was a tractor sitting outside her house. Man Mountain was sitting in the tractor.

She climbed up into his cab.

"You're hardly lost again!" she teased him.

He was bursting out of a tight suit. It stretched threateningly across his shoulders. She reckoned it was probably very uncomfortable on him.

"I'm not looking for Jane, I'm looking for you."

She knew what he was going to say, before he knew himself. She'd been waiting for it since the first time she'd met him, on her mercy mission to Temple, when Susie had pulled the cauldron of boiling nappies down on top of herself. Sometimes you just know these things, even in the most unlikely circumstances. But it had taken his near death experience and the curse of a fairy tree to coax out the proposal.

"Would you marry me?" he asked her.

23

After every social effort Cecily retreated to Old Dave's upstairs bedroom, and sat staring sightlessly at Old Dave's bed. She had never before felt this weight of sorrow, not even when her parents died, this boulder in her chest, beside her heart.

Cecily was a practical little woman, not given at all to fantastical notions. "Doubting Cecily" Dave had called her because she was unable to believe in anything she could not see: the soul, heaven, eternity. She tried, but she could not believe that after a lifetime in wellies her Dave could ever be comfortable with a pair of wings and a halo.

She'd been strangely comforted by the lovely poem Jane had read at his funeral. Something about death being nothing at all, a negligible accident.

"I am waiting for you, for an interval, somewhere very near, Just around the corner –" written by a godly man with an education, the type of man she respected, even if she didn't like, not an unemployed poet with a drink problem and dirty fingernails.

If Dave really was just out of sight, Cecily strained to hear a few snores, knock knock from the afterlife, but Temple was as still as a grave. Michael had gone home to the town and there wasn't a dog to stroke, or a cat to feed. On television everyone was laughing. It was disgusting.

Cecily became shaken and old. The fight seeped out of her and gathered in a puddle, like tears. There was no soda bread baked and no tea wet. She didn't pass one cheeky remark about Trevor Mountain's tight suit at the funeral, or his most recent disappointment in love.

"Linda's heart is broken too," Michael told his mother. There was so much potential for sneering. The oldest swinger in town finally finds a girl he wants to marry and she's already married . . .

Not even the flicker of a snide remark out of Cecily.

Michael told Jane, "I'm worried about her. She has no friends and no hobbies. Nothing to take her mind off it. Kathleen and Victor want her to stay with them, but she refuses point blank to leave the house. I'm torn between the both of you. You're sick and she's grieving. I can't cut myself in two. The sheep are starting to lamb and I'm a man down with my father dying."

Jane flicked her eyes at her husband. She knew what he was asking. Marriage to Michael was a master class in mind-reading; ten years and he still talked with his eyes.

"But she doesn't want me in the house with her, Michael. She made it impossible for me to live there after we got married."

"Just until the new house is built . . . you can help each other . . ."

Perhaps their mutual antipathy would give them both something original to think about.

"You can't possibly move back in with my mother! Didn't she make your life hell when you lived there previously?"

Kathleen had popped round to the council house for lunch though she was eating nothing but cabbage soup this week and drinking only black tea.

It didn't seem to matter how much exercise she took, on the Golf Course and in the bedroom, the weight kept piling on to Kathleen.

"I think you look radiant," said Victor and it was true that the spread of Kathleen's hips and waistline was more than compensated for by the swelling of her cleavage, the shine of her hair, and the prurient glint in her eye. She was full of erotic ideas – bare-bum dusting was the latest. She lay on the sofa eating chocolates, ordering about Victor who was naked but for a frilly apron over his modesty and a feather duster.

Rosie and Michelle at the bank swore she would lose half a stone in a week on the Cabbage Soup Diet so she was giving it a go. It was the latest last-ditch desperate attempt to trick her metabolism into working faster.

Chin up, it wasn't only cabbage soup –

"I can also eat as much fruit as I want, but not bananas . . ."

And tomorrow she was allowed a baked potato with butter. It was going to be the biggest potato in Ireland, she'd just been to the greengrocer and spent a full ten minutes poking through his bag of Golden Wonders, till she found a potato the size of a shoe.

Jane said firmly, "We're living with your mother only until our own house is built. The builders are already up to the roof. They're starting the turrets next week. I've checked!"

"But what if she comes knocking on your bedroom door in the middle of the night, insisting that she's having a heart attack and Michael has to get out of bed and go for the doctor?"

Why hadn't Rosie and Michelle warned her that she'd be full of wind, eating cabbage soup? Every time she moved she farted, and Susie and Patrick started sniggering. It was like she was sitting on a whoopee cushion.

"I'll break her legs," said Jane.

The bags were packed, the curtains half-pulled across the windows, it was time go.

"But I don't want you to leave," said Mrs Somerville.

Jane felt tears prick the back of her eyes. So stupid to start snivelling now, when for the past ten years she'd been patiently waiting for this moment, the end of her temporary adventure in Stove Pipe Town, the start of her happy-ever-after with Michael. It had taken hardly any time at all to pack a couple of suitcases with their clothes, and the record player and record collection, Patrick's reading books and drawings by Susie from off the wall.

But no furniture, or kitchen utensils or curtains. She was leaving it all behind her or giving it away. Oliver was taking the bunk beds, Mrs Somerville was taking the fireside chair, the alcoholics at the end of the terrace had come and asked for her cauldron to wash their clothes for they couldn't afford a twin tub and she'd given them plates and cups and bowls because they said they were always breaking their own.

Only the plastic sofa was left, sitting in the bare living-room against the far wall, where it had been sitting waiting for her when she'd moved in ten years before.

"I hope the next tenants get as much wear out of it as we did."

"What will we do about Patrick's extra lessons?" asked Diane.

Teaching him to read had been a neighbourly act at the

beginning, to help out Jane when she was so sick, one less thing for Jane to worry about. Now it had become almost a hobby for Diane. She was intrigued that Patrick couldn't distinguish between "b" and "d" or "b" and "q", and that he left out the little words in sentences – a, the, to, of – and that he often said a word that looked the same as the word in the sentence but meant something totally different, or used a totally different word which had the same meaning. She'd been to the library to read up on learning difficulties and it was her unprofessional opinion that Patrick was dyslexic, not stupid. His brain was wired in a special way and he needed a special way of learning to read. In fact she'd already ordered some books.

Jane said, "I'd very much like you to continue to help him, but from now on I'm going to pay you."

Jane didn't want to have to say goodbye to Oliver because she knew it was going to be awkward and sad.

Good friends are irreplaceable, but sexual tension is life's champagne, and it was fair to say that of all her neighbours it was Oliver who had made the council house years bearable . . . with their outrageous flirting since he'd started to help with the gardening and she'd started to lead him on, poor man with his wife so recently dead, and she'd been half-dressed half the time and provocative.

"Can you put baby oil on my back for me, please, I can't reach . . ."

She should be ashamed of herself, but she wasn't.

She'd used him, in abundance, to alleviate the tedium of her exile and half the fun had been never to step over the line where explosive flirting descended into sordid bed-hopping and adultery and she truly became a cheap little thing from the town.

And he'd used her too for it was only thanks to Jane that Oliver was still a man of tragic integrity, the nobly bereaved father of ten, who had not raced headlong into a second marriage to a second-rate replacement for Maeve. Jane had alleviated the tedium while he worked through the necessary steps of his grief.

Now she was leaving and it was a fresh start for both of them.

"You're welcome to dig up the gooseberry bushes," she told him. She was standing with her back pressed into the scullery wall, five months pregnant and starting to show, in a shapeless smock thing that made her look like the side of a house. Michael and the children were sitting outside in the Land Rover, waiting for her.

"Fuck the gooseberry bushes," he said, and for the first and only time his hand closed over her breast and the other took her firmly by a buttock and with one fluid, unresisting movement her body was glued to his body and he kissed her, deep and hard, until she thought both her head and her heart were going to burst.

Cecily said nothing about them moving into Temple, she said nothing about anything any more. She preferred to sit quietly in Old Dave's bedroom, straining to hear a few snores – knock knock from the afterlife.

Instead she heard Susie and Patrick running and laughing in the yard below, chasing Ruby and shouting, "Grandpa Dave says there are dogs in heaven!"

Cecily started to come out of herself. It was difficult not to when delicious smells came wafting up the stairs every day, home baking with exotic flavourings: ginger, coconut, lemon. Purdah had never smelt so good, or tasted so delicious, for Patrick brought every baking effort up the stairs for her to taste – "Try these, Granny!" – and Susie followed him with a cup of tea, carefully swaddled in a dishcloth so it didn't spill on her.

They sat on Old Dave's bed, side by side, patiently waiting for her to eat. They were unafraid of her grief, and incurious.

"Mummy says you're very sad, and why wouldn't you be? Grandpa Dave was a lovely man. There would be something wrong with you if you weren't sad that he died . . ."

Ruby followed them, slippy-tit, into the bedroom. She rubbed herself against Granny Temple's legs and stuck her nose up Granny Temple's skirt. She was hoping for a bite of the biscuits – today they were seductively cinnamon-flavoured and dusted with icing sugar . . .

"Take that dog back down the stairs this minute," said Granny Temple. Everyone knew she didn't like dogs in the house.

But half an hour later Ruby was back, softly up the back stairs when no one was looking. Cecily watched askance when she jumped up onto the bed and snuggled down on the patchwork quilt. The dirty dog!

"Get down the stairs!"

Ruby showed no sign of moving so Cecily took her by her collar, and dragged her down the stairs, through the kitchen where Jane was making a red-wine marinade and out into the courtyard to where Patrick and Susie, dressed in boiler suits, bobble hats and wellies were calling for her while Michael revved up the Land Rover and shouted oaths at them for keeping him waiting.

"Where was she? We're going to cap cattle and we need her to help us!"

(Patrick and Susie had quickly learned that 'capping cattle' had nothing to do with headwear for cows, and everything to do with being pulled away from the television and made to stand in a gap in the hedge and wave a stick and shout as the cattle thundered past, as big as motor cars and with minds of their own.)

"She was in the house," said Granny Temple severely, "Sleeping on your grandfather's bed!"

"Because she misses him too!"

And they were gone, piled into the Land Rover, bouncing out of the yard with Michael still shouting, Ruby barking and Susie blowing her kisses.

Now she was down the stairs, there didn't seem much point going back up, and the kitchen was warm and comfortable. A wireless was chattering in the corner, Jane was chopping vegetables.

"Victor and Kathleen are coming for dinner. I'm making beef bourguignon . . ."

Cecily inspected the preparations.

"You don't mean to feed the children food cooked in drink, do you? You'll give them a taste for it. Then you'll wonder why they become alcoholics when they grow up."

When Victor Rich and Kathleen pulled up in a new car that afternoon they found her in the thick of it. Drinking tea, baking soda bread and chatting to Susie and Patrick with her eyes trained on the back door. She was poised and ready to shout and throw things if Ruby dared come sneaking back into the house.

Cecily stretched her lips into a wide, false smile when Victor and Kathleen came into the kitchen.

"Come to show off your new car?"

"It's a company car, the bank pays for it."

"*'Do not store up for yourselves treasures on earth, where moth and rust destroy, and where thieves break in and steal.*

220

*But store up for yourselves treasures in heaven, where moth
and rust do not destroy, and where thieves do not break in
and steal. For where your treasure is, there your heart will be
also.'* Matthew 6, verses 19 to 21."

Kathleen stared at her mother in silent surprise. Everyone
did. Old Dave had had an eccentric fondness for quoting
scripture, but when he'd started Cecily had always stuck her
fingers in her ears and refused to listen to him.

Cecily shrugged. "I lived with Dave for forty years. Something
was bound to have rubbed off . . ."

"What are those ugly red things on your face?" asked Susie.

She was drawing Before and After pictures of Auntie
Kathleen. "Before" was a big fat blob, "After" a matchstick
person. The picture was for Auntie Kathleen's fridge, to inspire
her to keep up the good work, for after a week on the Cabbage
Soup Diet she'd lost five pounds of weight.

"Spots," said Kathleen. "They're a side-effect of the Cabbage
Soup Diet."

It had been a very stressful week, the week of the Cabbage
Soup Diet with Kathleen suffering from stomach cramps and
flatulence and Victor mildly resentful when she farted on him
in bed.

He'd tried to suggest that any dramatic weight loss in a week
was only water, and a crash diet would slow down her body
metabolism, rather than speed it up, because her body would
assume there was a famine and begin to hoard food. And when
she started eating normally again she would gain extra weight.

"What would you know? You've never been overweight
in your life!"

Now she was squeezed back into her jeans and feeling
fabulous. She was going to have a week off, then another

week of the Cabbage Soup Diet, and maybe lose another five pounds.

Cecily said, "I can't believe the size of you, Kathleen. You've got very fat, and it's all on your stomach. Are you sure that it's Jane that's expecting a baby and not you?"

24

In rural Ireland a son and his father are inseparable. When the son is too small to walk he is carried piggyback. When he grows bigger he takes his place at his father's elbow. He becomes an extension of his father's arm; he is his father's extra pair of hands. The time they spend together, sometimes busy, sometimes bored, not always friends but always together forges strong bonding between the son and his father. This is the rural Irish tradition.

In all Michael's memories Old Dave was right beside him, holding him on to the back of the plough horse, teaching him how to hand-milk a cow, carrying one end of a gate, while Michael carried the other.

Now Old Dave was dead and it was time for Patrick to step up to his father's elbow.

But Patrick hated the farm.

He hated the green spaces and the isolation. He hated the vague and gentle stupidity of dairy cows and the way their shit splashed across the milking-parlour. He especially hated the way Ruby chased every car up and down the avenue – pointlessly. If Patrick was a dog he'd have kept right on running out of the ornate wrought-iron gates and on and on down the road back to footpaths, street lighting and the white noise of neighbours shouting at each other and yelling for their children, and yelling at their children and children yelling and babies crying and televisions blaring and car horns honking. Civilisation.

Jane was stricken.

"But you liked it here well enough when you came to stay with Granny and Grandpa Dave, when I was sick and in hospital."

"I only liked it because Grandpa Dave bought me sweeties every day . . ."

It was lambing time at Temple and every afternoon after school Patrick was taken to the lambing sheds to inspect the flock.

Michael tried to make it fun for him: "This is a Suffolk, son, with a black head and short brown fleece. They're the Rolls Royce of good quality lamb production, real ladies these ewes . . . And this one is a Black Faced Mountain ewe. She has a delicate black face and long white fleece. She's as mad as they come, but it doesn't cost much to feed her and her horns are handy for holding on to . . ."

Stoically Patrick took a tight hold of her horns and pinned the ewe against the wall of the lambing shed with his knee. She had one scrawny lamb recently born. Michael stuck in his arm and, after a fumble, pulled out the twin.

"I broke the waterbag with my fingernails. It's a waste of time, us standing around waiting for nature to take its course . . ."

Tim from Next Door had a new Chopper bike; he'd given

Bare Bum Isaac his old one. Today, after school, they were going to cycle together to the public swimming-pool . . .

A pretty Ile de France hogget was in difficulties. Her overlarge lamb was stuck, its head was horrible and blue, the hogget was bellowing in pain.

"Dad! That poor little lamb is choking!"

"Roll up your sleeve, son, and pull it out!"

But the sight of the lamb's lifeless tongue bulging between blue lips made Patrick want to vomit. He shut his eyes tight and shook his head. It was as much as he could do not to turn and run.

Michael gently eased out the blue-faced lamb. With a wet whoosh its shoulder came free and the lamb was born. Michael rubbed it briskly with a ball of straw. Less than a minute later it was up and sucking on the mother.

"I'm going down to the house to wash my arm," said Michael.

He could taste his disappointment.

Patrick followed slowly.

Tim from Next Door was allowed to ride his new Chopper to the chip shop. His dad gave him money and he bought five fish suppers (one for his mammy, one for his daddy, and one each for himself and Valerie and Ernest); Tim was allowed to keep the change.

When Patrick announced that he'd like a Chopper Michael said, "You can't round up sheep with push-bike, son."

That night Patrick climbed out of his bed and squeezed himself in between Jane and Michael.

"Go back to your own bed, Patrick," said Michael, but the boy snuggled closer in to his mother, and wrapped himself round her and tried to nudge his father onto the floor. There wasn't enough room for all three of them in the old Irish double – it was a tight enough squeeze even without Patrick. Michael had two choices – his dead father's bed in the roof of the house, or sharing with Susie who kicked and talked in her sleep.

"I think the lambing shed has sickened him," said Jane.

"He'll soon learn," said Michael who thought an interest in farming was acquired by osmosis.

Saturday was special to Patrick. All week he struggled at school, laboriously and inaccurately copying from the blackboard, tongue-tied and embarrassed when asked to read in class, copying Tim from Next Door who sometimes knew the answer before Mrs Forsyth had asked the question.

On Saturday the boot was on the other foot, for this was when Tim and Patrick had walked together to Junior Soccer – and though Tim had real football boots it was Patrick who was the star. He was naturally brilliant with a ball on the end of his foot and he was always picked to be the captain, and he always picked Tim to be on his team . . .

Now Patrick spent Saturday at the market yard at the windswept foot of the mountain, where Michael taught him to stand with a hump on his back, among leather-skinned, purple-faced farmers, his woollen hat stretched down over his ears, and neatly folded pieces of newspaper in his wellies to keep out the damp.

"Did you have fun?" asked Jane.

Patrick cryptically answered, "It was *beyond* fun, Mum."

And for the first time in his un-academic life Patrick began to wish the weekend would be over so he could return to the concrete familiarity of the town school and the musical chatter of three hundred children. And rough and tumble football with Tim from Next Door on hard tarmac at break-time. Even now Patrick did not mix with the country children, bussed in from outlying farms, who pretended to be tractors in the playground.

"Shoot me," said Patrick, "if I ever try to turn into a Massey Ferguson."

He wasn't a cunning child and when he started to complain of a pain in his stomach, every Saturday morning after Michael finished the milking and before he left for the market yard, Jane was disposed to take him seriously.

"It might be a rumbling appendix," said Jane, and she took him to Dr Hennessey who listened carefully to what Jane told him, nodded sagely and examined him, poking and prodding his tight little stomach and fussing a lot with his stethoscope.

"Jump up and down, little boy! Do you feel pain?"

Patrick shook his head.

"Is it his imagination?" asked Jane.

"He's not imagining it – even though there's nothing physically wrong with him. And may I say he's a strapping child for seven! He tells me he loves vegetables and his favourite food is fish, so he's not lacking in healthy nutrition."

"What can I do?" asked Jane.

"Children have a sore stomach for the same reason as adults have a sore head – stress, anxiety. Identify the stress. Remove it and the pain in his stomach will disappear."

When Jane got home from the doctor's she announced, "Dr Hennessey says no sheep for a week. And listen, Michael, I think I'll invite the kids from Stove Pipe Town next Saturday. Could you take Cecily away for the day, in case she frightens them into fits?"

"I love you, Mummy!" said Patrick and for the first time since the start of the lambing he spent the whole night in his own bed.

After school, instead of going to the lambing sheds he stood in his granny's kitchen, and baked dainty, delicate iced biscuits.

"They're delicious," said Jane.

Patrick wasn't satisfied. "I think they've a bit too much cornflour in them. And the icing is lumpy . . ."

He made them again and they were delicious again, but Patrick said, "I think the oven wasn't hot enough . . ."

And the next time, "I don't think the eggs were fresh enough . . ."

Finally the iced biscuits were perfect.

"Now they're delicious," said Patrick and Jane helped him write down the super-refined and incredibly detailed recipe in a tiny notebook with a lock on it.

"He's doing it to spite me," said Michael hopefully because the alternative was too bitter to contemplate – that Patrick chose to bake biscuits because it pleased him, because he *preferred* baking biscuits to helping his father with the sheep.

Michael wasn't a praying man, but, *please God,* was it too much to ask that the heir to two hundred acres, a hundred milking cows, two hundred ewes and a three-storey-over-basement Georgian tall house might show an interest in his inheritance?

At the back of Michael's shallow, one-track, agriculturally orientated brain he could vaguely recall some of his father's thunderous crescendos of scripture, Old Testament threats about the heaping of punishments down the generations, New Testament parables about reaping what you sow . . .

"Do you think Patrick is punishing me for the council years?"

"You're never a loser till you stop trying," said Jane.

It wasn't a party exactly, not with Old Dave so recently dead, but when Jane went to Stove Pipe Town to collect the children she found them fizzing with excitement. Tim from Next Door was wearing his football strip and carrying a football under his arm. Claire Hennessey had two bottles of French wine, Isaac and Mary had a bag of potatoes and a bunch of leeks. They piled into the Jesus Bus, exuberant and noisy, Linda rode shotgun and helped with the middle verses of "Onward, Christian Soldiers".

She was wearing less make-up than usual and her clothes were almost decent and Jane noticed that it had been a while since she'd been near the bleach bottle for there was at least two inches of soft blonde hair, with the odd grey bit, growing out under the bleach.

When they got to the farm the children bolted into the wide blue yonder. Linda came into the kitchen for a cup of tea.

"What's new?" asked Jane

"I've decided to let myself go. I'm nearly forty and I don't care any more."

There was something horribly final in the way she said it.

"Don't you think it's just a lovers' tiff?" asked Jane for everyone knew that Trevor Mountain was mad about her, and had been for years. It seemed impossible that, having taken so long to get round to a proposal of marriage, they would not now live happily ever after.

But Linda only shook her head. The pain in her heart was still too intense to talk about it. Jane thought she looked close to tears.

"Where's your ironing-board, Jane? I'll just run through this little basket of ironing before I sit down. Is it in the laundry room?"

"Stop doing your martyr act, Linda."

"But that basket of ironing is calling to me," said Linda who was addicted to housework. She never left her own house without first mopping the kitchen floor.

Quietly Jane said, "Some would say that marriage isn't really all that it's cracked up to be."

Linda tossed her head. "Everyone who says that has already caught a husband!"

Just then Mary of the Sorrows came screaming into the house. She'd touched a live electric fence and shocked herself, her arm was still hurting and she was revved up to cry all afternoon.

"We went to look at the black and white cows and Susie told me to pull some long grass and touch the fence with the grass!"

Mary ran straight to Linda and climbed up onto her knee. She burrowed her head into Linda's breast and Linda comforted her. There was something surprisingly intimate about Linda and Mary together and Mary was beautifully dressed in a brand-new emerald-green trouser suit, with a pretty matching headscarf.

For years poor Mary had been the final destination for Valerie from Next Door's clothes. They filtered down through her sisters, Ciara and Niamh, who were tomboys and very rough, fond of falling over in mud and rolling. By the time they reached Mary the clothes were always torn and stained, boiled washed an ugly grey, and ironed with too hot an iron. The McBrides had always been shabbily dressed, but Mary had been the shabbiest.

"Dry your tears, darling," said Linda softly, "and I'll take for ice-cream later . . . just you and me, when we get home . . ."

In spite of herself, Cecily was having a wonderful time at the market yard. There were so many interesting people to talk to and none of them knew she'd been recently widowed, so none of them stared at her with a funeral face, embarrassed and unable to think of a thing to say. She'd had a lovely conversation with the jam and eggs woman about the shelf life of raspberry jam, and another long chat with the old dear selling Aran sweaters about the difficulty of knitting a raglan sleeve. She was enjoying a cup of strong tea and inspecting the bantam hens with a professional eye when an ancient old man recognised Ruby who was running beside her.

"I know that little dog! That's a pup from my Meg! I sold her to the old gentleman from the foot of the mountain."

"My husband, Dave." Then she added. "He's dead," and it was the first time that she'd managed to say it without bursting into hysterical tears. It was so much easier to talk up here, in the blustery wind and fitful sunshine.

The old fellow said, in a matter-of-fact voice, "My dear Maggie has been dead for twelve years and I still talk to her every day."

Michael was determined to make up for the council house years. He came home from the market yard with a pony. She was shaggy and plump and her appetite was enormous. Unless she had the bridle on her head and the bit in her mouth she ate anything that walked past her. She'd been 'Free To a Good Home' for two or three weeks before he'd taken a chance and loaded her into the empty cattle trailer.

"Better than a Chopper bike, don't you think?"

"More Black Faced Mountain ewe than Suffolk," said Patrick and he christened her Horny.

Horny wasn't the easiest pony in the world to learn on. She had a naughty habit of bucking off her rider into the hedge and biting him on the way down. And there was no saddle, so it wasn't as if Patrick, a total beginner, had a secure seat to start with.

Jane couldn't watch. Every time Patrick came flying off she expected to hear the snap of his neck breaking but every time he got up, winded and shaken, sometimes green with pain and fear and insisted that his father throw him back up onto Horny's back. To be bucked off again . . .

"It's just as well I'm fat," said Patrick. "The fat helps me bounce."

"I have to say I'm very impressed with him," said Michael. "He's black and blue. There's not many little boys could take the punishment."

By summer Patrick was a surprisingly competent jockey and short of lying down on the ground and rolling Horny couldn't get him off. More often than not, after the initial flurry of bucks, she settled herself and played nice.

"I'm proud of you, son," said Michael. "You've broken her spirit and mastered her."

"Thanks, Dad," said Patrick and at the first opportunity he rode Horny into the town, past the chip shop and the swimming-pool and the football pitches, triumphantly into Stove Pipe Town to give his friend Tim from Next Door rides up and down the street.

25

Finally the new house was built. It was exactly what Jane wanted. A faithful replica of the sleep-deprived pencil drawings from years before but now there were two turrets, one for Susie and one for Patrick, neither was padded and there was also a bathroom.

Jane and Cecily walked through the freshly finished shell of concrete floors and plaster walls. Tall narrow windows framed meadowsweet, birdsong and haymaking. It was pastoral perfection in the sunshine. They were praying in church that the lovely weather wouldn't break until the hay was in.

Cecily stole a few glances at Jane. She'd been watching her carefully for the past few months for she could see there was something not quite right. Jane had lost her serenity, which was her best feature. She was fickle and fey and withdrawn, lackadaisical with homework, less bothered about Patrick's brain than usual, content to let Cecily do the cooking and she did not once suggest mackerel for dinner.

"Because she's been so sick," said Michael. "The pregnancy hormones have left her exhausted."

Cecily insisted, "It's not hormones. Hormones make you bad-tempered and blotchy. She's worrying about something. Is she worrying that she's going to die, after the last time?"

If only. If only it was as simple as life and death.

"The consultant has said she can have an elective caesarean section, if she wants. The first Tuesday after the Twelfth fortnight – he's on holiday until then."

Cecily wasn't convinced that Jane would last until the middle of July. Her hands and feet were horribly swollen and she was breathless when she walked upstairs. Even now, after climbing the wrought-iron spiral staircase to show off the turrets and the master bedroom she'd had to sit down for a little rest.

"We can climb on up to the roof if you like," she told Cecily and she stoically led the way round and round up to the top.

"I've no head for heights," said Jane, who was holding tight to the banister rail, "but Michael says the view is magnificent."

Gingerly Cecily stepped out onto the roof. Could there be anything more beautiful than rural Ireland on a sunny day? A little breeze fluttered in her hair and she could see across the fields to where Michael was kicking hay with Ruby running mindlessly after him, to the river where Patrick was making Horny jump bales laid out in a row and to where Susie, a small spot of pink, was reading. Across the boundary of the farm, over the top of the trees she could see the new roof of Lisglasson shining in its magnificence. Since Bobby Flood had bought the place the sounds of renovation never ceased – new roof, new plumbing, electricity, mains water. The man had more money than sense.

It suddenly occurred to Cecily: this was the view that Dave had from heaven.

When she ducked back inside her cheeks were damp with tears.

Briskly she said, "Your things from the council house are going to look a bit lost in all this space, Jane dear. We have attics full of old-fashioned junk. You're welcome to take what you want."

So Jane visited the attics at Temple and selected some stately pieces of Temple furniture that her thoroughly modern mother-in-law had thrown there during the Swinging Sixties: a heavy velvet-covered chaise longue, a suit of armour, carved and canopied beds, enormous cut-glass chandeliers, a mirror decorated with gilt flowers, fruit and cherubs.

"These things are beautiful. And some of them are very valuable!"

"Not to me," said Cecily. "They gather ferocious dust and I've no time to be dusting. I'm a drip-dry woman myself."

"My mother knows the price of everything and value of nothing," Michael explained. "She wanted to pull out all the old windows in Temple when she married Dad. She said she didn't want to have to clean the little panes of glass. Dad had to get a preservation order from the Irish Georgian Society to stop her."

July was a festive month in rural Ireland, especially if the hay had been saved. The schools were closed, builders took their holidays and seaside towns were stuffed. On the twelfth of July there was a big band parade to commemorate the anniversary of an ancient battle somewhere near Drogheda, or was it Dundalk? An Irish town starting with "D" – but not Derry, Jane was sure of that even if she wasn't sure who'd been fighting.

Susie said, "William of Orange on a white horse, Mummy. With a waterfall of yellow hair down his back that was a wig."

"A wig in battle?"

"Maybe he took it off before he started."

"Who was he fighting?"

Patrick said, "A man called King James. He had a brown horse. And a brown wig."

"Why?"

"Why what?"

"Why were they fighting?"

A pause. A hesitation. Susie and Patrick looked at each other.

"Go and ask your granny why they were fighting."

Jane closed her eyes and tried to block out the noise of the Lambeg drum. Its thumping vibration carried clearly across the meadows from the village. Man Mountain had been carrying the drum up and down the street for a week, beating the living daylights out of it.

"Is it a competition?" she'd asked Michael.

"Trevor's looking for a wife. He's drumming up business."

Trevor's proposal, its earnestness and sincerity, had hardly mattered once Linda told him she had already been married.

"But what did you think?" Linda asked him, which was unfair since the whole point of Trevor Mountain and the reason he was affectionately referred to as "the village idiot but harmless" was that he didn't think. He let everybody else do the thinking for him.

So, never having loved before, his high ideals and infantile, idealist notions about love came from children's fairytales and the strict rules of the church. It was hearts and flowers and blushing virgins, marriage was a binding contract and divorce an anathema.

No wonder he couldn't get anybody to take him.

Formally he retracted his proposal.

"I cannot possibly marry you if you're a divorced woman," said Trevor and he went home and took off his tight suit.

Trevor's regret lingered. It made him foolish and sad. The furious beating of the Lambeg drum was only the latest in a long list of ridiculous efforts to sublimate his feelings. He had begun to drink heavily and his flashes of furious violence were the talk of the country.

"Why can't he come down from his moral high ground?" asked Jane. "Cut himself a bit of slack? Accept Linda for what she is, accept that we all make mistakes sometimes and we shouldn't be punished for them forever?"

What a pity Jane couldn't take her own advice and shake off the stain of her own night of indiscretion – whiskey and lewd dancing and what may or may not have followed. But it hung about her like a bad smell and every simple pleasure of her pregnancy, feeling the baby move in her belly, hearing its little heart racing at an antenatal appointment, left a bitter aftertaste of shame.

A guilty conscience can't kill you, but it can make your life not worth living.

Trevor was still banging his drum when Kathleen swept in on her broomstick, come to borrow Susie and Patrick for the Glorious Twelfth. She was the picture of sophistication today in a bright yellow dress to show off her lovely tan.

"Just back from a quick week in Spain. We played golf every day. Victor is thinking of buying an apartment there but I'd far rather stay in hotels and order room service."

The band parade for the Glorious Twelfth had been the one bright event of her dull country childhood, and she wouldn't miss it, not even now when exotic Spain with castanets, bullfighters and olives was the alternative.

"Shut the door," said Jane. "Quick! Michael is spreading slurry on the Forty Acres and I hate the smell of it in the house."

Kathleen flushed and clenched her fists. All her life she'd been unable to take an order without an argument. And even more so at this time of year for it was the marching season, her Unionist blood was boiling and she woke up every morning itching for a fight. Of course she'd seen the tractor and slurry tanker in the Forty Acres, she'd even screwed up her face in disgust at the slurry raindrops fanning out behind like a peacock's tail . . .

But why change the habits of a lifetime? With a magnificent pantomime show of suspicion she stuck out her ugly, large nose and sniffed loudly.

"I don't smell anything."

Jane laughed, delighted. "I don't believe you. I think you'd argue a black cow was white if you thought you'd get away with it."

Kathleen remained stubborn. "I can smell only Orange Lilies and Sweet William."

"Because your mother has pulled every flower in the garden to make a big bouquet for Old Dave's grave."

Susie and Patrick burst into the kitchen. They were cheerful and untidy with ruddy cheeks, scratched knees, dirty boots and freckles. Country living agreed with them. Their arms were full of flowers from Granny Temple's garden.

"Granny says that William of Orange and King James were fighting with each other because they felt like it!"

The morning of the twelfth of July was cloudy. Rain was forecast in the afternoon. The band parade was going to be a washout. Bobby Flood stood at the front door of Lisglasson morosely watching the weather. He hadn't been to a band parade for years, he'd been looking forward to the warm beer and flirting and the festival atmosphere, but not if it was going to rain. He'd only just recovered from his last exhausting tour of every nightclub, ballroom and village hall in Ireland, a diet of chips at unsociable hours, beer for breakfast and women throwing themselves at him. Fun while it lasted, for the first week anyway, but after a while he'd started to fantasise about a nice cup of tea. He always did. Then it was time to come home to his wife and son, so casually discarded and conveniently forgotten about when he was on the road.

They'd settled into Lisglasson and integrated easily. Today Millicent was helping with tea in a tent and Alex had gone riding with one of the twins.

"Come with us!" they'd both said, but he knew it was only out of politeness. Millie's women friends would be thrown into a frenzy if he appeared in the tea tent and Alex and the twin had eyes only for each other. He would be damp and neglected. He might catch cold, become hoarse and be unable to sing on *Top of the Pops*. Much better that he spend the day walking his grounds – the Lord of the Manor – in a raincoat and wellies, with a cashmere scarf carefully wrapped around his throat.

It was lonely at the top, but somebody had to do it.

"Do you really think you'll be all right in the house on your own?"

Cecily was nicely dressed in her good coat with the fur collar. She was going to visit Dave's grave and she was taking her bouquet of flowers. She wanted to tell him that she'd been to the roof of Jane's house and seen his view from heaven.

That lovely poem at the funeral, about death being nothing at all, a negligible accident – "*I am waiting for you, for an interval, somewhere very near, Just around the corner*" – didn't work for Doubting Cecily. She needed the physical presence of Dave to talk to him even if he was in the ground.

"Of course I'll be all right. It's only for a couple of hours. What can possibly happen to me in a couple of hours?"

Famous last words.

When Jane's waters broke she wasn't in the least surprised. She'd always known this baby was going to come when there was no one around to help her. She only hoped that no one would expect her to call it Orange Lily or Sweet William if it was born on the Glorious Twelfth. But more likely she'd be spared the decision, since her labour was bound to continue until well after midnight and into the 13th of July . . .

The bag was packed for the hospital, the Land Rover was sitting in the yard with the keys in it. The hospital was only five miles away along quiet country roads. And the pains had not yet started. There was no need to panic, so Jane didn't panic. She'd go and lie down. Rest a bit, in anticipation of the labour ahead. Eat something. The books recommended a light snack of slow-release carbohydrate to keep her energy up – porridge, pasta, potatoes and butter. She'd boil a floury potato and that would keep her going.

Trevor Mountain was an Orangeman and on the morning of the Glorious Twelfth he squeezed his powerful shoulders into his striped double-breasted suit. It was the suit's first outing since the day of Old Dave Temple's funeral and his inauspicious proposal of marriage to Linda. Trevor tried not to think about Linda but she had an unexpected habit of popping into his mind when he was least expecting her. Today was no exception.

Downstairs Mammy was cooking him breakfast: bacon, sausages, eggs, fried bread. She didn't want her wee Trevvie to get hungry when he was marching. She wasn't getting to the Glorious Twelfth for she had nobody to go with. If ever there was a day for a daughter-in-law, this was the day. It was a family occasion. There were no old women sitting lonely on the Twelfth.

Mammy hadn't said it at the time, but she thought it was a pity that Trevvie hadn't married the blonde. Mammy knew her from the doctor's surgery and she liked her. Linda was rough, but she was also kind, and you can't say fairer than that. Kindness was one of the most unrated virtues, especially as you grew older.

"You have nice day now, son!" She fastidiously brushed at the spotless shoulders of his suit and resisted the urge to hug him.

Trevor jumped into his old pick-up and checked the glove compartment for the bottle of whiskey he'd bought the night before. He never brought drink into the house in sacred respect for his mammy and the fact that his father had drunk himself to death. He'd take only a quick swig now, to wash down his breakfast and save the rest for after the marching.

Jane had never driven the Land Rover before, but she wasn't going to let that put her off. Not when she had contractions coming regularly every couple of minutes. They weren't too bad, two deep breaths and they passed – so far! She was optimistic that she could still get to the hospital by herself – she really had no choice in the matter – there was absolutely nobody around to rescue her.

Too late Jane began to regret that she hadn't made more of an effort with her neighbours. They were country people but they were still people, and they spoke the same language most of the time. There was no point lamenting Linda and Diane from Next Door today. Linda didn't have a car and Diane and Gerry were in Donegal for a fortnight, up to their ears in ice-cream and bingo.

It crossed Jane's mind that perhaps she should phone for an ambulance but it didn't seem serious enough – early labour – to disturb the ambulance service while they were out on duty at the Band Parade, ministering to blistered feet.

So Jane climbed up into the cab of the Land Rover and started slowly down the avenue under the canopy of stately beech trees, past the dilapidated gate-lodge. Out she pulled onto the country road and along the demesne wall of Lisglasson. There was only one problem. When a contraction struck she had to stop driving and grip the steering wheel and squeeze her eyes shut and count calmly until it passed. Only then could she drive on. She was temporarily halted thus when Trevor Mountain's pick-up came flying round the corner and shunted her from behind. The Land Rover did not have its handbrake engaged; the bump threw it forward, nose down into the ditch. Jane banged her head on the steering wheel and was knocked out.

Trevor Mountain jumped out of his pick-up and ran to the edge of the ditch. He recognised the Temples' Land Rover.

"Stupid place to leave a Land Rover," muttered Trevor who'd been sipping at the whiskey and his eyes were red-rimmed and blurry. He hadn't been going fast, he wasn't a fool, but there was a better chance that he might have seen it, sitting there, plonked, in the middle of the road and swerved on the corner if he'd been sober and concentrating.

No harm done. There was only a small fresh dent on the front of his pick-up and not any bit of a bump at all on the Land Rover. He might see the Temples at the Band Parade. He'd tell them he'd bumped their old Land Rover into the ditch. Then later, after the festivities, he'd come and pull it out for them with his digger.

It never once occurred to him to check if there was anybody trapped inside.

26

Though Bobby Flood was enjoying playing Lord of the Manor, he didn't actually think of himself as a gentleman and certainly not a country gentleman. He was a hard man, from a tough city neighbourhood, and it would take ten generations of genteel country living in rural Ireland to iron that out.

"There's no silver spoon in my mouth," boasted Bobby. He used his underprivileged upbringing as an excuse for everything, from his excesses of drink and drugs to the composing of Achilles' Heel's filthy lyrics.

When Bobby bought Lisglasson, requests for celebrity appearances had come thick and fast from his neighbours. He opened the local ploughing championship and donated signed records for a Christmas raffle. He was the guest speaker at the grammar school prize-giving – a tongue-in-cheek performance in front of a hundred spotless over-achievers, where he'd waffled regretfully about his misspent youth, though in truth he hadn't regretted it at all, not one glorious, wasted moment. He had never aspired to academia. He was worth a million pounds and he could not spell 'shoe'.

Now the initial euphoria had passed and Bobby was ready for anonymity and acceptance. He longed to walk down into the village for a pint in the old man's pub, and nobody staring. He felt resentful of the painted lady in Derryrose chemist shop. She'd short-changed him, considerably, and when challenged had defiantly remarked, "You're rolling in it. You can afford to pay extra!"

Finally Bobby began to understand why other country gentlemen, born and bred, were never seen about the place. They had learnt down the generations that when you're born with a silver spoon in your mouth there's always somebody wanting something.

So it was with the shoot at Lisglasson.

Bobby had no strong opinions about the shooting of game birds. It was a toff's sport, nothing to do with him. He'd never eaten pheasant and he didn't feel he was missing out.

The week he bought Lisglasson Bobby had been of a mind to close down the shoot until he met Albert the gamekeeper and was politely made to understand that it was a healthy earner for everyone in the village and he would become Public Enemy Number One if he closed it.

"The guns are corporate fat cats from the Big Smoke. They pay handsomely for the privilege of being here. They pay for the hearty shooting breakfast they get from the Village Spar and they pay for the soup kitchen that goes out with them for their lunch. They pay the young boys from the village to beat. It keeps them out of trouble during the winter months . . ."

Albert had laughed at Bobby's mystified expression. "Pheasants are highly strung, secretive birds. They hide when they see you coming. The beaters walk slowly in a line, smacking at bushes and trees and long grass, pushing the hidden birds towards the guns. They get paid for their trouble, they get a hot meal in the middle of the day and we send them home with at least one pheasant each for their dinner."

Bobby wasn't quite sure how it happened, how Albert had managed to convince him to hold fire on the shoot until after the shooting season. He'd even come away with a brace of pheasants and instructions on how to clean them and cook them.

"Albert says to dip them in hot water to loosen the feathers before plucking."

Millie took one look at the beautiful golden-brown birds, quite dead with their heads lolling limply, and she ran out of the kitchen screaming. Millie wasn't quite a vegetarian but she was an animal-lover and she preferred her meat oven-ready and sympathetically packaged and looking as unlike a fluffy animal as possible. So bacon was a big favourite in the Flood house, and stewing steak, chicken breast fillets provided the skin was removed, salmon in chunks. Bobby had to go to the fish market on Thursday because Millie couldn't bear to look at dead fish, or smell them.

Bobby was made of sterner stuff. He'd been half-starved growing up, one of seven children on a shipyard pay. Nobody had ever had to tell him to eat up his dinner and remember the starving children in Africa. His table manners disgusted Millie who was more finely bred. She objected to the way he shovelled food into his mouth and was not convinced by his explanation that he'd had to eat fast as a child or his brother sitting beside him would have grabbed it and eaten it for him.

So Bobby rolled up his sleeves and cleaned and plucked the birds himself. He stuck an onion up their bottoms and roasted them as Albert had advised. He picked feathers and shot out of his teeth afterwards.

On the day of the Glorious Twelfth, because it was wet and he couldn't go to the band parade, Bobby decided to stroll down by the gamekeeper's cottage and tell Albert that he'd finally decided to disband the shoot. He'd have done it sooner but that he'd been on tour since the season closed. Bobby was genuinely sorry if it interfered with the livelihood of the village people but all winter the behaviour of the guns had upset Millie. Many of them seemed to think that the Big House was a public convenience and more than once she'd turned round in the kitchen to find a large florid stranger dressed in green fiddling with his flies after using her bathroom – "like randy leprechauns, only bigger, and armed . . ."

"It's getting on my nerves," she warned Bobby, which was Millie's mousy way of saying that if he didn't close the shoot she would be wintering in the Caribbean, without him, again. Not that he really cared. It was a welcome respite from her endless requests that he take his elbows off the table when he was eating and her insistence that they drink out of china cups when he'd rather have a mug any day.

Occasionally it crossed Bobby's mind that now he was a rock star he should really trade in Millie for a faster model. It wasn't doing his lean, mean image any favours, to be married to Mrs Middle Class Housewife and soon they would be married twenty years. If he wasn't careful he'd be wearing a cardigan, and smoking a pipe instead of a reefer.

Bobby was tempted to walk to the gamekeeper's cottage, but decided at the last minute to take his new car. It was a

Rolls Royce and so grand that Millie thought he needed a special driver, in a uniform with a peaked cap. But Bobby hadn't bought a Roller to allow somebody else the fun of driving it so he fastidiously cleaned the muck from the bottom of his wellies and slid into the cream leather interior. Deep breath to inhale the new car smell and he ran appreciative fingers along the walnut dashboard and held the leather steering wheel as tenderly as he would a woman. He would be more impressive in the car, a man on a mission, when he told Albert that the glory days of the pheasant shoot were over.

Thank God for Bobby's sense of occasion, for had he walked he'd not have seen the Land Rover in the ditch and Jane might have been dead before she was found. When Bobby pulled over to investigate, more out of curiosity than concern, he found her hanging almost upside down in her seatbelt. There was a bump on her head, but that didn't bother him as much as the blood which was seeping between her legs. He could see she was heavily pregnant and it didn't require a medical degree to deduce that the bleeding meant something was seriously wrong. She needed to get to a hospital immediately.

Bobby wasn't a tall man, but he was as strong as an ox. Soon he had her wrestled out of her seatbelt and dragged up onto the road. Only then he realised that he knew her. She was the beautiful woman he'd danced with at the Electric Ballroom last autumn, the wild thing in the black halter-neck frock. He often thought of her now he was living in South Derry. He actually thought he'd seen her once, at the Thursday fish market, but she hadn't seemed to recognise him. He often wondered would he ever get a chance to chat to her again.

Had anybody cared to ask, Bobby would have said that

during the surreal drive, in his Rolls, to the hospital, Jane was comatose for the entire journey. In fact she'd been wide awake and, it was fair to say, hysterical, ranting about the curse of the fairy tree and the evils of drink on an honest woman.

"Listen, love," he'd told her in his pragmatic city voice, flat and hard like the concrete streets he'd walked over as a child, "calm down! You're going to take my eye out with the way your arms are flapping!"

"But I'm bloody dying!" she'd screamed straight back at him. She had a Derry accent – it was charming and almost foreign to his Belfast ear. He was immediately aroused by the sound of her voice, as he had been that night at the Electric Ballroom.

"And it's all your fault!"

"What an ungrateful girl you are when I'm trying to save your life! You're bleeding all over my leather seats and I haven't passed a remark on it. Yet!"

"It's your fault I'm pregnant!"

What!

And out it spilled, what she'd kept bottled up inside her for nine long months, eating away at her, some days better than others, the strain of wondering whether or not she'd had sex with bold Bobby Flood and whether or not the baby could possibly be his.

"You must understand, I was terribly drunk and I can't remember anything that happened. I'm not blaming you, not much, there's not much a man can do when a woman is determined to have her way with him, short of running for his life!"

Bobby glanced across at her. He felt strangely tender. She was bleeding to death in front of him, yet it was her conscience that was killing her.

"My friends say I disappeared with you during the interval of your show! They tried to get backstage to find me but the bouncers wouldn't let them through!"

Because he'd told the bouncers to let no one disturb them. He'd wanted to be alone with her, this exquisite woman, with her fathomless eyes and her filthy mouth. Alone together, against a wall. Her exuberant, wanton, hot passion had surprised her as much as it had excited him.

However, if she was going to die, and it wasn't looking good, he wanted her to die content. Bobby Flood was a hard man from a tough city neighbourhood, but there has always been more to being a gentleman than being born with a silver spoon in your mouth.

Bobby said, "I had to take you backstage, for you thought you were going to be sick and you didn't want your friends to see you. You kept saying 'That Diane will tell on me!'"

"You took me backstage because I thought I was going to be sick?" She relaxed, the tension went out of her, her fingers lightly brushed his thigh.

He thought she was fainting because he hadn't fully appreciated how tense she'd been.

He drove her right to the front door of the South Derry, a grand old hospital. It said *No Parking Ambulance Only* but he abandoned the Rolls and carried her himself, up the steps and in through the doors, followed the signposts, down the corridor, round the corner, and up another endless flight of shallow steps to the maternity ward.

"You smell nice," she murmured.

A crisply starched nurse took one look at them – the pregnant woman who was haemorrhaging and sliding into ugly shock and the vaguely familiar man carrying her.

"Emergency!" shouted the crisp, starched nurse and for

the first time since he'd bought Lisglasson and moved to the country Bobby wasn't the centre of attention, nudge-nudge wink-wink, feast your eyes on that then – he was part of a hospital drama, in the thick of it, while Jane was stripped and prepared for theatre. He might have backed away but that she was clinging to his hand and short of cutting off the hand and leaving it behind she wasn't letting go. And when the nurses loosened her grip to undress her she grabbed his hand again.

"You're going to be all right. You're in safe hands, love."

"My name is Jane."

So Bobby stayed, even after she was wheeled into theatre for her emergency operation. She was pale and weak. No one expected the baby to live.

Afterwards he was declared a hero and a knight in shining armour and his face was splashed across the local paper with the most acceptable shout line *"Local Hero"*, with a photograph of Jane's husband shaking his hand in humble gratitude – "You have saved my precious wife's life," said Michael Temple.

Now his neighbours came to shake him by the hand and thump him admiringly on the back and tell him what a great fellow he was, that he'd rescued the little woman from certain death in the ditch. He was stood pints in the old man's pub in the village and asked to tell the story over and over again – how he was taking the Roller for a run on the Glorious Twelfth when . . .

After a few of these liquid evenings, with encouragement and embellishment, it was generally believed that Bobby had found Jane trapped, semi-conscious in a burning Land Rover and that he'd risked his life rescuing her. That he'd loosened the cashmere scarf from round his own neck and placed it over her mouth so she didn't inhale toxic smoke as he dragged her away from the flames, that he'd carried her in his arms – five miles to the hospital.

"Oh Bobby, I'm so proud of you!" said Millie. It was the first time she'd said it in years.

"It was the least I could do, given the circumstances," said Bobby, who could not help but reflect uncomfortably about the many women, across Ireland, he'd seduced at the end of an Achilles' Heel concert. It was a trademark of his live performances, that he invite a beautiful girl up onto the stage to dance with him and he could always tell after one dance if she was up for it, a one-night stand, to boast about when she was old and fat and respectably married. It had never before occurred to Bobby that a one-night stand could cause shame and regret, and the life-long responsibility of an unplanned pregnancy.

Bobby couldn't let it go. Even after he'd had his leather seats cleaned and the local newspaper had taken him off the front page and was showing photographs of wet Orangemen. There was a particularly odd one of Trevor Mountain weightlifting the Lambeg drum above his head, with the buttons of his white shirt popped. His faintly confused drunken face bore marked resemblance to the Incredible Hunk on the TV: vicious and childlike, bereft of love.

Trevor had absolutely forgotten hitting the Land Rover so he never told the Temples that he'd caused the minor road accident which almost killed Jane. When questioned closely by the police, Jane told them, quite truthfully, that her eyes had been closed. She was looking the other way.

27

Victor booked a table at The Rainbow's End. It was the only posh restaurant for miles and it was said that Wilma the waitress knew her customers so well that she could take one look at any bridal party self-consciously posing at the folly for photographs and accurately predict whether the guests would be asking for coffee or tea with their wedding-cake.

He wanted to take Kathleen out for dinner, somewhere special, to celebrate the fact that finally she'd got the weight off. For suddenly she was two stones lighter!

"I can't believe it myself!" crowed Kathleen, for this was the first month in nine months that she hadn't embarked on yet another fast and furious crash diet, a triumph of hope over experience, with the inevitable downward spiral of desperation and self-loathing when another month ended and another wonder diet failed.

When she thought back over it, it was fair to say that the Cabbage Soup Diet had been the least mad of the lot of them, in spite of the flatulence and acne.

Kathleen was an intelligent woman and, though desperate to lose weight, she'd been only prepared to crash on a diet with a scientific basis. The diet cookies, imported at great expense from America had contained a special amino-acid combination that controlled hunger and they'd worked, for Kathleen had never felt hungry when she was eating them, but she didn't lose any weight either.

"I'm sure," said Victor, "that you're supposed to eat those diet cookies *instead* of dinner."

Next month she'd tried the grapefruit diet. It was simple and inexpensive: bacon was encouraged for breakfast, fried steak suggested for tea. All she had to do was eat half a grapefruit before every meal and, like magic, the fat would burn off.

"Not like magic! It's something to do with enzymes in the grapefruit reacting with insulin in your body to regulate fat metabolism."

But it hadn't worked. Kathleen thought perhaps she was allergic to grapefruit. There was an unpleasant metallic taste in her mouth and she'd felt dizzy and nauseous for the entire month.

"Are you sure you're not pregnant?" asked Rosie and Michelle when she fainted twice in one week, beside the water dispenser in the bank.

Victor scolded, "You never mentioned that you're only allowed eight hundred calories a day! Eight hundred calories isn't enough to keep a woman your size standing upright!"

During the fat months Kathleen weighed herself every morning but only after a visit to the loo and the removal of her negligée and wedding ring. With a sucking in of her belly and squeezing shut of her eyes she'd take the blind step on to the bathroom scales. Of course it didn't really matter what the scales said for Kathleen was not convinced by one bald figure. It was the banker in her which needed a selection of weights, from which to calculate an average, so every morning she moved them from their normal south-facing position beside the wash-hand basin, to at least four different places across the tiled bathroom floor, and she weighed in again and again. North-facing she always weighed a pound of flesh less.

"You're a slave to those scales," Victor complained.

"Not just these bathroom scales, *all* bathroom scales."

Kathleen couldn't visit a house but she asked to use their bathroom. Once she was locked in, she'd strip and weigh herself; it was becoming an addiction.

Victor had tried to counsel his wife.

"What does it matter what you weigh? Isn't it more important how you feel?"

"But I feel fat!"

Kathleen's morning weigh-in dictated her mood for the rest of the day. Rosie and Michelle and Frank from Accounts could take one look at her face as she entered the bank and they'd know whether it was suicide to offer her sugar with her mid-morning cup of tea.

Those who were charitable said, "Isn't it amazing the way she wears her heart on her sleeve?"

Those who were less charitable said, "Look at the face of thunder on Kathleen."

Cabbage soup, diet cookies, grapefruit, Atkins, Weight Watchers, G-Plan – tick a box, all tried, all failed. Kathleen lost interest in the pretty things in life: shopping for clothes, sex with her husband, a new lipstick, the latest perfume. Pretty things in life were for pretty people, not big fat losers.

Until she'd read about the Blood Type Diet in a Sunday newspaper. It was her favourite type of crash diet for it was grounded in scientific evidence.

"Researchers have discovered that chemical reactions occur between your blood and the food you eat, and by eating the right types of food for one's blood type, you can lose weight and keep healthy."

Monday morning, before the bank opened, she was first in the door to Dr Hennessey.

"I'd like to know my blood type."

Dr Hennessey was a kind old man who made house calls to the bedridden and worked weekends. Courteously he read her newspaper article, about how each blood type, O, A, B, AB, had evolved at certain points in history while Man's eating habits were evolving. Kathleen sincerely hoped that she was not the most common and most ancient blood group, O, which had evolved when Man was hunting and fishing. It would be another month of fried steak and Victor complaining that it was sticking between his teeth.

"The only way to lose weight is to stop eating," said Dr Hennessey.

Kathleen struggled to keep her voice calm to conceal her overwhelming urge to kill Dr Hennessey and eat him.

"With the greatest respect, Dr Hennessey, I've eaten hardly anything for the past six months and I'm still enormous. If I'd come in here and told you I thought I was pregnant, you'd have taken my blood without argument and had it tested for type."

"But you're not pregnant, are you?"

She strode out of the surgery with her face flaming. She was making for her car and a little cry when Linda caught up with her, Linda who had been sitting in the corridor, outside the doctor's door, holding hands with Trevor Mountain's nervous old mother who needed her ears syringed.

"Excuse me, Mrs Rich, I couldn't help but overhear you

256

asking for a blood-type test. Did you know that you can get kits in the chemists?"

"Thank you, Linda, but the doctor says I don't need my blood tested. He says I need my head examined!"

Linda laughed. She didn't know Kathleen, hardly at all, except for the odd occasion that they'd bumped into each other at Jane's house. Until now she'd always thought of her as a stuck-up cow.

"Sure, doesn't everybody know that he failed the bedside manner part of medical school! Come on back into the surgery and I'll make you a cup of tea."

"I couldn't possibly!"

"Of course you could! He has Mrs Mountain in after you, he's syringing her ears and she's a talking machine. He'll be at least half an hour."

Tea and sympathy – before long Kathleen was halfway down a packet of custard creams and sharing a condensed version of the fat months, while Linda smoked out of the waiting-room window.

"I just can't get the weight off. It doesn't matter what I eat or don't eat!"

Linda said, "What you need to do is to forget about what's going in to your mouth and concentrate on what is coming out the other end . . ."

The day Victor strolled into the bathroom and found his wife rigging up an enema bag to the shower rail round the bath was possibly the most disconcerting moment in his life. Until now, Victor's troubles had always been discussable with intimate golfing buddies. Nothing personal of course but plenty of serious stuff about bank mergers and competition with the Credit Union and the introduction of loans and credit to the common man.

Kathleen said, "I'm using filtered coffee. Linda says it stimulates a sluggish liver. There's still some left in the pot if you want a cup."

First he thought she'd gone barking mad and was trying to drown herself in black coffee.

"What are you doing, darling?"

Then he realised that her bag of coffee was not meant for drinking, at least not in the conventional sense.

"I'm giving myself an enema. Come and help with the KY jelly . . ."

Enough was enough. Victor reached the end of his tether.

With sheer utter bloody-minded male desperation he announced: "I'll buy you anything you want if you stop right now."

"But Linda says that people have been having enemas since the dawn of time. In fact, up until recently Dr Hennessey had a colon-irrigation machine in his office!"

"Kathleen, darling, you're not listening to me. I said I'll buy you anything you want if you stop right now."

"Anything?"

Suddenly a shrewd expression crossed Kathleen's bloated face. Victor was thrilled. Hurrah! The businesswoman was back and the crazy, fat bird with the dieting obsession temporarily forgotten about.

Eight for eight thirty – Victor and Kathleen were bang on time. They strolled hand in hand together into the lounge bar at The Rainbow's End. Kathleen was wearing a new dress, silk polyester with shoulder pads, scattered with enormous red poppies. Only Kathleen could have carried a dress like that, and only now that she was two stones lighter – a shadow of her former self. Without the weight loss she'd have looked like Flanders Fields in full bloom.

Kathleen couldn't stop smiling for this was a momentous occasion, it was the first month in nine months that she'd eaten without guilt and calorie-counting. Nothing had been weighed, not even herself.

"I'm locking these up," said Victor and he'd shoved the bathroom scales into the safe, along with the family silver.

Kathleen was graciously prepared to stop dieting, but she still desperately wanted to weigh herself. It wasn't so bad in the morning when she was rushing out to work and all day in the bank her brain was trained on money and figures, but not her own figure. It was during the long bright summer evenings when she was freely stuffing her face with Bounty bars and fizzy drinks and French fries that the addiction was at its strongest and the urge to weigh herself overwhelming.

Kathleen was nothing if not resourceful. Quietly she visited the gym in the local Leisure Centre – ostensibly to become a member but in reality only to weigh herself with the digital machine at the door of the professional athlete's office. Victor wouldn't be seen dead in the Leisure Centre – he'd never find out about her surreptitious weighing-in. It wasn't cheating if she didn't get caught . . .

Kathleen's cunning plan hadn't gone quite according to plan for the digital scales were broken. Disappointed, she quickly turned to leave, but not quick enough . . . the professional athlete pounced.

"You're new!" he'd said and he'd insisted on giving her a guided tour of the equipment. Then he encouraged her to take a gentle run on the treadmill. In spite of herself, Kathleen enjoyed running. Almost effortlessly she started to run. Quickly she became addicted to running.

"Swapping one addiction for another one," said Victor.

Soon she was running three miles in half an hour, twice a day, seven days a week, and hardly eating a bite – running suppressed her appetite.

"We're just popping out to the shop," said Rosie and Michelle at the bank. "Will we get you a bar of chocolate?"

"No thanks," said Kathleen, without regret, for since starting to run she had realised that she didn't have a taste for junk food, only for self-denial and now she was free to eat what she wanted there was nothing she enjoyed more than snacking on a Pink Lady and a glass of Irish tap water, which if you actually took the time to taste it was sweeter than Fanta orange.

At the end of the month Victor released the bathroom scales from captivity. Kathleen stripped off her clothes and her wedding ring – some habits are impossible to break – shut her eyes and stepped on.

"Ten and a half stone," said Victor.

She was lighter than she'd been the night of the Derry Emerald, a night she now thought back to with affection, though at the time it had felt as if all the world was picking on her, and in her newspaper photograph she'd been frowning with her head down.

"We'd like a bottle of champagne!" said Victor when Wilma flung menus at them.

"There's no champagne," she said.

Victor Rich was frankly surprised. It wasn't that he made a habit of ordering champagne when he was out, but The Rainbow's End was the number one wedding venue in South Derry and wasn't champagne *the* drink of celebration? Perhaps The Rainbow's End was the number one wedding venue in South Derry because it was the one and only wedding venue in South Derry?

Wilma said, "Them as wants fancy liquor brings their own, and we charge you a pound for the privilege."

"What can you offer us?"

Wilma hated this type of upstart customer, whose culinary expectations were better suited to the Big Smoke. Fancy dining was still in its infancy in South Derry and The Rainbow's End prided itself more on the generous size of its portions than the impressiveness of its wine list. Or the sensitivity of its waiting staff.

Terse, she explained that they served small bottles of red and white wine, with screw tops. And all of it was kept at room temperature.

"I can give you ice in your glass if you want it cold."

Victor said, "Shall I dash home, darling, and lift a bottle of Moet from out of the fridge?"

"I wouldn't bother," said Kathleen who was scanning the menu. "There's nothing here I want to eat. And they're offering chips with everything! I can make you chips at home! We can buy chips in the chip shop. Why are we coming out here to eat chips?"

Victor protested, "I'm sure there's more to the menu than just chips!"

Kathleen read, "Fried chicken and chips, sausages and chips, lamb chops and chips, steak and chips. And look at the price of the steak – you could buy half a cow in the butcher's for that!"

"Just relax. Drink in the ambiance. Enjoy yourself!"

Which was easier said than done, for Wilma stood over them, drumming her fingers and sighing with exaggerated emphasis.

Finally Kathleen stood up and clearly said, "I'm sorry, I

can't eat here. I have indigestion already and the food hasn't even arrived."

Wilma said, "Suit yourself. But there's nowhere else for miles."

Victor and Kathleen went back out to their car and considered their options.

"We can't go home yet," said Victor. "The night is still young and my tummy is rumbling. Will we dine at the chip shop? Champagne and chips, what do you think?"

Kathleen had a better idea. "Let's have an adventure! Let's go to the Chinese restaurant on Main Street! They're making a fortune, I've been managing the account. There must be *somebody* eats there . . ."

The Golden Trumpet was inauspiciously located above a rough pub, across from the local cinema festooned with colourful strobe lights. It was emptying-out time and the racket on the street was deafening with car horns blaring, boys fighting and women old enough to know better standing in huddles, with white legs and white stilettos, shrieking with laughter and sharing a cigarette.

"Do you think they're prostitutes?" Victor whispered with nervous disapproval.

Kathleen waved to one of the women. She waved back. "That's Linda from the doctor's surgery." She stepped over a man who was vomiting noisily into the gutter. "Come on, Little Lord Victor! Keep up," and she led the way up a badly lit threadbare staircase.

"I'm not sure about this," said Victor for he'd never eaten Chinese food before and he was sure it would upset his tummy and give him diarrhoea.

The Golden Trumpet was exotically lit with red lanterns. There were floating flowers at the intimate tables, there was a choice of chopsticks or forks and the waitress was a real Chinese person – Hong Kong Chinese she told them. She had a charming accent, a friendly smile and endless patience. When Victor finally and with trepidation agreed to try the crispy roast duck with orange sauce on the side she praised him as if he'd discovered the cure for cancer.

Kathleen reached across the table and took her husband's hand.

"Oh Victor, I know what you can buy me if I keep away from the bathroom scales!"

"A holiday in Hong Kong?"

"A restaurant!"

28

Jane was in hospital for almost a fortnight. Her emergency caesarean section had been major surgery, with a full anaesthetic and complications. Even now she was still in a lot of pain: cramping pain in her uterus as it contracted, wound pain along the vertical incision from the navel down, deferred pain from the anaesthetic in her shoulder. After the operation she'd woken up woozy and confused and was handed Alice – impossibly perfect after what she'd just been through.

"Is she really my baby?" asked Jane for Alice bore no resemblance to angry red Susie, or the vermix-coated package that was Patrick.

It was only after a long sleep and a cocktail of painkillers that Jane looked at her new daughter and realised she was the picture of Grandma Cecily with white skin, a strong nose, thick, strong wiry black hair and glittering black eyes.

"What have I done to deserve you?"

For the first few days after the operation – the drugs were

very strong – Jane had only intermittent flashes of full consciousness. Most of the time she was high on morphine and idiotically smiling. She received visitors and chatted to them; when the bell rang for the end of visiting time she wondered if it was all a dream.

"Whatever you're on," said the redhead in the bed beside her, "would you pass it over?"

She'd just had her fourth son, born on the side of the road on the way to the hospital, delivered by a policeman who would dine out on the story till the day he died.

"Jimmy was cutting silage and I had to wait till the field was finished. I sent the boys down to him, to tell him to get a move on or he'd be delivering the baby himself – and when we finally did get on the road, the town was blocked off because of the Band Parade."

Theoretically she didn't need to be in the hospital at all. The little redheaded baby was the picture of robust health, as were her three other sons who stampeded the ward, bouncing on beds, eating and drinking anything that wasn't nailed down while their mother sat oblivious in the middle of it, breast-feeding the baby, "It gets the weight off" and occasionally raising her voice to roar at them.

"I'm staying here until they kick me out. I've not had my dinner made for me since I was in here last, having Sidney."

She was gone before Jane regained full consciousness but she left behind a packet of disposable knickers, and her phone number. *"You're always welcome."* The ward was a less vibrant place without her.

Michael said, "That's Jimmy Carson's wife – he used to bully me at school."

"I think he's met his match."

As Jane gradually came down off the drugs, and her

dream-like bubble dispersed, and her interludes of absolute consciousness became longer she realised that Cecily was her most consistent visitor. Twice a day she raced in at visiting time, and could hardly contain herself with small-talk until the enchanting bundle of Alice was brought from the hospital nursery and placed in her eager waiting arms.

"The first time ever I saw your face . . ."

It was love at first sight and she was utterly without sense in her infatuation. Alice was bombarded with yet another foolish and inappropriate gift – a musical toy with flashing lights and sparkly music which frightened her and made her cry, or baby clothes in rich dark colours. Alice was dressed in a ruby velvet babygro and a photograph was taken of her cradled in her granny's arms staring into the middle distance.

"I think she was filling her nappy when that photograph was taken," said Jane.

The stream of Jane's visitors was endless. Everybody came at least once, even Oliver from up the street, with Linda and Mary – he brought a box of gooseberries. Diane brought a book on the benefits of breast-feeding, though she hadn't tried it herself.

"I can't bear anybody touching my breasts – not even My Gerry."

Mrs Somerville knit some very nice cardigans. Susie and Patrick brought iced biscuits and flowers pulled out of the hedge. When Susie poked Alice in the eye everyone said it was an accident.

The only person who was conspicuous by her absence was Kathleen.

"Did she come when I was sleeping?" asked Jane, for there was a magnificent bouquet of pink roses in a vase beside her bed, with a tasteful card in Kathleen's elegant hand:

"An enchanting sister for Susie and Patrick – well done!"
As if she'd won Alice, first prize, in a competition.

Michael shook his head. "She left them at the front desk. Don't take it personally, pet – she's furiously jealous. It's only to be expected."

"Jealous of me?" asked Jane. She found that hard to believe.

Michael shrugged. "She's a good person. She'll get over it, eventually."

It's only human nature to compare your situation in life with that of your closest friend: her house, her job, her holidays, her clothes, her car. The list is endless. And it's not just material things. It's her kind husband, her charming children, even her ability to have a child when it's simply not happening for you.

Here was Kathleen, a successful businesswoman, happily married, newly thin, with a husband who had just offered to buy her the earth. And she'd have sacrificed it all up in a flash for the chance to hold a baby in her arms and call it "mine".

"It's God's will and you have to accept it," said Victor.

"Perhaps. But I don't have to accept it graciously."

Kathleen had struggled all her life to control her passionate nature. She knew there was no way she could go into the hospital and congratulate Jane on the birth of Alice without also wanting to put a pillow over her face and smother her.

She couldn't even bear to read about it. She ripped the *"Local Hero"* newspaper into a thousand pieces. Something poisonous was wrecking her head. A pregnant customer laughed in the bank and Kathleen thought she was laughing at her. Victor found her out the back, kicking a bin and crying.

"It's going to take time for me to come to terms with the awful unfairness of my infertility."

So he took her away on another holiday, though they were only just back from Spain. This time they toured Ireland, visiting restaurants with five stars in the *Discover Ireland* brochure. He called it research for Kathleen's restaurant project; Kathleen called it "my baby".

In Dublin they dined in the loveliest restaurant, with Michelin stars and everything. It was called The Townhouse and it was full of light and air, irreproachable in its simplicity. The Georgian dining-room looked so like a cleaned-up version of the parlour at Temple that Kathleen suffered what could only be called an out-of-body experience when she was taken to her table. She saw Cecily's horsehair sofa set and antimacassars burning, the heavy ugly curtains stripped away, the white marble fireplace opened up. She saw the old brown stained shutters freshly painted, the floorboards varnished and the ancient glass and pewter chandelier cleaned and lit and throwing a million soft sparkles across an exquisite dining-room. Cecily wouldn't switch on the chandelier, because of the cost of the thirty-five bulbs burning.

"Are you feeling all right, darling?" asked Victor.

"I've just felt my baby move for the first time."

She was carrying an imposing notebook. She left it open on the table beside her and she asked the waitress a lot of demanding questions: "Are your vegetables organic?" "When was this piece of fish caught?" "From what breed of sheep did this leg of lamb come?"

This most excellent restaurant had all the answers and the proprietor, Henri La Salle, came out of the kitchens to explain how he made ice-cream with stout – there was definitely more to it than opening a bottle of Guinness and pouring it over a scoop of vanilla.

"He thinks you're a food critic for a magazine," said Victor.

"I wish I was. I'd write that Jane's vichyssoise tastes better than what I got here."

Victor unfurled his wife's clenched hand and kissed it. "I think you've just won your first battle against the green-eyed monster."

"Tell me, Victor, what's the most enchanting dining experience you've ever had? Not just the food, but everything – the restaurant, conversation, wine, ambience . . ."

"Apart from the Chinese on Main Street?"

This was something they did brilliantly together – brainstorm: it was tantric sex for their brains. And a golf course was the best place to practise it, for they could march along briskly, breathing deeply in unison, prolonging and anticipating the exquisite pleasure of an orgasmic idea finally coming together.

And so it was at the Royal Portrush, in a gale-force head wind coming off the Atlantic, with a view of crashing white-topped waves, that they cast back their minds together to sun-drenched lunches in Spain, formal bank dinners at grand hotels, afternoon tea in pretty English pubs, morning coffee in Bewleys, their wedding reception at Derryrose Golf Club . . .

Finally, with a grunt of satisfaction, together they reached one conclusion.

"Jane's first dinner party at the council house, just after we got engaged."

Jane was painting the kitchen walls Tuscan Earth, from Fired Earth, cost the earth, when Kathleen swept in on her broomstick.

It was now a month since the birth of Alice and this was the first time Kathleen had called since the morning of the Glorious Twelfth, when she'd taken Susie and Patrick to the band parade and Jane had almost died in a ditch.

It could have been awkward for both of them until Kathleen said, "These kitchen walls are a very strange colour. What did you call it? Tuscan Earth? I can't say I like it."

Jane hid a smile. "Michael doesn't like it either. He thinks sage green would have been better." Gingerly she descended the stepladder and kissed her sister-in-law's cheek.

Kathleen scolded, "I'm sure you shouldn't be up that stepladder. You're bound to be weak from the surgery."

"I'm fine. I want to get the house painted before the baptism. I'm planning a lunch party for afterwards. Kill two birds with one stone. We'll invite everybody for a grand inspection."

Kathleen bounced a packet of disposable nappies briskly onto the kitchen table. She waited defensively for Jane to comment. But Jane passed no remarks.

"Where are Susie and Patrick?"

"They're outside, building a hospital in the orchard. Once I've finished painting I'm to join them for an operation. Susie wants to cut open my tummy and check there are no more babies inside. She's not convinced the surgeon in the South Derry checked carefully enough when I went in to have Alice. She thinks, since I still have a big tummy, there may be another one left inside me. And Patrick hasn't quite grasped the facts of life. He's hoping to open me up and find a litter of pups. He'd like collie dogs, like Ruby, thank you very much!"

"Let me repeat what you've just said," said Jane. "You want to turn your mother's parlour into a restaurant. You want to serve food to a two-star Michelin standard, and you want me to be your cook."

They were sitting at the kitchen table. They had just lunched on lettuce and mint soup; it was delicious with Cecily's soda bread. Now they were drinking coffee and eating tiny bite-size pieces of chocolate fudge. Each was decorated with a raspberry and dusted with icing sugar, Patrick had thrown them together that morning.

Kathleen had been expansively outlining her vision for a restaurant at Temple. They would start small to begin with – advertise in the local paper: *Care to dine at a country house?*

"When you think of where else they have to choose from, I think we'll be overrun!"

Jane nodded. She'd been out to The Rainbow's End once, when she and Michael were courting, for a farmer function thing and she'd ridiculed every mouthful of the three-course dinner: the soup was salty, the turkey dry, the sherry trifle had not tasted of sherry.

"What does your mother think of the idea?" asked Jane.

Kathleen hesitated. It had not been the most auspicious of interviews, the one she'd had with her mother. She realised now that she should have taken Victor with her, for moral support, for Cecily was better behaved when Victor was around. But she'd been so excited, and so determined to impose her brilliant idea on her mother that she'd not allowed herself to consider anything other than unmitigated enthusiasm.

Unfortunately for Kathleen, Grandma Cecily had developed a one-track mind since Alice was born and could not answer a question but she had to mention the baby.

"You want to take over my parlour, and make it into a restaurant? But where will Alice nap? I always push her pram into the parlour when it's time for a nap."

271

"You want to cook for the restaurant in my kitchen? But how will I boil Alice's nappies, if you're using the Aga for cooking?"

Susie and Patrick burst into the kitchen, followed closely by Cecily who was all business with a big blue pram.

"Alice is crying, Alice is crying. She sounds just like a kitten."

Kathleen stiffened. This was what she'd been dreading, the small muffled sound of a small baby crying for its mother.

"She's hungry," said Cecily, who every day pushed Alice in her pram round the road, showing her off to the neighbours, praising those who praised Alice, viciously criticising those who didn't.

Without fanfare Jane lifted her small swaddled daughter out of the pram, unwrapped her and tucked her under her T-shirt. Alice latched on and started to feed.

Susie and Patrick watched with interest.

"Alice sucks Mummy's udder when she's feeding. Like a calf."

"Her poo is bright yellow."

Cecily dug into the pocket of her quilted coat and with a little exclamation of practised surprise found a packet of Polo Mints which she quickly split with her finger and shared with Susie and Patrick.

"Come along, children, come up to the farmhouse with me and leave your mother in peace."

She frogmarched them out of the kitchen.

"Your mother thinks breast-feeding is something only animals do," Jane explained. And in fairness it was something she had never once considered with Susie and Patrick, but this time

Annabel Carson, her new best friend, had helped her a lot at the start by introducing her to the medicinal benefits of whiskey.

When Jane first saw the bottle she'd said, "But I don't drink any more! And certainly not whiskey! It was whiskey that got me into this trouble in the first place!"

"It's not for drinking! It's for putting on your breasts, to harden them up when the baby chews on them . . ."

Now the breast-feeding was second nature and so much easier than the tyranny of washing and sterilising bottles. It meant that Jane was rather tied to Alice, just at the minute when she was very newborn, but it also meant she had a magnificent pair of large, engorged breasts and for the first time ever in her life she had the questionable pleasure of talking to Michael and having him answer her cleavage instead of her eyes.

"Tell me more about your restaurant," said Jane. "Where did you get such an unusual idea?"

Kathleen unclenched her fists. Took a deep breath. Relaxed. It was only a little baby after all.

"It's all thanks to you!" she said cheerfully. "That first night you had us for dinner, when Victor and I got engaged, it was the most enchanting dinner party of our lives. The surroundings were so unusual and of course the food was delicious. I think good food should be the cornerstone of our restaurant at Temple. We'll use only seasonal produce, and our motto will be 'nothing out of a packet'."

"It sounds amazing but don't you think you should hire a cook with proper qualifications? People are more impressed by qualifications than experience, especially if they have no qualifications themselves."

Kathleen thought for a moment. "In that case you'll have

to do a cookery course. Not that you have anything to learn – but if anybody asks we can say you studied at the *Something* School of Culinary Art. Leave it with me! There's still time to get you squeezed on to a course somewhere before the cookery schools open again in September!"

"Aren't you forgetting I have three small children?"

"I will look after the children."

"You will look after the children?"

"Of course! I mean, how hard can it be?"

29

It has always been said that the only way to get over one man is to go out with another one. Especially when the man in question is Trevor Mountain, who loved but only until he saw the warts.

"I never meant to hurt you," said Trevor Mountain when he formally retracted his proposal of marriage to Linda.

These clumsy words had hurt her far more than if he'd called her unkind names or slapped her around a bit, or slept with her friend, which was what she was used to at the end of a relationship.

Linda kept a brave face most of the time. She made jolly jokes at her own expense.

"There's no fool like an old fool," she said. It was such a useful cliché to suit an occasion like this. And she tried to keep her chest out, shoulders back and chin up. But the stigma hung about her like a shroud and she suffered an awful urge to tell every new man she met that she'd been recently disappointed in love. And then she wondered why eligible bachelors ran away from her screaming and those who paid her attention were the scallywags with the oldest excuse in the book: "My wife doesn't understand me any more."

A stream of unsuitable lovers followed, whom Linda ridiculed afterwards: "He had hairy nostrils and a cough." They offered nothing but a bit of a laugh, a couple of drinks, a slap and a tickle – she wasn't grateful exactly but it was better than another night in front of the telly.

In the morning she looked at her miserable, remorseful face in the mirror and knew she had fallen into a downward spiral to the scrapings at the bottom of life's barrel. This was her legacy from Trevor Mountain: that she thought she didn't deserve anything better.

Diane from Next Door was incensed. She had never liked Trevor Mountain, having accurately judged him on first sight as a man with broad shoulders and no brain. But she liked Linda's succession of lovers even less. Her curtains were not the only curtains to twitch with disapproval when another married man cluttered up Stove Pipe Town in a flash car, with stinky aftershave. The best that could be said for them was that they did have other homes to go to, so they did not loiter making the place untidy.

"Please stop the madness, Linda. Trevor Mountain wasn't good enough for you!"

Linda was contrite. She knew she was making a fool of herself and that her neighbours were talking about her and their reserves of sympathy were finite. She'd seen contempt on the face of the wife-beater, but maybe that was her imagination.

"What would you suggest I do, Diane, to get over my broken heart?"

"You need to make love to a millionaire!"

The "girls", and none of them was getting any younger, took drastic action. It was ages since they'd had a night out in Derry City. It was time to hire the minibus! Because they preferred to travel as a gang, safety in numbers, and everyone had family plans for the summer holidays, they agreed on a Saturday night at the end of August.

This was the day Oliver had been dreading since Maeve died.

Ciara got her period.

Ciara was thirteen. She was the oldest of Oliver's three daughters, and a tomboy. He had always thought of her as an honorary boy and had dressed her, without much thought, in her brothers' cast-off clothing, when there were slim pickings from Valerie from next Door.

Today she was standing in bloodstained Y-fronts, so innocent.

"I'm bleeding out of my bum. Do you think I'm dying, Daddy?"

This was the most terrifying ordeal of Oliver's life, worse even than the death of beloved Maeve. He was no longer a single parent, raising a shower of children. Today he had also crossed a line. Now he was the father of a thirteen-year-old daughter who had developed the necessary equipment to make him a grandfather. And she still thought babies were born under gooseberry bushes.

Oliver was a conscientious parent – he had been very particular to explain the facts of life to his sons about erections, acne and facial hair, man to man, in a group, when the oldest boy's voice had broken. These were the signs that you were no longer a child. Please lock the bathroom door in future.

The reason that he hadn't taught Ciara the facts of life for girls was because he had only a sketchy idea of what they were himself.

Girls grew breasts. That was obvious and easily dealt with. There was an efficient, motherly woman in charge of lingerie in the local department store. "Leave it to me, Mr McBride." She'd fitted Ciara with a Junior First.

Menstruation was another business entirely and until now he'd thought of it dispassionately as a biological equation: you couldn't get pregnant until you'd started to menstruate, menstruation stopped when you were pregnant.

"Dad, how am I going to stop the bleeding?"

Now Oliver realised that menstruation was also emotional and educational. And he would only have himself to blame if Ciara conceived a child through ignorance. Not that she was even vaguely interested in boyfriends, not with seven brothers, but forewarned was forearmed – you never carried a loaded pistol without safety training . . .

Where were the nuns when you needed them? Maeve had been clearly taught what was socially acceptable with boys in conservative sixties' Ireland and more importantly, what wasn't. Oliver remembered, with affectionate amusement, the courting years when she'd refused to sit on his knee until there was a telephone directory wedged between her bottom and his lap. The nuns had advised it, she'd told him solemnly.

At the time he'd laughed at her healthy respect for the fires of hell – today he thought it was a very sad state of affairs that the nuns didn't teach in the convent school any more. Sex education, if it was taught at all, was a biological diagram and sniggering at the back of the class.

Today the nuns' heavy-handed advice didn't seem heavy-handed enough.

For the first time since Maeve died, Oliver clearly thought: I wish there was a woman about the place.

"Where are you going, Dad?" asked Ciara who was wrecked with stomach cramps and lying on the sofa, with a hot-water bottle, and the *Jackie* comic.

"I'm going to find a woman," said Oliver, and he was only half joking.

Linda was alone in her council house, she was not expecting visitors. She was mildly depressed – pale blue, not navy. Tonight was her big night out in the minibus with "the girls" and she really couldn't care less. It was going to be just another lonely night out with a bunch of married women, sharing a bottle of vodka and a few laughs. They were content to brush up on the old flirting but if a man came too close they flashed their wedding rings and ran a mile. They did not really approve of Linda because she lowered the tone of their evening with her sluttish clothing and brazen attitude. Sometimes when she met a man and kept them waiting, they sneered quietly, "She really has no self-respect, has she?" It's so easy to ignore desperation when you're going home to a warm bed and a tolerant husband.

"Cheer up, Linda," she told her miserable face in the mirror. "Today is the day you might meet Mr Wonderful."

But she was sorely tempted to duck out and stay at home, pretend she wasn't feeling well. "Women's problems" she was going to say and it was nearly the truth for what was Trevor Mountain's legacy if it wasn't a problem and she wasn't a woman.

Oliver knocked on Linda's front door. Such was her current reputation that he'd cautiously waited until the middle of the day, and he took Mary with him, as a chaperone, for Linda was particularly fond of Mary, and mothered her, when Mary never had a mother. They often went shopping together, and Linda bought her sparkly hairclips and painted her fingernails and put lipstick on her, and hugged her so that sometimes Mary's tears actually stopped.

"Linda! Linda!"

The door opened. Mary ran to hug her.

Oliver tried not to look shocked. He'd been braced to find an unclean bit of fluff, a glass of wine in one hand, a cigarette in the other, with her latest man lying with his feet up on the living-room sofa, watching the racing on the television.

But Linda was alone in her house and without make-up and careful dressing she had no sexual aura. She was wearing a quilted body-warmer thing that was so enormously large on her that it could only ever have belonged to Man Mountain and for the first time Oliver noticed that her nails were bitten, and her eyes were sad.

"Would you like to come in?" She made it sound like a challenge.

Her house was spotless. And furnished with pretty framed Impressionist prints. There were pink flowers on the wallpaper and a family of carefully dusted china ladies on the fireplace – they had names and tissue-lined boxes to live in, you ordered them with coupons from out of the newspaper. Linda had the whole collection, and Oliver knew instinctively that if he lifted one of them and put it back an inch out of place she would notice and would wait until he'd gone, then move it back to its allocated location.

"Please, may I touch 'Mary'?" said Mary.

"Sit down, Oliver," said Linda, but he felt awkward and untidy in such a feminine environment and there was only the large soft sofa in front of the television. The small table pushed against the wall had the hard chairs trapped behind it, and anyway, Linda was sitting there, sewing.

"It's for Mary. I saw the material in the sale. I thought she might like a frock made out of it. Pull off your dungarees, Mary darling, and try it on for size – be careful of the pins!"

Still he stood awkwardly in the middle of the room, embarrassed and unsure how to describe his cry for help.

Until Mary, with the pleasing innocence of eight, gave them a twirl in her half-finished, handmade frock and announced, "Can I wear this to Ciara's funeral, Daddy?"

"What is Ciara dying of?" asked Linda, and the ice was broken.

Diane from Next Door shoved a glass into Linda's hand.

"Don't ask what it is! Just drink it in one. It's a magic pheromone cocktail and once it starts to work we'll have to beat the eligible bachelors of Derry City away from you!"

Linda drank it quickly. It tasted like nothing she'd ever tasted before but whatever it was it was potent, and by the time they reached Derry she was singing, "The Wheels of the Bus Go Round and Round" loudly at the top of her voice.

This was going to be the best night of her life.

Afterwards Oliver always wondered what woke him. In spite of everything he was a heavy sleeper. The children had learnt early that they could call for him in the night till they grew hoarse and he would not hear them. Quickly they had learned to be heavy deep sleepers too.

Oliver had always had an amazing talent for blanking out background noise. There had been no choice in the matter when he'd been studying for bank exams in a living-room cluttered with small children and babies and a pregnant wife who could spoon-feed one infant, distract another and proofread a summary for him at the same time.

And the sounds of drunken argument and the screeching of car tyres were commonplace in Stove Pipe Town. The alcoholics at the end of the terrace were always picking fights and throwing things and Ernest from Next Door liked to practise handbrake turns late at night in "My Gerry's" Ford Capri when his mother was sleeping and couldn't stop him.

But tonight these sounds had woken him. Oliver got out of bed to investigate.

Huddled on his doorstep, with her face badly smacked about and her lip bleeding, was Linda. She had her keys in her hand, she'd been trying to let herself in through his front door by mistake, but now she'd passed out, or fallen asleep, on the doorstep.

"You'll get cold in that mini-skirt," said Oliver and he picked her up in a fireman's lift over his shoulder and gently manhandled her into his living-room which was a mess as always. He cleared a space on the floor and put her in the recovery position with a large towel under her head and the basin out of the sink. Oliver didn't drink but he'd been round the block as a young man and he was confident that when Linda woke up her first reflex would be to vomit, copiously.

She was muttering. "I got a man! Forty-five. Works for the Civil Service in City Hall. A nice modest man with glasses. I told the girls to go on home without me. He said he would leave me home. Diane wanted me to come home. She was *insistent*. 'I can't leave you here' she kept saying. 'Please come home with us, Linda!' but I wouldn't listen to her. He was a nice modest man with glasses. Forty-five. Works for the Civil Service in City Hall . . ."

Oliver sat with her the rest of the night. He mopped up when she vomited, he stroked her hair when she cried. It was surprisingly soft, just as her soft tears of self-indulgent self-pity were surprisingly moving.

It was difficult to reconcile this unhappy bruised old tart with the kind woman who had spent half the afternoon gently explaining the facts of life to Ciara – biological, emotional, educational: "Don't believe a word they tell you. They'll say anything to get into your knickers. They'll promise you the sun, the moon and the stars. Afterwards you'll never see them again . . ."

Now Oliver understood why the women of Arabia were veiled in black at the onset of puberty. Suddenly it didn't seem like such a drastic measure any longer when you thought about how many feckless men there were in the world – walking, talking, violent volcanoes of testosterone.

The minute his sons woke up he was going to review their understanding of the facts of life for boys. This time he was going to make it very clear that surging testosterone was not an excuse for disrespectful behaviour towards women who were lovely, inconsistent creatures, much given to the changing of their minds. At all times they should be handled lightly and with care.

"Like flammable liquid," said Oliver.

30

Kathleen had another brilliant idea. They were just shooting out of her. This was how it felt to be brilliant; it felt brilliant!

"Steady on, Victor!" said Kathleen for his hand was straying across the bed sheets. It was poised to land, with devastating accuracy, on an erogenous zone. When it landed, it would immediately banish all creative thought.

Kathleen wriggled away from the dangerous hand and quickly grabbed the notebook on the bedside table, specially placed there since the inauspicious evening of her first brilliant idea when Victor's hand had crept across the bed sheets and she hadn't bothered to write down what she was thinking and after lovemaking he'd thought her cranky because their passion was spent and the brilliant idea was forgotten.

"You interfered with my concentration!"

He was huffed. "I'm sure there are lots of women who can think creatively and make love to their husbands at the same time."

She wasn't amused. "Men think with only one organ, Victor, and it's not the brain!"

There'd been a week of smouldering and flouncing while Victor learnt his lesson: that he who pulls his hand away, lives to love another day.

Victor tried not to feel frustrated but it almost seemed as if his creeping hand was the source of Kathleen's inspiration for without fail when he felt amorous, she felt inspired. Victor tried to cheat the hand by pouncing at different times of the evening and in different locations: while they were dining, or watching the news together or when Kathleen was showering after a run. It didn't make a bit of difference. Up went his erection, out came her notebook and pencil. Victor was beginning to feel violated and not in a nice way.

"What is your brilliant idea, my darling?"

If he stretched his neck he could read *"dress rehearsal"* and *"eclectic mix"* and *"Alice's baptism"* in bold print, underlined.

"We need a trial run of my table," said Kathleen.

Kathleen's table was one of her many brilliant ideas. And special thanks to the old dear at the Golf Club who'd won Dinner for Two in the Ladies' Day raffle and after a couple of stiff sherries, admitted, "Well, I'll not be taking my husband with me, for what on earth would we talk about all night? He's interested only in politics and I'm interested only in golf."

A firework went off in Kathleen's brain. She had discovered an untapped market – everyone in the world who loves to eat out but dreads a night of dull conversation with a long-term spouse.

"If they were all sitting together at the one table they could chat to each other!"

Victor was amused, but also impressed. "You intend using your mother's parlour as a knocking shop?"

"I said 'chat,' not 'chat up'!"

"Same difference!"

Kathleen scoured every auction room and furniture warehouse in Ireland until she found a twelve-seat table with carved matching chairs, sold cheap because nobody wanted to cook for twelve any more, unless they were getting paid for it.

This table would be the centrepiece of Kathleen's restaurant.

She brought it home and cleaned it, polished it, shone it, draped it in antique white linen, dressed it with Irish Wedgwood, Newbridge silver and Waterford crystal – it was another brilliant idea, to use her wedding presents that were still in their fancy packaging.

"Such a waste when they're only for looking at."

Kathleen's table sat, fully dressed, in Kathleen's good room. Often she slipped in to visit it, after a long day at the bank. Its splendour never failed to make her smile. It reminded her of a bride, fully decked for her husband and still virginal, waiting for the appointed hour, when she would leave the seclusion of her mother's good room to take centre stage, on the first day of the rest of her life.

For there was just one minor detail in the grand scheme of Kathleen's brilliant ideas: Cecily hadn't said "No" to the idea of a country-house restaurant in her parlour, but she still hadn't said "Yes".

"We'll see," said Cecily.

Victor's carefully folded hands were on top of the bedspread and his face was inscrutable. He was the perfect picture of a house-trained husband, though inside his hormones were boiling. If Kathleen did not soon stop scribbling he was going to have to take a cold shower.

Kathleen said, "What I propose is that Jane invites twelve for a lunch party after Alice's baptism. She can choose whoever she likes and cook whatever she wants provided it's seasonal, fresh and organic. We'll put my table in her living-room and use the Irish Wedgwood, Waterford crystal and Newbridge silver. We'll have to start praying now that she doesn't invite Trevor Mountain for he's bound to break one of my glasses . . ."

"You are proposing to upstage Alice's baptism."

It was a criticism, not a question.

Kathleen put down the notebook and snuggled closer into Victor. Softly she unfolded his hands and kissed them. She kissed his mouth. It was stiff and unyielding but she continued to kiss him until he relented and kissed her back. Then she relaxed back into the bed and allowed his hand to stray where it wanted.

Afterwards, when she knew he was beyond caring she said, "It's about time Alice was baptised. I am *facilitating* the baptism . . ."

Alice was now six months old which was traditionally rather late for a baptism. It wasn't that Jane had forgotten, just that the furnishing and finishing of her new house was taking longer than expected. These things always do. The building of a house, like the rearing of a child, is always a work in progress; there is always room for improvement.

First she'd wanted to wait till the outside was painted. It wasn't asking a lot and Michael had agreed since gawky grey plaster makes any house, no matter how fine, look unfinished: "And I'll not have anybody saying we ran out of money."

But there were forty days of rain after the painter arrived. He sat in the stainless-steel kitchen, drinking cups of tea and eating Cecily's soda bread, waiting for a break in the clouds, until Michael finally remarked, "Maybe we should have built a boat instead of a house."

It was the wettest autumn on record and by the end of it the rain had washed away the old lane, leaving a boggy impassable track. They'd had to order ten tons of gravel to throw down and use a tractor with clean wheels to compact it, so the painter's van didn't get lost down a hole when it finally stopped raining and he was able to paint the outside a lovely grey-green colour which matched the grey-green roof tiles, so the house blended utterly into its surroundings.

"We live in a tree-house!" said Patrick.

"Please can we have the baptism now?" asked Cecily for soon Alice would be too big for the Temple christening-gown which was an antique thing in bleached white cotton, made for tiny newborns in the days when babies were baptised immediately after birth, in case they died. Without a baptism they couldn't be buried on church soil and their innocent little bodies were left outside the church walls, in ground that was not consecrated, as a solemn reminder to the next young mum to get her priorities right. Baptism was a holy necessity, not an excuse for a lunch party and the showing off of one's new house.

But by then Jane had developed a hankering for pitch-pine floorboards, like the floors at Temple, where each board was nearly an inch thick, warm underfoot, lightly sprung and beautiful to admire. But short of taking a crowbar and prising them up . . .

"I don't think they'd look right in a new house," said Michael who had very real concerns that one day he might come in from the milking and find her on her hands and knees nailing them down in her tree-house while his mother phoned the police to report the mysterious theft of a roomful of old floorboards.

"The originals wouldn't, you're right! But my new best friend Annabel Carson tells me you can buy old floorboards from linen mills and whiskey distilleries and libraries and have them resawn into wide planks. She bought them for Granny Carson's granny flat. She's given me the number of a place near Derry that delivers."

Michael said, "Wouldn't a nice linoleum do, with floorboards painted on it?"

"Now can we have the baptism?" asked Cecily, for if you believed everything you were told, a baby who was not baptised was left floating in limbo, not good enough for heaven, not bad enough for hell.

Jane had laughed at her mother-in-law. "If this child dies it will be because you have killed her with kindness!"

Kathleen came bearing gifts. It was something she'd learnt late in life, but better late than never, that the catching of flies is easier with honey than vinegar.

She wasn't asking for much, not if you looked at it from her point of view, and Jane had always planned to have a lunch party to celebrate Alice's baptism.

It was Sunday afternoon and Jane's tree-house was strangely quiet. Usually Kathleen was swarmed before she'd even opened the car door – by Susie dishing out compliments: "Your hair is lovely, Auntie Kathleen," and Patrick demanding, "What have you brought us, Auntie Kathleen?"

"Is your mother watching, children?" she'd ask and, once they were sure that Jane couldn't see, indulgent Auntie

Kathleen would covertly hand over a bag of sweeties and shoo them away to the bottom of the garden to eat them. This was their little secret, Kathleen and Susie and Patrick, for though Jane did not forbid sweeties she did not approve of them either.

"The only time Patrick ever tried swinging from the chandelier in Granny's parlour, singing 'Onward, Christian Soldiers' at the top of his voice was after a packet of Smarties – the sugar makes him mad!"

"Knock knock!" shouted Kathleen from the threshold of the tree-house.

"Come on in!" shouted Jane. "You're just the woman I'm looking for! I'm learning about nouvelle cuisine this week – French cooking without the fat and I have to give a presentation at the Catering College tomorrow morning. Will you taste something for me and give me your honest opinion?"

Kathleen was ushered into the kitchen and a plate of food thrust in front of her.

"Do you think there's too much pepper in the pâté?"

Kathleen rolled the pâté round her tongue. It was fabulously rich, with a tang of something: "Have you made this pâté with mackerel?"

"I have! Do you think my tutor will be impressed?"

Jane's cookery course at the Catering College in Derry was another of Kathleen's brilliant ideas. It was designed for experienced cooks, on day-release from full-time employment, who wanted to brush up on new culinary fashions and skills. There was only one day of classes a week – on Monday when most restaurants were closed. The rest of the course work was cooking assignments. Then there was a work-placement project for the entire month of February, in an approved restaurant, and a certificate at the end.

"Minimal disruption to your life!" said Kathleen who was usually never around on Sunday afternoon to watch Jane organising clean clothes and clean uniforms for Monday, or to help her check her assignments and the children's homework, make packed lunches and polish shoes, find Susie's library book and Patrick's football socks, cook a casserole and express more breast milk with a hand pump – Jane did this every day, punctually, then she froze her milk in Tupperware boxes, in the ice-box of the stainless-steel fridge.

"Five ready meals for Alice for Monday!"

Sometimes it got a bit manic so Michael took the children away in the Rapier for a mystery tour and ice-cream.

On Monday morning Jane drove out of the gates of Temple without a backward glance for her conscience was clear and her household was under control.

It sounded like a lot of bother; it was a lot of bother, but Jane wouldn't have changed it for the world. It had always been her ambition to go to Catering College and learn to be a professional cook, until she'd met Michael and married him.

Now, thanks to Kathleen, she was getting a second chance.

Kathleen had brought a bag of winter clothes for Jane with her usual story: how she'd tried them on in the shop and thought them beautiful, and had been seduced to buy because they were a bargain, but when she brought them home she'd discovered that they didn't suit . . .

In fact, this time, Kathleen had spent Saturday exclusively shopping for Jane. In particular, she'd been looking for an outfit for Jane to wear to her daughter's baptism. There was a Lady Di craze sweeping the fashion world, with pie-crust frills and voluminous skirts and everyone getting her hair cut into a pageboy – so pretty if you were under five or over ninety, but just awful on everybody else.

Kathleen had shopped long and hard to find an elegant sophisticated coat dress for Jane in deep plum velvet, with fur at the cuffs and collar; Cossack almost. And perfect with burgundy leather boots. It almost broke her heart to hand those over, she wanted them so desperately for herself.

"Try them on," urged Kathleen, "and I'll do the washing-up."

Jane tried on her new clothes in silence. This was an exquisite outfit on her: the plum velvet brought out the violet in her eyes, the fitted coatdress hugged her slender body. She might have searched for a month and have never found anything so lovely.

"I've just been to see my mother," said Kathleen. She tried to keep the sour note out of her voice for once again she'd been unsuccessful in her attempts to persuade Cecily to agree to the restaurant at Temple. "But no. It's not as if she has any other pressing plans for the rest of her life . . ."

Kathleen tried every day to be patient, but she desperately wanted to open at Easter. It was another brilliant idea. After six weeks fasting for Lent she knew her customers wouldn't be fussy about what she fed them. And there was always the extensive wine list as back-up if Jane burnt the soup. A couple of glasses after six weeks of abstinence would go to anybody's head, in the nicest possible way.

But Cecily wouldn't be rushed.

"It's not that I'm against the idea," she'd say for she was a practical little woman and had never been one for nostalgia. Temple was awfully empty now – there were rooms and bedrooms that she never went into any more, except to open the windows on a breezy day.

And living alone was a lonely business, punctuated by boring and pointless rituals. Often she didn't bother dishing up her dinner onto a plate, but ate it straight from the saucepan; sometimes she didn't bother cooking at all. Sunday afternoon in the uncomfortable parlour was particularly melancholic without Old Dave to poke fun at.

Increasingly it crossed Cecily's mind that if she agreed to Kathleen's restaurant Temple would be full of chatter all the time. Chatter and food. Kathleen thought maybe five courses and always a set menu of seasonal produce.

"We'd start with soup and your soda bread, Mother."

"So you'd expect me to help with the catering? What if I poisoned somebody?"

"With soda bread? Is that possible?"

Jane allowed the latest instalment in the Cecily – Kathleen battle of wills to gently wash over her head. She'd heard it all before, or something like it, for every unpleasant confrontation was a variation on the same theme, and afterwards Kathleen would phone her and say "My mother is a bad-tempered twisted old woman! I'm her only daughter and she won't oblige me."

And Cecily would come marching down the gravel lane to scold and seek solace.

"I wish she'd remember her Bible! '*Honour thy father and thy mother*' and all that."

Stuck firmly in the middle Jane sometimes thought fondly of Stove Pipe Town where she and her neighbours had lived on top of each other in tiny houses with thin walls, yet everyone had managed to maintain a dignified interpersonal distance.

Now, humming softly, she pulled her long dark hair up

into a chignon at the back of her head and swished up and down in the high boots, so high she was almost floating. She knew instinctively that Kathleen had bought this outfit especially for her. And that she wanted something. There was a keen, hunting look in Kathleen's eyes. Best put her out of her misery.

"Well, whatever it is that you want from me, Kathleen, the answer is 'yes'."

31

1st Derryrose was not a pretty church. There was no picturesque lynch gate or ancient graveyard. No antique headstones with lichen-encrusted inscriptions. No yew trees. Just a wide expanse of carefully maintained tarmac and inside the pews were as hard and uncompromising as a sinner's soul.

Years before there had been two churches and many had chosen to worship in the formal and old-fashioned surroundings of Lisglasson's picturesque and charming private chapel down by the lough. Morning Prayer was always packed at nine o'clock after the milking.

The rector was a likeable old fellow who lived in a tied cottage on Lisglasson estate. A poor relation who supplemented his stipend with a market garden, he was incumbent on Lord Laurence. Six days a week he drove round South Derry in a grocery van, selling vegetables. On the seventh day he washed his hands, put on his robes, got down on his knees and read the lesson out of the Prayer Book in a deep, musical voice that Michael and Kathleen were convinced was the voice of God when they were children. His wife taught in the village school.

When he died there were no applicants for the vacancy at Lisglasson and the old-fashioned chapel closed. The faithful were invited to worship in 1st Derryrose with its no-frills preaching and packed pews. Robust Evangelism suited some, like Old Dave Temple, but many others fell by the wayside. Cecily had stopped attending the first Christmas when everyone held hands and sang "Happy Birthday, Baby Jesus".

Today was Alice's baptism. Jane's chosen twelve, an eclectic mix of farmers and townies out of Stove Pipe Town were huddled together on the steps of 1st Derryrose and the only thing any of them had in common was their acute nervousness about entering the church.

"I've heard they make you pray in public!" said Diane who was self-conscious in a hat and gloves. "I've written out what I'm going to say, if I'm picked . . ."

"I've heard that they speak in tongues," said Linda. "What am I going to do? I'm hopeless at languages!"

She was finally wearing something that suited her – an A-line frock that flattered her narrow shoulders, big breasts and small hands, and it floated out over her ample hips. Her hair was its natural soft blonde and for once she'd left off the scary red lipstick. Mary was holding her hand.

Ciara said, "Don't worry, Linda, we'll help you. I'm learning French at school and Daddy speaks really good Irish."

"Cheer up, everybody!" said Kathleen who was resplendent in Prince of Wales check. "It's a baptism, not a funeral." She led the way right to the front of the church. "So everyone can see us!"

She was closely followed by Diane and Gerry, then Victor Rich and Cecily, Annabel Carson and Jimmy. Linda and Oliver and the family of ten brought up the straggling rear, Linda blushing in spite of herself at the frank and curious sightseeing of the country congregation. Didn't they know it was rude to stare?

Oliver smiled at her discomfiture. "It's just a new way of making heads turn, isn't it?"

Trevor Mountain stared at Linda from the choir, where he sang every Sunday in a loud, tuneful bass and shared a hymn-book with Bobby Flood. His big stupid heart leapt in its mighty chest and he sang louder because he hoped she'd look round at him. But she was far too busy ushering the McBride family into two pews. Oliver sat in front with five strapping boys who wore school uniforms because it was the only decent clothing they had. Linda sat behind with the younger children. The three girls were in lovely dresses that she'd sewn herself and thick black tights and school shoes; their hair was brushed until it was shining.

Two hours it had taken her this morning, to help Oliver get the children ready for church.

The hot water had run out after the seven boys were washed so she'd brought the girls into her own house and bathed them in her own bathroom with bluebell-scented bath oil, while Oliver polished shoes and shaved.

Linda couldn't help beaming with modest pride at the shining family sitting around her; Trevor didn't notice her leaning forward to lightly brush some fluff from the shoulder of Oliver's dark suit.

Bobby Flood hadn't seen Jane since the afternoon of Alice's birth, when her face had been distorted with pain and fear.

Before that he'd only ever seen her plastered or pregnant. And until Jane actually walked to the front of the church with Alice Bobby Flood hadn't consciously considered the baby. He only knew that there was a baby and her name was Alice, for he sometimes happened upon the old granny in the Village Spar or the post office where she'd be loudly boasting, "Alice held her own bottle this morning!"

Bobby had never been tempted to take a peep at the child under the cell blankets. For what would he do, if he looked at her and found his own green eyes staring back at him?

In an effort to take his mind off it Bobby had thrown himself into work. His new album had a working title of *The Walls Come Tumbling Down*. It was still at the lyrical stage, when he wandered around in a dreamlike state, with his mind carefully emptied of day-to-day minutiae, thinking beautiful thoughts.

Until his well-documented drying out Bobby had relied heavily on drink and drugs for his inspiration. Now he carried a dictionary and sometimes he happened on an interesting, random word which triggered extraordinary, creative thought. Some of Bobby's more poetic lines had sprung from this unconventional approach to songwriting and it was this which gave Achilles' Heel their star quality and their cult status and their critical acclaim. Bobby Flood had won a knighthood in the New Year's Honours List for his Services to Rock Music.

While Sir Bobby indulged in his lyrical phase, the East Wing of Lisglasson was being converted into a sound-recording studio and the whole first floor of the main part of the house transformed into four large apartments. This was where the rest of his band would live, each with his own entourage, while the album was being composed and recorded.

298

"I suppose we'll have to get caterers in," said Sir Bobby, for there wasn't even a chip shop in Lisglasson village.

"We'll cross that bridge when we come it," said Lady Millicent, who fully intended to be at the far end of the world when the rabble arrived, though she didn't even live in the main part of the house, finding it vast and draughty and unfriendly; she stuck to the cosy West Wing.

Bobby stared long and hard at the elfin child carried in Jane's arms, dressed in plain white cotton. There was plenty of time for staring for baptism in 1st Derryrose was a long hard formal business, with special hymns and audience participation. All members of the congregation were asked to help rear the child; this had always been Old Dave Temple's excuse for meddling in the business of his neighbours and their children.

Patrick Temple read a piece out of the Bible about how Jesus loved little children; Susie sang "Jesus Loves Me". Reverend Simms took the baby and threw water over her head and formally pronounced her "Cecily Alice".

It was an emotional moment and Bobby was overwhelmed. He'd been hitting the bottle quite heavy, the year his son Alex was born, and he couldn't have honestly told you if Alex was baptised or not. He had hardly any memories of Alex as a baby for the music industry was not child-friendly and Bobby had been far too macho to change a nappy, or give a bottle.

Bobby regretted that now. If he could have his time again, he'd not arrogantly squander his chance to share in the rearing of his own flesh and blood . . .

Bobby Flood whispered to Trevor Mountain, "What an enigma!"

Trevor assumed Bobby was referring to Linda, since he

had eyes for nobody else. Trevvie wasn't sure what an enigma was but he was immediately jealous – how dare Bobby Flood notice his woman?

After church Trevor Mountain took the scenic route home, through Stove Pipe Town. He hesitated briefly outside Linda's council house, but the street was strangely quiet and her house was empty. Everyone was at Temple.

Twelve adults were invited for lunch. And a million kids – but nobody cared what they thought of the cooking – they were getting bangers and mash in the kitchen. Michael had thrown down another ten ton of stones out the back, to make an area for ball kicking and skipping and running around. Horny was tacked up and tethered to the bin.

Kathleen's table took pride of place in the middle of the emerald living-room. It was draped in antique white linen, dressed with Irish Wedgwood, Newbridge silver and Waterford crystal. Kathleen had a seating plan and there were place names on stiffened card, neatly printed by Susie. One chair was empty. It wasn't deliberate. Mrs Somerville couldn't come. She had pneumonia. Kathleen thought it very inconsiderate of her.

"Now, please, everyone sit down and stick out your elbows and see if there's enough room for you to eat comfortably. And rock a bit on the legs of your chairs. I want to check none of them are shaky. Does everyone have enough leg-room?"

She positioned herself in the middle of the table with her Notebook of Brilliant Ideas. Oliver was seated beside her for there was something momentous she wanted to ask him but until she picked the right moment she was content to help Jane in the kitchen.

Bobby Flood pulled up in front of Temple in his Rolls. He

knew this wasn't Jane's house. He knew she lived at the bottom of the lane, in the tree-house with the turrets. He could see a Rapunzel tower from his bedroom window at Lisglasson now the leaves were off the trees.

Bobby Flood was not a modest man. What you saw was what you got, on stage and in life; a rock star must have ego to have charisma. Bobby could see Jane was entertaining for there were cars parked in the lane. He knew he'd cause at best a sensation on arrival, at worst a disruption, but he was going in with all guns blazing with a legacy for Alice. He would call it a baptism present and if anyone asked he'd say he had a vested interest in the infant having saved her life before she was born.

Bobby had stared long and hard at Alice in church and he could honestly say that she didn't even vaguely resemble him. This was what gave Bobby the confidence to do what he had to do. If Alice had been a boy or if he'd seen even the flicker of himself in her face he'd have known to leave well alone. Bobby had been at Lisglasson long enough to know now that country memories can stretch back for generations.

"I can't take all this," said Jane.

She was alone in the kitchen when he came to the door. Straining the turkey jus into the gravy, her hair had come loose from its topknot and was curling in tendrils round her face.

"It's not for you," he said. "It's for Alice."

Jane opened her mouth to refuse again but Kathleen burst into the kitchen. She was splattered with soup and swearing.

"We're going to have to hire waitresses, Jane. I'm utterly useless! I've just dropped a plate of vichyssoise on your wooden floor – thank God I didn't break the Wedgwood!"

She stuck her wrist under the cold tap. "I've burnt myself . . ."

"Allow me to help," said Bobby. "I waited tables in a fancy diner when Millie and me were saving to get married . . ."

He swept up the last four plates of soup from the counter, up his arm like something out of the movies, and carried them quickly out of the kitchen.

"Should I curtsy when he comes back?" asked Kathleen. "Now he's a Knight of the Realm?"

"You can kiss him for all I care," said Jane.

She was faintly affronted that the most famous rock star in Ireland had so casually turned up on her doorstep. And he was dressed to kill in a very sexy outfit – jeans, a leather jacket and dealer boots – the sort of clothes she was always trying to persuade Michael to wear and always failing.

"You dress like an old man!" she'd told him every day since she'd married him for she'd been reared among sexy city dressers and Michael always wore a formal dark suit when he wasn't wearing a boiler suit. Or country casual corduroy with turn-ups and brogues. Or tweed that went baggy round the bottom.

"It's such a waste!" said Jane, for Michael had particularly good legs – they were muscular and toned from walking after cows, running after sheep, strolling down to the village pub, and taking his family for Farm Walks.

"I'm not wearing jeans!" he told her, even though she got down on her hands and knees with the tape measure and ran it up his inside leg, from instep to groin.

"Thirty-three inches."

Then she'd measured his waist. It was thirty-three inches too.

"Thirty-three by thirty-three. Wow!"

"I'm *not* wearing jeans," he repeated for it was his

conservative country opinion that denim was sluttish on men, the male equivalent of the mini-skirt.

Bobby Flood returned to the kitchen.

"What's next, love?"

Jane solemnly regarded the most famous rock star in Ireland, dispassionately and with disappointment. She'd been his number one fan forever – since the summer of the Derry Emerald, when she was seventeen and had gone to the Town Hall to see him, in her brand new black halter-neck frock.

It was the first gig she'd ever been to and the first gig he'd ever played in Derry. Shy and young and overwhelmed, she'd watched him singing and gyrating on stage. He'd invited a girl up to dance with him . . . she'd wished it was her.

Up close and sober Jane realised she didn't find Bobby Flood attractive. Even in jeans. His legs were shorter than Michael's.

"Thank you for helping," said Jane politely, "but I think you've done quite enough already."

"Sir Bobby," said Kathleen, "if it wouldn't be too much bother, would you care to join our lunch party?" She spoke obsequiously but the keen hunting look was in her eye and before he had time to think of a tactful refusal Bobby was ushered into the emerald living-room, seated in Mrs Somerville's empty chair and introduced to Cecily.

"Sir Bobby Flood, Services to Rock Music. Sir Bobby, this is my mother Cecily Temple."

Cecily was a fan of royalty. She'd been very impressed with Bobby's knighthood when she'd read about it in the newspaper. She said, "Did you have to get down on one knee? Were you tapped on the shoulder with a sword? Was it Her Majesty? What was she wearing? Was she looking well?"

"It was Prince Charles. He said his mum was off in the Commonwealth somewhere."

"I'm told he has beautiful skin," said Cecily.

"And a beautiful wife," said Bobby.

Kathleen presented her new guest with a plate of vichyssoise. And stood over him while he ate it. Diligently Bobby spooned the soup into his mouth. He could feel Kathleen's hot breath on his neck – in spite of himself, he was faintly aroused.

"Delicious!" said Bobby. "What's next?"

Jane said, "Roast turkey with potato mousse, buttery cabbage and a warm salad of baby leeks."

"What made you choose turkey?" asked Kathleen for it was the least sexy bird on the market and conjured up horrible memories of indigestion and disappointment when she was a child and Santa Claus hadn't brought anything she'd wanted, again.

From her end of the table Cecily said proudly, "It was my idea. Trevor Mountain's mother sells her surplus half price, now that Christmas is over. They tick all the boxes, Kathleen, for they're organic, seasonal and fresh. I went myself to choose this one, for you know those Mountains are as cute as weasels and if Jane had gone they'd have tried to *do her.*"

"Mrs Mountain deals in all manner of poultry," Jane announced solemnly. "Ducks and geese and guinea fowl. Mrs Temple has offered to source other organic seasonal produce from the smallholders up the mountain when I'm gone to Dublin for my work placement."

Cecily added importantly, "There's a country woman comes to the market yard sometimes – she makes lovely cheese from goat's milk. She bought the goats to help with her son's eczema and there was always some milk left over so she taught herself cheese-making out of a library book . . ."

"I take it, Mother," said Kathleen carefully, "that you're finally reconciled to the idea of a restaurant at Temple?"

Finally Cecily said the magic words.

"Wasn't it my idea to start with?"

Cecily's capitulation left Kathleen free to concentrate on Oliver McBride. She was still waiting for the right moment.

Her latest brilliant idea was to take a sabbatical from the bank while she got her restaurant organised.

She had burst into Victor's office on Friday afternoon and told him, "I'd like thirteen weeks off. We can call it maternity leave if you like."

Victor had looked over the rims of his spectacles. It was disconcerting but exciting how Kathleen sprang these things on him without him ever guessing. Here she was, buoyant with impulse, but his bank manager's office was hardly the time or the place.

"When would you like your maternity leave to commence, Mrs Rich?"

"When Jane goes to Dublin for her work placement."

Victor frowned. "But that's next week! You're not leaving me much time to find a replacement."

"No need to look. I've found you someone already."

She was confident of that. Why wouldn't Oliver McBride take the job when she was about to hand it to him on a plate? He'd been the assistant bank manager for years. He was experienced and well respected. If Victor Rich didn't like him it was for personal reasons not professional. And all his children were at school now, even Mary, so his house was empty from nine until three, and even then there were activities for the older children – football, chess club, swimming.

So Kathleen picked her moment carefully, before she sprang her brilliant idea on Oliver. Not too early in the meal in case he refused emphatically and it created an unpleasant atmosphere but not as late as the Tipsy Pudding with Mulled Wine in case it went his head. He was a Pioneer and it would take only a sniff of alcohol to put him under the table. This narrowed down her window of opportunity to some time during the turkey dinner.

Oliver said, "But I couldn't possibly come back to work, Kathleen. It's been years since I worked in the bank. It's been years since I worked!"

"It's only while Jane is in Dublin and until the restaurant is up and running."

Miserably Oliver played with the food on his plate. They were his baby leeks in the warm salad, and his potatoes in the mousse, but he should have known there was no such thing as a free lunch and that Kathleen Rich had singled him out to sit beside her because she wanted something.

It wasn't that Oliver didn't want to work, for contrary to popular opinion there are very few people in the world who genuinely prefer to stay at home every day, living on the breadline, never having money for anything except the bare necessities.

It was just that for a long time after Maeve died he hadn't been able to see anything clearly. Some primitive part of his brain had told him to get up in the morning and mind the children but the intricate and tricky details of his work at the bank – numbers, figures, formulae – had simply fallen out of his head; he hadn't been able to count to ten without pausing after six and puzzling.

Dr Hennessey told him, "You're suffering from shock. Give it time, man, she's only just dead."

And maybe if he'd had time and a bit of compassionate support from his boss, the sophisticated part of brain might have started to work again. Instead Victor Rich had summonsed him into his bank manager's office and formally asked him to consider an early retirement.

"But I'm only thirty-five!" said Oliver.

"You are the father of ten small children. They're your sole responsibility now your wife is dead."

Oliver had been too taken aback to try to negotiate part-time work or flexible hours or a job-share.

Quietly he offered to resign and Victor Rich hadn't stopped him.

"There are plenty of competent staff members within our banking team who will have no problem stepping into your shoes."

Gradually Oliver's brain returned to its normal high voltage and he realised, too late, that Victor Rich had punched very low in his petty and vindictive determination to get rid of him out of the bank.

"Victor Rich must hate my guts," said Oliver. Disillusioned, he turned his back on the corporate ladder.

"*Please* will you come back and cover for me?" Kathleen asked again.

Oliver told her firmly but with regret, "I honestly can't see how it could be juggled. I'm still the father of ten children. They're still my sole responsibility and my wife is still dead."

Linda spoke up from her side of the table.

"I'll help you, Oliver. I'll do the early shifts at the doctor's surgery and be home every day in time to collect the younger children from school."

Diane spoke up.

"I'll help you, Oliver. I'll walk them to school in the morning with Tim. We'll give their teachers my phone number as an emergency contact. If a child is sick I'll take charge."

Finally Victor Rich said what he should have said eight

years before when Oliver had received the phone call to the bank that his wife was in hospital, having her baby and something had gone wrong and he must come immediately.

"I have to go to the hospital," Oliver had apologised.

"Another baby!" said Victor, and he'd found it particularly difficult to keep a sneering tone of suppressed jealousy out of his voice, for this was Oliver's tenth child in ten years and he himself didn't even have a wife any more. "Can't it wait till visiting time?"

So Oliver waited till visiting time. But by visiting time Maeve was dead.

Now Victor leaned across the table and said, "I'll help you, Oliver. Any way I can. You only have to ask."

Kathleen said gaily, "This is going to be a learning experience for both of us, Oliver! We can compare notes! You can phone me for banking advice and I'll phone you if I have any concerns about the children!"

For Jane was going to Dublin for a month and Kathleen was determined not to worry her with day-to-day trivialities.

"Don't worry about a thing!" Kathleen told her "I'm in charge and we're going to have a wonderful time!"

32

His first day back at work, Oliver phoned to ask Kathleen about sorting codes. Some had changed since his compulsory resignation and he hesitated to approach Victor Rich; it is easier to forgive a knife in the back than it is to forget about it.

Kathleen heard the shrill shrieking of the telephone and lifted it but there was such a racket going on round her that she wasn't sure who she was talking to. Patrick had been manic since breakfast, since eating a bowl of Frosties.

Susie had tried to warn her. "Mummy doesn't allow us to eat sugar-coated breakfast cereal. She says it makes Patrick mad!"

"I should hardly think so!" said Kathleen. Jane was such a fusspot when it came to the children's food – the list of what they weren't allowed to eat was stuck to the door of the stainless-steel fridge; it was alphabetical and exhaustive. Indulgent Auntie Kathleen thought that perhaps Susie and Patrick were the only children in South Derry who had never had Frosties for breakfast.

Within ten minutes she was eating her words. Instead of quietly brushing his teeth and getting his schoolbag ready Patrick had stripped off naked, put his Y fronts on top of his head and was running madly through the tree-house screeching.

"Who's speaking please?" Kathleen roared into the phone – first chance she got, the Frosties were going into the bin and everything else on Jane's list.

"It's Oliver McBride!" shouted Oliver but the noise was too deafening for her to hear him.

Kathleen took two of Susie's prettiest outfits from the wardrobe and presented them with a flourish.

"Would madam prefer a dark blue jersey dress or a red and purple corduroy pinafore?"

Susie pointed to the jersey dress. "But I don't want to wear a polo neck with it."

"Darling, you always wear this cream polo neck with this dress. They match."

"I don't want to wear a polo neck."

"If you won't wear the polo neck you'll have to wear the pinafore. There's a red long sleeved T-shirt to go with it."

Quietly Susie changed into the red T-shirt and the pinafore. She allowed Kathleen to help her drag on the matching red tights. Then she said, "I want to wear my new trainers."

"No, darling. You know the rule. You wear your red shoes with red tights and your trainers with trousers."

Softly Susie began to cry. "I want to wear my trainers! I want to wear my trainers!"

"Please stop crying, Susie. I cannot allow you to wear trainers with a dress –"

"I want to wear my trainers! I want to wear my trainers!"

"Then you'll have to take off the pinafore and the red T-shirt and the red tights."

Kathleen laid out three pairs of trousers on the bed.

"I want to wear my trouser suit that Mary of the Sorrows gave me!"

"Susie, you can't wear it. It's grubby and old and there are holes in the knees. Please choose something from the top of the bed . . ."

"I want to wear my trouser suit that Mary of the Sorrows gave me!"

When Michael came in from the milking he found Kathleen standing in the middle of the stainless-steel kitchen, gulping at a large Bloody Mary and frantically dialling the bank.

"What are you doing?"

"What does it look like?"

Oliver said, "Let her wear what she wants, Kathleen! Save your fire power for the important rows."

When Kathleen smelt urine in her wellie she at first assumed it was Ruby the dog. The naughty thing must have slipped in through the back door and lifted her leg when she was preoccupied with Baby Alice, fifteen bags of shopping, the school bags and the swimming bags –

"Susie, Patrick, is the dog upstairs with you?"

Kathleen didn't want to start shouting again, not after this morning when she'd been trying to hurry them out to the bus and Patrick had jumped up and down in a puddle at the back door until his shoes and socks and the bottom of his trousers were filthy.

"What did you do that for, Patrick?"

He'd refused to change into clean trousers and he wouldn't take off his socks. He kept saying "You can't tell me what to do, you're not my mummy!" and Susie was shouting "We're going to miss the bus, Auntie Kathleen!" and Alice was squealing from her car seat.

Kathleen had snapped and smacked Patrick. "*Get your trousers and socks changed and get into the car!*" she'd roared.

Nobody spoke. There was an ugly red mark on Patrick's leg. Her fingers were brightly outlined on his pale skin.

Patrick changed his clothes and they climbed into the car. She set off down the lane with oaths and revving. They missed the bus at the gates of Temple but chased it successfully into the village. The children got onto the bus and went to school without even closing the car door behind them. She picked them up after swimming lessons and they didn't speak to her.

Now her wellie was saturated in urine.

"Is the dog in the house, children?"

They were very subdued, shifty even, particularly Patrick.

"Ruby's away with Daddy, to fetch the pregnant ewes from the foot of the mountain."

When Michael came home from the foot of the mountain he found Kathleen slumped at the kitchen table, gulping at a large Bloody Mary.

"Kathleen! It's four in the afternoon! What's wrong with you?"

"I slapped your son for jumping in the puddle at the back door this morning. When he got home from school he peed in one of my wellies."

Michael said, "I should've filled in that hole ages ago. I'll throw down some stones before the milking."

Was it really only a week since Jane had driven off into the wide blue yonder?

Kathleen could safely say that it had been the most challenging week of her life for Susie and Patrick had treated her like a servant.

"Get me a drink of water, Auntie Kathleen."

"Where are my school tights, Auntie Kathleen?"

"Why have you not made chocolate Rice Krispie buns for the Bring 'n' Buy Sale?"

"No, you can't come into my bedroom, Auntie Kathleen, it's private."

And she'd turned into a fishwife.

"You're not getting a drink of water until you say 'please', Patrick!"

"How would I know where your tights are, Susie, they're far too small for me to wear!"

"I can't make chocolate Rice Krispie buns, because I forgot to buy Rice Krispies! Would chocolate Cornflake buns do instead?"

"How am I going to change your sheets if you won't let me into your bedroom?"

And she couldn't get out to the gym for a run, unless she starting planning at least two hours in advance. It had to be morning, when Susie and Patrick were at school, preferably during Alice's rest time – but she had to be fast asleep and swaddled when she was left with Cecily for this was the only time that Cecily could be trusted to follow her strict instructions to leave the baby alone. Left to her own devices,

Cecily nursed Alice all morning and she got over-handled and overtired and Kathleen had hell to pay in the afternoon when she also had Susie and Patrick's dinner to make, their homework to supervise and extra driving around for after school activities – Patrick visited Diane from Next Door three afternoons a week for his reading grinds and Susie had swimming and Girls' Brigade.

And even then, in the morning, if Alice started to screech, or needed her nappy changed, or needed a bottle, it was another half an hour. Kathleen had started to wear gym gear and a shell suit all the time, in the optimistic hope of a window of athletic opportunity . . .

"What did you expect it to be like?" asked Oliver.

One week down, three weeks to go – Kathleen marked the calendar with a chunky red marker pen.

It was Saturday night and she was getting a pass out. Victor was taking her to the Opera House though frankly she'd have settled for a night's unbroken sleep in her own bed.

"How have you been?" asked Victor politely when she finally got into his car with him, after emptying the dishwasher, brushing the kitchen floor and putting on another load of washing.

He'd seen her only briefly during the week and at inopportune moments – when she was struggling with a screaming baby in the butcher's, or roaring at Susie and Patrick for wrecking the Children's Corner in the bank. And though he loved his wife he'd been moderately disgusted by her physical appearance for her hair had been hanging in greasy strands and her face was not washed and she seemed always to be dressed in a pink and lilac shell suit which he remembered her buying as a bit of a joke during her diet binge.

Kathleen said, "Best week of my life! I understand now why Jane has no problem staying thin. She doesn't have time to eat!"

She was fast asleep in the passenger seat before Victor reached the main gates of Temple.

33

Michael missed Jane and it wasn't just Jane in the bed or Jane in the kitchen, though of course he missed those too. In ten years together they'd never spent a night apart, except when she was in hospital and that didn't count because it was circumstances beyond her control.

Now she was spending a month away from him and he couldn't help wondering if she might develop a taste for it.

The first week he'd taken her to Dublin though she'd cheerfully offered to go by bus.

"I've checked the timetable and phoned the Bus Office. The Express will stop for me on the main road at three minutes past five. I'll be in Dublin by ten o'clock."

"No wife of mine is travelling by public transport," said Michael who had a horrible picture of Jane struggling with her leather suitcase, unable to successfully hail a cab, in torrential rain, at night; an innocent in a foreign land.

She was booked to stay in Flowers Hotel and it was important to him that he inspect the room before she was allowed in it, though of course with Kathleen at the organising there would be nothing to worry about. But he still had to know there was a lock on the door and no fire escape outside the window where a rapist might climb up to her.

"You watch too many cop shows on TV," said Jane, but the fact was that Michael had always lived in the country and Dublin was as foreign to him as Tokyo or New York.

"If I give you this hammer, will you put it under your pillow when you're sleeping, in case somebody breaks in to the room to murder you?"

"I will not!"

They left straight after the milking on Sunday morning. It was going to be tight, the turnaround, for it took four hours to get to Dublin, a meandering route through Cookstown, Dungannon, Armagh, Newry, Dundalk, Drogheda and little Balbriggan on the sea front before reaching the city itself, which he'd only ever driven through once, to take her to the final of Ireland's Emerald in 1971 and that time they'd got so lost they'd had to park up on a street called North Circular which they seemed to be driving around in a circle and ask a taxi driver to take them the last mile.

"Why don't you ask Mountain to do the evening milking?" said Jane, for Michael's old Rapier had a top speed of fifty, with the wind behind it, going down a hill. And already they were stuck in Derryrose Village while the decent and devout of deepest South Derry, with Trevor Mountain among them, queued to get into the church car park.

"No time!" said Michael which was prophetic for when they finally reached Dublin after four hours and thirty-five minutes he realised that he had exactly fourteen minutes to

317

spend a penny and stretch his legs before setting off again, homeward bound. A hundred full-breasted dairy cows had a hot date with him, in the milking-parlour, at four o'clock.

"Why did you have to pick a restaurant so far away? Isn't The Rainbow's End a restaurant? Couldn't you have had a work placement there?"

Jane said, "You've no idea how lucky I am to get a placement in The Townhouse – they're a very exclusive establishment."

It was true that The Townhouse never took students. Henri La Salle, the proprietor, had made that clear many times to the catering colleges of Ireland. But it was also true that Henri La Salle had never before had to deal with Kathleen Rich who was determined to have Jane's modest culinary qualifications enhanced with the gold-plated endorsement of having trained at The Townhouse, which everyone had heard of even if no one had ever eaten there.

"Far too dear and they charge you for tap water . . ."

After a dozen rebukes by telephone she'd turned up on Henri La Salle's doorstep with a thermos flask of Jane's vichyssoise.

"Which part of 'No' don't you understand, Mrs Rich?"

"I've just driven this soup a hundred and forty miles from South Derry. Taste it and tell me that it's not better than the signature vichyssoise you serve in The Townhouse."

She'd unscrewed the lid of the thermos flask and wafted it under his nose. In spite of himself Henri La Salle had sniffed. And hesitated. There was something enchanting about the top notes of the vichyssoise; it had a glass-shattering purity which Henri rarely smelt, even in his own restaurant. It made him think of flagstoned country kitchens, sturdy round-shouldered country women, friable rich soil between his fingers . . .

While he was lost in this reverie Kathleen deftly poured the soup and with great ceremony offered it to Henri to taste . . .

The minute he put the spoon to his mouth she knew she had him . . .

Michael listened vaguely to his wife's excited chatter. He hadn't a clue what she was talking about.

"Vichyssoise . . . that's just a fancy name for the leek and potato soup you make every day, isn't it?"

Jane grinned. "There's no chance of my head swelling when I'm married to you, is there?"

Buried in the country all his life, up a long lane, Michael knew nothing of the art of goodbye. He didn't know that it's always easier to be the one who goes, than to be the one who is left behind.

It was only when he was back at Temple, back in his boiler suit, back in the milking-parlour, that he fully realised that Jane was gone away and she wasn't coming back for a month.

"Don't you get time off? Isn't it a legal requirement?"

"It'll be half a day now and then and I'll always be on call. Kathleen says it's very important to show willing when you're new to a job!"

"What will you do on your half-day off?"

"In a large, beautiful city like Dublin, with art galleries, museums, concert halls, libraries and old churches?"

Sometimes he desperately needed to talk to her. It was like a pain or an addiction and it always happened in the middle of the night. He'd wake up, he who had never had trouble sleeping, and lie tossing. He was torn between his urge to phone her and his sensible consideration; it was the middle of the night, she would be sleeping, he would wake her.

Instead he went downstairs and made a cup of tea and desperately wrote down what he wanted to say: how he missed her with a pain that he couldn't locate, how the house was empty without her, how looking at her photograph didn't help but banging his head off a wall relieved some of the pressure.

His handwriting was a scrawl. He couldn't find a pencil so he wrote with crayon. He couldn't find a piece of paper so he used toilet roll. It was a passionate love letter, from a man who didn't know the difference between "b" and "d" until he was fifteen.

One of Jane's more fanciful ideas for her house had been to dispense with curtains.

"What's the point when we're at the end of a long lane? There's nobody to see in. I want to be able to see out!"

It was an inspired idea for daytime, especially in the living-room with its emerald green walls and large windows; in a dusky twilight it was difficult sometimes to see where the living-room ended and the field outside began.

Night was a different matter entirely. Michael was not an imaginative man and Jane was so slender she took up hardly any space but sitting in front of the television with Kathleen passed out on the sofa beside him, dribbling and shouting out in her sleep – "Stop that!" and "Come back here!" and "Hand over those sweeties!" – he felt very alone, and worse than lonely, he felt watched by eyes in the dark that he couldn't quite see.

"I think I'm going mad!" said Michael.

When anybody asked, Michael told them that Jane was having a wonderful time in Dublin. And people were constantly asking, people he hardly knew, most of them men. For example, the school bus driver said. "It must be nice for her, going back to the Big Smoke. That's where you found her, wasn't it?" as if she was unique and rare, something he'd searched for, fought for and carried home victorious after perils and adventures.

Victor Rich said, "She'll be a triumph in The Townhouse for there's not a finer nose in Ireland."

Bobby Flood added, "Nor a finer arse."

Since gatecrashing Alice's baptism, Sir Bobby had become a feature round Temple. Himself and Cecily were thick as thieves and every morning he temporarily stopped his lyrical wanderings and parked himself in Cecily's kitchen. Sometimes he sang his new songs to her and to Alice who sat on his knee and kept time with a wooden spoon beaten against the table.

Cecily was an inspiring critic. "You can't rhyme 'enchanting' with 'gallanting' – 'gallanting' isn't even a word!"

"Yes, it is!" and he dived deep into his dictionary:

"'*Gallant: a young man who tries to impress women with his fashionable clothes or daring acts.*'"

"Gallant is a noun, Bobby. That means it's a naming word. 'Gallanting' is a verb and it's not in the dictionary so you can't use it. Not even in a pop song. I'm sorry . . ."

Michael came in from the milking and helped himself

quietly to a cup of strong tea and listened, mystified, to the banter crossing the table.

Was this really his mother, who'd been an old bag for so long that he couldn't remember her ever being anything else? His mother who seemed to have done something with her hair for it looked less like silage than usual? Who was wearing lipstick? Who was flirting with Bobby Flood?

"What verb would you suggest I use, Cecily?"

Cecily dusted the soda-bread flour from her hands and smiled an engaging smile.

"Read me the chorus line again, Bobby . . ."

Of course, Michael did hope that Jane was having a wonderful time, that she wasn't homesick, or unhappy, or fretting. The fact that she hadn't phoned him was a good sign, wasn't it? Sometimes he loitered unnecessarily long in her stainless-steel kitchen, watching the phone, and picking it up to make sure it was working. At his mother's house he stuck a notepad and pen beside the phone in the hall, just in case she phoned there and Cecily forgot to tell him. But she didn't phone.

"You should get yourself a telephone answering machine," said Kathleen.

A couple of times Michael tried to phone Jane. Not to The Townhouse in case it got her into trouble but to the hotel where she was staying. Except the man on the desk said he was very sorry but he couldn't put phone calls through to Mrs Temple without her authorisation. This was a security measure that Michael himself had implemented during the fourteen-minute drop-off at the start of her work placement. He'd thought it might save Jane hassle from unwelcome callers; he had not at the time fully realised that he might also be classified as "unwelcome".

Michael became frantic. Never before in their marriage had Jane not been immediately available to him.

After the milking he went into his mother's house for strong tea and soda bread and solace.

Bobby Flood was parked in the kitchen again, nursing Alice and singing. Today he was trying to persuade Cecily that "enchanting" could rhyme successfully with "dancing".

Michael wished Bobby would go home.

"He can't go home," said Cecily. "That wife of his is bad to him. She's always complaining about something. It's no wonder he took drink and popped pills when you think of what he's had to listen to for the past twenty years. She won't let him rest his elbows on the table when he's eating and she's obsessed with the positioning of the toilet seat after he's finished in the bathroom, even though our Bobby told her: 'Sweetheart, Millie, when I was a-rearing, we had a redbrick privy at the end of the garden. It was a bucket, and there was no toilet seat.'"

Michael burst out: "I've not heard from Jane in over a week. Do you think she might have been knocked down, and is lying concussed in a hospital, and can't remember her name?"

Bobby said, "More likely she's out having fun. A good-looking woman like Jane, young and free in Dublin – she might never come back to you . . ."

This was, of course, exactly what Michael had been too afraid to think. He immediately rushed home and upstairs, into their bedroom and flicked frantically through Jane's wardrobe. What a relief! Her black halter-neck frock was still hanging. He buried his face in its folds. It smelt of her.

Kathleen said, "I don't know what you're fussing about. You *know* restaurants don't keep regular hours. That's the point of them, that they're open for fine dining and entertainment when the rest of the world has stopped work. Weekends at The Townhouse are especially busy for on Sunday they serve a world-renowned buffet lunch and there are three sittings."

34

Rupert Glass got out of the car and looked up the higgledy piggledy village street. Its straggle of houses was just as he remembered: butcher, baker, pub, undertaker, the Village Spar which sold everything else.

Rupert had spent a lot of time in Lisglasson village when he was growing up. It was so boring at the Big House, with his mother lying full drunk in the drawing-room and four bossy older sisters schooling ghastly horses over show-off fences. Even now Rupert found it hard to believe that there were men in world prepared to marry such hearty, horsy women, the life and soul of every house party, when there were so many other more alluring types to choose from.

"Because there's no mystery about them!"

Lord Laurence made that sound like a good thing, yet Rupert had noticed, in his formative years, that his father was almost invisible about the place. It was a skill that Rupert inherited. Nobody noticed when he quietly slipped away to the village pitch and joined in with the local boys in free-for-all football, without rules and hierarchy. He told them his name was Bert, as if anybody cared for boys are not snobbish and Rupert took the hard tackles with stoicism and tried not to look ridiculously pleased when somebody passed the ball to him.

Sometimes his sisters rode past, hacking out on their highly strung horses, groomed within an inch of their lives, so haughty with their noses in the air. They spoke a private language: "He's behind the bit, Prudence,", "Kick on there, Jenny!" They never noticed their little brother, crouching behind the goal posts pretending to tie his shoelaces. The very fact of his ordinariness was his most successful camouflage.

Sometimes he was invited home, to somebody's house for tea, where he would remember always to say "Please" and "Thank you"; they were words he never used in his own house.

The village mothers felt sorry for Rupert who was a skinny little runt, unkempt and uncared for. But for his awfully nice turn of phrase – "I say, what a scrummy cake, Mrs Murphy!" – he might have been anybody, or nobody. They told their rough and ready sons to be kind to him.

Rupert's sisters had been educated at home until they were old enough to join the upper-class conveyor belt of prep school, boarding school and finishing school that would shunt them gently through childhood, girlhood and young adulthood until they emerged at the other end as perfectly polished marriage material with *no mystery*.

Their tutor was an effeminate man with soft hands. He wore bow ties and had a posh accent; it was as much his job to teach the girls to talk proper as it was to teach them to read. Lady Glass had borrowed him from a friend who had advised she get the Irish accents fixed before prep school or she'd be out a fortune in elocution lessons when the time came.

Rupert watched, with fascinated horror, his sisters walking through the rooms of Lisglasson, with books balanced on their heads, reciting in strangulated English: "*The rain in Spain falls mainly on the plain!*"

When it was his turn, he rebelled. He did not want to be educated at home by a poof and he did not want to change his accent. It sounded perfectly fine on the football pitches when he was shouting "Go, Jimmy!" and "Goal!"

"But you sound like a peasant, darling!"

"What wrong with that?"

Rupert appealed to his father. Lord Laurence was more visible about the place now his overwhelming daughters were at school. He could be found daily talking to the flowers in the garden or comfortably crouched in the kennels, sharing his dinner with the dogs.

"Please let me go to the village school, Father. I want to make friends with my neighbours."

"But doesn't your mother invite little boys up to the house for you to play with?"

Rupert scoffed. "They're not my friends! They're the sons of *her* friends!"

Lord Laurence hesitated. He had no friends either, though he had always longed for them. A few familiar faces with a shared history, casually dropping by unannounced for a cup of tea and a chat, not this horribly restrained, formal atmosphere, where even his wife booked him in for a conversation. Dogs were a man's best friend but Laurence wouldn't be sitting in the sunshine, sharing his dinner with them if there'd been anybody else to eat with.

These were the happiest years of Rupert's life, the primary school years. He sat between Michael Temple who smelled of cows and Trevor Mountain who was frankly mad and given to climbing out of the window and running away when he got his spellings wrong.

The village school was part of Lisglasson estate and there was only one teacher, the rector's wife. She really had her work cut out for her for her youngest student was not quite four and not quite toilet-trained and her oldest was Trevor Mountain who was still in her classroom learning to read when he'd grown a moustache and his voice had broken. And though some of the children were from the village, most of them were from nearby farms. They helped with the morning milking before they walked to school and when it was the lambing season or the calving or the potato gathering they didn't come at all.

"You horrible lot!" shrieked Mrs Rector who was middle-aged and menopausal and much given to shrieking.

At first Rupert was terrified, for he was used to being ignored. Quickly he learned to read her face and to know if her shrieking was anger or only emphasis.

At break-time they kicked a ball in the playground, or wrestled, or chased the girls. Rupert always chased the same one. Her name was Poppy; she had a Mono Lisa smile and was fleet of foot: "You'll never catch me, Rupert Glass!"

This pleased him rather, for he wouldn't have known what to do with her if he had caught her.

It was the making of him, the village school. Rupert didn't lose his Irish accent but he learnt how to make friends, how to be a team player, and how stand up for himself. When the Carson twins tried to beat up Michael, Rupert was first to his rescue, with his skinny hands bunched into fists.

Michael told him, "Put your thumb on the outside of the

fingers or it'll get broken when you punch and always punch hard into the chest between ribcages or you'll hurt your hand."

This simple piece of advice was one of the most useful things Rupert ever learned. It proved invaluable his first year at English public school when his classmates heard his accent and shouted "Paddy!" It took only a few scuffles in the dorms after lights out for them to realise that "Paddy" didn't pull his punches.

Lisglasson School closed after Rupert left. It was only his presence there which had kept it open at all for the school board decreed it uneconomical and the teaching was so poor that nobody ever passed the eleven-plus.

"Country children deserve better than this!" said the school board and a bus was organised to take them to the big bright school in the town where the headmaster and his team of truancy inspectors took a very dim view of any father who kept his child at home to help with the farming.

Lord Laurence sold the schoolhouse to an artist who made a very fetching studio of it.

All through English public school Rupert liked to delude himself that he was impervious to the superior education his parents were paying for, that he was still part of the proletariat. In the holidays he raced out of Lisglasson and down into the village, seeking out his old friends, who were always pleased to see him. This is a beautiful thing about boys, that they will continue to like you in spite of the silver spoon in your mouth. The girls were less forgiving. Poppy was married at sixteen to an ignorant brute of a builder who beat her up when he caught her smiling at him.

Gradually, like brainwashing, Rupert's expensive education

crept up on him. French is so much easier to learn when ordering a croissant in Paris, the history of Ancient Greece is so much more interesting when taught in the shadow of the Acropolis.

At eighteen, in spite of his best endeavours, he emerged from English public school a gentleman.

"What will it be?" asked Lord Laurence. "The Church, the Army, the City?" for by now the money was all spent and it was generally accepted that Lisglasson would have to be sold and Rupert must find a job.

Impoverished and eccentric though he was, Lord Laurence Frederick Rupert Glass was still tenth Baron Glass of Lisglasson in the County of Derry and he was still part of an exclusive network of terribly grand old boys in prominent establishment positions. A word in the right ear or an introduction to the right fellow and Rupert would be set up for life.

"The television!" said Rupert, and he charmed his way into Broadcasting House.

Rupert started at the bottom with employment so insignificant it did not have a job description. He lived in London with his unmarried sister, Prudence, in Daddy's flat in Chelsea, but only from Monday to Friday for the weekend started on Friday morning when they packed up the Golf GTi and travelled to grand country houses for Hunt Balls, shooting parties and school reunions. These houses were often the size of Lisglasson, or bigger, but unlike Lisglasson they had running water, bathrooms and electricity. There were armies of staff, in tidy uniforms. They addressed him as "Sir", and announced him at dinner as "The Honourable

Rupert Glass" which made him feel pompous and important until a title-free schoolfriend would shout "Paddy!" and the moment would be broken. Then the gold-digging girls would give him the glad eye while carefully checking his pedigree. Those who could face the thought of deepest South Derry would contrive to sit beside him at dinner and flirt with him into his face. At night they would bed-hop into his bed where he'd do his gentlemanly best to show them a good time.

"I don't fancy any of them!" Rupert complained.

"Then don't sleep with them!" said Prudence, who had earned for herself the unfair reputation of frigidity, when in fact she was only old-fashioned.

The simple fact was that the village school had ruined Rupert in his formative years. He'd seen the green grass over the fence and he knew there was more to life than a suitable wife with a healthy breeding pedigree. Poppy's enigmatic smile haunted him and he wasn't going to be content until he'd found a girl who was fleet of foot and made him do the chasing.

It took ten more years of country-house bed-hopping before Prudence finally caught a husband and Rupert finally realised he was homesick. He missed home. Not the Big House for he'd never liked living there, but Lisglasson village and South Derry and Ireland. It wasn't the same in England; he wasn't the same in England. There was a job going in Broadcasting House in Belfast. Rupert asked for a transfer.

"Are you quite sure?" asked the suits in London, for Belfast was a BBC outpost. It was where aspiring presenters started their careers before moving onwards and upwards to the bright lights of national television. And Rupert's career was going in the right direction fast, for the viewers loved him, especially the women – it was his pleasing mix of public school polish and Irish charm. After a successful run on *Blue Peter*, with guest appearances on *Saturday Swap Shop* and John Craven's *Newsround* he was hotly tipped to soon make the leap from Children's Television to the big time. His name was being seriously considered for *Top of the Pops*.

"It's career suicide to move back to Belfast," they cautioned him.

But of course he wouldn't listen. The Honourable Rupert Glass had carved for himself a noteworthy path in the real world but he still was heir to an aristocratic title and had inherited the arrogant self-belief that accompanies it.

In the end they reached a compromise. Rupert was borrowed by BBC2, which was funding an ambitious project called *From Our Local Correspondent* – a collation of feature-length documentaries, one each from a BBC regional outpost.

Rupert was given three months to research a unique and interesting documentary about the residents of Northern Ireland.

The *Belfast Telegraph* was complimentary on the flight back home and Rupert, crushed into the window seat, flicked through it.

The man sitting beside him heard him ask for "A cup of tea, if it wouldn't be too much bother, thanks awfully" and said, "First time into the North, is it?"

"Not at all," said Rupert in his soft hybrid voice of strangulated English with Irish vowels. "I'm from Ireland. I'm Irish. I'm going home."

Rupert left the car at the bottom of the village street and walked towards his ancestor's magnificent ornamental carved gates. He walked slowly, savouring the sunshine and the familiar smells of warm bread from the bakery and stale beer from the pub. Clutched in his hand was the *Belfast Telegraph* from the flight, carefully folded so the page on the top was the Business Section:

Lisglasson Shoot Closes. Business Men Weep

The Belfast business community received the sad news today that the pheasant shoot at Lisglasson, South Derry, is to close. The pheasant shoot has been a popular venue for corporate entertainment for many years. The pheasant-shooting season runs from 1st October until 1st February. The season has closed and the shoot has closed with it.

Lisglasson is the ancestral home of Lord Laurence Glass but was recently bought by Sir Bobby Flood, lead singer of Belfast rock band Achilles' Heel. Bobby Flood was knighted in the New Year's Honours list for his Services to Rock Music. He is not a fan of pheasant shooting and his wife, Lady Millicent, is a vegetarian and a lifelong campaigner against cruelty to animals.

So far, so predictable. Rupert was also an animal lover; he had never been a fan of the pheasant shoot. Not if he was starving would he put a piece of pheasant in his mouth.

It was the next part of the article which interested him.

Mr Albert Armstrong who was gamekeeper at Lisglasson for twenty-five years has been poached, no pun intended, by a large estate in County Tyrone.

This meant that for the first time ever the gamekeeper's cottage at Lisglasson lay empty.

Rupert had no fixed address in Ireland. There was no family house in Dublin, not even a holiday cottage on the North Antrim coast. When Lord Laurence sold Lisglasson, his move to England was forever. For the first time since Cromwell, there was no Glass at Lisglasson.

There was free-for-all football on the village pitch as always and Rupert watched for a minute. Today, being Saturday, it was men and boys together, Rupert thought he recognised some of them.

That monster in the middle, running with his head down, without much of clue, just had to be Trevor Mountain. Was he even running in the right direction? Did he care?

The little boy running alongside him, dribbling a ball on the end of his foot, looking around for someone to pass it to and shouting "Mountain, look up!" bore striking resemblance to Michael Temple, the dairy farmer he'd sat beside in the village school, who had taught him how to use his fists and how to punch straight.

And the dark, fit, handsome one in jeans and an anorak, running in to tackle young Temple – could that really be Sir Bobby Flood, lead singer of Achilles' Heel and current owner of Lisglasson?

Rupert hesitated at the edge of the pitch. He didn't expect anyone to recognise him for he was no longer a skinny little runt with bad teeth. Now he was a handsome and charismatic television presenter, well dressed and well groomed, a metrosexual man who had regular manicures, Turkish wet shaves and massages.

But he was still the boy who loved football and had loved being part of the village gang.

"Over here!" he shouted. "Pass it to me, young Temple! Your father always passed it to me!"

Patrick looked over and kicked the ball towards him. Rupert threw down the *Belfast Telegraph* and his overcoat, and ran joyfully onto the football pitch.

35

Flowers Hotel was just down the street from The Townhouse, they were both on the same ancient Georgian row. The Townhouse took up one house, Flowers Hotel was four houses knocked into each other. The street was stately and charming but not twee. It had black railings and wrought-iron lampposts and at ten o'clock on Sunday morning Michael had no problem finding a parking space.

It was Trevor Mountain's idea that he spend a couple of days in Dublin with Jane.

"For I can see you're fair worn out with missing her."

They'd been sitting together in the old man's pub in Lisglasson, after another game of football, with Bobby Flood, Rupert and Patrick. The men were each drinking a pint of Smithwicks. Patrick had Fanta orange and a straw. Everyone had a packet of crisps.

It was three weeks since Jane had gone to Dublin and though she'd phoned a couple times and spoken to him, Michael thought the calls unsatisfactorily brief.

"I can't control this call box! It says 'Push Button A' when I hear the beeps, but then it swallows the money . . ."

The phone calls had reassured him that she was alive and well but they'd also left him frustrated and tearful. He didn't want thirty seconds of small-talk. He wanted to drink out of her teacup, to eat off the side of her plate, to sit with her watching television, to hug her in bed.

He wanted his wife. It was written in bold print across his forehead.

"I'll do the milking for you," said Mountain, "and young Patrick here can help me."

Patrick beamed. He had a particular affection for Trevor Mountain, who took him for spins in his pick-up and had found him the first frogspawn for the Nature Table at school. Trevor had taught him how to belch and stretch like a man.

"They've the same mental age," said Kathleen.

Michael said, "That's very decent of you Trevor, for Jane's homesick and not settling."

"I'm thinking it's not Jane that's homesick," said Mountain.

Michael parked up and rushed straight into Flowers Hotel.

He told Reception, "Room 25. Jane Temple. My wife. Please call her and tell her I'm here."

"Mrs Temple left the building at six o'clock this morning. She arranged a wake-up call for five. Our night watchman unlocked the front door especially for her."

"What was she wearing?" asked Michael and then he wondered why the staff on Reception wouldn't allow him up to her room.

"But I'm her husband!" Michael protested.

"Of course you are," they said.

He went back out to the car, rolled down the seat and fell

asleep with the *Sunday Press* over his face. He was booked into the first sitting of the internationally acclaimed Sunday buffet at The Townhouse. In only a couple of hours he'd see his darling wife again. If anybody rapped the car window he'd pretend to be a foreigner.

"No speak English," he'd say and maybe they'd leave him alone.

Michael wasn't sure how long he'd slept for, in the Rapier, on the street between Flowers Hotel and The Townhouse. He only knew when he heard the gentle tapping on the car window that he'd been asleep for quite a while, with the *Sunday Press* over his face.

Michael was loath to take off the newspaper and wake up properly. This was the best sleep he'd had in three weeks, since Jane had left him and he'd started to worry about eyes in the dark. Three weeks of broken sleep can be easily managed by most people but Michael was carrying residual exhaustion, being a dairy farmer; it was one of the perks of his job. All the early rising and the long days in the fresh air ground you down in the end. Dairy farmers were old men at forty.

"Early to bed, early to rise," Michael always said because if he didn't get to bed early, he had an embarrassing habit of dozing off in socially inappropriate venues: the dentist's chair during root-canal treatment, in the barber's when the new boy had tried an Indian head massage. And every church service he'd ever been to that lasted longer than half an hour. Even the day he married Jane, he'd dozed off at the top table during the toast to the bridesmaids.

"Power naps," Michael called them.

The knocking on the window of the car continued. It was friendly and persistent, unwilling to take "No" for an answer. Michael lifted the *Sunday Press* from his face.

The first thing he noticed with a little jolt of surprise was that it was dark. The second, with a huge jolt of pleasure, that it was Jane. He wrenched open the car door and jumped out and hugged her. She felt even finer than he remembered.

"You've not been eating!" He buried his face in her hair. "And your hair smells funny."

She was wearing her beautiful coatdress that Kathleen had bought her for Alice's baptism. And the high-heeled boots though they both knew, intuitively, that Kathleen expected her to hand them back, sooner rather than later.

Michael added, "And you're dressed to kill!"

He didn't mean it to sound like an accusation, but in a way it was. For how dare she be in Dublin looking marvellous when he was at Temple missing her? She gave him a little twirl, on the frosty city street. There was something else different about her . . .

She said, "Well, you haven't changed a bit! You still look like a dairy farmer who's a long way from home! Please, will you kiss me now?"

So he closed his eyes and kissed her. It was strange at first for she felt different and smelt different and he'd been loyally kissing only the one woman, in his dreams and his reality, since he'd met her: Jane, his Derry Emerald, from whom he expected no surprises. But she tasted the same as always and she kissed the same as always and that helped.

She said, "I saw your name on the customer list for our first sitting at the buffet this morning. Oh Michael! I was so excited I could hardly chop my vegetables. And I asked Henri to allow you sit in the alcove, it's the best seat in the restaurant and permanently reserved for visiting dignitaries who might turn up without a booking and of course you can't turn them away. On Friday night that actor popped in, you know the one that has all the girlfriends, he was going on the *Late Late Show* and he thought my vichyssoise was delicious . . ."

Michael felt strangely disorientated.

"What time is it, Jane?"

"Six o'clock."

"In the morning or at night?"

"At night."

It hadn't really bothered her that Michael was "no show" for lunch for he'd been missing meals since she married him. There was always some crisis on the farm and she'd grown resigned, over the years, to taking second place to fifty milking cows, and then a hundred milking cows and two hundred ewes and the silage and everything else.

She'd learnt to feel pleased when he was there and feel nothing when he wasn't. So it had never occurred to her to panic. Or to worry that he might have had an accident. Or to speculate that he might be asleep in his car, two minutes' walk down the street.

"I left at six this morning," Michael told her sadly. "I wanted to eat in your fancy restaurant. I wanted you to show me the art galleries, museums, concert halls, libraries and old churches. But instead I've been lying here sleeping all day."

Jane flicked her eyes at her husband. He was still the most handsome man she'd ever seen, with his hard face and enigmatic eyes. His shoulders were broad and his cheeks were ruddy. There was a splash of cow-shit on his earlobe and a sprinkle of grey in his hair. He was wearing his very best checked cotton shirt and jeans – sexy Wranglers with a button fly that she'd bought him for Christmas – thirty-three by thirty-three, they'd been hanging in his cupboard unworn even though she'd sometimes brought them out and waved them enticingly in front of him and made provocative suggestions.

"I'll wear my black halter-neck frock, *with no knickers*, if you try them on . . ."

"Hell will freeze over before I wear them!"

Now Jane cheerfully told her husband, "All is not lost! We can still go out for dinner. The Townhouse serves an à la carte menu until ten. Come into the hotel with me first and I'll have a quick wash. I smell of kitchens and cooking."

She was ridiculously pleased that he was wearing his jeans and impressed that he'd paired them so nicely with his favourite country check shirt. All around her for three weeks there'd been Dublin men in acid-coloured city shirts with scary stripes and big shoulder-pads to disguise their lack of genuine muscle. And soft hands. Everywhere she looked, the men had soft hands. There were few things less attractive in a man, except perhaps a soft penis. To think that she often complained about Michael's rough hands laddering her tights when he was groping her leg . . .

She was never going to complain again.

"Hold on a minute," said Michael and he stuck his head into the back seat of the Rapier and pulled out her black halter-neck frock.

"I think we have a deal?" said Michael.

Jane's bedroom was right at the top of Flowers Hotel, above the street lighting and the traffic. Tall narrow sash windows looked out over the rooftops of Dublin. The room was illuminated with starlight.

Michael sat on a chintz-covered armchair and watched his wife unfastening the endless buttons at the front of her coatdress. Her heavy dark hair flowed down her back. Under the dress she wore a silk camisole and the tiniest wisp of lace panties.

"I don't usually dress in such uncomfortable underwear for work. But I thought you were coming to lunch . . ."

"Leave the boots on," he told her, his voice husky with desire. "You look good enough to eat."

She laughed and shook back her hair. "I certainly *smell* good enough to eat! I smell of roast beef, roast potatoes, gravy – you're not coming one step closer until I've washed, in case you forget yourself and try to take a bite out of me!"

So he'd run her a bath and filled it with complimentary bubbles. He washed her hair and carefully soaped her body, between every toe, fastidiously, as she'd often done for him, after a long day at the farm. Jane shut her eyes and tried to relax. She was still tense from work, her adrenaline was still pumping, her head was still buzzing. There was a dull ache between her shoulder blades and her feet were horribly swollen.

The water was perhaps a little bit colder than she preferred and Michael was pulling the head off her, as he vigorously rubbed in the shampoo. He could not have washed her more thoroughly with a Brillo pad and bleach.

And he wouldn't stop talking when what she really longed for was restful silence. As if the news from Temple couldn't wait. As if anything interesting had happened in the past ten years since he'd taken her to live there, after their honeymoon, and had abandoned her on the grassy road to run after escaping sheep. She was still waiting to be carried over a threshold.

He told her that Rupert Glass was renting the gamekeeper's cottage and researching a television documentary for BBC2 called *The Good Old Days*.

"It's about how the old traditions of rural Ireland are changing. He's been up at the Big House to interview our Bobby and to see round the new sound-recording studio and the renovations. He's going to talk about how there was a Glass at Lisglasson since Cromwell, but now that's all gone forever . . . And he's been down the lane to see your house. He's going to talk about how for centuries the young farmer's wife always moved in with her in-laws, and lived with them until the old pair died, but that's all changing now too. He's been to see our new milking-parlour and he's even been into my mother's house to inspect the new restaurant at Temple. We've it all cleaned up for the grand Easter opening. The East Belfast Mission took away the horsehair sofa set and the electric bar heater. The fireplace has been opened and the chimney swept and we're burning a barrow-load of turf from the mountain every day to warm up the room. Kathleen's fancy table is sitting in state and Rupert is coming to the first dinner party – himself and the whole of Achilles' Heel. He's bringing the camera crew with him and he's going to do a piece on rural diversification and alternative farming enterprises."

Michael helped his wife out of the bath, wrapped her in the towel and vigorously rubbed her dry. He laid her on the top of the bed and massaged baby oil into her aching back until the pain between her shoulder blades was subdued.

"Do you know that expression about Mohammed and the Mountain?" she asked him.

He raised his eyebrows. "Trevor Mountain?"

343

She shook her head. She was too tired to talk. The bed was clean and inviting.

"I thought," said Michael, "that maybe after dinner we could go out to a night club for a dance?"

Jane was hovering in the delicious suspension between sleeping and waking. She had just enough energy left to murmur, "Early to bed, early to rise," before she fell asleep.

36

The twelfth of July was a glorious day. The sun was hot and the sky was a blissful, unbroken blue.

"Do you think he ordered the weather?" asked Michael, for today was Bobby Flood's first big splash as Lord of the Manor – he was hosting a summer garden party in the grounds of Lisglasson, and everyone was invited.

"Nothing would surprise me," said Jane. She was cool and collected in brand new linen – something she'd chosen herself, not from the sales, not hand-made and not hand-me-down from Kathleen.

It was the first time ever in her life that Jane had bought her own clothes. It was the first time ever in her life she had money to call her own. In the space of a few short months, she'd become a professional cook as well as a mother of three.

"Now I've double the workload and half the time to do it," said Jane.

"Cut a few corners!" said Cecily. "Honestly, Jane, children

don't need to be bathed every night. When Michael was a youngster he was bathed once a week."

"And the odd bag of chips won't kill them!" said Michael.

"And some television programmes are educational as well as fun," said Susie.

Jane had learned quickly how to juggle the demands of career and family for since Temple Restaurant's grand opening at Easter, there hadn't been a weekend when they hadn't been fully booked.

TV exposure had helped at the start and it honestly seemed that everybody in Ireland had watched *The Good Old Days* and admired the restaurant in its full magnificent splendour with a turf fire burning in the marble fireplace, the chandelier throwing sparkles, and Kathleen seated at the piano, churning out Chopin and chatting . . .

"The elegance of a bygone era," whispered Rupert's seductive voice-over, "with food and wine to die for."

And the glamour of Achilles' Heel, the whole band, rock royalty, insisting they ate there every night, while recording *The Walls Come Tumbling Down*.

Bobby Flood had confided to the camera, "Five courses every evening, and nothing out of a packet!"

It had resulted in a minor degree of celebrity. The restaurant was now open on Thursday, Friday and Saturday, and the waiting-list was still enormous.

It was only in sacred respect for Old Dave – "*Remember the Sabbath day, to keep it holy,*" Exodus 20, verse 8 – that Kathleen didn't agree to three Sunday brunches, back to back, and afternoon tea for another busload of tourists.

"Are you ever coming back to the bank?" Victor asked her on a regular basis, at least once a week, since the end of her self-appointed maternity leave.

"I'm sorry," said Kathleen, "I can't! The maternity leave is over and I've fallen in love with my baby. There's no way in the world you can drag me back to figures and mergers and working for somebody else!"

This week Emerald Heritage had written. The company who had once declared Lisglasson too boring to buy were hoping to include a visit to Temple as part of their Northern Charm package. In the letter they'd expressed disappointment that there was no accommodation available – market research indicated that their wealthy American clientele base were keen to sample the exclusive ambiance of a working Irish farm.

"We've no particular plans at the minute," said Kathleen but already in her mind's eye she could picture the three main bedrooms on the first floor of Temple tarted up with four-poster beds, their fireplaces opened and swept, and en suite bathrooms installed in the dressing-rooms.

"You propose to take over the three main bedrooms?" said Cecily. "Where would I sleep?"

"It's only when guests are in residence! Half a dozen, now and then! I was thinking we could renovate the gate-lodge for you. We're going to have to do something with it for it's making the place untidy in its current dilapidated state. I took the liberty of having a structural engineer look at it. He says the roof is perfect. There's very little damp and absolutely no rot. Really, it just needs cleaning up! What do you think, Mother?"

Cecily had opened her mouth to say "Over my dead body! Temple is my house and I'm not moving!" but she felt strangely excited by the thought of living in the gate-lodge. Its last occupants, an elderly couple, had been very comfortable and happy there – Mr Murphy had helped Dave with the cows, his wife had ironed Cecily's laundry. Cecily had often strolled down the avenue for a chat with Mrs Murphy in the early years when living with Dave was so stressful.

"Knock knock!" shouted Cecily from the threshold of the tree-house. "Where's my birthday girl?"

"Grandma!" shouted Alice and she stampeded out of the emerald living-room on stout little legs, arms pumping, and into her granny's arms.

Cecily was looking well. Her black hair was freshly tinted and set and she was wearing a flowing pink dress set off with a pink picture hat. She had ropes of imitation pearls round her neck and her toenails were painted and peeping through silver sandals.

"What a lovely new outfit!" said Jane.

Cecily gave her twirl. "I was afraid I looked like mutton dressed as lamb so I tried it on for Bobby. He told me Queen Elizabeth wore something very similar at the opening of Ascot in June – he saw her on the television. And I just said to myself, 'If it's good enough for Her Majesty then it's good enough for Cecily Temple' . . ."

Just like Jane, this was also the first time in Cecily's life that she had money of her own, to spend on clothes that were fun and frivolous and did not have to last forever. She was officially recognised as Temple's Assistant Head Cook, with all the pomp and circumstance surrounding it, for she baked the signature soda bread and Jane trusted her to make stocks and marinades. And of course she sourced original and unique fresh produce and haggled with Mrs Mountain about the price of the poultry.

In truth, though, Cecily was one of the principal

attractions at Temple and very popular in the drawing-room where the guests met and mingled before dinner. She offered them generous lashings of drink and spiced up flagging conversation, being utterly without tact or discretion and a devil for asking bald questions.

After a couple of drinks she occasionally sang while Kathleen played the piano.

Today Cecily was helping Bobby organise Lisglasson Garden Party. She was due at Lisglasson at nine, for breakfast and last-minute fussing – she was in charge of twenty-five smallholders, coming to peddle their wares to the general public. Cecily had to make sure they were organised neatly alongside the formal lawns.

"Aren't you running a little bit late?" asked Jane.

"There's always time to give Alice another birthday kiss," said Cecily.

Lisglasson was festooned with bunting – it was pink and green, Bobby's favourite colours – "For happiness and hope," said Bobby.

Bobby had a lot to celebrate. *The Walls Come Tumbling Down* was completed and recorded and due for release at Christmas. A huge tour of the United States was planned for early next year. And what better way to celebrate than to invite all his neighbours together and throw a big party for everyone!

For the children there was a bouncing castle, commissioned at great expense from the Big Smoke. Fully inflated, it dominated the formal lawn. Trevor Mountain was in charge of its supervision and he was organising races through it from one end to the other; an "obstacle course," he called it.

Diane and Gerry had brought a blanket, their own picnic

and a thermos flask. You could never be sure at these events, about the price of the drink and the quality of the barbequed meat. Diane had even packed an umbrella in case it started to rain but she told people it was a parasol to take the bad look off it. And she'd picked their picnic site carefully. They were sitting with their backs to the demesne wall, facing the pony-jumping. Patrick Temple had just won the Mini trophy, jumping bareback on Horny; it was quite an achievement and everyone clapped.

Diane felt uncomfortable and out of place. She was wishing Linda and Oliver would hurry up.

"Go on without us! We'll meet you there! We're cycling!" they'd said.

"Such a strange thing to buy to celebrate Oliver's permanent position at the bank!" said Diane as all twelve of them, two adults and ten children had mounted their new bicycles and set off Indian style, out of Stove Pipe Town, with Oliver leading from the front and Linda bringing up the straggling rear.

"It's been nearly an hour," said Diane anxiously, "I hope they've not had an accident."

Her heart plummeted when Annabel Carson and her husband stopped to chat. Jane's new best friend was a hearty and barking woman who could not open her mouth but she said something outrageous and memorable. She'd been the life and soul of Alice's baptismal lunch, and Diane also knew her from the primary-school gate – she was one of the gang from the posh end of town who boasted so boldly about her children's achievements.

Annabel said, "How lovely to see you, Diane! And didn't young Patrick ride well! What a wonderful confidence-boost for him, to win the Mini-jumping! Life can be terribly tough for a child with learning difficulties . . . Jane says she has you to thank that he's learnt to read at all! She says you're an amazing teacher."

Modestly Diane said, "Dyslexia is a special interest of mine. Patrick learned to read using the Orton-Gillingham Multisensory Method – it's a phonemic approach to reading –"

Annabel interrupted. "I'm concerned about our Nigel. He's ten and his reading is hopeless. Is there some way he can be tested for dyslexia?"

Then Jimmy Carson spoke. He was a large florid man, in a checked shirt and hunting-yellow tie, the caricature of a hunting, shooting, fishing squire.

"Dyslexic is a posh word for stupid," said Jimmy.

Annabel eyeballed her husband. "Allow me to introduce Jimmy. Jimmy can't tie his shoelaces and doesn't know his left hand from his right and can't tell the time on a clock with hands – you'll notice he's wearing a digital watch. Yet he's the smartest man in the country when it comes to talking big and swindling the tax man!"

Suddenly Diane began to long for the undemanding companionship of her Gerry who was patting Horny and asking Patrick, "Is your little pony a boy or a girl?"

Annabel said, "I'd be very grateful if you'd consider Nigel for tuition – maybe now in the summer holidays, before school starts again in September? And my friend Vanessa is very worried about her Fiona – her end-of-term report was terribly disappointing. And as for Sebastian Molyneux! He's *never* going to pass the eleven-plus without extra coaching."

Suddenly Diane had three new students and she was starting to see the world with different eyes. These terrifying women at the school gate – the louder they boasted, the more insecure they felt. They weren't really any different to her, for

351

when Ernest and Valerie didn't perform as well as expected she simply stuck out her chin and told shameless lies.

"All As and Bs in her O Levels," she'd said about Valerie, when in fact she'd got one A and one B and the rest were C.

"What's wrong with C?" asked Valerie who found schoolwork a bit of a struggle and had tried very hard and was pleased she'd passed anything.

"I don't know." Ernest was doubtful and perplexed. "She did the same last year with me. And I *failed* O Level Maths."

Later in the afternoon, when the heat had gone out of the day and the shadows were starting to lengthen, Bobby Flood cornered Jane by the bouncing castle.

"You've not cashed that cheque I gave you," he said.

She smiled at him, under her lashes. All right, so she didn't fancy him, but he was still the most famous rock star in Ireland, and his short shorts left little to the imagination. It would be rude not to flirt a little bit.

"I'm not intending to cash it, Bobby."

"But . . ."

Michael was showing Alice some brand-new fluffy yellow chicks, in the corner of the lawn beside the produce stalls when he noticed the pair of them talking – Jane and Bobby, head to head, tête-à-tête – he knew immediately that Bobby was hitting on his wife.

"Not another one!" said Michael for it was always happening at the restaurant too.

"My compliments to the chef," the diners would say, after a successful dinner and when Jane was ushered into the dining-room all men present would unanimously rise and offer to help her with the washing-up.

"We'd better rescue your mother," said Michael and he

swept up Alice into his arms and marched over to the bouncing castle.

He was just in time hear Jane firmly say, "But Alice is the picture of her Grandma Cecily. She takes after Michael's side of the family."

"I'll race you, Bobby Flood," said Michael, "through the bouncing castle."

"Ready . . . Steady . . .!" shouted Mountain.

Michael thrust Alice into her mother's arms, but Bobby was already ahead, running for the thin, pink slit. He wasn't a man who waited for "Go".

"Cheat!" roared Michael and chased after him.

Together they plunged into the heavy plastic heaving depths of the pink and green bouncing castle. There was a ladder and a rope to pull yourself up to the next level, Bobby grabbed the rope, Michael grabbed Bobby and there was a wrestling match between the two men, that could only be partially explained by competitive urges and testosterone.

"What are they doing in there?" asked Jane.

Mountain said sagely, "Trying to get the upper hand."

"It sounds like they're killing each other."

The highlight of the afternoon was a gig by Achilles' Heel. Bobby's neighbours were to be the first to hear *The Walls Come Tumbling Down*.

Bobby was still flushed from his race when he took the microphone and started to sing. "Enchanting Alice" was a ballad. It was dedicated to Cecily Temple . . .

When the music started Alice wriggled and wriggled in Jane's arms until she set her down. This was her song! The song she'd been helping to write, in the kitchen of Grandma's house. She recognised it the minute she heard it, for hadn't she been sitting on the bold Bobby's knee, beating time with a wooden spoon while Cecily and he argued the toss on the lyrics?

Alice broke free from her mummy's hand and stumbled forward onto the lawn. She'd only just learnt how to walk and she was still unsteady on her feet. She took up a prime position, directly in front of the band.

"Ba ba!" she shouted. It was her way of shouting "Bobby". Blowing him kisses and waving she began to dance to the music, wriggling her nappy and keeping smart time. It was a remarkably accomplished performance, for a baby who'd just turned one.

"Ba ba!" she shouted again, and over the din of the music, Bobby was sure she was shouting "Da da!"

The End

If you enjoyed *Enchanting Alice* by Anne Dunlop
why not try *Cinderella's Sister* also published by Poolbeg

Here's a sneak preview of Chapter one.

Anne Dunlop

Cinderella's Sister

POOLBEG

1

All our lives Camilla and I have been so physically identical – with our dark-red hair and hazel eyes and smooth peachy skin that tans such an envied, unfreckled, golden colour on the slightest exposure to the sun – that even our mother has never been able to tell us apart.

It started the moment we were removed from the faultless hospital nursery and our name-tags were taken off.

Mummy was presented with one sleeping cherub dressed head to toe in pink; Daddy was presented with the other.

The brisk, meticulous midwife announced, "Now, Mrs Reverend Simms, this is Francesca. Reverend Simms, you have Camilla."

Mummy was doubtful. "Are you sure this one is Francesca?"

The midwife had already met my mother. The day we

were born she'd asked, "Mrs Reverend Simms, how are you going to feed your babies?"

Mummy, confused, had said, "How? Don't you mean *who* is going to feed them?"

So this time the midwife tried to be helpful.

"Mrs Reverend Simms, it might be easier for you if you didn't dress them identically. Not at the start anyway."

But Mummy wouldn't listen. In Mummy's mind there was only one advantage in having identical twin daughters and that was to make them look as alike as possible. So we wore identical Babygros, slept in identical cots and played with identical dolls.

"But I thought that was Camilla." Daddy did his best but he was never singing from the same hymn sheet as my mother. "I thought you said Camilla did all the screaming."

"Why do you do it, Madeline?" Aunt Grace scolded. "Most people look for bargains in life. Two daughters for the price of one. What you are creating is one daughter for the price of two."

Mummy was unrepentant.

"I'm the first to admit that it's perfectly possible that the one who answers to Francesca could actually have been baptised Camilla. But I can't see that it'll make much difference in the long run. Mixing them up. I've always thought individuality overrated."

Mummy's best efforts were in vain because even with identical haircuts, anoraks, shoes and parents, Camilla was always the brighter variation on the theme. In school uniform or pyjamas she sparkled and I always had my nose stuck in a book.

"I cannot believe they came out of the same womb,"

said Aunt Grace. "Are you *quite* sure they have the same father?"

My father is the minister of a small country congregation of farmers. 1st Derryrose is a modest, unadorned and enormously practical church with acres of shiny black tarmac for parking and no trees, not even a traditional yew or laburnum to weep over the tidy formations of headstones. Derryrose Manse sits beside the church. Our garden was the graveyard and our closest neighbours were the dead.

Camilla and I grew up in a surreal type of isolated splendour. Suitable friends were invited for tea, but under my mother's critical gaze they were always on their best behaviour, and they were always afraid of the graveyard.

Sometimes we got invited back again but Mummy insisted she come too, just in case we said things that weren't suitable for a minister's daughters to say.

"Yes, Mummy, no Mummy, three bags full, Mummy," said Camilla.

Before long Mummy had frightened off our school friends and we had one approved playmate – Sam Dawson, whose father was an anaesthetist in the South Derry and whose mother was Mummy's only friend. While Sam played hide and seek with us in the graveyard, Mrs Reverend Simms and Mrs Doctor Dawson impressed each other with their childrearing theories. Children should be seen and not heard. Spare the rod and spoil the child. Give me the child till he's five, and I'll show you the man . . .

"Do you think we'll both have to marry Sam when we're older?" Camilla mused.

"Both at the same time," I asked, "or can we take turns with him?"

Camilla had charm, charisma and confidence. She laughed loudly when she was happy, screamed loudly when she was angry and wept bitter tears when she didn't get her own way. She was careless, affectionate and flirtatious. She was the life and soul of the party. People always asked, "Where's Camilla?"

"She's utterly without hidden depth," said Mummy in bemused exasperation. "And so loud and chatty and amusing Francesca never gets a chance, poor little mouse."

Aunt Grace shook her head sadly. "Poor Camilla, destined to a life of attention-seeking antics. Hardly any surprise really, when you look at the other one."

I was perfectly content to be known as 'the other one'. I knew my place. And more than anyone I missed Camilla's infectious good humour and high spirits when she wasn't around. We had such fun; Camilla's favourite game was 'Confusion' when she changed into me.

"Let's play Confusion," she'd whisper and her mischievous eyes would become suddenly solemn, her expressive face serene. The bounce left her step, rebelliousness left her mouth, her cracking fizzing energy was perfectly distilled into an innocent otherworldliness. She became an enigma, an angel, a girl from a fairytale.

"Do I really look like that?"

"Let's ask Mummy."

Mummy never suspected a thing. I watched from a safe distance, fascinated.

"Where's Camilla?" asked Mummy.

Before bed every night, when I was saying my prayers, I fervently prayed that I would die first because I could never imagine the loneliness of life without her.

Aunt Grace was disgusted. "You're making those little girls into freaks, Madeline."

She had stiff words with my father and, with the kind-hearted ambition of exposing us to a more gregarious, 'normal' childhood, Camilla and I were removed periodically from the ordered and aseptic calm of the Manse and introduced to the warm, noisy, untidy world of Lisglasson Lodge, where Aunt Grace lived with her rough, tough sons Frank and Philip, her darling, petted daughter Naomi and her chain-smoking, hard-drinking husband, Uncle Denis.

"From the sublime to the ridiculous," sniffed Mummy.

Lisglasson Lodge had once been the dower house on the Lisglasson estate. Designed by an imaginative Edwardian, it was as impractical as it was lovely. It had fourteen-foot-high ceilings, cast-iron fireplaces in every room and huge windows in the drawing room.

Upstairs the main bedroom looked over a wild-flower meadow and a thousand acres of Lisglasson parkland.

At Lisglasson Lodge, while Aunt Grace sat with her feet up reading a book, Camilla learned to ride Ginger the pony – she was a risk-taking natural – and Naomi and I played hunt the thimble with Mrs Murphy the housekeeper. Mrs Murphy was a big, strong countrywoman with several grown-up children of her own. She cooked for us with a cigarette balanced between her lips; when ash sometimes fell into the food she said: "Tastier than salt." If we were feeling unwell, or had a temperature she gave us extra-big spoonfuls of medicine with bread and jam to kill the taste. She never wasted good weather – the first blink of sun we were put into our wellies and sent outside to pull blackberries for jam, or hunt for hens' eggs in the yard, or to pull bunches of flowers in the wild-flower meadow.

It was from Mrs Murphy that we learnt that Santa Claus (she called him 'Santy') leaves only a bag of coal for naughty children, and she wasn't afraid to wash out Naomi's mouth with soap and water when she started swearing ("Thou shalt not take the Lord's name in vain, Naomi Walsh!") or put Frank and Philip over her knee and spank them when they were 'bold'. Camilla and I tried to copy her soft accent. "It's grand," we'd say to each other, and "That's right, so".

Mummy strongly disapproved of our visits to Lisglasson Lodge. She strongly disapproved of Aunt Grace taking us to see *Darby O'Gill and the Little People* at the cinema. She strongly disapproved of Aunt Grace taking us to the seaside on Sunday instead of church. She strongly disapproved of Aunt Grace buying us sweets. She strongly disapproved of Aunt Grace inviting us for sleepovers and letting us choose our own bedtime.

"I wish you would remember your Bible, Grace. '*A man reaps what he sows . . .*'."

Aunt Grace was unrepentant. "I promise we'll put '*She knew the price of everything and the value of nothing*' on your headstone when you die, Madeline."

When we were teenagers Camilla loved boys ("the more the merrier, so many boys, so little time") and boys loved Camilla and not just because she loosened her school tie and opened the buttons on her school shirt to expose the plump ripe peachy swollenness of her pubescent breasts. And not just because she rolled up her school skirt to reveal subtle flashes of tanned, toned thighs. Camilla was fast but she was never cheap. And she loved to keep them guessing, sitting quietly beside me at the front of the school bus, with her knees pressed demurely together, pretending to read one of my books – one of the shorter ones. With pictures.

"I can't see the point of books. Why read about Lucy Glitters when I can live her?"

"I've been hearing Chinese Whispers," said Mummy anxiously, "in church on Sunday. When we walk together up to the front to our pew. I hear the word '*slapper*'. What's a slapper?"

But then of course Camilla went too far. Not satisfied with the admiration of every other boy in South Derry she wanted Alex Flood too. Alex Flood's parents had recently bought Lisglasson, he was Aunt Grace's neighbour and his mother, Lady Millicent, was Mummy's new best friend.

Officially Alex Flood wasn't my boyfriend – we didn't 'shift' – but we spent every spare minute together. I know I bored Camilla to sobs talking about him in bed at night.

"And then Alex said . . ."

"And then I said . . ."

"And then Alex said . . ."

Derryrose Manse had many bedrooms but Camilla and I always shared a room, hugging in a double bed to keep warm.

After months of 'And then Alex said . . .', 'And then I said . . .', Camilla finally said, "Is all you ever do talk?"

"Yes," I said, suddenly embarrassed. "What else would we be doing?"

"That *nastiness*."

"You mean sex?" I shook my head. "No. Of course not."

"Wouldn't you *like* to?"

I hesitated. Fatally. My identical twin leapt for the kill.

"Don't you think Alex might like to? I mean, what seventeen-year-old boy *doesn't* want to have sex?"

"But he's never even kissed me!"

"Have you asked him to?"

I felt myself blush in the dark. Of course, I hadn't. I really was not that sort of girl.

Camilla called me Francesca the Puritan.

"It's one of three things then," Camilla announced authoritatively. "He's frigid, he's gay, or he doesn't fancy you."

"I'm nearly sure he fancies me," I said firmly for sometimes when we were out riding together I felt the heat of his eyes on me, and my legs would melt to jelly. And when we were in his car together, with the windows steamed up, sharing a packet of crisps, our fingers would sometimes touch. And linger. "Intimacy has nothing to do with how naked you are . . ."

"Well, I think he's frigid," Camilla insisted. "Would you like me to find out for you?"

What was I supposed to say? No, no, no? But that just wasn't me. I never chased men or buses . . . and I trusted Camilla.

"I think Alex's feelings might be hurt, if he thought I was sharing him with you."

"But he doesn't have to know. Of course, I can be you!" Camilla boasted.

Even when we were seventeen it still took very few physical adjustments for Camilla to cause confusion. We swapped clothes. She combed her hair off her face and secured it back with my Alice band. She washed her face free of make-up. She cut her fingernails.

She stooped a little when she stood and toed in a little when she walked. It was Francesca standing in front of me.

Mummy said, "Francesca darling, why don't you wear some

8

lipstick this evening when you go out with Alex? Brainy girls are allowed to look pretty too, you know."

And wicked Camilla smiled my hesitant, innocent smile and said, "Perhaps I will, if Camilla will lend me some."

It was the end of Alex of course. The next time he didn't even come into my house.

From the doorstep he said, "I'm sorry, Francesca. I can't see you any more." And he turned on his heel and walked away.

"What did you do to him, Camilla?"

Camilla shrugged. "There's *definitely* something wrong with that boy. He wouldn't even kiss me. And as for anything else . . ."

"So he is frigid."

"Or gay . . ."

I know I should have gone after him. And said I was sorry. And said I just didn't know what had got into me. And said that I still respected him. I could even have blamed Camilla and said she'd put me up to it. But I never did.

I was the silly, proud girl who never chased men or buses.

And I had 'A' Levels looming. And it was so much easier to agree with my sister. Maybe he was frigid, or gay, or maybe he just didn't fancy me.

Mummy said, "Cheer up, Francesca. You're a lovely girl. You'll meet somebody else."

Aunt Grace was furious. She was very fond of Alex Flood, and she'd harboured high hopes of a proper romance blossoming between us.

Soon afterwards she and Mummy joined forces to consult with a matchmaker "before Camilla goes to university and *really* gets into trouble".

I was curious. "How does the matchmaker do it? How does he match people? Does he use a computer? Or a crystal ball?"

"Mr Moss is not a fortune-teller, he's a matchmaker! He started off as schoolmaster, he taught me when I was girl, and he taught your father. He told me that once you've taught a lot of young people in their formative years you realise that there are very few truly unique people in the world. The majority of us shake down into certain stereotypes and we're easily matched with each other. How do you think I found your dashing Uncle Denis?"

"Really? But I thought you married for love!"

"Oh, Francesca, you're such a *romantic*! Just like your father – and look at the botched job he made when he married Madeline. *She's* not suited to the role of a minister's wife, poor woman. She's far too obsessed with keeping up appearances. If only Roger had listened to me and asked Mr Moss to find him a wife instead of going to a prayer meeting and falling in love with the youngest woman there. Love at first sight is so *unreliable* . . ."

"But what does Mr Moss actually *do*? Do you have to fill in a questionnaire? Does he have a book with photographs and you pick somebody you like the look of? Does he play psychological games with you to reveal your innermost thoughts?"

So I went too. Mummy, Aunt Grace, Camilla and me squashed into Aunt Grace's sports car, hurtling through wet country lanes under cover of darkness because Mummy could hear Chinese Whispers again, *"Bad reputation. They'll never get a nice boy to take her . . ."*

Camilla was sulky and a bit frightened. "You can't force me to marry somebody I don't like."

"Where is your sense of adventure, my dear?" Aunt Grace asked her impatiently. "We're not forcing you to do anything.

We're merely taking you to meet Mr Moss, who will interview you and suggest a young man he thinks might suit you. Whether or not you decide to marry the young man has absolutely nothing to do with Mr Moss."

Mr Moss said, "I have the perfect man for her. Adam Robinson. He's a young minister, recently ordained, lives in a lovely big old Manse with stables. Nice young fellow but very quiet. He needs a confident girl to help him win over the congregation."

Camilla cheered up a bit. "Better the devil you know, I suppose."

Mummy and Aunt Grace were thrilled. "How amazing!"

"Not really," said the matchmaker modestly. "She's a very commonplace girl. And the pretty, flighty ones are always the easiest to match. Men never refuse them." He pointed to me. "I'm so glad it wasn't this girl you needed matched. I've nothing to suit her. Never in forty years of matchmaking have I been able to match this type of girl."

Mummy immediately took offence. "What's wrong with Francesca?"

"She's already matched. I can see it in her eyes."

Aunt Grace never stopped hoping that Alex Flood and I might kiss and make up.

"Alex rode by about half an hour ago. He's gone to look for foxes in the little wood at the end of the avenue. Why don't you walk down and talk to him?"

"What would I say?"

Aunt Grace sighed. She was a tough old boot who didn't invite pity but Life had been unkind to her. Darling, petted Naomi, 'my one and only', had died young and she'd adopted me as her protégée – my lost romance with Alex Flood was an affront to her sensibilities.

"I'm sure you'll think of something. You never stopped talking about him before Camilla ruined your chances! Time heals almost everything, Francesca, even wounded pride . . ."

"Camilla says there are plenty more fish in the sea."

"Only if you're a herring or a mackerel! If you're not a herring or a mackerel there really aren't that many fish in the sea. It makes my blood boil when I think of the way you allowed her to manipulate you. What was it she said? She was doing you a favour, finding out if he was frigid or gay! Some favour!"

"I won't make the same mistake again."

Will Dallas was well briefed about Camilla before he came to Ireland for our wedding.

"Not the tattoo thing again," said Will. "If I hear once more about Camilla's tattoo . . ."

Free postage*
Worldwide

on our web site
www.poolbeg.com

Direct to your home!

If you enjoyed this book why
not visit our website

and get another book delivered straight to
your home or to a friend's home!

www.poolbeg.com

All orders are despatched within 24 hours

* See web site for details